"Brilliantly written and thoroughly researched historical detail comes to life with novelistic flair in Kevin Cahill's Sand Creek. Informative without being boring or dry, this novel is remarkably unbiased in its presenting of the story of the Sand Creek Massacre, revealing in detail how fear, misunderstanding, and a few violent men on both sides led to so many lives being lost."

- Colorado Country Life Magazine

1864 . . .

The Civil War had swallowed a nation whole in a struggle over power and providence, splitting the country's heart, and slaughtering the white sons of America's founding fathers.

But on the plains of Bleeding Kansas, America's true natives are embroiled in a life or death struggle, indifferent to the political collision between blue and gray. The inevitable war between ancient native culture and Anglican progress in the New World is about to explode on the dark and frigid banks of a Colorado river that the Cheyennes call *Ponoeohe*.

Kevin Cahill dramatically assembles the labyrinth of power, politics and controversy that surrounded one of the most notorious events in the history of the American West. His remarkably insightful resurrection of the true-life Indians, soldiers and settlers involved in the Sand Creek Massacre provides a poignant look at the monumental struggle for life on the Plains.

Novels by Kevin Cahill

Sand Creek

Letters to a Rose

The Last Café

Knights of Harvest

Simon Sez

Available in hardcover, paperback,
e-book, and Audible formats at Amazon.com.

More information at
www.kclonewolf.com

Author contact
mailto: admin@kclonewolf.com

KNIGHTS OF HARVEST

KEVIN CAHILL

LoneWolf

This Paperback Second Edition published 12.01.2020
ISBN-10 0-9969544-8-1
ISBN-13 978-0-9969544-8-8
by KC LoneWolf,
Colorado Springs, CO USA
admin@KClonewolf.com

Paperback First Edition published 11.02.2004:
ISBN-10: 1-4208-0964-4
ISBN-13: 978-1420809640
Library of Congress Control Number: 2004098874
by Author House
Bloomington, Indiana

Printed in the United States of America

Kindle Second Edition published 04.25.2020
by KC LoneWolf,
Colorado Springs, CO USA
ASIN: B002F9MA3O
Also available at Amazon Audible.

Author contact information:admin@KClonewolf.com

For my parents
Lauren & Lee Cahill

HARVEST

"... and on their heads were as it were crowns like gold, and their faces were as the faces of men. And they had hair as the hair of women, and their teeth were as the teeth of lions. And they had breastplates, as it were breastplates of iron; and the sound of their wings was as the sound of chariots of many horses running into battle."

Revelations 9:7-9

I

Thousands of birds. Sparrows and starlings, crows, robins. Prairie falcons and chicken hawks. Thousands of them. They drew passionate halos over a scorched and cracked land that stretched to the horizon like a worn rubber band about to snap. They soared high, retreating to the cooler air and dotting the morning sky. More and more joined the frenzy as the sun's silver ridge brought fire to the parched terrain.

New morning heat stirred.

Heat.

It was everywhere; suffocating. It barely abated overnight as sultry remnants of yesterday's horrid sun hovered over the ground, awaiting energy from the dawn. The birds climbed higher, seeking relief from both the smothering air and their unconscionable fear.

Below, thermal updrafts ushered other passengers of the wind.

Vultures . . . Buzzards . . . Diners.

Below them, a mournful howl, perhaps of a coyote or hound. And everywhere, it was hot; getting hotter.

At least, mercifully, the night was over.

The heat swelled, although the sun was but a sliver of white diamonds on the edge of the world. Yesterday's one-hundred-twelve degrees awoke and swirled up from the dirt on strands of invisible silk. The birds above squealed in the dying breezes, and a bizarre symphony of buzzing ricocheted across the land below.

Flies . . .

Seth Cameron awoke to their enraged buzzing. He grimaced and rubbed his face, sucking for stale air and grasping at the untidy reality behind his closed eyes. His sleep had been dreamless, yet he prayed to his god this sudden awareness was just a terrible nightmare. It was like the many mornings that Seth Cameron's mind, often savaged by whiskey, boiled in realization of the dawn. But Cameron was sober today. In fact, he begged his god to punish him with a hangover that might provide a logical explanation for this horrible morning.

Flies buzzed.

Seth refused to open his eyes. He knew exactly where he was and what he heard. He knew what he smelled - the festering scent of rotting flesh and hot blood. Seth could only lie in his own sweat and pray he might never see again. This was no dream, of that he was certain. He prayed for death.

Seth's eyes finally opened, and he returned to the world he left behind just hours ago. The nightmare was real.

Overhead, the birds winged in uncontrolled panic. They flew on a headless tack, startled by the guttural screams of Seth Cameron, who knelt in the weeds two hundred feet below. They soared high over the Linville Reeves farm, across the vast wheat fields, seeking escape from Seth's screams. Doom, panic, and fear frolicked in their primitive minds. Fear of the heat, the wind, the screams - each other.

Like magic and the magician: the two are never one and the same.

The birds returned to the Linville Reeves farm, flaring in on fence posts, rooftops, in the trees and on the ground. They gathered together, nervously cackling and perking to the ominous cry of a hound not far down the road.

The flies relentlessly buzzed.

Seth Cameron stood on his knees, his gut still heaving as he pulled himself up on first one foot and then the other. He staggered backward, his eyes never leaving the flies and their fleshy breakfast. He groped at his mouth with blood-caked hands, trying to stuff the bile down his throat. He heard himself scream again as he tried to run, but the hypnotic buzzing held his legs firmly. The enraged buzzing manacled him to the ground and mercilessly held his eyes on their grisly breakfast.

Finally, Seth turned away and ordered his legs to run. He dragged himself through the wheat field, passing a hay barn and the adjoining pigpens that flanked a chicken house. Seth covered his ears, his legs pushing harder. He never looked at the small cabin behind a modest farmhouse - the cabin he had called 'home' for over five years. He ran faster on wobbly legs - past the farmhouse and brushing by his old pickup truck, a gift given him by his boss, Linville Reeves. Like Linville, the truck was dead, too. Pushing on, Seth reached County Road 84 and scrubbed his bleeding feet down the rocky path.

"God, please help me," he gasped through his tears. "Just help me get to town. Please, God, just let there be a town left..."

* * *

Tick . . .tick . . .tick . . .

Dreams to reality . . . Reality to dreams.

Carly Farrel purred as she reached across the bed and found the strong chest of Kenny Jackson - K.J., as he was known to fellow officers at the Attica Sheriff's Department. Jackson smacked his lips and took Carly's hand without opening his eyes. Carly laced her fingers in his and drifted back to a light sleep.

Tick . . .tick . . .tick . . .

Through an open window, a sad, lonely howl drifted over the bedroom. It rode the sultry breeze coming from the expansive farmlands due south. The howl was that of a hound, or perhaps a coyote. Carly pursed her lips and tried to swallow. It was so damned hot.

Tick . . .tick . . .tick . . .

The howl grew louder. Ken Jackson's breath suddenly stopped, his eyes popping. His mind said he was sleeping, but his eyes betrayed the ruse. He breathed again and smacked his dry lips. For some reason, something felt good - but very wrong at the same time.

Carly felt Jackson move. She opened her eyes.

Tick . . .tick . . .tick . . .

"Crapola!" Carly bolted upright.

Jackson's eyes bugged, feeling as if a buzz saw just sectioned his frontal lobes. A strange dream of lights vaporized in his mind. Carly's voice might have just as well come from the barrel of a .45.

"Kenny!" she cried. "It's seven-thirty! You forgot to set the alarm again!" She leaped and scrambled to the bathroom.

Jackson groggily watched Carly's naked body pound out. Under better circumstances, the sight might have given him reason for hope, but her harsh voice erased even the slightest carnal notion that might have entered his webby brain.

Tick . . .tick . . .tick . . .

His head bobbed to the clock. 7:33. Roll call was dangerously twenty-seven minutes away.

"I'm a dead man," Jackson muttered. He jumped from the bed and jammed his little toe into the nightstand. He spat a curse as he hobbled to the bathroom . . .

* * *

An inky shadow wobbled behind the little farmer on County 84. Seth's gait was stiff. His unsteady legs grew heavier with every step as he felt a weight pull on his shoulders - the weight of demons with bloated bellies perched on his soul. Seth Cameron's mind was slipping. He tried to concentrate on the road ahead, considering each step, each rock, each pebble; but he could not block out the horror of what he left behind on the farm. He glanced up, hoping Attica would soon peek over the horizon and tell him he was safe - that life was as it had been yesterday when he drove this very road with Linville Reeves on a trip to the market. Seth prayed he would soon see Rusty's Tavern at the edge of town, and he'd find Bill Candy sweeping out the grain and feed store next door. He prayed he'd see Moses Homan snoozing in his rocking chair outside the ConOil gas station, holding a can of lukewarm orange soda near his crotch. But mostly, Seth prayed he would suddenly wake up in the Attica lockup, sleeping off the worst hangover of his life.

Seth pushed harder, but was overcome by sudden darkness.

Terrified, he stopped.

"Seth, honey. Seth?"
It was Momma's voice. He whirls in the darkness and sees the headless, shaking corpse of his mother. Her splintered spine protrudes from her shoulders, and a river of blood spurts on her cotton slip. Her torso screws into the floor.

"No!" Seth screamed.
The sun burned his face. His eyes open, Seth was alone on County Road 84. His body trembled as he swallowed mucus from his throat.
"Gotta get to town," he whispered. He shoved his legs forward. "Gotta get to town . . ."

* * *

A distant howl was barely audible in the dimly lit room of Marcus Andrew Payne. His small cubicle was just large enough for a single bed, a table and wash basin, a three-drawer chest, and a feeble rocking chair. A skinny yellow cat snoozed in the chair. She perked when she first heard the dog's howl, but, sensing little danger in distant sounds, she settled back down to dreams of mice and tuna cans. The only audible sound in the darkness was a deep, scratchy voice that hummed a mindless, monotonic tune.
Marcus Payne sat on the floor in the corner among dozens of empty beer cans and dead Scotch bottles. Last night was as bad as any since Lori died. A bodiless voice left deep scars on his brain overnight, and the welcome morning light in the window gave Payne reason to hum. He wasn't happy, but singing kept him awake.
However, within the retched haze of his mind, Payne knew last night's nightmares were different from the others. He knew all about illusions and reality, because he was a magician - a sorcerer of sorts. Last night wasn't a dream. Payne knew it. Last night evoked the same feeling he felt just minutes before he found Lori Payne lying in pieces at the foot

of the stairs. It was a memory no amount of booze could drown.

On the table was a pencil sketch of Lori, impeccably drawn on a tattered yellow legal pad. Payne drew it early last evening before the beer and whiskey overtook him. Lori's eyes looked at him hauntingly, but Payne also felt the eyes of something else on him. He looked at 'Remington,' the cat. Her green eyes stared right through him.

"What are you gawking at?" Payne asked.

Remington blinked once and warily put her head on her paws. She was cautious, for her survival instincts were keen...

* * *

Two more miles, maybe? Attica can't be much farther away, Seth thought. It was only five miles from the Reeves farm. His legs felt like petrified logs as he dragged them through the dust. The hot breeze consumed him. In this recent heat wave, the wind was a caustic enemy. Seth tried to fix himself on the road by pushing visions of last night to the musty cellar in his brain, but the heat was taking its toll. As Seth pressed forward, the other terrible vision - that of his long-deceased mother - crept up the cellar steps like an oily spider.

Seth tried to run, hoping he could stay ahead of it. He ran as hard as he could, but he suddenly stumbled and pounded into the gravel. He could do nothing but weep. His tears welled and dropped, making tiny mud balls in the dust. Wet, sandy tails streaked his face, and his nose spat blood.

"If I ain't dead already," he whimpered, "take me, God..."

In his quiet darkness, they come.

Seth is aware of the dark sky - the blackest night. He peers ahead and sees his mother's disembodied head, and now, two long silver hands reach for him.

Seth cries out. "Get away from me!" The cold, metallic hands are coming at him, reaching from a steel armor breastplate. "Leave me be!" He scoots back on his haunches, swinging his skinny arms in the darkness. In the black sky, Seth sees the head of Linville Reeves drifting toward him, its eye sockets dark and wide, and its mouth retching. Seth is drowning as if helplessly caught in the hard current of a red mountain river narrows . . .

"Stop it!"

Seth sat in the dirt of County Road 84. He sucked the hot air, peering between the cracks of his fingers. The sun was brilliant, glaring at Seth like a malevolent god. In another moment, he was back on his feet and scrubbing toward Attica...

* * *

Carly Farrel stood at attention, always in control. She watched Sheriff Virgil White from the corner of her eye. The balding sheriff sauntered into roll call with a clipboard under one thick arm. A coffee cup filled with ice water hung from his hand. White looked like an old oak tree. Ken Jackson stood behind Carly in the second row. He was less composed, but miraculously on time with all buttons buttoned and zippers zipped.

Sheriff White scanned his clipboard and looked up at his troops. They stood in undisciplined formation, trying to crowd under a pitiful ceiling fan overhead.

"Aw, jeez," White said, waving them down. "At ease, already. It's too hot for this."

The day shift officers lightened and collectively sat in school desks scattered around the room. Jackson struggled into his desk. His muscular thighs just didn't fit. A wave of fluttering police hats only stirred up the hot air.

Sheriff White hitched his pants over a well-constructed beer belly and slammed his clipboard on the podium. He looked around disdainfully. The second floor of the Attica County Courthouse could be used to bake chicken today. It was a sturdy building that had served the county seat forty-seven years, but it was a merciless oven when the few window air-conditioners were overwhelmed by a heat wave like this. A new police and court building was going up three blocks away near the river, but construction wouldn't be completed until next spring.

White rolled up his sleeves and undid the top two buttons of his shirt. He pulled a handkerchief from his pocket and dabbed his forehead while he listened to his officers chatter and whine.

"Ladies and boys," he said, "let's not push this any further than we have to, okay?" The random conversation settled. "Before anybody asks - no, the air-conditioning ain't gonna be serviced today. The damned AC company is overloaded, and they won't get here until at least tomorrow."

Mumbled complaints rolled over the room.

White raised his hand. "Now now, children, don't cry. At least you can get out of here and stake out a nice, cool doughnut shop." White didn't smile at the smattering of embarrassed laughs. "Okay, here's the agenda for today in this tropical paradise. Blake and Monroe will continue their watch on the Pierson farm today. Word's out that Jimmy Pierson and his boys are gonna ship their wild weed any day now, at which time we're gonna bust the biggest dope crop of the decade. Jimmy's as crazy as your momma's brother, so everybody keep your ears open for a backup call."

White shifted his weight and dabbed the sweat. "Many of you know by now that Officer Clare Lewis got into a ruckus with some drunk local at Rusty's last night. She got a busted nose for her trouble. I'm glad to report Officer Lewis held her own. She buried her boot in the bonehead's crotch, successfully completing a fifty-two-yard field goal." The officers let out with cheers and applause. White couldn't help but smile. "Bar wars, people, are getting very ugly in this heat, so keep your guard up. Officer Lewis is taking a few days at home, so offer a phone call or a tulip . . ."

* * *

Marcus Payne screwed his brow. He turned an ear to the distant howl and looked at his shaded window. Goddam death, he thought, it's out there - I smell it.

Remington purred and arched her shiny back. Payne watched her straighten and extend each leg for a good stretch. She circled the rocking chair three times and dropped down to rest. Payne shook his head and asked himself - how can life be that easy? He stood and tried to stretch his own back, unable to match Remington's grace. He reached for the ceiling, his bones popping, and grabbed at the air several times to awaken his fingers. Payne felt older than forty-three this morning, and he seriously considered dropping down on the bed for ten or twelve more hours of sleep. The cursed needles of Hangover Madness suddenly pierced his brain. He quickly bent over to dike a flood of sparkling stars in his skull, and he staggered like an unbalanced top. Payne sat in a heap and rubbed his abused forehead, growling at the booze that suddenly turned on him.

Several minutes passed before his shopworn head cleared. He swallowed a thick ball of nausea and looked across the room.

"Remington," he said to the ambivalent cat, "this would be easier if I were an alcoholic."

Remmy stared back as Payne stood and shuffled to the table. He put the drawing of Lori Payne on his bed and reached into the wash basin. The cool water felt good on his face. His ears perked to the sound of the dog's howl - a lonely cry. He dried his face and gave the window shade a hard tug. It snapped and recoiled with a crisp, CLACK CLACKETY CLACK CLACK!

The room exploded in brilliant sunlight, and Remington jumped to her feet with wide eyes. It took only a moment to realize she had been had again by her crazy two-legged roommate. She calmed and hopped off the chair, carefully measuring Payne. He had never raised a hand in anger, so Remmy's mood was moderately trustful. She arched her back and rubbed against Payne's leg.

Payne snatched her up and put her close to his heart. She rolled her eyes and turned on the motor as Payne scratched her ears. Marcus Payne, once the best-known criminal defense attorney in the country, stood in his stocking feet and peered out the window. His gaze ambled to the Attica water tower, where the dog's howl wafted over the trees.

"Something's out there, Remmy," he whispered . . .

* * *

The water tower! Thank God! Seth Cameron's heart raced when he saw the tower pierce the horizon. His blood gave new life to his legs. He now believed he could make it. Momma's voice pounded through his brain, but Seth could ignore it now that he knew Attica was still standing. He could ignore the steel hands and silver eyes that stared at him, the roar of some ungodly engine whining in his ears, and the screams of Linville Reeves and his butchered family. He ran, and it suddenly felt good.

The water tower was bigger now, as was the unmistakable outline of Rusty's Tavern at the tower's base. Rusty's roof consisted of two rounded peaks painted hot pink. Rusty Wade proclaimed the colors were his idea. A large sign sat atop metal braces next to the water tower, boasting: All Nude Babes 'N Tall Cold Brews!

Seth ran as hard as he could, sweat draining from his pores. The sun burned his brow, but he forged ahead.

Have to get to town before everybody dies, his twisted mind cried.

He ran until the tower was almost over him, and then his legs collapsed, his body grinding into the dusty road. Seth rolled onto his back, his chest heaving dirt and gravel.

A huge shadow covered him. "Seth? Seth Cameron?"

"Momma?" Seth said.

"What in hell happened to you?"

Seth felt a hand on his chest, but he couldn't find the strength to look up. He feared they finally had him. It took all night, but they had him.

"What got hold of you, boy? Shit, this is just what I need right now! C'mon Seth, don't you go die on me."

Seth finally looked up. The sun rimmed the shadowed face, but there was a familiarity in the voice. "Momma?" he said.

"God dang. Somebody sure beat the hell outa you."

Seth blocked the sunlight with a feeble hand. Through his dirty fingers he saw a round, bearded face and a stalk of thick red hair. Seth gratefully dropped his head back. It's Rusty Wade, he thought . . . it's Rusty . . .

* * *

Ken Jackson covered his mouth to hide a yawn. He took a drink from a cold soda can, putting on his sunglasses to hide any telltale signs of boredom. Sheriff White droned on. Jackson's eyes wandered to Carly and found her staring at him. She smiled and blew a tiny kiss. Jackson quickly looked away.

"People," White continued, "when you get a chance, swing into the farmland. Since this heat wave started, three people have died of heat strokes - all in their eighties. The most recent was Carroll Driftmeyer's old granddaddy. He cooked in his shed for two days before anybody found him." White disgustedly waved off the comments. "Yeah, I know. Point is, ya don't want to find something like that, so keep your eyes open and stop by the farms and ranches when ya got the chance. This is the nineteenth straight day we're gonna go over a hundred. It ain't any fun for anybody, but put out some extra effort and maybe you'll be a hero. That's it, and, by the way, use the damn air-conditioning in your units sparingly."

Jackson led the whines, "C'mon, Virg, give us a break. You want roasted cops?"

White sighed and dabbed his sweat while several other officers chimed in. "I know . . . I know. Roasted weenies in some cases." Good laughter rolled over the room. "Look, I got an average of two to three units overheating per shift. Roll down the windows. If anybody misses a call because of an overheated unit, I'm gonna be real unhappy. Have a nice goddam day." With those words, the same he had used to end every roll call for twenty-three years as Attica County Sheriff, White snatched his clipboard and retreated.

The officers lethargically snaked toward the door into the main lobby of the sheriff's office. From there, they shuffled down the large double staircase. Jackson and Carly walked with Officer Jerry Monroe.

"So, when's the wedding?" Monroe asked.

"Would you shut up," Jackson whispered, glaring at his best friend. He turned to Carly, giving her an unspoken scold as she giggled. "Why not let's make an announcement to the whole world?"

"Hey, lighten up," Monroe said, enjoying the joke. "How long do you think you can keep it a secret around this place?"

"Give us time," Jackson coolly said. "We'd just as soon be discreet, if you don't mind."

"Nothing to me," Monroe said, shrugging. "Hell, you two aren't exactly breaking new ground here. Cops sleep with cops all the time."

Carly couldn't hide her laughter as they reached the main floor. Jackson gave her an exasperated nudge. "Don't encourage him. It isn't funny."

"I'm enjoying it," Carly said.

"C'mon, K.J.," Monroe said. "It's not like you to let a woman embarrass you. It must be love." Monroe fluttered his eyebrows.

"That's not the point," Jackson said, nervously scanning to see who might be nosing in.

"Then what's the rub?" Monroe said. "I mean, look at this fine, lovely woman here. Any man should be proud to call her his sweetheart."

"Why, thank you, Officer Monroe," Carly said.

"Hush up," Jackson whispered. "Jerry, do I have to spell it out? Look at her. Look at me. What do you see?"

"A babe and a boob?"

Carly and Monroe yucked again.

"You know what I'm talking about," Jackson said. "It's bad enough we're fishing off the company pier, but this part of the state ain't exactly a liberal hotbed. Some of you white folks don't approve of your women - you know - mixing their drinks."

"You're an alcoholic?" Monroe said.

Carly laughed.

"Aw, man," Jackson sighed. "Okay, you two make a big joke out of it. I just hope you don't laugh when you find me hanging from a tree someday."

"Kenny," Carly said, "give some of us credit. This isn't the dark ages - no pun intended."

"No?" Jackson said. "You come from Harrisburg, Miss City Girl. You haven't lived here that long. I've been here all my life. Monroe can tell you about the subtle messages he and I have received over the years we've been friends."

"Excuse me," Monroe said, gently brushing Jackson's shoulder. "Let me get that chip off there."

Jackson sighed as Carly and Monroe laughed again. "You two are a riot."

Carly rubbed Jackson's elbow and winked. "I'll see you later." She walked outside and headed for her patrol car.

Monroe stood with Jackson and watched her leave. Monroe leaned heavily on Jackson's shoulder. "Hark! I hear your heart pinging, big fella. It's about damned time, too. After all your wayward romances, I was starting to think maybe you didn't like girls anymore."

"I still don't." Jackson gave Monroe a sly wink. "But, my man, Carly ain't a girl. That is a woman. A woo-man."

"Look out, the big fella's in love!"

"Let's go earn a buck." Jackson brushed Monroe aside and headed for the doors.

"Right behind you," Monroe said. "Hey, did you hear that dog howling this morning?"

Jackson shook his head. "All I heard this morning was a lecture about alarm clocks."

"Real strange," Monroe said. "The damned thing woke me and Ruthie up at dawn. Sounded like a damned were-wolf."

Behind them, a desperate voice echoed through the court-house lobby. "Hey, somebody help!"

Jackson and Monroe turned and saw Rusty Wade standing in the front doorway. Rusty held Seth Cameron up with his big freckled arm. Seth hung over Wade's shoulder like a bad suit - a position most of the cops had seen Seth in before. The burly Wade walked Seth in and eased him onto a couch in the outer foyer.

Jackson and Monroe shared a knowing stare. They walked over as Rusty climbed out from under Seth.

"Hey, that's real decent of you, Rusty," Monroe said. "Since when did you start delivering?"

"I found him in front of my place this morning," Wade said. "He was face-down in the road. Damn fool coulda got run over."

Jackson reached Seth first. Monroe glared at Rusty. "Why don't you just set up a row of cots outside that saloon of yours?"

Rusty's wiry red hair and beard fluttered as he shook his head. He put his hands out defensively. "Look, man, he wasn't even in my place last night."

Jackson knelt and examined Seth. "Uh-huh, Rusty. How do you know who was there with all the head-bashing going on?"

"I didn't have nothing to do with your cop getting her nose busted. Hell, I warned her there was trouble, but she came in without any backup. But little Seth, I swear he wasn't there."

Jackson ignored Rusty and looked in Seth's glazed eyes.

"Are you sure he wasn't loading up last night?" Monroe asked.

The big biker crossed himself. "On my mom's grave, man. Hell, you know he works full-time in the fields. He never comes in during harvest."

"Look at his clothes, Jerry," Jackson said, grabbing Seth's pajamas shirt.

"Looks like bloodstains. He got rolled," Monroe said.

"In bed?" Jackson took Seth by the shoulders and deliberately spoke in his face. "Seth? You hear me?"

Seth's eyes pinballed, his head wavering. "I ain't dead yet," he said. Tears welled in his eyes. "We gotta stop 'em before they kill us all."

Jackson looked at Monroe. Monroe could afford only a confused shrug.

Rusty Wade bent over, his hands on his knees. "Man, let me know what you been drinking and I'll buy a dozen cases."

"Thank you, Rusty," Monroe said, grabbing Wade by his huge tattooed arm. He shoved him toward the door. "Hit the road. And let me tell you something: You best collect your shit, pal, 'cause we're gonna be looking at you real close, hear? If y'all don't start behaving yourselves, you may find that dump locked up for good."

Rusty lumbered to the door, whining innocently. "Monroe, I'm cool. I didn't tell them boys to mess with your cop."

"Yeah?" Monroe said before giving Rusty a final shove out the door. "Clean up your act, or maybe the liquor board will pay you a visit and start checking the ages of those dancers of yours." He slammed the door in Rusty's face.

Sheriff White ambled down the stairs, his attention dropping to Seth Cameron. A tall, silver-haired gentleman with coal black eyes followed him.

"What's going on here?" White asked Monroe.

"Not sure, Virg," Monroe said. "Seth's got some problems here."

White walked over to Seth, who still wavered in Jackson's grasp. "He loaded?"

"I don't think so," Jackson said. "Check this out." He pulled up Cameron's shirt, exposing a deep black bruise on Seth's rib cage.

"He got kicked but good," White said, cocking his head. "Let's get him to the hospital and have him checked out. Was he in on the brawl at Rusty's last night?"

Jackson shook his head. "Wade found him outside the bar this morning, but he says Seth wasn't there."

White knelt next to Jackson and held Seth's head steady. "Seth boy? Who did this to you?"

Seth's eyes chillingly pierced White. "I ain't dead yet," his voice trembled. "But Linville . . ." Seth dropped his head and wept.

White stood up and looked at Monroe. "Linville?"

"What about Linville?" Jackson asked Seth.

"They killed Momma."

Jackson looked at White and Monroe. The silver-haired stranger watched from a distance without expression. Jackson immediately noticed his black eyes.

"Sheriff?" the man said.

White waved him off. "In a minute. K.J., my gut's got a twist right now. Go out to Linville Reeves' place and see if he knows anything about this. Monroe, drive Seth to the hospital."

"They's no need for doctors," Seth said. "They's all dead."

"Who's dead, Seth?" Jackson said.

"Forget it, K.J. He's blown out. Go on, get your butt out to Linville's."

Jackson nodded and stood. Sheriff White moved in and reached for Seth's arm. "C'mon, Seth, stand up."

Suddenly, White's throat was caught in a deadly vise.

Seth sprang and clamped the sheriff with unbelievable force. The little man's eyes burned with a fire that heated the sweltering courthouse.

"Noooo!" Seth screamed. His grip tightened on White's throat.

The big sheriff dropped to one knee, stunned. He grabbed Seth's hand and violently sucked for air as Jackson and Monroe pounced. Seth whipped his free arm and caught Monroe across the forehead. Monroe fell back, his eyes blinded by the blow. Seth brought his arm back around and hit Jackson across the jaw.

"Nooo!" Seth cried, his eyes rolling.

Jackson dumbly crawled back and tried to pull Seth's hand from White's throat. The sheriff turned blue, his mouth contorted and bubbling with foam.

Jackson doubled his fist and smashed Seth's temple. Unfazed, Seth gritted his teeth and clamped White's throat harder. Jackson desperately wrapped his arm around Seth's neck. He pulled back as Monroe and three other cops jumped in. They wrestled Seth and Sheriff White to the ground, the little man still screaming. Monroe pulled his nightstick and cracked it across Seth's purple ribs. Seth doubled and released White, exhaling another scream as he clutched his battered side. White staggered back, holding his throat and gasping for air.

The cops held Seth down for cuffing as the courthouse tumbled in a chaotic swirl. Jackson rolled to Sheriff White and tried to help him to his feet, but White shoved Jackson's hands away. "I'm okay!" he coughed as he bent over to catch his breath.

Seth didn't resist. He wobbled as he stood with help from the firm hands of Jerry Monroe. His wicked fire flamed out.

"God damned bastard," White said, straightening himself. "What the hell's wrong with him?"

Seth's eyes wandered the cops as he spoke. "Ain't no use. I can't help myself. They's inside of me . . . inside my head. Kill me. Kill me before I kill somebody . . ." He slumped into Monroe's arms.

"Get him outa here!" White ordered, still rubbing his throat. Monroe obeyed and led Seth outside.

Jackson put his hand on White's shoulder. "You okay, boss?"

White helplessly looked at Jackson and shook his head. "I thought he was gonna bust my neck, K.J."

Jackson nodded and took a deep breath. He suspiciously looked at the silver-haired gentleman, who had watched the entire event without offering any help.

"I'll get out to Linville's," Jackson said to White, still looking at the stranger. The man returned the stare with those hollow, black eyes . . .

2

Jackson put the pedal to the floor. He gunned down Lakehurst Avenue, rolling past the suggestive twin spires over seedy Rusty's Tavern. Lakehurst turned to gravel at the water tower and became County 84, a twenty-mile farm road that eventually hooked up with Highway 30. In-between were six large farms, some of the richest and most productive fields in the state. The black-and-white negotiated the change from pavement to gravel with ease, its powerful engine growling at the morning heat. Jackson maintained his speed as the car spewed a brown cloud of dust high into the stagnant air. The dust obliterated the view in Jackson's mirror, preventing him from noticing a large black sedan picking up his trail half a mile behind.

Jackson rolled his window up and flipped on the air-conditioner. Rules are made to be broken, he thought, as he dragged a fist across his dampened forehead.

He plucked the radio microphone and spoke clearly. "Fifty-six."

The dispatcher quickly responded. "Fifty-six."

"I'll be code six at the Linville Reeves farm. Five miles south on County 84; ETA eight minutes."

The dispatcher acknowledged, and Jackson gave the car more gas. He sped down 84, passing two farmhouses, several grain elevators, and countless fence posts and trees. The temperature had already hit ninety-seven degrees, and it wasn't even midmorning yet. Jackson looked out across a barren field as the Leggitt farm flew past. Sam Leggitt was losing dozens of chickens to the heat, and it wouldn't be long before his pond went dry. He was worried. Damned worried. The ground dried and cracked over a month ago, wiping out

Leggitt's, as well as every other farmer's corn. The wheat wasn't in much better shape, but everyone was bringing in what they could. It was a war against the elements, and the sun was taking as many farmers down as it was destroying crops. This drought passed severe two weeks ago. The heat was literally burning up the region, and there was no sign of relief.

Jackson estimated his arrival at the Reeves farm at one minute. His stomach tightened when the big farmhouse appeared on the horizon. Linville Reeves' farm was the oldest in the county, having passed through four Reeves generations. If Jackson were to wager, he'd bet Linville Reeves was surviving the drought better than anyone. He knew Reeves from his days as a kid when he hired on during summer vacations. Linville was a miser and a shrewd businessman, who, Jackson was certain, had plenty of money shoved into CDs and mutual funds all over the state.

But Jackson felt uneasy as he watched the house grow larger. Something was wrong out here. After Seth Cameron's bizarre behavior in the courthouse, it didn't require ten years of police experience for Jackson to figure that out. There was something else creaking like a rusty door hinge in Jackson's mind. Seth was a little rummy, no doubt about it, but he'd never been violent. His staggering around like a zombie at this time of year was completely wrong, too. Linville Reeves was a taskmaster who put up with no bullshit from Seth when there was work to be done. What's more, Seth worked that farm like a dog. It's the only thing he'd ever done well in his thirty-eight years. Linville's farmhand simply wouldn't be wandering the streets drunk during one of the most critical harvests in years. That was a plain fact.

Jackson scanned the farm grounds for some sign of life. It was just past nine a.m. Breakfast should be long gone, and the place ought to be alive with action. Reeves wasn't showing much business sense, as far as Jackson could see. He pulled into a long drive leading to the main house, looking for big Jake, Linville's dog, or a moving tractor - anything to reassure Jackson that this situation wasn't going to turn sour. Instead, he discovered an odd, almost unbelievable sight. He leaned over the dash to look up.

Birds - hundreds of them in the trees, on the fences, the rooftops - everywhere.

Jackson slowed to a crawl. He'd never seen so many birds in one place. The windmill stood guard over the house, turning slowly and steadily in a hot breeze. The birds nervously inspected the invader Jackson. He pulled into the shade of a large elm tree and parked next to Seth Cameron's old pickup truck. The farmhouse was surrounded by dried brown grass. A beaten path led out to the barn. Next to the barn were the chicken houses, and beyond were pigpens. Reeves' land stretched beyond the horizon, interrupted only by a small cabin behind the main house where Seth Cameron lived.

Jackson sat for a moment, gently lowering his window and surveying the eerie scene. He saw no sign of life other than the birds. They cackled, awaiting Jackson, who clicked the door open and gingerly set his left foot out. His eyes darted around the birds as a nervous voice trickled down his spine. It was that reliable squeaky hinge in Jackson's brain warning it was time to watch his ass. He never considered ignoring that old hinge.

He stepped away from the car and called out. "Linville?"

At once, the birds exploded and broke for the sky in an incredible frenzy. Jackson instinctively crouched. He scampered back to the open door of his car. The birds screamed at the sun and drove upward in a swirling mass. Jackson shuddered as he watched them pull away toward the south, screaming as they arced northward over the wheat fields. They circled four or five times and sporadically fluttered back in, landing on the fences, trees, and rooftops. Finally, they all returned, and Jackson found himself again in their nervous company.

He drew a long breath. "This is one bizarre scene," he whispered to himself. He took a step forward and abruptly stopped, expecting another feathered eruption. The birds, apparently accustomed to his presence now, didn't react. They just cackled and pecked at one another while the big cop walked toward the farmhouse. As he approached the door,

Jackson got a whiff of something that instantly tightened his skin. The odor was elusive from here, but he knew what it was. He'd found a few dead bodies over the years. It's a smell you don't forget.

A steady pulse whipped on Jackson's temple as he walked up three steps to the porch. Sweat rolled from his hat and moistened his collar. He opened the screen door, the hinges singing to him like a tone-deaf old lady. It sang the same song he heard in his head. He tapped lightly on the wooden front door.

"Anybody home?"

The door creaked open. Jackson watched the sunlight trace a white slit into the house, mentally filing a note that the door was ajar. He slowly entered. The living room window was covered with heavy curtains. Jackson groped the wall for a light switch. He finally found one and clicked it, but nothing happened. His heart galloped now. Quickly, he slid to the curtains and drew them open. The room filled with hot sunlight. It reassured Jackson, but the voice in his head kept up its steady tune.

He searched, but found nothing unusual. The room was neat and orderly, a chair here, a sofa there, the television standing silently next to the china drawer. Mary Reeves' knitting sat on the couch. On the floor by the couch was a wrinkled copy of the *Attica Sentinel*. An old western novel sprawled on its face on the coffee table.

It looked like any other family room, but Jackson knew what was missing. Life...

He continued to look around, searching for answers. His attention was drawn to the television set, or, rather, the electric clock on the wall above. Jackson squinted and cocked his head. The clock read 2:14. Its hands were still. He filed this oddity in his brain, moving through the dining room and into the kitchen. Again, nothing unusual. He remembered how Mary Reeves kept her kitchen. It was typically neat without so much as a breakfast dish or coffee cup in sight. On the wall, the clock was dead at 2:15.

Jackson exited and walked down the hallway to the bed-rooms, his hand now firmly on his weapon. His heart kept its steady rhythm as he stepped carefully down the dark tunnel. The first bedroom belonged to Lisa Reeves, Linville and Mary's granddaughter. Jackson opened the door and peered in, his thoughts on the little freckled teen-ager. Orphaned at the age of eight after her parents died in an automobile acci-dent, Lisa was taken in by her grandparents. In the following years, Lisa had gained the unflattering reputation in Attica as the classic farmer's daughter. Small town gossip credited Lisa with giving more than a few farm boys a journey into man-hood in a variety of unsavory ways. Jackson looked in at the typically girlish bedroom, finding lace curtains, bobby pins, boy-crazed rock posters, and a small bed. Nothing in here gave a hint to the mystery; however, Jackson noticed Lisa's bed sheet haphazardly thrown back. The curtains were open. Jackson's instincts suggested a hasty exit might have been made from here.

He left Lisa's bedroom and crept to the guestroom. Nothing there was disturbed. The bed was neatly made. Jackson's next stop was the master bedroom, where he found the Reeves bed unmade, the sheet thrown to the floor and the curtains pulled open.

Jackson returned to the living room after searching the rest of the house. Okay, K.J., he thought, family's gone, front door's open, and everybody beat it in a hurry. He rubbed his chin and kept scanning while his mind whirred. It's harvest, he thought, but nobody's around - not here, not out in the fields. And what about Seth? Old Reeves wouldn't let Cameron go far without looking for him and getting him back to work. And Seth wasn't the kind to cross Linville, anyway.

He quickly retreated outside, certain he wasn't going to find an easy solution. Too much evidence was piling up to the contrary. The outdoor blast furnace slapped his face when he stepped back outside. A ground search was the next logical procedure, but he wasn't going to do that alone. Jackson started for the car to call for backup, but he stopped when he heard a sound he hadn't previously noticed. The sound didn't come from the birds that still loitered around the farm by the hundreds. Jackson cocked his ear.

Buzzing.

Under the din of bird cackling, Jackson detected ominous buzzing. Flies? He squinted and scanned the grounds. He knew he should call for backup before taking another step, but he was drawn to the buzzing. Slowly, he followed the sound. His nose again picked up the distinct scent of death. As he rounded the corner of the house, another smell joined the strange mix. Something burned out here, he thought.

Jackson curiously looked around until he caught sight of an electrical junction box on the side of the house. It was literally melted to the wall, hanging like a mushy chocolate bar from its moorings. The power line was melted into the box, but the other end was still connected to the utility pole thirty yards away.

"What the hell," Jackson whispered, his voice trailing off. He cocked his head, inspecting the box and flinching at the death-smell, which was stronger here. He finally diverted his eyes and backed away. He turned and headed toward the barn, where the sound of buzzing flies was louder. His steps were slow and deliberate as he approached the huge wooden doors. When he reached the barn, he took a deep breath of foul air.

"Yo, Linville Reeves! It's me – K.J. You in there?"

Jackson's heart raced while he listened for a response. He heard nothing but the loud buzzing of flies inside.

He pulled his weapon and moved away from the line of fire as he reached for the doors. He shoved one open, its hinges squawking at the hot morning. The sun gave light to the barn, and Jackson froze. His mind tried to sort out what he saw, but the grotesque sight and overpowering stench assaulted him. Before him was a once powerful plough horse, now stiffly sprawled on the barn floor. Its wooden-like legs pointed at the ceiling, and its belly, covered with an army of huge flies, was cleanly cut from throat to loins.

"Christ, not again." Jackson swallowed a wad of nausea as he cautiously walked in. He pulled his handkerchief and put

it over his nose as he approached the bloated carcass and disgustedly surveyed the second such animal mutilation found
in the last two weeks. The other was a prized bull found in a
neighboring county - its testicles and brain removed.

A patch of sun lit the horse, and Jackson could see this
mutilation was extensive. His hands trembled as he looked at
the animal's empty body cavity. A portion of its head and ears
was missing, and all of its skin was smoothly peeled from the
left side of its face. Despite the incredible ravaging, Jackson
found no blood in the animal, and none on the floor surrounding it.

Jackson's trance broke as a horsefly lighted on his face. He
swatted it and staggered back to the door. Despite his revulsion, he could not pull his eyes from the horse. Morbid fascination glued him to the carcass, and he was overcome by the
memory of school days when he took his first glimpse of life
in the form of a dissected frog. That was in a clean biology lab,
not on a dirty barn floor, but the incisions looked similar.
Jackson backed out until the sun fell on him. The hot air
slapped his face. He collected his thoughts, fighting a suspicion that this was not the only atrocity lurking about. Slowly,
he approached the chicken house and opened the door.

The smell in here was overwhelming. Jackson gritted his
teeth and covered them with his handkerchief, never walking
inside. He choked as he looked at endless rows of dead chickens. They had obviously succumbed to the ungodly heat
inside. At the far end of the house, three large fans sat, stilled
by the power outage. Jackson's stomach wrenched, and he
started to turn away when his eyes stopped on another
bizarre sight. On the floor, he found three hens lying neatly in
a row. They were all dissected in a similar manner as the
horse. Jackson shook his head in confusion. All three birds
had not a trace of blood under them. The smell finally coaxed
him from the doorway. He walked back under the sun, now
wiping his brow and dabbing both hands on his pants.

"Be cool, K.J.," he whispered to himself as he walked to
the back of the farmhouse. He moved past the barn and out
toward Seth Cameron's cabin. His thoughts were on Seth's

violent outburst at the courthouse, and his words, 'they's all dead.' His eyes remained firmly on the door of the cabin, and he listened for any sounds of life inside. All he heard were the damned flies. He stopped a few feet from the door and cocked his head to the right, his eyes again alighting on something they didn't at first comprehend. Thirty yards to the south, a huge sow carcass stuck out of the ground next to the pigpens. Surrounding the corpse were four huge black birds, picking out breakfast tidbits. The other pigs appeared more interested in hiding in the shade of a lean-to.

Jackson breathed harder now, unwilling to move any closer. He could see the sow had a gaping hole in its belly, and much of the skin on its face was peeled back. Jackson shook his head as if it might dislodge the vision from his brain.

"God," he softly pleaded, "you want to help me out on this one? What's going on here?"

His heart kicked the wall of his chest. He demanded his senses remain keen in this incredible assault of unreality. His eyes slowly drifted over the sow's carcass and suddenly fell on a pink-white mass lying in the wheat field another forty yards beyond. Around the mass were more black birds enjoying a grisly feast. Jackson's blood felt like acid.

"God almighty . . ."

Jackson found the Reeves family.

He inexplicably wanted to turn and run, but he'd been a cop too long to entertain the urge. He slowly holstered his weapon as he began to walk on frozen legs. Each step pieced more of the horror together. The buzzards at first eyed Jackson's approach as an invader to be thwarted until his size became apparent. They yielded to the law of nature and fluttered away. Jackson's breath shortened when the pink lump turned into three separate objects surrounded by bloody night clothing strewn about. His eyes moistened as he finally reached Mary Reeves' cold, hard body.

Her dead eyes stared at the sun. She was nude - in the center of her chest a large knife. Only the handle was visible. Lisa Reeves' body laid not more than ten feet from Mary's. The girl's naked body was twisted and balled tightly. Jackson could make out several knife wounds. Lisa's eyes stared at Jackson's boots.

He suddenly felt air suck into his lungs when his eyes reached the body of Linville Reeves. He first saw Linville's white feet, and then tracked up past the man's scraped and battered knees. Jackson trembled at the gaping hole in Linville's groin. Where Reeves' penis should be, an incision began at his abdomen. It smoothly ran to his throat, leaving a fleshy wake ten inches wide. Inside Reeves' chest cavity was an empty, bloodless hole where his internal organs once were. His mouth was plastered in a hideous silent scream. At his brow, another clean incision ran the circumference of his skull. His eyes and the top of his head were gone. . .

Jackson wildly wheeled around, now shaking in the white heat of morning. He felt Linville's brainless corpse blowing its stench on his neck. Jackson's knees collapsed. He hit the ground on all fours as a hot wave of soda pop, bran muffin and acid exploded from his mouth. He choked and retched into the dirt and straw, and, after his stomach was empty, he heaved as if his guts might follow. The heat closed in as he tried to relax his body. Flies danced around his sweat-soaked hat, and his ears were pierced by the ominous howl of a dog in the distance. He had to escape - at any cost, he had to get away, even if he had to crawl.

Jackson finally dragged himself from the dirt and stood on uncooperative legs. His steps were boozy until he finally found the strength to run. The wind slapped his face, and his strength reluctantly returned. When he reached the farmhouse, he slowed and fought for control. Jackson bent and propped his stiffened arms on his knees, all the time reorganizing every tangled piece of his mind. He straightened and rubbed his eyes, hawking the slime from his throat and spitting it into the dust. Call for help and watch your back, he told himself as he made his way back to the patrol car.

He slumped into the driver's seat and grabbed the steering wheel for balance. After taking a few breaths, he plucked the radio microphone from the dash.

Terror suddenly lanced his heart.

A shadow covered the passenger side window. Jackson bolted from the car, drawing his gun. A tall man stood on the opposite side of the car.

"Hold your ass right there!" Jackson hollered, leveling his weapon at the stranger.

The man froze and raised his hands. "Easy, Officer."

"Not a goddam move." Jackson sidestepped around the front of his unit.

"I wouldn't think of it."

Jackson warily sized up the silver-haired man he'd seen this morning at the courthouse. "Put your hands on the car and don't goddam move."

The man complied as Jackson moved in. "Please, be careful with your weapon."

"Shut up." Jackson put the barrel on the man's neck. He quickly ran his hands up and down each leg and then along the sides of his suit jacket. He stopped when he found a holstered 9mm semiautomatic. He quickly pulled the weapon. "You so much as yawn and I'll drop your ass, understand?"

"Clearly."

Jackson pulled a loaded clip from the weapon and dropped it on the ground. He gingerly laid the weapon on the hood. He seized the man's left arm and pulled it back, and then grabbed the right and pulled it down and handcuffed him. "Now, turn around slow and tell me who the hell you are." The stranger obeyed as Jackson reached and pulled the man's sunglasses off. He backed one step, looking into a pair of cold, black eyes.

"My identification is in my jacket pocket."

Jackson reached in the man's suit pocket and found a wallet, mindful of a large black sedan parked near the road. "You got company in that vehicle?"

"There are two armed men in the car. We're all on the same side, I assure you."

Jackson felt a wiry ball of panic catch in his throat as he glanced again at the car. He then looked at the wallet, which contained a badge and ID, which read: Special Agent J. Carswall. Central Intelligence Bureau. A photograph of the man bore a good likeness. "You're a fed?" Jackson said.

"I prefer 'Special Agent,' but I never seem to be able to get anyone to call me that," Carswall said.

Jackson slowly holstered his gun. "You're lucky they aren't calling you 'dead' right now, pal." He unlocked the handcuffs. "Do they train you to sneak up on cops, or are you just stupid?"

Carswall put his wallet back in his pocket. "I'm sorry. I didn't realize I was sneaking."

Jackson returned Carswall's gun and walked back around the car. "What are you doing here?"

Carswall retrieved the clip and reassembled his weapon. "I followed you. The incident back at the courthouse stirred my curiosity."

"Yeah? Well, stir your ass back to your car and stay out of my way."

Carswall followed Jackson. "What happened out here?"

Jackson looked over the tall man and decided that perhaps they were on the same team after all. "You wouldn't believe me if I told you."

Carswall gently grabbed Jackson's muscular arm. "Try me."

"This is local," Jackson said, looking at Carswall's hand.

"Humor me."

Jackson took a deep breath. "I got three murders, Mr. Special Agent. I got a farm that looks like a butcher shop."

"Is it another animal mutilation?"

Jackson suspiciously glared at Carswall. "Yeah, there are animals out there. But you didn't hear me. I said I got three murders."

Carswall's eyes nearly burned through his mirrored sunglasses. He drew very close. "Listen carefully, Officer. Call your sheriff and tell him I'm here and am commandeering this investigation."

"Say what?"

The agent gave a signal toward his car, and the vehicle suddenly raced up. "There's no time to explain. Just make the call immediately."

Two men quickly emerged from the car.

"Commandeering? What are you -"

"Make the call!" Carswall said, turning to his men. "Scramble, gentlemen." The agents quickly retrieved several large metal cases from the car and headed for the farmhouse. Carswall looked at Jackson. "Where are the bodies?"

Jackson stupidly waved toward the wheat field. "Behind the house. In the field."

Carswall whistled at his men and pointed at the field.

"What the hell is this?" Jackson demanded.

The silver-haired gentleman patted Jackson's shoulder. "Son, it's imperative you stay sharp and follow my instructions very carefully. I realize this appears out of line, but this situation is critical - it is a matter of national security."

"National security?"

"I can't explain it right now because we have to move fast. Just call your sheriff and tell him we need a coroner and backup. Cordon this area at the entrance and see that nobody but Sheriff White is allowed back here. Nobody, do you understand?"

Jackson helplessly watched Carswall walk away. He sat in his patrol car and rubbed the sweat from his eyes. The heat sapped nearly all his remaining strength. Jackson seized a breath and keyed his microphone, but a sudden thought stopped him short. He craned his neck and curiously looked out the windshield.

"Where the hell are the birds?" he whispered . . .

3

The oppressive heat smothered Linville Reeves' farm like a thick woolen blanket. Sirens cried in the air, joining the sorrowful, persistent howl of the hound somewhere over the horizon. Two emergency vehicles sat along County 84 with their overheads flashing a monotonous blue-red rhythm. A skinny paramedic stood with his partner by one ambulance. They smoked cigarettes and complained about the heat. They were told to stay put near a cluster of trees – luckily, the only shady spot along the road.

Sheriff Virgil White's patrol car sat next to Jackson's on the property. White stood near the farmhouse porch with Special Agent Jonathan Carswall. Jackson remained by his unit, talking with Jerry Monroe, who was the first to respond to Jackson's call for help. Jackson's orders were to not discuss what he had seen with anyone, and he had to fend off Monroe's curious questions. Another patrol car pulled up, followed by the medical examiner's van. The vehicles pulled up to a barricade of yellow crime tape strung along the perimeter of the yard. Their engines died in a plume of dust.

Dr. George Baker pried all 380 pounds from his van, his piggish body pouring out like an overfilled bladder that rippled when it hit the ground. Baker looked more like a garage mechanic than a doctor, and his personality was just this side of a weasel. A fat weasel. He grunted as he bent under the yellow tape, throwing a patronizing nod to the officers as he emerged on the other side. The coroner dabbed himself, using a white towel to wipe a ring of sweat from several folds of skin under his chin. Monroe smirked and gave Jackson a nudge as the fat man passed by. Baker waddled to White and Carswall, and Jackson followed.

Carswall spoke to White as they approached. Although the agent wore sunglasses, Jackson felt the man's steely eyes on him. The conversation didn't appear friendly.

"Look," White said, "this is my town, Inspector. Dead citizens are my goddam responsibility!"

"I understand, Sheriff," Carswall said. "I'm simply saying that we will conduct our investigation in concert with yours."

White took off his hat and wiped his brow. "So far you're the one conducting this 'concert.' I got a multiple homicide out here – that is, according to the goddam rumor. Now get the hell out of my way!"

"Sheriff, please just allow me to brief you before we go back there."

"So brief already."

"The area must be sealed. Be certain your officers do not answer any questions from the media."

"Media? This is farm country. The only media we got around here is an ink-drunk reporter who can't spell."

"Nevertheless, you must gag your department. I'll explain why later."

White looked at Dr. Baker, whose hair was spitting oil down his face. He lamely introduced the M.E. to Carswall. "Now, what say we get on with this before we all get heatstroke."

"Very well," Carswall said, walking down the steps. White, Baker and Jackson followed. Carswall stopped. "Just the sheriff and the medical examiner, Officer Jackson," he said.

"Hold it," White said. "K.J. found them."

"Just you and the medical examiner, Sheriff." There was no compromise in Carswall's voice.

Jackson warily looked at Carswall. He waved them off. "I've seen enough anyway." He turned and retreated to the shade.

White and Baker disappeared behind the house as Jackson reached the big elm tree. He mopped his head, looking out at the pigpens, where one of Carswall's men just finished poking around the sow carcass. The agent slowly walked through the wheat field, apparently searching for something. He bent over and picked up what looked like a shotgun. He inspected it for a moment and then tucked it under his arm and walked on. Jackson's eyes diverted to an area just south of the agent. K.J. squinted in the blinding sunlight, cupping his hand over his brow for shade. The ground out there appeared to be burned in a large circle.

A big voice boomed just inches off Jackson's shoulder. "Top of the morning, Officer Jackson!"

Jackson jumped, turning to meet the toothy grin of Dan Williams. "Willy, how the hell did you get in here?"

"Officer Monroe's taking a leak," Williams said with a big grin. "I, in turn, seized the moment."

Jackson grabbed the reporter's arm and turned him toward the road. "You're out of here."

"Easy, Constable, we fair-haired types bruise easily."

"Back behind the tape. Let's go."

"Come on, Jackson," Williams said. His breath reeked of pipe tobacco and gin. "This is my big moment. We haven't had a decent homicide in years."

Jackson stopped and glared at the lanky reporter. He decided to avoid a jousting match. "Who told you that?"

Williams still grinned, his bright blue eyes sparkling through a patch of sandy, straw-like hair. "I have a big nose." His eyes wandered over Jackson's shoulder and saw Sheriff White poking around in the distant field with a trio of 'suits' he didn't recognize.

Jackson got in Williams' face. "C'mon, Willy, be a good boy. I don't want to have to beat you."

Williams let out a satisfied chuckle as he plodded down the long drive. "What gives with the gutted pig? You guys having a barbecue? I'm starved."

Jackson cursed under his breath. "Move it!"

"How about a statement for the evening edition. I'll quote you."

"I'm gonna quote *you* if you don't get out of here," Jackson said, still shoving. "You'll get a statement from Sheriff White." He led Williams under the yellow crime tape just as Jerry

Monroe emerged from the trees.

"Morning, Jerry!" Williams said.

"What the hell?" Monroe said. "Dammit, where did he come from?"

Jackson glared at Monroe. "Jer, you make sure he stays back here. If he moves, shoot him . . . twice."

"Sorry, K.J.," Monroe said, embarrassed. He gave Williams a shove just to salve his pride.

"Police brutality," Williams said, pulling a plastic flask from his jacket. He took a pull and offered it to the cops. Jackson would have given a nut for a belt right now, but instead, he gave Williams a hard stare. Williams shrugged. "Come on. Why else would I wear a sport coat in this blast furnace? It's got deep pockets." He winked.

Jackson wasn't amused. "Willy, you stay back, you hear? I'm not playing with you. This isn't the day to be messing with me."

Williams raised the flask and nodded as he watched Jackson head back to the farmhouse. He then curiously looked out to the fields, where Sheriff White, George Baker and the strangers covered up what looked like bodies . . .

4

Seth Cameron's eyes dropped. He took short breaths, barely recalling someone poking a needle into his arm just moments ago. Through closed eyes he saw a glimmer of tiny sparking lights.

Sleep.

The thought was inviting. Seth could scarcely move. He heard voices coming from outside, lilting through his consciousness. It was talk of murder.

" . . . killed somebody . . ."

"Who?"

"Nobody's talking, but I think it's Linville."

Seth breathed harder. He looked into the sparkling lights and saw Linville Reeves . . .

He sees Linville's head open up and his eyes plucked from their sockets. A heavy shadow moves toward Seth.

"I can't move! I swear!"

Mary Reeves squeals. Seth watches his knife ram her helpless body. She tries to catch the blade, but it's too late.

"I can't stop!"

Seth jumped from his sleep and stared at the cold, white ceiling. He tugged at his manacled wrists as if he might break loose. Across the room, a large officer warily sat by the window. He glanced up from a fishing magazine and cautiously studied Seth for a moment until satisfied. He then returned to *Rod and Stream,* not particularly comfortable with the privilege of sitting in an air-conditioned hospital room all day.

Seth laid his head down and closed his eyes. He thought he heard his momma calling. Within the cavern of his mind a red river ran, fed by Linville Reeves' ravaged body . . .

"I can't move! I swear!"

By the river's edge, Momma sits spread-eagle against a wall. A shattered bone protrudes from her neck.

"No!"

Darkness shrouded Seth's mind. His dreams subsided, and he fell into a discordant sleep. He remained that way for a long time. He was lost. It was over for now, but this was only beginning. Seth was about to embark on a long journey home to Momma . . .

* * *

Jackson stared at his computer monitor without a word. His mind remained on the sight of Linville Reeves' mangled corpse. The station churned around him - officers milling about, phones ringing, pitiful fans whirring.

Carly watched K.J. from a safe distance. She wanted to come up and touch him - to find something to say that might bring Jackson out of the funk he'd brought from that farm. For now, she could only sit and wonder: What in God's name went on out there this morning? The stuffy air was heavy with speculation and innuendo.

Jackson glumly stood and walked into Sheriff White's office. White sat with his chair turned away from the door. He stared out the window.

"Virg," Jackson said, "I don't know what the hell to put in my report." He slumped into a chair next to White's desk.

"How's that?" White said without looking away from the steamy afternoon.

Jackson shook his head. "I got a report to file, but I don't know how to put what I found out there into words."

White slowly turned his chair and propped one leg on his desk. "You best sit tight until Carswall fills us in."

"That's another problem, Virg." He pointed an accusing finger at White. "You let that fed take over."

"And you're out of line." White pulled his leg down and

leaned hard on the desk.

"What business is this of the feds? This is local." Jackson suspiciously looked at White. "Unless it's related to that bull mutilation in Rockford last week."

"What do you mean?"

"That farmer reported a UFO the night before he found the bull. Maybe this fed is -"

"Hold it, bubba. There ain't nothing that relates the Rockford incident to this. That town's been a damned carnival sideshow since that bullshit UFO story came out. I don't want any rumors like that spreading around here." White's old eyes betrayed his defiance, and Jackson noticed. The sheriff's fatigue had been showing up often during his last year before retirement. This wasn't the first time Jackson had scraped his nails on White's blackboard.

George Baker knocked on the door and peeked in. "This a private meeting?"

"Come," White said.

Baker shut the door behind him. He plodded in and sat in front of the small fan on White's desk, pressing his face against the fan guard. His tenor voice was shaky. "Jesus Jiminy, what's with the air-conditioning in this place?"

"Busted," White said.

"The richest county in the state, and they expect me to work in this goddam oven?"

Jackson scowled at Baker. He often wondered how a man smart enough to get a medical degree could allow his own body to become such a disaster. The fan scattered the smell of Baker's sweat around the room. Jackson disgustedly fanned his nose.

White sniffed. "Dammit, George, you spend so much time around stiffs - you're starting to smell like one."

Baker looked hurt. "Well, pardon the turds outa me. It's a hundred and ten out there, you know?" He pulled a stale doughnut from his pocket and munched.

White looked at Jackson and rolled his eyes. "What's up, Bake?"

Baker continued eating as he spoke. "That G-man called

and said to meet him here."

"You had time to look over the bodies?" White said.

Baker shrugged. "I had a look. Seems cut and dried to me."

"Cut and dried?" Jackson said with an astonished laugh.

"Sorry," Baker said. "Poor choice of words."

"What are you talking about, cut and dried?" Jackson said.

"K.J.," White interrupted. He fished for his handkerchief and soaked it in a pitcher of ice water. A satisfied growl rolled from his throat as he dabbed his face. "Relax, son. Look, keep this to yourself, but Seth all but confessed."

Jackson sat back and stared at White. "Confessed? Everything?"

"In so many words, yeah."

"Wait a minute," Jackson said. "Seth told you he cut up those animals? He said he chopped up Linville?"

White stopped dabbing and looked first at Baker, who shared his confusion, and then back at Jackson. "Did what to Linville?"

Jackson felt his stomach turn over. "Killed him. Butchered him - the women - the horse - the pig . . ." He curiously looked at White and Baker. Both returned blank stares.

"What are you talking about?" White said.

Jackson didn't like the look on White's face. "I'm talking about the murder of Linville Reeves; or maybe you didn't hear about it?" The sarcasm instantly fell from Jackson, for both Baker and White looked at him as if he was crazy. "What's wrong with you guys?"

"What's wrong with *us?*" Baker's voice was a squeal.

White raised his hand as if to tell Baker to shut up. He carefully studied Jackson. "K.J., are you saying you saw Linville?"

"What?" Jackson said, trying to laugh. "Hell, yes I saw him. And I have a hard time buying little Seth Cameron as a cold-blooded butcher. Where's the evidence? He should have had blood all over him!"

"Jackson," White said. "We haven't found hide nor hair of Linville."

Jackson's mouth dropped, and his blood suddenly iced. The fan's gentle whir was the only sound in the room. He held his hands out as if he might be trying to hold the room steady. "Are you saying you didn't see Linville out there next to the two women?"

"Are you saying you did?"

"Oh, shit," Jackson said, falling back in his chair.

"What's this about a horse?" White said.

"In the barn - a goddam horse. And those hens in the chicken house - all of them were gutted just like the pig. You saw them, didn't you?"

White dabbed his brow. "We saw the pig. We didn't go into the barn or the chicken house. The fed told me they searched them before I got there."

"That son of a bitch," Jackson whispered. "Virgil, you gotta believe me. Linville Reeves was lying out there with Mary and Lisa. He was gutted - no, not gutted - he was goddam dissected like a lab rat!"

"Are you nuts?" Baker laughed.

Jackson ignored Baker. "Virg, Linville was there. I saw him!"

"K.J., all I saw were the two women. The feds are out there looking for Linville right now with five of our guys."

"Damn!" Jackson stood and paced. "They took him! God dammit, they took him right out from under me!"

"You better go climb in a cold tub, Jackson," Baker said. A giggle squirted from his crusty lips.

Jackson grabbed Baker by the loosened knot in his tie. "I got an idea! Say something else! Go ahead! Say something!"

"K.J.!" White hollered. "Back off! Now!"

Jackson shoved Baker into his chair.

Baker wheezed, a river of sweat pouring over his brow. He tried to right his cumbersome frame. "Virgil, I don't have to take this shit from no . . .no . . ."

"No what?" Jackson turned back and glared at the coroner. "No nigger?"

"That ain't what I was gonna say! Asshole cop! That's what I had in mind!"

"Shut up, both of you!" White ordered. He took Jackson by the arm and wrestled him back into his chair.

"I'll sue your ass, Jackson! I'll sue the whole goddam city!"

White turned and put a finger to Baker's nose. "You ain't gonna sue nobody, Bake. And if you say another word, I'll let him kick your fat butt, hear?" The sheriff held his glare on Baker, who indignantly tried to straighten his collar. White ran his hand through his hair. "It's too damned hot for this crap, boys. Now both of you cool your jets and stop sucking the air out of this place."

Jackson, his breath short, tried to calm himself. "They took him, Virgil."

White draped a leg over his desk and propped himself up. He looked squarely in Jackson's eyes. "You're sure of this, K.J.?"

"I saw him, Virgil! He was out there with the women. He was cut open. His balls were cut off; his damned brain was cut out!"

"Oh, Chrissakes!" Baker cried.

"Georgie," White calmly said, pointing at Baker, "I told you to hush up, now. One more time, and I swear to God I'll break your arm." Baker rolled his eyes, but he wasn't about to say another word. White came back to Jackson. "Son, I ain't saying I don't believe you. But all we saw was Mary and Lisa Reeves poked full of holes; them, and a pig all chopped into pieces."

"Chopped? Virg, that pig was dissected. The wounds were clean."

"It looked torn up to me," White said.

"Then Carswall tore it up. He chopped it up, and he took Linville's body away! He was cut open just like that bull in Rockford!"

"Okay!" White said. "Just relax and we'll try to make sense of this."

"Sheriff," Baker cautiously said. "Can I say something without being smacked?"

"Long as it ain't something stupid," White said.

"Just for the sake of argument, let's say Linville was murdered like Jackson says. How the hell could that G-man cover up something like that? Even if he hid the body, it's got to turn up sooner or later. If Linville's been 'dissected' like Jackson says, there's no way to hide it."

White looked back at Jackson. "Hate to admit it, but he's got a point. Carswall was dumping his drawers about us keeping the press away. Something like this gets out and the whole place would go up in smoke. Maybe he's just trying to keep the lid on until we come up with some answers."

"By hiding the body?" Jackson said. "That bastard sucked you in! You're the damned sheriff here!"

"Back off!" White said. "Right now I got nothing else to go on. Until he shows his hand, I got to wait him out. Why don't you do me a favor and save your campaign for the voters? You ain't wearing this badge yet, pal. I'm still running this show, and if you cross me, I'll see you hauling trash next year; you got that?"

Jackson gritted his teeth and calmly sat back with his hands defensively raised. "My mistake."

"Apology accepted," White said, walking to the window. He suddenly focused on Jonathan Carswall, who entered the courthouse downstairs. "Okay, here comes that fed. Do me a favor, K.J., keep your mouth shut, and let me do the talking..."

Jonathan Carswall entered White's office without knocking. He barely looked at anyone as he stood next to White's desk. "Gentlemen, I'm glad you're all here," he said with that emotionless glaze in his eyes.

"We dropped everything," White sarcastically said.

Carswall never changed his expression. "I apologize for being so dictatorial this morning, Sheriff White. I assure you, our intervention was necessary, and now I'll explain."

White poured himself some water, but he didn't offer his pitcher to anyone else. "I'm all ears. Suppose you start with why you chased me away when I got a multiple homicide in my town."

"I sent you to interrogate the suspect," Carswall said. He

backed the sheriff down with a wave. "Wait. Let's take this from the top. First, Dr. Baker, I trust you've scheduled autopsies of the women?"

"Yeah," Baker said, more concerned with shoving another doughnut down his throat.

"Good," Carswall said. "Officer Jackson, we're filing a report for you since we conducted the on-site investigation. You won't need to file one yourself."

"Why am I not surprised?" Jackson grumbled.

Carswall ignored Jackson. "Sheriff, does the suspect have a story?"

"He says he did it," White cautiously said.

"Did he say he killed Linville?" Jackson said.

White glared at Jackson. "No names. His words were, 'I killed them,' that's all."

Carswall nodded. "It's likely he did, but you must be careful to persuade this man to be specific. We still know nothing about the fate of the third victim, if he indeed is a victim. Perhaps we can help you question him about Mr. Reeves."

"Inspector," White said, "I got a little problem with that. It seems we have a difference of opinion on the subject of Linville Reeves' whereabouts. Officer Jackson tells me you might have an idea where he is."

"I might?" Carswall threw a perplexed stare at Jackson.

"He says he saw Linville's body with the others," White said.

"You did?" Carswall said.

"What the hell is this?" Jackson said. "You know he was out there, and you know what happened to him."

"Officer Jackson, I have no idea what you're talking about. We found two females."

"Bullshit!"

"K.J., be cool," White said.

Carswall shook his head. "Sir, when we arrived, I found you at your car. You were obviously distraught, and you mumbled something about a murder, but you said nothing about how many victims."

"Wrong! I said I had three murders!"

"I'm sorry to differ, but you were nearly incoherent. You were about to collapse from the heat. Perhaps in your condition, you thought you saw three."

"Hey, pal, I got your condition right here. I know what I saw!"

White stood between the two. "Look, K.J., you knew the Reeves family pretty well; they were friends. Hell, I know I damn near blew my eggs after seeing those poor ladies. Maybe the heat got to you."

"I know what I saw!" Jackson looked at White, who was of no help at all. He then looked at Carswall. Jackson knew he was clearly outnumbered. This wasn't the time to challenge anybody. He sighed and rubbed his face as if he really was about to concede. "Shit, I don't know. Maybe you're right. I ain't sure what the hell I saw out there. Virg, if you don't need me anymore, I could use some personal time."

White knew Jackson long enough to recognize the ruse, but he didn't let on. He also knew in his heart that Jackson had long since cut his own path around here. He was the department's best player. "Yeah," White said, "you got it."

"Indeed, Officer Jackson," Carswall said. "You did a good job today. And Dr. Baker, I'm finished with you for now. I want to speak privately with the sheriff."

Baker was happy to leap from his hiding place and waddle out. Jackson slowly followed, tossing a hard stare at White as he pulled the door shut behind him. White walked to his desk and pulled a cigar from his shirt pocket. He sat on the desk and lit the stogie, puffing huge smoke clouds into the room.

"Sheriff," Carswall said, "I don't mean to be rude, but in this stuffy room, that cigar is stifling on a day like this. If you don't mind?"

White took a deliberate pull and blew smoke into Carswall's face. "Yeah, I do mind. This here's a smoke-free building, but I like to think of this as - what's it your boss likes to call it - executive privilege?" He smiled, but Carswall didn't. "What do you say we cut to the bone, pal?"

Undaunted, Carswall fanned the smoke. "I'm not sure I follow."

"Attica's been my town for twenty-three years now. Eighteen years before that I pounded a city beat, so there really ain't many flavors of shit I haven't tasted, you know?"

"It's an impressive record, Sheriff. But you only served on the Harrisburg Police Department for seventeen years and nine months." Carswall's steely black eyes were triumphant.

White took another drag. "Well, well," White said. "Despite all that covert homework you've done, there's something you don't know about me. When somebody kills my citizens, I get real upset; but when somebody fucks with my investigation, I can get downright ugly. Now, pretty little government badge or not, if I don't get some straight answers from you, I'm gonna ram this stogie right up your ass. Do we understand each other?"

Carswall's face reddened, but his voice remained calm. "Sheriff White, we're only beginning to understand each other."

"Good," White said, still madly puffing in Carswall's face. "Now, I got two of my neighbors lying in the morgue with holes in them, and I probably got another one out there in the weeds somewhere. I got a fed who comes here this morning asking me about UFO sightings in the area, and next thing I know, he's following my cops around and taking over a crime scene. Call me stupid, but these are pretty goddam strange circumstances. The taxpayers don't expect nothing from feds like you, but they're gonna want me to explain all this. I don't plan to spend my retirement answering questions like, why did I let some shit-ass bureaucrat keep me from finding the bastard who killed one of Attica's most respected families."

Carswall clenched his fist, his face now crimson. "Sheriff, your insolence aside, the importance of this incident supersedes any personal offense I might take. I suggest you save your bullying for chicken thieves. To use the only language you apparently understand, if you want to fuck with me, you better have a big dick."

White leaned back and chewed his cigar. It would take a moment before they broke their clench and resumed the conversation, but White felt as if his power was slipping.

Jonathan Carswall was certain he'd take it all away before this was over . . .

* * *

Marcus Payne sat at the window for three hours. His eyes fluttered from a soft nap. A siren in the distance pushed through the window screen. He'd heard more sirens on just this one day than he might hear in six months in this town. Payne rubbed his chin and peered out into the brilliant sunlight. He wondered if all the excitement out there might relate to the odd lights he saw in the sky last night.

His attention dropped back to the legal pad on his lap. He took a hard swig of whiskey and mindlessly watched his hand draw, sighing as the paper filled with meaningless lines. The siren outside had irretrievably broken his mood. He tossed the pad and pencil on the floor.

Remington crawled out from under Payne's bed and inched to an empty whiskey bottle with a curious sniff. She inspected the pad and pencil before checking out Payne, who watched her. Bored with what she found, Remmy lazily walked out into the hallway and headed for the sandbox.

Payne, his chin resting in his cupped hand, watched the cat disappear. He turned his attention back to the window. The siren was gone, but something wicked was still in the air...

* * *

Virgil White stood with a doctor outside Seth Cameron's hospital room. After a short conversation, White entered. Seth was still sedated, the doctor said, but he might be able to talk. White nodded at Officer Jimmy Royko, who sat in a corner with his chair propped against the wall.

"Wake up," White half-whispered.

Royko perked and dropped his chair to the floor. "Hey, boss."

"You been here all day?"

"Feels like all week."

"Take five. I wanna talk to Seth."

"You sure you want to be alone with him? It ain't a good feeling, Virg, trust me."

"Eh, look at him. He hasn't been stirring, has he?"

"Not much." Royko stood and stretched. He wandered to the door. "I'll be out in the hall, just in case."

The sheriff watched Royko depart. He looked back at Seth, who stared blankly from his bed. The little man was still restrained, but he showed no interest in moving. "Seth? You awake?"

Seth didn't answer.

White walked up and cocked his head. "Seth? I want to talk to you. You hear me?"

Seth's eyes lazily danced to White. "I hear ya," he said. His voice was sluggish.

"I want to talk to you about what happened last night."

"I already told ya, Sheriff. I done it."

"Okay, Seth, just hold on. Let's take it from the top. You remember what I told you this morning? I told you about your rights? I said you got a right to have a lawyer here anytime you and me talked."

"I don't need no lawyer. I done it."

"You're saying that you killed Linville, Mary, and Lisa Reeves?"

"I didn't have no control over it, Sheriff. It was like this morning when I hurt you. Yeah, I killed Mary and Lisa, but I couldn't help myself. Them bastards put something in my head, and I can't do nothing to stop myself."

"Slow down."

"Them bastards killed Linville."

White felt his ulcer spit acid. His conversation with Jonathan Carswall this afternoon after Baker and Jackson left twirled in his mind. "Who are you talking about, Seth?"

"They killed Linville, and they made me kill Mary and Lisa."

White watched Seth cautiously. "You didn't kill Linville?"

"No."

"Come on, Seth. You killed all three of them, didn't you?"

"Them bastards killed Linville. I swears."

"Seth, you're talking crazy. I want the truth."

"I ain't crazy," Seth said. Tears welled in his eyes.

"Let's take it one by one, Seth. We found Mary Reeves out on the farm with a knife in her. Did you kill her?"

Seth, his eyes still closed, sucked back the tears. "Yeah, I told ya I did."

"Lisa Reeves was right next to Mary. She was stabbed, too. Did you kill Lisa?"

"I don't know. I reckon I did."

"Did you kill Linville?"

"Them . . . them bastards. They killed him."

"Who are they?"

"Them bastards in the sky. Aw, shit - you ain't gonna believe me."

"Seth, I think you killed Linville."

"What's it matter? If you think it, that's how you're gonna think."

"I think you did it, Seth. You got yourself all boozed up, and you and Linville got into it. Next thing you knew, the liquor had you blind and you went on a killing spree. Ain't that about the way it happened, Seth?"

"Okay! I done it! Just leave me be!" He wept, his arms pulling at the leather restraints.

White breathed heavily, looking at this sad excuse for a man. He turned and cursed this whole damned situation.

It was a sudden flash . . .

In an instant, Seth came up and clamped his hands on the sheriff's throat, lifting White off his feet. In one incredible burst of strength, Seth tossed White across the room as if the sheriff were nothing more than a tiny rag doll. White instinctively turned his shoulder as he hit the window. A spray of glass showered his head and back.

Officer Royko pounded through the door and jumped at Cameron. He tried to wrestle Seth off the bed, but the little man was too strong. Seth came down on Royko and began choking him.

White groggily pulled himself up. A terrible gash in his

scalp spewed blood into his eyes. He staggered to Royko and tried to pry Seth's hands from the cop's throat. An orderly ran in and jumped into the fray. On his heels was a doctor, who first hollered out the door for the floor nurse to bring a sedative. White pulled Cameron's hands away from Royko, but Seth's rage then turned on the orderly. He grabbed the man's arm and twisted it until his forearm snapped with a hollow pop! The orderly bellowed and fell as White pulled his gun and cracked the butt end across Seth's forehead.

The little man fell back and released the screaming orderly, who crumpled to the floor, tucking his broken arm to his chest. A nurse ran in as White and Royko pounced on Seth and held him down. The doctor hastily snatched a hypodermic needle from the nurse.

"Put him down!" White cried.

The doctor checked the needle and quickly jammed it into Seth's upper arm. Seth struggled for another minute and then wavered. His eyes finally fluttered, his head dropping to the floor. White and Royko eased their grip, both stumbling back in terror. The nurse tended to the injured orderly as White clamped his hand over his head wound. He staggered to Seth's bed.

"God damn," White said. "Look at this."

The doctor and Royko stared incredulously at Seth's bed. White grabbed the leather restraints, which had been ripped from their moorings . . .

5

An uncomfortable, almost unfriendly dinner put Jackson and Carly on edge. They hastily ate without saying much. Jackson then retreated to the shower, where he planned to cool down and wash off his sullen mood. Carly went into the living room and put on some soft music. She slumped into Jackson's favorite chair, hoping he might land there soon.

Jackson appeared in a moment with a towel over his head. He wore a pair of old, tattered running shorts that bore the number 31, and the words, 'Jack Magic' underneath. They were a prized possession from his high school football days when he led the state for three years in rushing and touchdowns scored. His bare chest was even bigger than it was in those days, and his arms now looked like tree trunks. He stood before Carly with the towel still covering his face.

Carly smiled. "Has that big grizzly turned back into my little teddy bear now?"

Jackson weakly growled. Carly got up and rubbed the towel over his head. She led him to the chair and gave him a good shove. He dropped down, taking her with him. They nestled in and Carly put her head on his hard shoulder. For a moment they simply enjoyed a good hug.

"You ready to talk to me?" Carly said.

Jackson, his eyes contentedly closed, rubbed her arm. "I'm sorry about the attitude."

"Did you see the paper this afternoon?"

"I didn't see anything after I left the courthouse," Jackson said. "I took a drive to some dried up corn field and sat there, wishing we never got up this morning."

"You were front page news. Attica Police discover grisly

murders and animal mutilation."

Jackson's eyes popped open. "It said that? Damn, I gotta hand it to Willy - he's a drunk, but he ain't stupid."

"The story said two women were murdered, and one man is missing. Some guy named Cameron is in custody. The whole thing was compared to that UFO sighting in Rockford last week."

"Oh, man, Williams - that sonofabitch," Jackson said. He shook his head. "Virgil's gonna have a stroke when he reads that."

"He already read it," Carly said. "You should have seen the station. We were swamped with calls when the news broke - people reporting UFOs, prowlers - one lady called and asked if we could put her cats in protective custody."

"Oh, damn," Jackson said, finally sharing a laugh with Carly.

They leaned back and held each other for several anxious moments. Carly ran her hand over Jackson's chest. "What happened out there?"

Jackson sighed and looked into her eyes. The words didn't come easily. "I don't know, to tell you the truth. I've seen some strange things on this job, but today was beyond belief."

"So there was an animal mutilation along with the murders?"

Jackson shook his head. "It's not the right word for it. I saw dissected animals, like somebody took a scalpel and operated on them. They were opened up with clean incisions, and there wasn't any blood anywhere – not a goddam trace. But that's the good news."

Carly felt Jackson's body tighten. She sat up and looked at him. "What else?"

"I don't even know how to say it," Jackson sighed. He looked at the ceiling, fighting off the images of that farm. "I knew those people. They were friends. Mary Reeves looked like - it was terrible, babe."

"I'm sorry, Kenny."

He took her hand. "I'm alone out here. Something's going on, and I'm twisting in the wind. Right after I found them, this dude who claims he's with the CIB suddenly appears from nowhere. He took over the entire investigation and shut us out. He's covering up something."

"Covering up what?"

Jackson stared vacantly at Carly, his mind still on the farm. "I found Linville Reeves out there in that field."

"But I thought he was missing."

"He may be missing, but I saw him. Carswall and his boys took the body and hid it before my backup arrived."

"What? Why would they do that?"

"Because Linville Reeves was dissected like those animals."

Carly's mouth dropped open. "My god," she whispered.

Jackson swallowed hard, trying to believe what he just said was true. "His body was . . . damn, Carly, it was empty. His balls were cut off, his organs were gone, and his head . . ."

"Kenny." She grabbed his trembling hand.

Jackson drew a hard breath, sucking back a fear that tried to choke him. "The top of his head was gone. His brain was - gone . . ." He looked at Carly as if he might have to convince her.

She could only give Jackson an unbelieving stare, but she tried to gather her thoughts. "What kind of monster would do something like that?"

"You mean you believe me?"

"What do you mean by that? Of course I do."

"I'm having a hell of a time convincing anybody I wasn't some rookie with heatstroke out there."

"Did you tell Virgil?"

"Yeah," he said, frustration leaking from his voice. "But the last thing Virgil wants is somebody souring his retirement party next year. Carswall's playing us for fools, and Virg is the head clown."

"How can they hide a crime like this?"

"What I want to know is, why was Carswall there in the first place? He was hanging around this morning when Seth came in, and he followed me out to the farm. That bull in Rockford was mutilated like the animals I saw today, and the old guy who reported it said he saw a UFO that night. These things have been going on for years, but until now it's always been passed off to some old farmer high on bad moonshine."

"But that was before the old farmer was the victim," Carly agreed.

"Exactly," Jackson said. "Linville gets dissected, and suddenly the place is crawling with feds. Next thing you know, Linville disappears and everybody's looking at me like I need sedation."

"What about Cameron? Did he give Virgil a story?"

"White said he confessed to killing Mary and Lisa. But whatever he says happened to Linville isn't gonna matter if the feds have the body. Seth's got no credibility. He's a rummy."

"I still don't understand why they'd try to cover this up."

Jackson shrugged. "Maybe this time they can't come up with an explanation that's gonna satisfy the public."

Carly nervously rubbed her arms. "This is crazy, Kenny."

"I'd lay odds that Seth's got one hell of a story. Ain't no way Carswall's gonna let it get out, and he's got a hammer over White's head."

"Why would Virgil give in?"

"Baby, he's got a sweet pension and maybe fifteen more years of life without problems, providing he doesn't cross somebody who could take it all away. We're talking about a government agency with a heavy reputation for eliminating problems, you know."

Carly took a long breath. "And they know you saw Linville."

"Yeah, that's my problem."

"What are we going to do?"

Jackson looked into her terrific eyes. The word 'we' had never meant much to him until now. He put his big hand on her cheek. "We keep a low profile. I'm going to let Carswall go right on believing I'm a dumb small town nigger flatfoot with heatstroke."

Carly gave Kenny a sour look. "Something tells me he's going to find out the truth before this is over."

Jackson smiled. "I told you that you weren't too bright getting mixed up with me."

"Oh, shut up," Carly whispered. She put her head back on his shoulder . . .

* * *

Marcus Payne sat on the roof outside his window. Remington purred in his lap, bobbing her head as Payne scratched her ears. He suspiciously watched the sun vanish from the horizon. The hot air stirred into a breeze while Payne listened to the sizzle of cicadas in the trees. Fireflies twinkled in the dusk like tiny electrified angels. The smell of heat was thick, and Payne could only sit very still to manage any comfort.

Soft music leaked through the window, vintage stuff as old as the woman who owned this boarding house. Payne sighed softly, looking into the growing darkness and trying to separate last night's dreams from what might have been reality. He recalled seeing lights and dreaming of murder. Nightmares were as common to Payne as breathing since Lori Payne died, but the lights were something new. In fact, Payne wondered if it had really been a dream at all . . .

* * *

'Spider' Saunders' squeal was distinctive. It sounded like a pig. He pulled a big stick from the pond and watched a thick bull snake wrap around it. "Go on," he said, laughing at his dirty buddy, Al Pike, "touch it. It ain't poisonous!"

Pike recoiled instinctively. His lean, almost comical body twitched and trembled. "Get away!"

Spider laughed. "He won't hurt you none!"

"Get away! I'll kick your fat ass, I swear to God!"

Spider still laughed as he dropped the stick back into the pond. The snake disappeared into the muck. "He was one big boy," Spider said, reaching for another beer from a well-stocked ice chest.

"I hate them goddam things," Pike muttered, taking a beer for himself. A belch popped out with his words. "I came out here for the beer and bullfrogs, not no fuckin' boa contractor."

"Constrictor," Spider laughed.

"Whatever." Pike took a pull from his beer. He plugged one nostril and blew a wad of green mucus from his nose.

Spider disgustedly shook his head. "You can't hide class," he said. He sat on the muddy bank and lit a reefer. The smell of pot wafted through the woods. He sucked in and held it, passing the joint back to Pike and speaking as he exhaled, "Hell, it's too hot for giggin' tonight. What say we just get real stupid and go to Rusty's and chase pussy?"

"Okay by me," Pike said. He threw another belch that echoed across the water and mixed with the clicks and chirps on the pond.

Spider tossed a louder croak, and they burst into laughter. They were already pretty damned stupid. "Listen to them bugs."

Pike plopped down into the mud. "Yeah, a fuckin' bug choir."

Spider was twenty-nine, a welder by trade. Al Pike was a petty thief on parole. The boys attended the tenth grade together - the happiest three years of their lives, they liked to joke. Spider blew off school and started welding, and Al took up stealing. Al was out of stir for three months now, and he was getting tired of honest work. 'Finding' beer and pot money was a hell of a lot easier than earning it. Tonight, Al was going to suggest they take out a convenience store in Rockford this weekend. Get Spider wasted enough, and he'd rip off his own mama.

Pike checked the beer cooler. Plenty of beer. Plenty of weed. Plenty of stupid. The problem was, they were both going to die in a few minutes.

Spider's beer was already gone. He snagged another and popped the top. "I love it out here, you know? 'Bout the only cool spot around. Hell, them bugs chirpin' ain't nothin' compared to the old lady on my case all the time."

"I'm thinkin' more 'bout that pussy at Rusty's. Let's go get us some whores."

"Okay by me. Okay me moo, huh-huh." Spider just surpassed stupid. His eyes resembled cut glass.

"Woah," Pike said, suddenly perking. He sat up and looked at the starry sky. "You see that?"

"See what?"

"Right up there." He pointed a muddy finger. "A big 'ol flash right up there."

Spider wasn't very interested, but he looked. "I don't see nothing."

"It ain't there now. It was a flash; then it was gone."

"Shootin' star. Real big deal, Al. Big beal, huh-huh." He laughed badly.

"Shee-it, that wasn't no shootin' star. It looked like a fuckin' explosion."

"Yeah? I didn't hear no explosion. You need another beer. Nara - poya - paranoia. Huh-huh!"

"Damn," Pike whispered, leaning back down and taking another long pull. He curiously watched the sky.

"Wanna have a fart contest?"

"Shuddap. Listen . . ."

Spider blew more smoke and looked at Pike. "What?"

"Just shuddap." Pike slowly got up on his knees, putting his beer can in the mud.

"What's with you?"

"Listen!" Pike scanned the pond like an animal with the eyes of a dangerous predator on him.

"I don't hear nothin'."

"Yeah," Pike whispered. "Neither do I."

Spider finally caught on. The pond was entirely silent, as if someone had flipped a switch and turned off every sound in the valley. The only sound was the gentle hiss of a gas lantern at their feet. "Where'd all them bugs go?" Spider almost whispered.

"I don't know," Pike said.

"What the . . .aw, shit." The lantern suddenly fizzed out. It dropped them headlong into the moonless dark. "I can't see a damn thing. Where's your lighter?"

"Listen," Pike said, groping for Spider's arm.

Spider stopped and heard what he could only believe was a low hum coming from somewhere off in the distance. He squinted, but it didn't help. All he could see were black-blue shadows. "What's that?"

Pike squinted. "Sounds like maybe a motor, or an engine." The hum grew louder. As it did, the ground began to buzz. "What in hell?"

"Feels like an earthquake," Spider said.

"You know, hoss," Pike said, "I ain't so hot on stayin' out here no more."

"You and me both," Spider said. They bumped into each other and groped for the beer chest and lantern. "You got any feel for which way the truck is?"

"Yeah, I think -"

Pike's words were cut in half by an incredible shriek overhead. Spider squealed and put his hands over his ears, while Pike instinctively dropped to his knees and covered his head. They looked up and saw a blur of light and shadow. The roar followed close behind.

"Holy fuck!" Spider cried. He knelt with Pike and watched the huge shadow glide through the sky until it reached the other side of the pond. It suddenly changed direction and darted five hundred yards downrange, moving at an unbelievable speed. There, it simply hovered with a still tremendous roar.

"What the hell is that goddam thing? A helicopter?" Spider hollered.

"That fucker's bigger than any chopper I ever seen!" Pike trembled next to Spider. A blue beam of light jumped to the ground and swiveled, lighting up an acre of ground. The craft made a sudden lateral move. It slowed about one hundred yards from the men and hovered again. The light fired to the ground and swiveled.

"They's searchin' for something?" Spider said.

"Hoss," Pike said, "whoever they are, or whatever they're looking for, we best get the hell outa here!" He took off.

Spider clumsily followed, stumbling every other step. He heard Pike up ahead, but it was too dark to see him. Within seconds, the approaching roar knocked him to the ground. Spider tried to stand, but he was frozen, his arms and legs numb. A blinding blue tunnel of light suddenly fell over him, and Spider saw trees and brush as if it were daytime. He also saw Pike standing motionless just a few yards away. Pike's eyes bulged in the terrible light. Spider tried to scream, but he couldn't hear himself. In a minute, they both screamed; in another, the swamp fell dark and still . . .

6

R eed Aaron stepped out of Seth Cameron's hospital room, lugging a tattered leather briefcase as if it weighed a hundred pounds. He stopped outside for a moment and simply stared at the closing door. Two Attica police officers nodded at Aaron and walked back in to resume watch over Seth. It was mercifully cooler in here than it was outside, but Aaron was still uncomfortably warm. Perhaps the extra fifteen pounds he'd accumulated over the last ten years made it so, or maybe it was the stress from a job that was losing its appeal lately, but Aaron was beginning to feel old for the first time in his life. The past ninety minutes with Seth Cameron did nothing to lessen his fear. It was only eleven a.m., but Aaron felt as if he'd put in a sixteen-hour day. He shook his head and trudged down the hospital corridor. Sheriff White rounded the corner and met him.

"You done, Counsel?" White asked.

"I can't pull anything over on you, can I, Virgil," Aaron said, wiping his neck with a handkerchief. He walked around White and headed for the elevators.

White followed Aaron, his bandaged hand tucked close to his belly. "You figure Seth's checked into the Schizoid Hotel?"

Aaron tried to hold back a smile. Despite twenty-some years of searching for a logical reason to dislike White, Aaron hadn't succeeded. "I think that's for a psychiatrist to decide. Do I look like a psychiatrist?"

"Hell, it don't take a shrink to see his pilot light's out."

"Thank you, Doctor White," Aaron said, pushing the elevator call button. "Now, do you want to sentence him, or maybe just shoot him and save the taxpayers some money?"

"Easy, Counsel," White said, defensively raising his bandaged hand.

Aaron glanced at White's hand and the bandage on his head. "I hear you tried to jump out the window yesterday. Try carbon monoxide, it's painless and leaves very little mess for the coroner."

"Thanks for the advice, Counsel, but it was your client who tried to give me early retirement," White said. "So where you going? I got a case to file. Let's make the confession legal while you're here."

"Nice try, Virgil. No confession. And, by the way, now that Seth is officially represented by the Public Defender's Office, no more interrogations unless I'm present."

"Look, he declined counsel at first. I gave him a break, holding off until you were here before I took his statement."

"Congratulations, you're a fine man, Virgil, but he's not confessing."

"He already did - off the record, anyway."

"Objection, Your Honor; hearsay."

"Come on, Reed. Let's wrap this up now. A blind man can see he's guilty."

"I'll be sure to remember that if you're called to jury duty."

"Jury?" White said. "The heat getting to you? The guy is certifiable. You want to take a mental case to trial?"

"Virgil, you and I aren't qualified to make a mental evaluation of Seth. I'll look into that before arraignment. And, why am I discussing this with you?" Aaron turned and waited for the elevator.

"So, I just wasted my morning getting all this paperwork ready? Thanks, Counsel. And by the way, you're pissing in the wind if you think that boy can skate."

"Thank you, Judge White."

The sheriff shook his head. "I guess that's what separates me from you. I see this old boy who carves up innocent folks, and you see an opportunity to dust off your law books."

"Is that so?"

"Yeah, and I'll tell you something else. A lot of people in town owed debts to Linville Reeves that can't be measured in dollars - things like the helping hand he offered his neighbors in this drought, and maybe a thousand things he and his kin have done for this town the past century. Seth Cameron ain't given Attica nothing but a boil on its ass since the day his ma got her head blown off by that lowlife pimp. Off the record or not, he confessed to stone-cold murder. People around here don't think much of killers - or the lawyer who defends them, if you get my drift."

The elevator doors opened. Ken Jackson and Dan Williams were inside. Aaron turned to White. "Very touching speech, Father White. You ought to carry a violin to accompany yourself. But let me remind you it's your job to collect evidence and present your case to the D.A. Nowhere in your duties do I recall your need to present sermons and veiled threats."

"Come on, Reed, that wasn't a threat. You ought to know friendly advice when you hear it."

"Thank you. I appreciate it, I really do, but the taxpayers pay me to defend my client, just like they pay you to do whatever it is you do. Court adjourned."

White sighed and shook his head. "Lawyers," he huffed. "How can you look at yourself in the mirror every day?"

Aaron stepped into the elevator. "I don't own a mirror."

The doors closed before Jackson or Williams could exit. Jackson wanted to say something, but he was intrigued by the look Aaron gave Williams. Willy grinned through the smell of gin and pipe tobacco. Aaron rolled his eyes in disgust. "Is there no God?"

"Well," Williams said, "wasn't that an interesting exchange?" He reached through Aaron's arm and hit the emergency stop button. The elevator bounced to a halt between floors. Aaron slowly turned to the nosey reporter. Jackson felt like an uninvited guest.

"I first want to thank you for coming by for this exclusive interview," Williams said, still grinning.

"My pleasure," Aaron sighed.

"Officer Jackson," Williams said, "I believe you know the esteemed Public Defender Aaron?"

Aaron, who'd tripped this snare before, played along to

get it over with. He acknowledged Jackson. "He didn't try to bite you on the way up, did he?"

Jackson pointed at the door. "I . . .uh . . .wanted to get out."

"Technically, it's kidnapping, Officer Jackson," Aaron said, "but I don't think I could make it stick. You and I know the kind of mentality we're dealing with here. Now, Mr. Williams, would you mind making your point? I have a hell of a day ahead of me."

"I protest," Williams said. "What do you mean, 'the kind of mentality?'"

"Willy," Aaron said, "do you have any idea what the penalty is for taking city employees hostage?"

"No," Williams said, "but this won't take long. The combination of heat and claustrophobia should shorten the time it'll take me to pick you clean. Let's start, as the big city reporters say, with a comment."

"No. Can we go now?"

"I asked for a comment. Those were an answer and a question. Try again."

"I don't have any comment," Aaron said.

"Let's start with Cameron. What did he tell you?"

"I'll release a statement this afternoon."

"Do you believe the confession he made to Virgil?"

"Why do we have to go through this every time, Willy?"

"Hold it," Williams said, "you're asking me a question. It doesn't work that way. I ask the questions, and you dodge them. Boy, you'd think after all these years you'd know that."

"Sorry," Aaron sighed.

"Why were there federal agents at the murder scene?"

"Ask them."

"I did," Williams said. "Special Agent Jonathan Carswall must have majored in 'Asshole' at spy college."

Jackson hid a smile. It felt good not being Williams' prey for once, but at the same time he felt sorry for Aaron - even if he was a lawyer.

"Can we go now?" Aaron said.

Williams plucked his briar pipe from a pocket and fished

for his lighter. "Did Seth see any flying saucers?"

Aaron grew suddenly uncomfortable. "I said I have no comment."

"Uh-oh. I just hit a nerve. So, he did see a UFO, just like the incident in Rockford a few weeks ago?"

"Look, Willy, that's enough. And if you light that pipe in here, I can have Jackson arrest you."

Williams lit his pipe. "How about Linville? Has the M.E. done the autopsy yet?"

Jackson perked. "Say what?"

Williams and Aaron looked at Jackson as if they were surprised he could talk. Aaron spoke to Williams, but his eyes didn't leave Jackson. "He released a preliminary this morning."

"Hold it," Jackson said. "Did you say, Linville?"

"Yes," Williams said, "you know, farmer, missing person, it was in the paper."

"Shut up, Willy," Jackson barked. He turned again to Aaron. "Linville was found?"

Aaron felt a ball of gluey suspicion roll down his back. He spoke cautiously. "They found the body in the field late last night."

"And Baker filed a report already?" Jackson said.

"Like I said, just a preliminary," Aaron said. "He's going to perform an autopsy today."

"Did the report give a cause of death?"

"Hold on," Williams interrupted. "I'm the interviewer. I'll ask the questions. What was the cause of death, Reed?"

Aaron sighed. "Look, Officer Jackson, no offense intended, but my life stinks enough right now. You're just feeding this guy."

"What was in the report, Mr. Aaron?" Jackson said with finality.

Aaron measured Jackson. "Like I said, the autopsy is scheduled today, but the prelim shows a single gunshot to the head."

"What?"

Williams puffed his pipe. "Problem, Jackson?"

Jackson suddenly felt cornered. His eyes darted between the two men. "Did you see the body, Mr. Aaron?"

"No," Aaron said. His brow lowered.

"Maybe you ought to have a look."

"The plot twists," Williams grinned. "Officer, I gather from your surprise that you might not agree with the Medical Examiner's opinion?"

"You don't gather anything but flies, Willy," Jackson said. "All I'm saying is maybe the Public Defender ought to have a look at the body." His glare fixed on Aaron, who remained unexpectedly calm.

"Good idea," Williams said. He released the elevator. "Maybe we should all go."

* * *

Dr. George Baker's mouth was just too full. There simply was no room for the coffee he tried to pour in. He lurched forward, and pound cake spewed on his lab coat as Jackson, Aaron, and Williams walked through the door. Baker sponged himself, curiously gawking at the trio.

"Hello, George," Williams said. He pulled the pipe from his mouth. "Wearing your breakfast again, I see."

"What do you guys want?" Baker grunted.

"Be a good sport and let us have a look at Linville Reeves," Williams said.

"What? Are you crazy? Get outa here."

"Why is that a problem?" Aaron said. "I'm the Public Defender assigned to the case, you know? Officer Jackson here is a key actor in the investigation, and Willy - he's scum, but he's with us."

"Scum?"

"Shut up, Willy," Aaron said. "How about it, Doctor?"

"What are you guys? Ghouls?"

"Maybe you got something to hide?" Jackson said.

"Hide?" Baker said, glaring at Jackson. "What do you mean, hide? Hell, if you want to look at a dead body, go ahead." He tossed a final hateful glance at Jackson and led the trio through a door. They pounded a long corridor and turned into the morgue. Baker approached a bank of steel doors and chose one with a hastily scratched label that read 'Reeves, L.' He clenched the cake in his teeth, and he rolled out a stainless steel stretcher. Upon it was a body, covered by a thin sheet. Baker pulled the sheet back.

Williams and Aaron felt their stomachs churn as they looked at the shredded body of Lisa Reeves. She was yellow-white, her skin cold and waxy. Her eyes were half-open, and the wounds on her body were black and purple, accented by the hideous zipper-like autopsy scars.

Baker munched his cake. "Oops, wrong 'L. Reeves.'"

Aaron looked away.

"We want to see Linville," Jackson said.

"Sure," Baker said. "Why not? I wouldn't want to ruin your fun, but you better grab hold of your gut." Baker stuffed the cake in his big jowls. He covered Lisa and slammed the stretcher back into the vault. "Let's see, here's the other Reeves, L." He opened the vault and pulled out the stretcher.

Jackson's blood raced as he looked over the covered remains. At last, he thought, somebody else is going to see this - a lawyer and a reporter, no less. Baker pulled the sheet back, and Jackson's heart twisted.

Aaron cocked his head and looked at the body. Although he'd seen this kind of wound before, he never found a way to keep from being nauseated by it - particularly one this grisly. Secretly, he experienced a second, unusual emotion of disappointment. He thought he might see something different.

The body was of the same cold and waxy consistency. The front portion of the head was entirely gone. A shotgun blast had taken away all of the corpse's face and had blown most of the skull and its contents away. In fact, there was very little head left on the bloody white sheet except for the rear portion of the neck. The rest of the body, however, was untouched, and it bore a remarkable resemblance in size and weight to Linville Reeves.

"Gunshot," Baker said triumphantly. "Shotgun, I'd say. Of course, fifteen years in this business ain't much, but I have a weenie hunch he got hit from pretty short range. Weapons have a tendency to kind of explode anything real close when they go off." He smiled with gooey teeth.

"Good god grief," Williams whispered, his eyes helplessly glued to the gore on the stretcher.

Jackson hovered over the cadaver, but Williams had seen enough. He walked to the door.

Aaron turned, but Jackson grabbed his arm, still staring at the body. "Officer?" Aaron said.

"I want you to look at something," Jackson said quietly. He threw the sheet off the body.

Aaron's stomach burned. "I really don't like this, Jackson. Would you make your point - in a hurry?"

"What are you doing?" Baker asked.

"Shut up," Jackson ordered. "Mr. Aaron, look at his feet."

"What?"

"Just look at them."

Aaron disgustedly pushed his eyes to the body's feet. "What about them? They're feet."

"Any scars on them?" Jackson said.

Aaron, his teeth grinding, quickly looked them over. "I don't see anything."

Jackson threw the sheet at the corpse.

Baker covered the body and shut it back in the vault. "C'mon, Jackson, beat it. Your boss will kick my ass if he knows I let you guys in here . . ."

Jackson reluctantly followed Williams and Aaron outside. The heat was stifling.

Williams plugged his hands in his pockets. "Counselor, if you aren't going to help me, I do have a deadline." He sauntered to his car and climbed in.

Aaron reached his car as Williams drove away. As he fished for his car keys, he noticed Jackson sheepishly following at a distance. "Officer? Something on your mind?"

Jackson looked Aaron over. Scooting up next to a defense lawyer just didn't feel right. It was the nature of their confrontational professions, but Jackson knew that Aaron was his only chance. "Mr. Aaron," he said, "you may think I'm crazy, but that body in there isn't Linville Reeves."

Aaron's reaction was unexpected; no look of disbelief - just a calm, noncommittal stare.

Jackson pensively scrubbed the pavement with his boot. "Oh, yeah, it's damn good. Without a head, it probably could pass for Linville, providing the right people take care of the autopsy report."

"Do you want to elaborate?"

Jackson's cold stare ripped through Aaron. "That body in there is not Linville Reeves."

Aaron drew a hard breath. He watched his own foot nervously trace a circle in the gravel. "Ordinarily, I'd say this wasn't a wise idea, but maybe we ought to go have a cup of coffee..."

* * *

The Honey Pot Cafe couldn't be called a 'greasy spoon,' but it surely wouldn't rate four stars either. It did boast the best chili cheeseburger in the state, and most of the trucking trade agreed the coffee was strong enough to keep you off amphetamines for five hundred miles. Jackson asked the waitress for a refill of iced tea, but Aaron turned down more coffee. The graying attorney's health wasn't the best, and what Jackson just told him turned his stomach sour.

Aaron loosened his tie and pushed the empty cup away. "You're the only one who can verify that Reeves was out there when the other victims were found?"

"Me, and Carswall and his boys."

"Have you told anyone else?"

"I told Virgil, but I don't think he wanted to believe me. I don't think anyone knows where he stands anymore."

Aaron nodded.

"Carswall knows I saw Linville. I told Baker, Virg, and..."

Aaron awaited Jackson, who suddenly looked hesitant. "Who else?"

Jackson waited for the waitress to deliver his drink. After

she left, he lowered his voice. "My girlfriend. She's a cop."

"I see. Jackson, if what you're telling me is true, this Carswall fellow must be watching you carefully."

"He did me like I was a poor old nigger with a bad imagination. I don't plan to let him think anything different."

Aaron nervously chuckled. He had never been comfortable with the word 'nigger.' "Son, you have to admit what you just told me is pretty farfetched."

"Is it?" Jackson said. "When I told you Linville was cut up like a lab rat, you didn't even blink. That's because Seth told you the same story this morning, right?"

Aaron remained stone-faced. "I'm sorry, but that's privileged . . ."

"What's more, he probably told you Linville was killed by something that came out of the sky that night. Tell me I'm wrong, and I'll pick up the check and we never had this conversation."

Aaron tossed a heavy sigh and shook his head disapprovingly. "I never was much good at poker."

"I heard Seth. He said 'they killed Linville.' I also know what happened in Rockford is similar to this incident. Something's going on, Mr. Aaron, and that fed is neck-deep in it. Maybe Seth told you a story that, under other circumstances, would give you an easy insanity plea. But you gotta admit that Carswall's interference with a local homicide changes the rules."

Aaron nervously fiddled with his empty coffee cup. He was hesitant to confide in Jackson, but he felt he had little choice now. "Ok, Officer Jackson, we have to talk, but from this point on – we didn't have this conversation, clear?"

"You got it," Jackson said.

Aaron cupped his chin in his folded hands. "All the time I sat with Seth this morning, I kept asking myself, why does this man sound like he's telling the truth? He described some kind of aircraft down to small details. And he described his assailants, complete with helmets, steel armor - some kind of unspeakable torture."

Jackson triumphantly slapped the table. "I knew it."

"Look, Jackson, I'll admit Seth intrigues me, but he is an unstable little alcoholic with a ton of evidence against him. I can't tell a jury those people were the victims of some brutal extraterrestrial highwaymen. They'd throw a net over me. His knife was in Mary, and his prints are on it. His clothes had Lisa and Mary's blood on them. A shotgun was found, and it was fired one time. There are prints on the gun, and I have a feeling they're going to match Seth's. I think that body in the morgue is indeed Linville Reeves. Everything fits."

"Does it?" Jackson said.

Aaron contemplated Jackson's dark eyes. "Wait a minute. You made me look at Linville's feet. What was that about?"

Jackson smiled and cocked a brow. "When I was in high school, I worked for Linville. One day we dug out an old tree stump, and Linville brought an axe down on his left foot. It cut through his boot right down to the bone. I carried him to the house and Mary bandaged him up. But that stiff in the morgue didn't have a scar on either foot, did it?"

Aaron pulled off his wire-rimmed glasses and leaned back in the booth. His ordered, logical mind had no room for this gem. "Did he ever see a doctor?"

"Linville liked to brag that he had no use for doctors. Most farm folks don't have time for them unless they got a hand or a leg hanging by the skin. Hell, he was back hobbling in the fields two days after he got hurt, but I saw that leg, and I guarantee it left a nasty scar."

"But there's no medical record to confirm the injury. Dental records are useless for an identification when a head's blown off, and, if he never went to a doctor, there're probably no blood records. And I doubt I could sell the county on expensive DNA testing with so much evidence going another direction."

"Damn it, Mr. Aaron, stop being a lawyer for a minute and look at what's going on! You got feds interfering with a local investigation. I saw Linville's mutilated corpse and several dissected animals that Carswall subsequently hijacked. Seth claims he saw a UFO, which happens to resemble that mutilation incident in Rockford. Carswall has a private sit-down with Sheriff White, who rolls over and conveniently leads Seth into a confession without a lawyer present. Can you honestly tell me you don't suspect the truth is being systematically buried out in that wheat field?"

"What I'm saying, Officer, is you are long on accusations, but woefully short on proof. You and Cameron are the only witnesses with a dispute here; and neither one of you has anything but a story that nobody in his right mind would believe. I can only present a defense based on evidence, not paranoid speculation of a government conspiracy."

"Damn," Jackson sighed. "Look, I'm in Carswall's way. I'm taking a big chance talking to you right now, but you're my only shot. If you don't buy any of this, and you just want to cut a deal for Cameron, then tell me now. I want to know who I can trust."

Aaron contemplated Jackson's dark eyes. "Look, I'm an old lawyer, Jackson. I've spent my career right here in Attica where it's safe. If Carswall is covering something up, he's banking on the fact that nobody around here has the experience or the nerve to take him on. But, for what it's worth, I believe you."

"Then take them on," Jackson said. "I'll help you."

"Take them on? Just like that? I should take on the government, armed with an old alkie who claims aliens killed those people, and a half-crazed cop who believes him? I don't mean to sound as old as I am, but this is a league I've never played in."

They sat in silence for a moment, both lost in thought. Jackson reluctantly understood where Aaron was coming from, but it didn't weaken his resolve. He finally broached a subject that had twisted his mind since tossing and turning all of the previous night. "How about your old pal?"

"Pal?"

"Payne."

Aaron had to smile. "Do you know him?"

"Marcus Payne? You kidding? Not to mention reading about him, I've run into him a few times out at the old Rusman mansion on prowler calls. His landlady gets nervous when he sits out on the roof."

"Yes," Aaron sighed, "that's Marcus."

"No offense, but 'law enforcement' and 'defense attorney' are mutually exclusive terms. And 'Payne' is the first name every cop learns to hate - at least, it used to be before he quit. I guess I was disappointed the first time I met him. No horns or fangs, just a pretty pathetic case these days."

"Indeed," Aaron sadly said.

"Have you and him been friends a long time?"

"Marcus is my brother."

"Brother?" Jackson said. "I didn't know that."

"Well," Aaron said, "I say 'brother,' but actually, Marcus was adopted. He was orphaned at the age of eleven. My parents were very close to his family, and they took him in. Marcus was a gifted kid; an enormous I.Q." Aaron had to laugh. "I was in my last year of law school when Marcus was fifteen. The bastard tutored me through the bar exam. He treated me as the classic big brother - worshiped me - but secretly, I was enamored with him. He was an accomplished musician, an artist, and even a talented athlete. He excelled in anything he attempted, and, I suppose because he admired me, he followed me into law."

"And now he sits out at that old mansion, drinking and staring at the stars," Jackson said. "As much as I don't like you lawyer-types, I feel sorry for the guy."

"Lawyer-types?" Aaron indignantly said.

Jackson gave his infectious smile. "I'm a cop. I don't like lawyers who defend bad guys. But the way things rolled over on his wife shouldn't happen to anybody. I have some cop friends up in Harrisburg who were at the murder scene that night. Those were some seriously sick animals that killed her."

"It broke Marcus," Aaron agreed. "He still blames himself."

"From what I hear, he couldn't have seen it coming."

"He's not convinced," Aaron said. "You know, you may not believe it, but some of us indeed have a conscience. It's our job to protect the civil rights of the accused, whether you like it or not. Marcus got caught up in a situation that led from one bizarre occurrence to another, all leading to Lori's murder. You may see him as a coldhearted criminal attorney, but he is a compassionate, caring man. And, despite his unorthodox style, he was a brilliant attorney."

"And now he just sits up there all the time?"

"A temporary grieving period, I hope," Aaron said.

"Maybe now's the time to light a fire under him," Jackson hopefully said.

"I don't know. I'll admit, your story would have lit him up two years ago, but I don't know how he might react now. Attica's a long fall from the Supreme Court."

"Mr. Aaron, Marcus Payne's tried hundreds of sensational murder cases. What's the harm in talking to him about this one?"

"I don't know if he'd even discuss it."

"You'll never know if you don't ask. Look, you may not like it, but you're in this thing now. You got me in your corner, but who the hell am I? Marcus Payne is a legend. Maybe you could get him back on his feet. This may be one crazy marriage, but I'd say we might make a hell of a team."

Aaron felt Jackson's energy infect him. There was something almost mystifying about this cop's determination that made Aaron feel perhaps a little younger and stronger. He tossed Jackson a wary glance. "Officer Jackson . . ."

"My friends call me K.J."

Aaron smiled. "There's something I don't understand. If what you suspect about this Carswall character is true, then we may be dealing with a pretty ruthless opponent. You're risking your neck for Seth Cameron. Is he that important to you?"

"Seth?" Jackson said. "I don't know. After all, maybe he did kill Mary and Lisa. But there's more to this than Seth falling in a bear trap, Mr. Aaron."

"Call me Reed."

Jackson returned Aaron's smile. "All my life I've had to walk a thin line that you white folks just don't understand. Guys like you may honestly want to, but that's not the same as understanding. My mom died giving birth to me. My daddy had nothing but me and his pitiful sharecropper life. It was the best he could do to buy him and me a little house in the colored section. Daddy always wanted to buy a farm, but he never could. He brought me up to believe that I could do better than him. He said I could be or do anything I had a mind to, so long as I did the right thing. He told me, 'Kennyboy, there ain't nobody in this world can take away your honor; only you can do that by taking the wrong road.' Reed, three people were murdered yesterday, and Carswall's setting Seth up for the fall. If I let him get away with it, then I haven't learned a damn thing my old man taught me."

Aaron contemplated this kid, suddenly feeling pretty small. "K.J., let's take a ride."

* * *

Aaron's sluggish car pulled into the long drive leading into the Ben Rusman estate. Once the pride of old Senator Rusman, the place had long since lost its grandeur to time and neglect. The grounds were brown and weedy, lined with dead or dying trees. A rickety, three-story house was the gnarled centerpiece of Attica's link to a stately past. It was now but an old and musty boarding house. The estate's demise was due wholly to its spinster heir, Marie Rusman, the senator's youngest child. Even in her prime, Marie was quite batty, and now in her late seventies, she was senile and dim-witted as well. Marie had squandered most of the Rusman fortune to slick lawyers, swindlers, and shirttail relatives. The remaining half-million or so was kept mostly in cash stuffed under rugs, in cookie jars, and in a hundred or so other hiding places. Unknown to anyone, Marie's will was written on a paper towel in her bathroom, bequeathing all her remaining wealth to the two dozen cats that freely roamed her property.

Marie Rusman stood in front of a stairway leading to a once magnificent veranda. She tended a ratty garden, unaware of Aaron and Jackson's approach. Aaron turned off the engine, and the two watched Marie.

"Bless her heart," Aaron said, "she shouldn't be out in this heat."

Marie turned when she heard the car doors slam. She squinted under a wide-brimmed hat, recognizing Aaron, but suspiciously glaring at the colored cop. "Oh, no," Marie said, "I told him to stay off the roof, but does he listen to me? Are you going to arrest him?"

"No, Marie," Aaron said. "Nothing like that. We just stopped by to visit."

Marie quickly shifted back to her wilted flowers. "I'm sorry my roses are dead. The heat killed them. Should I file a report?"

Jackson smiled at Aaron, who ruefully tried to keep Marie on track. "Dear, you shouldn't be out in this sun."

"The devil's work," Marie said. "Heat is the devil's work. The devil's out here ruining my roses and killing, killing, killing."

"I'm not sure I follow you, dear," Aaron said.

She turned and pointed at Jackson's nose. "You should arrest the devil instead of killing my roses."

"I . . .what?" Jackson said.

"Marie," Aaron interrupted, "this is my friend, Officer Ken Jackson."

"Pleased, ma'am," Jackson said. He took off his hat and wiped his brow. "We've met before."

"You're a colored," Marie said. "Can you fix my garden?"

"I, uh."

Aaron pulled Jackson up the stairs. "We're going to say hello to Mr. Payne, dear. You better come inside and have a lemonade."

"Don't arrest poor Mr. Payne!"

The two stopped on the staircase. "Dear?" Aaron said.

She plodded up the stairs with remarkable ease. "I know he's a day late in his rent, but I forgive him. Please don't put him in jail."

"This is a social call," Aaron said. "Besides, Marie, I pay his rent. Remember? I paid you last week."

She stopped and glared at Aaron. A blank pall fell over

her face as she turned and went back down to her garden without a word.

Aaron winked at Jackson with an 'oh, well' shrug, and they went up to the veranda.

"Be sure to tell him he's late with his rent!"

Aaron didn't reply as he led Jackson to the door. They entered a large foyer. Their ears were greeted by the sound of old music coming from an equally ancient record player in the corner. An elderly man sat in a rocker next to it, looking at a magazine. The old fellow gave Aaron and Jackson a smile as they walked by.

"How are ya, Eddie?" he muttered.

Aaron nodded and took Jackson up a long staircase. "Goddam nuthouse," he mumbled.

Jackson agreed. "I've wandered through this place a time or two."

They rounded the second floor landing and started up the next set of stairs, both puffing in the sultry stairwell. "Smell that?" Aaron said. "Senility - old people spoiling."

Jackson stifled a laugh. "I ain't gonna get old. No way."

"Best of luck, pal. That was my plan, too." They reached the third floor and turned down a long corridor. "Marc's room is at the end. It's the smallest one in the whole damned place."

"Why'd he take it?"

"Same size as a prison cell, I guess." They reached the door and Aaron knocked. "Oh Noble One? Are you in there?" He gave the door a healthy push and it creaked open. The room was empty. A bare bed was loaded with papers and beer cans, and the floor had to be plowed for the two to pass.

"Damn," Jackson said, "some housekeeper."

"Actually, it's pretty clean today," Aaron said. He looked around the dismantled room and spotted one of Payne's drawings on the floor. Aaron picked it up and shook his head. "My god, look at this."

Jackson looked at the pencil drawing of an eerily beautiful woman. Her eyes looked as if they were alive. "Did he draw this?"

Aaron nodded, swallowing a ball of sadness down his

throat. His eyes grew moist. "Lori," he whispered. "It could be a photograph."

Jackson took the drawing. "She's beautiful." He turned the paper over and read Payne's hastily scribbled words: 'time is too short.'

A huge voice shattered the silence. "Trespassers!" Payne's head hung upside down in the window. He peered in from the roof like an enraged bat. "Thieves!"

Jackson stepped back.

"You scared the crap out of me!" Aaron whispered, holding his heart.

"Tally-ho!" Payne said with an upside down smile.

"What are you doing out there?" Aaron grumbled.

"Catching rays," Payne said.

"Get in here before you break your neck!"

Jackson dumbly watched Aaron reach for Payne like a nervous, befuddled mother. Aaron tried to grab Payne's hand but got slapped for his trouble.

"I can do this," Payne said. "Leave me alone."

"Get in here!"

Payne's head disappeared.

Aaron twisted and tried to look up. "Stop fooling around, Marc." Suddenly, a wild-eyed cat flew at him with all four paws bared and primed to shred the attorney. Remington yowled and planted herself in Aaron's chest.

"Mother mercy!" Aaron cried. He wrestled Remington, but the match was already lost. The cat dug into his shoulders and used his back as a ladder to reach the floor. "Ya-ouch-dammit-to-hell!"

Remington darted out the door. If Jackson had not been so bewildered by this entire scene, he would have laughed.

"Oops!" Payne hollered as he fell through the window. He clumsily staggered into Aaron. "Pardon me, crazy person coming through!"

"Cut it out," Aaron barked.

Payne ignored Aaron and collected himself. He took a deep breath and wiped the sweat from his brow. He then reached for Jackson's hand. "Marc Payne, a pleasure to meet you."

Jackson quizzically looked at Payne's hand and shook it. "Ken Jackson."

Payne offered both hands. "Careful with the cuffs, Officer, I chafe easily. I won't speak to you until I call my lawyer. His name is Aaron, and he'll have your badge for this."

"Would you shut up?" Aaron said.

Jackson finally let out a laugh. "Man, you two are a couple of strange individuals!"

"Nice meeting you, too," Payne said, calmly turning to Aaron. "Now that we're past the formalities, get out."

"Marcus, would you please calm down?" Aaron said.

"I'm calm. Get out."

"We want to talk to you," Aaron said.

"Oh?" Payne said. "Why didn't you say so? I'm always happy to talk. What's the agenda?" He plopped down on the bed.

Aaron took a long breath and sat in Remington's rocking chair, while Jackson shyly leaned against a wall. The room settled and grew uncomfortably quiet. Aaron shook his head, looking at Payne, who leaned back in his tattered blue jeans and sweatshirt.

Finally, Aaron broke the spell. "How are you feeling, Marc?"

Payne could hardly believe that question. He gazed around his room, which looked as if a giant flood had just receded. "Well, thanks. You?"

"Look, Marc, we didn't come by to chase you off the roof. I have a problem."

"Irregularity? Try more fruit."

"Will you stop with the jokes?"

"Who's joking? You look constipated."

"Officer Jackson and I spent the morning discussing a problem we thought you might be able to help us solve."

"Am I scaring Marie again?"

Aaron chuckled. "No, Marcus, it's a little bigger this time."

Payne looked at Jackson. His eyes seemed to burn right through him. "Sirens," Payne said.

"What?" Aaron said.

"Something's cooking."

"That's an understatement," Jackson said.

"Murder," Payne theatrically whispered, bobbing his eyebrows.

Aaron shared a nervous glance with Jackson. "You heard?"

Payne sighed and leaned against the wall. "No, I'm a good guesser."

"Linville Reeves, his wife and granddaughter, Marc," Aaron said. "They were murdered yesterday."

Payne suddenly turned off the wise guy routine. He carefully pulled a cigarette from his shirt pocket and lit it. "That's a little strong for Attica, isn't it?"

"Seth Cameron's in custody," Aaron said. "He confessed."

Payne stopped in mid smoke. "Little Seth? You gotta be kidding."

Aaron shook his head. "I wish I was. The evidence is strong."

Payne took a drag. "I've known little Seth since we were kids. He's a sad case, but murder? What happened?"

Aaron looked at Jackson, who stood stoically by the wall. He wasn't going to leave it, either. "Well," Aaron said, rubbing the back of his neck, "you know a client-attorney relationship is privileged."

Payne puffed, looking at Jackson and rolling his eyes. "Here it comes . . ."

"Of course," Aaron said, "if this were a professional consultation, I'd be at liberty to discuss it with you."

Payne laid his head back and closed his eyes. "Nap time."

"Marcus, I need your help."

"Okay, I'll help you to the door."

"Advice," Aaron said, "that's all. This thing is too big for me. I need you."

"You can't afford me," Payne puffed.

"Let me tell you about it."

"Press on, brother," Payne said, "but you're on the clock."

"This is a strange one, Marcus."

"You said Seth confessed," Payne said. "It's hard to pull rabbits out of an empty hat. The guy's broke, so plea him out of a lethal injection and take me to lunch."

"It's not that simple."

"Come on, I'm hungry."

"Dammit, Marcus, would you hear me out?"

"Sure, I live for murder, or don't you read the papers?"

Aaron grew irritated. "Don't you think it's time you stop beating yourself up? It sure chaps my keister."

Payne smiled at Jackson. "We're not losing you with all this legal talk, are we?"

Jackson felt very hot. "Maybe I ought to wait outside."

"Sit down," Payne ordered. "You bought a ticket to buddy up with old chapped-butt over here; besides, I kind of like you."

"Just let me tell you about the case," Aaron said, watching Jackson cautiously sit on the table.

"So tell me, but watch your step; you're under oath," Payne said.

"I'm not asking for anything, even though you ought to stop rotting in this nuthouse and get back to practicing law where you belong. Hell, you never get out of here. You're breaking my little daughter's heart. She thinks her uncle doesn't love her anymore."

Payne sighed and looked at Jackson. "You have any brothers, Jackson?"

"No," Jackson said.

"Lucky you. I got one who doubles as a mother."

"Okay," Aaron said. "The sermon is over."

"For now," Payne said.

"Look, Marcus," Aaron said, sitting on the edge of his chair like a pleading child, "this is the most unbelievable case I've ever seen, or, at least, the craziest story I've ever heard - but I can't tell it without first prefacing it with my skepticism, which -"

"Get on with it!" Payne bellowed. "God, I hate lawyers!"

Aaron related the events of the Reeves murders for over an hour. Payne listened without commenting, oblivious to anything else in the room. Jackson added a comment or two, but he stayed quiet most of the time. Instead, he watched Payne's incredible eyes. He read accounts of Payne's mystical command of his senses, his inflection, and the gentle nuances of his inborn charm. Payne's eyes made up the nucleus of this magical mental machine, Jackson thought. They were transparent, but they could also be solid as stone. Jackson knew he would stand helpless before Payne if he tried to lie. On the way to the Rusman mansion, Aaron mentioned Payne's eyes. He commented, "They're his forte. His eyes are as important as his vast intelligence; they can lull you to sleep, and then slice you in half . . ."

Aaron continued his long-winded explanation while Payne patiently listened.

"We saw the body in the morgue this morning," Aaron said. "The M.E.'s preliminary report is consistent with what we saw."

Payne awaited the sudden silence. He lit his tenth cigarette. "So you think Seth killed the women, but you haven't said much about Linville."

Aaron looked at Jackson. "I honestly don't know."

Payne took a deep drag and exhaled a cloud of smoke. "Sounds to me like Seth threw a rod; either him, or you, Jackson."

"I know what I saw," Jackson said, suddenly uncomfortable with jumping to his own defense. "He was dissected, Mr. Payne. It looked like a surgeon cut him open - just like the animals."

Payne rested his head on his chin. "How much time went by until the sheriff got out there?"

"About twenty minutes," Jackson said.

"That's plenty of time for a pro to contaminate the evidence," Payne said to Aaron.

Aaron nodded, feeling a surge of excitement at the long dormant fire in Payne's eyes.

"How long was Linville missing?" Payne asked.

Jackson calculated. "They say he was found late last night. Could have been twelve, fourteen hours."

"And he was found out in the same field?" Payne asked.

"That's the report," Aaron said.

"It's pretty hard to find a body in a wheat field in the middle of the night. If the buzzards were picking at the other bodies, seems they would have pointed Linville out, too," Payne said.

"Not if Carswall stashed him in the barn," Jackson said.

Payne smirked. "So, the body you saw in the morgue wasn't in pieces?" Payne said.

"It wasn't Linville," Jackson said. "I'll admit it is the same size and weight, but it doesn't happen to have a damn head to make a positive ID."

"Officer Jackson says Linville had a deep scar on his foot from an accident years ago," Aaron said. "This corpse had no scar. I know it sounds absurd, but the corpse just might very well be an impostor."

"Absurd?" Payne said, matter-of-factly. "You're dealing with feds, big brother. There are plenty of homeless folks who can vanish and never be missed. In fact, when you're dealing with a rotting, headless body, a fake stiff doesn't have to be all that perfect. The art dwells in the lie. You might not be able to fool expert criminalists without problems, but here in the sticks, you've got George Baker working with two beakers and an alcohol lamp. A fed hands that overstuffed quack a custom-made piece of evidence, tells him what the autopsy will say, growls about the hazards of crossing his government, and you got a sealed package."

"How do we bring it to the surface?" Aaron said.

"Sticky," Payne said, flicking an ash in a beer can. "The dead women are the kickers - they're the linchpin to the state's best evidence, along with two positive murder weapons. It puts two strikes past Seth, because your jury will attach the third murder to the two that everyone knows he did. A headless Linville and a blown shotgun are convenient window dressing. You have to prove the third body isn't Linville with blood matches, DNA -"

"Jackson says Linville never went to a doctor for any-thing."

"Then you're screwed on an ID," Payne said. "I'll guaran-tee they've eliminated any trace of Linville's DNA in that farmhouse by now. If they're serious enough to plant a replacement corpse, then you can forget trivial matters like an autopsy - which is probably being fabricated right now. They can lead your medical examiner down any path they choose. Those are loose ends compared to killing some patsy and stuffing him in Linville's coffin."

"How about prints?" Aaron said.

"I doubt that old farmer's ever been printed in his life, but your fed buddy probably fixed that by now anyway - just print the corpse and duplicate them into a phony record."

"My god," Aaron said. "What the hell are they covering up?"

"I think you know. If that Rockford UFO incident has teeth, there's a universe of possibilities," Payne said with a wry smile. "Universe . . .get it?"

Aaron kept shaking his head as if he might recover his sanity. "This is crazy. We're accusing our own government of murder?"

Payne huffed a laugh. "Reed, my big, naive brother, I told you that practicing in this little town was bad for your health. In the dictionary, look up, 'Power,' 'Politics,' 'Money.' Do you really still believe this is a government by and for The People? If you do, then explain just who The People are to your black friend here."

Jackson smirked as Aaron's eyes barely touched him.

Aaron shuddered. "Marcus, you're one cynical son of a bitch."

"Did you come here for advice," Payne snapped, "or shall we just say 'fuck it,' get drunk, and let your client hang to dry?"

Aaron rubbed his burning stomach. "Okay, you made your point. Where does that leave us?"

"I'd say you're so far behind this Carswall chap that you ought to give up on life and move in here with me."

"That's your advice?" Aaron said.

Payne shrugged. "Here's your alternative. If the front door's locked, then go around back and break in. Instead of trying to prove your client is innocent, attack his accuser and make the jury forget who's on trial. Drop bombs and throw smoke, and maybe you can kill the prosecutor. Remember, reasonable doubt can't convict. The D.A. needs twelve votes, but you only need one. Go out and dig up something to scare the shit out of one measly juror. Just be careful where you dig with this Carswall lurking about."

Aaron leaned forward and rubbed his eyes. "I'm over my head, Marcus. I need you."

Payne sighed and leaned against the wall.

"Look, I can fix it so you can come aboard the P.D.'s office."

Payne looked first at Aaron and then Jackson, who had obviously been sizing him up from the minute they met. He then let his eyes wander his room, the place that had lately been turning his stomach. "I'm walking the edge, Reed," he finally said with surprising frankness. "I can't say for sure from day to day how long I can last anymore."

"That's because you're wasting away in this self-imposed exile, Marcus," Aaron said. "Occupational therapy is what you need. And don't tell me that Lori wouldn't agree. What the hell would she say if she could see you now?"

Payne's eyes pierced Aaron, at first spewing venom, but then with sad recognition. "I'm spinning the chamber and clicking a gun at my head, and you want me to help you defend a man who says his alleged victims were murdered by ghouls in a spaceship? You want me to spit in the face of a government agency that makes its living in political assassinations and espionage? Occupational therapy?"

Aaron smiled. "For you, it's pretty tame."

"Mr. Payne," Jackson said, "maybe it's none of my business, but you don't look too busy around here. I'm sorry about what happened to your wife, but maybe it's time to let it go. You don't know me, and got no reason to give a damn, but I'm in deep sewage. I need your help."

Payne rolled his eyes and huffed at Aaron. "Where'd you get this guy - off the front of a cereal box?"

"He hates lawyers," Aaron said.

"I knew there was something about him I liked," Payne said. He stretched his long arms and took a deep breath. "So tell me, Jackson, do you believe Seth?"

Jackson shrugged. "All I know is, Carswall's lying. From all the years I've known Seth, there's no way he could make up a story like this."

"He's no rocket scientist, if you'll pardon the pun," Aaron said. "But, his descriptions were too lucid and exact for a fabrication by a lunatic; and, Marcus, his description of Linville's murder coincides with Ken's description of the body he saw."

Payne slowly perused each man and lit another cigarette. He shook his head, secretly recalling his nightmares the night before last. "Do either of you know what you're walking into?"

"Do we have any choice?" Aaron asked. "Help me, Marcus."

Payne looked at the floor, hating himself for what he was about to do. It didn't really matter, for he hated himself anyway. "Okay, fellas, I'm in, but if I decide the water has too many sharks, we quit - no discussion, no argument."

"Incredible!" Aaron said, clapping his hands. "You've got a deal!"

"One thing, Officer . . ."

"Call me K.J."

"One thing, Officer," Payne insisted. "You're bucking serious odds, messing with a fed like Carswall. Killing is a job perk for people like him. The time may come for you to run for your goddam life. If I say run, ask no questions and sprint like you have four linebackers on your ass. Clear?"

"I got it." Jackson wasn't going to question why Payne happened to use such a coincidental analogy. It obviously had to do with what Aaron called 'Payne's Magic.'

"You said something about a girlfriend. She's wise to this?"

"Yeah. She can take care of herself."

"You take care of her, too," Payne said.

Jackson nodded and suddenly thought of the sketch on Payne's table.

Aaron grew nervous with the direction this was heading. Besides, he could barely contain his excitement. "Wonderful, Marcus, I'll arrange everything. We'll have to get your clothes out of storage; I wouldn't want my staff seeing you dressed like this. You'd scare them to death. You'll need to shave, and I have to make room in my office for you . . ."

Payne sat, his shoulders hunched, listening to Aaron drone on. He wondered if he just made the biggest mistake of his life . . .

7

Jonathan Carswall sat on a park bench in Laurel Square at precisely fifteen minutes past twelve o'clock. He opened a bag of popcorn and began tossing kernels to the pigeons waddling about. Laurel Square was a concrete and tree oasis in the center of Harrisburg's financial district. The city suffered the same heat that was drying up Attica, but here it was more humid. Carswall took off his jacket and loosened his tie and shirt collar. Laurel Square buzzed with brown bag executives, secretaries, street artists, vendors, in-line skaters, and a few volatile gang bangers. A handful of happy teen-agers hopped barefoot in the fountain. The city surrounding Laurel Square was insane with taxi and bus traffic, its clatter bouncing off endless rows of skyscrapers, while people of all sizes, shapes and colors bounced off each other below. It was an ordinary late summer day in the city.

Carswall spotted a nattily dressed man walking his way. The elderly fellow sat on the bench and pulled a monogrammed handkerchief from his pocket. He wiped his lips and eyes and smiled at the hungry pigeons. A handsomely gray man in his late sixties or early seventies, his health appeared frail. His belly poked under his vest, and his shoulders had a distinct droop. While Carswall fed the birds, the man put the handkerchief back in his pocket.

"It's good to see you again, Jonathan."

Carswall nodded faintly. "You're feeling well, Baytree?"

"Eh, you know, a few 'old man' problems. It's kind of you to ask."

"How are things at the Capital?"

"Confused and chaotic - utterly normal." He huffed a chuckle that turned into a cough.

"Your e-mail sounded urgent."

"It regards Specter. We've confirmed three more sightings in the Attica County area. The Defense Department is now on full alert."

"Any identification?"

"We're still on a learning curve - but making progress. Whatever it is, it's unlike anything ever catalogued. To date, we have six incidents; thankfully, none with corpses falling into the hands of civilians. For some reason, Specter keeps returning to your area. We believe a pattern has developed. It may give us a target."

"Target?" Carswall said.

"Specter must be stopped now, at any cost. Who knows what it may do next . . ."

"Aggression against an unknown enemy?"

"I know what you're thinking, Jonathan; it's a risk, but it's just a matter of time before we end up with another Attica. The consequences of exposure are far worse."

"Where does the President stand?"

"He's outside, and hopefully will remain there."

"That's good. This is no time for politicians. I'm just a humble soldier, but I shudder to think what might happen if he knew everything."

"Providing he is kept preoccupied with other matters, he won't. I have it on good authority that a terrorist strike overseas in the next 48 hours will divert both him and the media. If he does find out, it's an entirely different problem we'd have to address. But let's not buy trouble."

Carswall never looked away from the birds. "This information doesn't warrant a personal visit from you, Baytree. You're here for something else."

Baytree sighed and wiped his mouth again. "It's just a field contact, Jonathan. Don't read any more into it. In my shoes, you'd do the same thing. Your action to date is exemplary, but Attica is unique."

"I'm handling it."

"Indeed. But you know company procedures well enough to understand the need for an obligatory contact in light of your last report. Attica is becoming very nasty business."

"Whatever is required."

"Jonathan, I personally came here to reiterate the severity of our problem. We want to be sure you understand that your situation can't be compromised. Mistakes would be costly. We anticipate you may have to initiate sanctions, and we want to be certain you are equipped with enough personnel to employ critical maintenance afterwards."

"Are you questioning my ability?"

"Look, Jonathan, it was pure, dumb luck that our trackers detected Specter over Attica that night. Had we not moved you into position in time, this entire affair might be raging out of control. We might not be so fortunate next time. Attica must be isolated at any cost. Don't take my scrutiny personally."

Carswall's face was crimson. He reached into his shirt pocket and pulled out a small white box of nitro pills. "The situation is under control," he said, popping a pill under his tongue.

Baytree watched with concern. "Control is relative to the controller, Jonathan. May I expect success from you?"

"I would," Carswall said, his anger quelling.

"Bring me up to speed."

"The homicide investigation is contained, but we're preparing for the possibility of a trial."

"Trial?"

"Baytree, it's a small town with small minds, but I drew a road map even the simplest fool can follow. The suspect committed two murders, and the third has been taken care of. Under normal circumstances, the D.A. could dispose the case with a plea bargain; however, as I mentioned in my report, there may be a complication."

"Marcus Payne," Baytree said.

Carswall nodded. "His unfortunate presence, and his relationship to the public defender are ominous signs. The man's a brilliant opportunist and I expect his involvement. I'll know soon."

"Can you prevent it?"

"I have enough fires to put out, Baytree. Payne is a rogue

- his psychological profile suggests he's self-destructive. I'd prefer exploiting that."

"How about the police officer?"

"He is difficult to read. He belies his dossier. For someone expected to replace the sheriff, he doesn't appear very bright."

"Don't underestimate him. Power, even on a small scale, is power nonetheless. Your alternatives with him are limited, you know."

"Alternatives are always limited, Baytree. I'm watching him."

Baytree wiped his mouth again. "Then that's it, Jonathan. You see? That wasn't so bad, was it?"

"I'm paid well to do what I do, Baytree. I wouldn't be here if I weren't your best agent. You'll have to excuse me if I'm insulted by this visit."

The old man finally looked at Carswall, but could only see himself reflected in the mirrored sunglasses. He stood and wandered into the masses in Laurel Square. Carswall watched him leave, and then departed in the other direction . . .

* * *

The night was warm and clear. Temperature: eighty-nine degrees. Winds, south by southwest at twelve knots. Katie Lyle finished her coffee as she prepared to close the Rockford Centennial Airfield tower for the night. It was a long and busy shift, typical of a late summer evening. When she reached the door, a voice suddenly crackled over the loudspeaker.

"Centennial, Arroyo NR5656, five miles west of outer marker. Request permission to land."

Katie's heart nearly popped from her chest when she heard that voice. Had it been any other, she would have gone out the door and left the pilot to land on his own. She ran to the radio, donned her headset, and keyed the microphone.

"Arroyo NR5656, you're clear to land on 17-R."

"Good evening, Centennial," the voice said.

"Arroyo NR5656, please follow proper communication procedures," Katie said with a wry smile.

"Okie-dokie."

Katie laughed. The bastard, she thought, he made it after all. Time and again, she scolded herself for these late-night liaisons. God knows she had enough trouble raising two kids without a husband. Falling for a married doctor who flew in every so often for candlelight dinner and screaming sex was exciting but hardly the basis for a future. But Katie had endured twelve years of physical abuse from an alcoholic jerk. A rich and handsome doctor eight years younger than her, married or not, made her feel alive again.

His voice broke over the speakers. "Centennial, I see traffic at three o'clock. Are you sure I'm clear to land?"

Katie curiously looked at the radar screen. "Arroyo, I don't see anything -"

A sudden loud whine ripped over her headset. She yanked it off, putting her hands to her ears. "Damn!" she cried. The whine shook the loudspeakers. In a moment, the noise subsided and Katie put her headset back on. "Arroyo NR5656 - Whoo, did you just get your eardrums shattered?"

An uncomfortable silence followed. Katie listened to an obnoxious static rattle over the air. She started to call the plane again when the pilot's frantic, disjointed voice suddenly crackled on.

"Arroyo . . .56 . . .flying at . . .egrees! . . ."

Katie strained to hear, but the voice continued to break up. "Arroyo," she said, "say again?" She looked at the radar screen and saw the plane, but on the left edge was a new blip that appeared only on one radar pass.

"Centennial!" the voice cracked. "Something huge went by . . . an incredible . . . ten o'clock . . . like a jet . . ."

"Arroyo?" A wave of panic poured down her throat.

"The son of . . . almost hit me! . . ."

"Carl?" Katie said. "Arroyo, do you copy?" She checked the monitor, finding the Arroyo and the other blip again - this time it was on the right side of the screen.

" . . .God damn! . . . It's huge! . . . It's coming back at me!"

Katie's hands shook. "Arroyo! Carl? Do you hear me?" She looked out the tower windows and saw nothing but distant stars in the black night.

The voice popped back on, iced with terror. "Katie! It's after me! . . . green lights . . . unning along the side! . . ."

Another earsplitting whine broke over Katie's headset. "Carl?" she cried. She saw both blips flicker and disappear. The plane was gone. "Carl!"

The radio fell silent, except for an ominous static buzz.

"Oh, my god," she whispered. She quickly turned and grabbed the telephone. It would take several minutes for her to calm herself enough to call the Civil Air Patrol . . .

* * *

Ken Jackson's eyes popped when he heard Carswall's voice on the phone.

"Officer Jackson? Carswall here."

Jackson looked at the receiver in stunned silence and then put it back to his ear. "It's two a.m. . . . ."

"This will only take a moment."

"What do you want?"

"Regarding the homicide investigation," Carswall said, "did Sheriff White make it clear that the particulars of the case should be kept in strict confidence?"

Jackson's heart pumped hard. "What's your point?"

"I trust your trip to the morgue today with the Public Defender and that reporter was strictly routine?"

Jackson looked at Carly, who perked and sat up next to him. "I went with them to see Linville Reeves' body. Did you count the times I took a dump today, too?"

"Officer Jackson, I don't believe I have to remind you of your obligation to not compromise due process?"

"Hey, my obligation is to three homicide victims. You don't have to tell me how to do my job, but you might explain why you don't want me to do it."

"Sheriff White will bring you up to speed, that's all I will tell you for now. But yesterday you insisted you saw something that didn't exist, so my concern is not unreasonable."

Jackson held his temper in check. "Look, I saw the body in

the morgue. I don't know what happened to me out on that farm, but I admit it - I fucked up, okay?"

"Then may I assume you considered this when you spoke with the Public Defender and Mr. Williams?"

"Look, Aaron has a lot of clout in this town. I can't afford to make a damn fool of myself in front of him or the press this close to the election. I told both of them that I found two bodies, and that's it. This job is all I got, so I ain't gonna get in your way."

"Very well," Carswall said. "It's a difficult social climate we live in. I encourage you to take care of your own interests and not compromise yourself. Pleasant dreams."

Jackson slammed the receiver and dropped back into bed. Carly came down on him quickly. "I guess I don't have to ask what that was all about," she said.

"Did I sound convincing?"

"Hey, you make a great weasel."

Jackson huffed a sigh. "Maybe. But there's no mistaking it; he fired one right across my bow."

"I don't believe this," Carly said. "It's a nightmare."

"One thing's for sure, that call tells me everything we suspect is true."

"Are you sure?"

"Baby, they killed somebody to take Linville's place! It's a cover-up, plain and simple. How sure do I have to be?"

"Okay! I'm on your side, remember?"

"I'm sorry," Jackson said. He wrapped her in his arms. "Those bastards are watching every move I make."

Carly almost laughed. "You may not believe it, but before you got home tonight, I scoured the house for bugs."

Jackson agreed. "There's nothing wrong with a healthy case of paranoia right now. Our security system is good, but I'll set a few traps to let us know if we get visitors."

They held each other in what suddenly seemed like a terribly dark room. Carly finally spoke. "Do you really think Seth is telling the truth?"

"I'd just as soon not answer that one. I'd feel less certifiable if we just concentrate on the murders for now."

"No argument here. So, I hate to say this, but we need to find Linville's body."

"Yep," Jackson whispered. "Hey, you're the former big-city homicide detective. Start detecting."

"Okay. The first person I'd question is the officer who discovered the crime. What's your gut tell you?"

"I know we're dealing with murders, but those damned animals keep bugging me. It just can't be a coincidence that there was an animal mutilation in Rockford last week, and the farmer there says he saw a UFO."

"Then let's assume there's a link. Go with your instincts, Kenny. Keep talking."

"I figure if you're gonna frame Seth for three murders, that dissected sow had to be a major problem. It was too big to drag away before White showed up; besides, I would have seen them if they tried. I just didn't have my shit together to notice that they hacked it up."

"Okay, they had to include the sow in the frame-up, so obviously they didn't want anyone to see the dissection."

"Payne thinks they'll try to sell a theory that it was just another target on Seth's blind rampage. But I swear, Carly, I didn't see any blood on it - or on Linville. I won't be able to prove that now, because they got the carcass out of there, and nobody's gonna see it."

"But there were other dead animals on the scene."

"Right. Forget hiding dead chickens, that was easy, but they kept everyone away from the barn where the dissected horse was. Overnight, when they had White and the department chasing rabbits, they managed to make Linville and the horse disappear, and they planted some poor, dead homeless fool out in that field."

Carly shuddered. "Since they had to go that far, my guess is this murder is as big a mystery to them as it is to us; so maybe the evidence on that horse is just as important to them as inspecting Linville's body."

"Maybe they're stashed somewhere together."

"Okay," Carly said. "Big-city detective has an idea."

"That makes one of us. Fire away, girl."

"I remember reading that the Humane Society investigated these mutilation incidents. I had a college friend who's now a veterinarian in Harrisburg - she does volunteer work for them. I'll see what she knows."

"Okay, but hold off for now. We need to lay low for awhile and try to get Carswall off our back. We need to make it look like we bailed, and I'll have to go underground whenever I communicate with Aaron or Payne."

"Hey, I worked undercover for ten years. I know a few tricks," Carly said. "So, what do you think of Payne? Does he live up to the legend?"

"Hell, he's four moves ahead of the rest of the world. You gotta sprint to keep up with him. But he's wounded. You know his wife was murdered."

"I wasn't in on that case, but I heard that 'murder' hardly describes it," Carly said. "It was a hit, wasn't it?"

"Yeah, Aaron filled me in. Payne had a case back east - some mob capo was going to roll into the witness protection program. Turning out the little scumbag was small pickings for Payne, and he was preoccupied with bigger trials. The snitch was hidden away, so the mob sent him a message by killing Payne's wife. She was raped and tortured right in their own house."

"My god."

"Payne flew in that weekend and found her. Aaron says it damn near destroyed the guy."

"How did he end up here?"

"Him and Aaron grew up in Attica. Payne tossed it all and moved into the old Rusman boarding house - been living there the last six months, drinking himself to death."

"Do you think we can trust him?"

"I thought he was a damn train wreck when I first met him, but Aaron insists that's just the way he is. But in the two hours we discussed this mess, he came up with a dozen angles that me and Aaron never even considered."

The phone rang again.

"Doesn't anybody sleep in this town?" Carly whimpered.

"Carswall probably forgot to mention the thumb screws."

Jackson picked up. "What!" he barked.

On the other end of the line, Virgil White was in a rage. "Jackson, who the fuck do you think you are? I just got off the phone with that son of a bitch Carswall! He says you been sucking up to Aaron and Williams - said you three went body hunting today. Is that true?"

"Yeah," Jackson said.

"Lemme tell you something, K.J., we're both gonna get dragged through the fire if you keep up this bullshit about Linville! Seth blew his damn head off! Ain't the body good enough for you?"

Jackson swallowed his pride. "Yeah, it is. Look, I ran into Aaron and Willy at the hospital. They were going to the morgue to check out Linville, and I tagged along because I just had to see him for myself. I saw, and I'm done, okay?"

"Carswall said you and Aaron spent most of the day together. What about that?"

"Aw, you know goddam lawyers. We just took a drive, and he asked a few questions. I didn't say anything about Linville. Shit, it was so goddam hot out there, and seeing Mary and Lisa like that, I think I just blew a fuse and thought I saw him, too. But now it's pretty obvious I'm wrong, okay? All I told Aaron was I found the girls, and then the feds stepped in."

White cooled down. "K.J., you gotta watch your step, son. Carswall's loaded for bear."

"No shit. He called me, too. I ain't messing with him." Jackson looked at Carly and shrugged.

"You best think about the company you keep. Goddam Willy's gonna run a story tomorrow. He said he 'owed it to me' to tell me in advance. Somehow, he got by the guard and had a little chat with Seth tonight. He says Seth told him about a UFO and butchers in silver suits who cut Linville to ribbons. You know anything about that?"

"I didn't say anything to Willy!" Jackson said.

"You told me you saw Linville - "

"And I'm telling you now I didn't see shit! Whatever Willy prints, it didn't come from me!"

"Dammit, K.J., we gotta put a lid on this."

"Put a lid on what?"

There was a lengthy silence on the other end of the line. Jackson waited, listening to White's heavy breaths. It was apparent that Virgil was hitting the sauce heavily tonight. "Yesterday, after you left my office, Carswall came clean on what happened," White finally said.

"You want to tell me?"

White was quiet again. Jackson motioned to Carly to go pick up the extension. She darted into the other room.

"We're in a shit stew, pal," White said. "He offered us a deal, and we gotta take it."

"I'm listening."

"The government's covering something pretty goddam terrible, and there ain't nothing we can do about it. Seth's screwed, K.J. He's gonna be sacrificed."

"What?"

"The feds put a fix on the whole investigation, and Seth's gonna fall. We can't stop it."

Jackson could hear White take a long drink. "C'mon, Virg. What's the story?"

"Okay," White said. "You heard of Arrowhead up in Mason County?"

"Yeah, I've heard of it."

"A government installation, K.J. They manufactured components for nuclear weapons there during the cold war. Weapons that this country doesn't manufacture any more, at least, not so's anybody would know - you get my drift?"

Jackson sighed. "Ok, so you and me are in on a big secret that every other idiot with a room-temperature IQ probably suspects, Virg. It ain't exactly front page news."

"No? Look, wise guy, if exposing this country's violation of a major arms treaty ain't a ball buster to you, it sure has Carswall's nuts in a pinch."

"What's it got to do with a triple homicide in Attica?"

"It's a double edge, K.J. You ever notice these cattle mutilation incidents cropped up over the last thirty years - just about the same time we been waiting for the goddam planet to go up in smoke? Whenever an animal gets cut up in some field, seems there's always a big UFO mystery tied to it. The feds are behind it."

"What the hell for?"

"It's a goddam smoke screen. Look, K.J., there was a UFO over Linville's farm the other night. It was the same one that farmer saw over Rockford the week before. Thing is, this so-called unidentified flying object ain't just popping in from some Planet X."

"Carswall told you this?"

"Hang on to your ass, pal. He told me everything. What was flying over Linville's place was a souped-up military chopper the feds use to conduct tests. The bastards rigged the chopper to make it look like something that just blew in on a cosmic wind. They do it to scare the shit outa anybody who might see it."

Jackson heaved an unbelieving laugh.

"Think about it, K.J. Nobody takes a UFO sighting serious. You set that chopper down in the middle of nowhere and one or two hicks see it, you suddenly got a UFO story for the supermarket tabloids.

"That's where Arrowhead comes in. Everybody knows that place has enough nuclear waste buried to melt down the planet. The feds insist they're cleaning it up, and since, according to them, nuclear weapons production is a thing of the past, then nothing hinkey should be going on. But environmental groups ride their ass constantly about the cleanup. If any bad long-term effects were discovered, it might trigger private investigations into the plant."

"I'm lost, Virg," Jackson said.

"The feds have been monitoring animals all these years to see if there is any long-term effect on the food chain, but they do it secretly, so's not to raise any suspicion."

"Why?"

"To cover their ass and get out ahead of any problems that might be found. They set up this UFO ruse, dissect an animal, and if they're seen, they leak the mystery to the morons in the press. In two weeks, there's so much bullshit spread around that nobody's interested anymore."

Jackson found it difficult to play along, but he tried. "So, you're saying that's what happened on Linville's farm?"

"Yeah, but they fucked up this time. They targeted the Reeves farm since it's isolated, but the chopper pilot didn't realize he came in too close to the farmhouse. He and his partner hop out, and the idiots don't know they woke up the family. They kill the sow and start dissecting it, but the next thing they know, Linville and Seth come out and surprise them. Linville starts shooting at 'em like they were ducks on a pond. Hell, those clowns land in some crazy aircraft and start butchering that sow - Linville and Seth must have thought they were going to war with the universe.

"The women were out there, too, screaming and carrying on, and one of the feds returns fire at Linville but caps Mary in the chest instead. Linville freaks out, so Seth tries to wrestle the shotgun from him, and the damned thing goes off right in Linville's face. That's it - now Seth flips out, and Lisa's hysterical. The feds rush them, and the fight is on. That poor old alkie probably thought it was the end of the world. He has his knife, and somehow he ends up putting it right into Lisa - two or three times. They said it was dark, and Seth was so fucked up that he was swinging that knife at everything. Finally, the feds knocked him cold.

"Now they're screwed - big time - so these geniuses decide to make it look like a psycho murder so they can set Seth up for the fall. The bastards stripped the women down and spread them out. They took that goddam knife handle and banged the girls up to make it look like a sex crime, and they stab Lisa a few more times to back up the psycho ruse. Then these fuckers cut the slug out of Mary, and they put the knife into her chest to destroy the gunshot wound."

"C'mon, Virg," Jackson said, "this is unbelievable."

"Believe it, K.J.," White said. "Carswall's one hard-core case. He tells me this like he's describing a ball game."

"So, how did he explain the fact that Linville was missing for so long?"

"They hauled Linville away to make it look like Seth shot

him first and then chased the women down. That way it blows any theory that Linville might have had a chance to defend the girls. Those sick bastards must have scooped up what was left of his head and moved that evidence, too. Then they chopped up the pig to cover the dissection. They sanitized the whole murder scene, and gift wrapped a theory for the D.A. to paint Seth as your garden-variety psycho. Shit, poor Seth was half whacked out before this happened, so it's easy to see why he's out of his goddam mind now."

Jackson shook his head. Play the game, he told himself, play the game. "How could they do something like that and think they can get away with it?"

"They're feds, K.J. They got reasons no normal person can understand. The whole goddam thing was done to cover up this insane agenda they got with Arrowhead."

"Okay, let's say the feds did need to test samples taken from animals. Why would they create this bizarre UFO and cattle mutilation ruse, when they could just raise and monitor their own livestock somewhere near Arrowhead?"

"I asked Carswall the same thing, K.J. He said, for one thing, they have to monitor multiple generations of livestock. He says every test site is unique to its environment, so they gotta monitor animals that have been breeding for years in the same locations."

"Couldn't they just buy animals from the farmers?"

"No way. Like he said, these environmental nuts watch Arrowhead all the time, and they're always looking for legal leverage to move in close. If the feds just randomly bought animals, Carswall says it would raise a red flag. That's why I say it's a double edge. First, Arrowhead is supposedly an obsolete nuclear weapons plant that ain't as obsolete as the government wants us to believe. The second big problem is, they have a serious health and environmental disaster on their hands."

"Woah, what do you mean by that?"

"Ten years ago, traces of plutonium started showing in the blood of the animals they been harvesting. Now they're finding it in the food and crops. It's in the ground water, K.J. In this past decade there's been a 150 percent increase in cancer deaths in Attica and Mason County."

"Virg, this is nuts."

"Yeah? The feds admitting that Arrowhead is the leading cause of cancer in this state is nuts. Admitting that Arrowhead is also violating a global nuclear arms reduction treaty is downright suicidal - that is, for anybody with a mind to expose it. I got an idea from him that if we want to go on some crusade here, either you or me, or somebody we care about ain't gonna be around long."

"Did he threaten you?"

"The fucker didn't say it outright, K.J. He gave me this shit about bein' a partner with the government now, whether I like it or not. He didn't say he'd croak me, but he made it clear that if I tried to do something about it, then maybe somebody close to me might have some kind of accident. And he mentioned you and Carly, too."

Jackson felt a jolt to his heart. "What do you mean - Carly?"

"He told me about you and her, K.J. I didn't know, and it ain't my business, but the bastard knows everything about us, so Carly's in the same jackpot. I don't think the son of a bitch is lying, pal, and I sure as hell ain't willing to find out. That's the deal he offered - all we gotta do is keep our mouths shut."

"What about Seth? Let alone the government causes the deaths of three of our friends - Seth takes a lethal injection for it, and we're just supposed to walk away?"

"No! Carswall guarantees he can fix it so Seth will avoid the needle if he cops to the murders, or pleads insanity. Hell, Seth's better off locked up in a hospital anyway. But if the case goes to trial, Carswall says he can't guarantee anything. Look, I ain't happy with this shit either. Linville was my friend, too. I can't change what happened, but I sure as hell can do some-thing to keep us alive. You better think about that and admit we're licked."

"Shit," Jackson sighed. He took a minute to make White believe the con. "So what do we do?"

"First, stay clear of Aaron. Don't tell this to anybody but

Carly, elsewise there ain't gonna be nowhere to hide."

Jackson hesitated for another moment. "I guess we don't have any choice . . ."

"K.J.," White said, "Carswall has complete control of this investigation and the media, and he's covering his tracks as we speak. So listen to the advice of an old bastard who's been smart enough to stay alive in a short-term business: You and me ain't nothing but janitors. Somebody makes a mess, and we clean it up. When one of us gets whacked, somebody else is driving our beat the next day. You got everything going for you. You got a good lady, you're a damned good cop, and you're gonna be a great sheriff. But you'd better know if you jack with this fed, you're gonna lose it all . . ."

Carly came back in the bedroom after Jackson hung up. She nestled in his arms. "You're a pretty good liar when you want to be."

"We're both gonna have to get pretty good at it."

"I'm afraid Carswall's better than both of us," Carly said. "Can you believe that spin?"

Jackson shook his head. "I never would have thought anybody could con Virgil. He's scared shitless."

"I guess we can take him off the list of trustees."

"It's a damn short list . . ."

* * *

Marcus Payne's serenity was shattered by an ungodly scream. He bolted from his bed, his eyes wide. He blinked at the sweat pouring from his forehead. His undershorts were clammy from a combination of sweat and the humidity that hung in his room like a wet towel. He quickly scanned the room, realizing the scream was just another trick his mind played from time to time.

He took a deep breath and walked to the window, lighting a cigarette along the way. He looked out into the dark and typically windy night as he puffed smoke through his nose and thought about Seth Cameron. For the first time in what seemed forever, Payne thought about something besides a darkened staircase and pieces of Lori's body strewn along the stairs.

Seth Cameron . . .

One word dominated Payne's thoughts when Seth came to mind. Since he heard about the murders in Attica, the word wafted through his brain, sometimes intertwining with thoughts of Seth and thoughts of himself.

Acquittal . . .

JUDGMENT

"Execute ye judgment and righteousness, and deliver the spoiled out of the hand of the oppressor: and do no wrong, do no violence to the stranger, the fatherless, nor the widow, neither shed innocent blood in this place."

Jeremiah 22:3

8

ATTICA SENTINEL

CAMERON JURY SELECTION CONTINUES; ATTORNEYS PREP FOR 'UFO TRIAL'

by Dan Williams

Renowned defense attorney Marcus Andrew Payne and Attica Public Defender Reed Aaron continue to grapple with D.A. Roland Whittaker, as jury selection for the triple-slaying trial of Seth Cameron enters its second day.

The media-dubbed 'UFO Trial' draws continued national attention to Cameron's bizarre claim that he was forced to murder Mary and Lisa Reeves by inhabitants of an unidentified flying object last summer. Cameron alleges that the craft landed on the Linville Reeves farm, where he was employed.

Cameron, also charged with the murder of Linville Reeves, relented on his initial confession to authorities and later told the *Sentinel* that Reeves was killed by the UFO aliens.

Adding to the furor of the pending trial is Payne's return to legal practice after a lengthy absence. Payne's reputation as indomitable in criminal litigation spans twenty years. His many high-profile victories include the acquittal of reputed mob boss Joey "Checkers" Domenico on murder and racketeering charges, and his successful defense of baseball hall-of-famer Bobby Harlow, for the murder of Harlow's wife, Jenny...

"Watch this," Payne said. Aaron looked up from his desk, peering over a pair of reading glasses. Payne held a small green doll resembling some kind of outer space creature. He squeezed it and the doll's eyes bulged to twice their original size. "Die, space scum, die!" Payne yelled as he squirted those ugly eyes in and out.

Aaron scowled behind a mountain of legal pads, files, documents, and hamburger wrappers. "Where the hell did you get that?"

"Grocery store down the street," Payne said, still playing with the doll. "They have a ton of them in a bin next to the UFO books and 'UFO Trial' t-shirts. The manager thanked me for all the space gadget business he's done the last five months."

Aaron shook his head. "This town's lost its mind."

"I told him we expect royalties." Payne bulged the purple eyes again.

"Can we get on with this?"

"Lead on, Counselor." He tossed the doll on the desk and propped his feet in the middle of Aaron's legal pads.

Aaron took off his glasses and rubbed his eyes. He blew an exhausted breath and checked his watch. "Lord, it's one a.m. We've been at this since eight this morning - last morning."

"I have my second wind. Let's go until breakfast."

"God, no. My child bride will divorce me if we don't get this trial rolling soon. She already thinks these late-night sessions with you are more than business. She thinks something unnatural is going on between us."

Payne took a long drag from his cigarette. "Tell Sybil we're just exploring an alternative lifestyle. Let's go a few more minutes. I want to review Dr. Skelton's testimony again."

Aaron sighed and dutifully fished through his papers. "Right; Skelton, Skelton, here we go." He bugged his eyes so he could read the medical report. "I don't know, Marcus, this is such radical testimony."

"We'll decide how much to present based on the prosecution's case. By then I should have the jury on a liquid diet. Seth's CT scan is a potential bomb, but a good prosecutor could shred it."

"How do you read Dr. Skelton?"

"He'll be a teddy bear on the stand. We have to see if the jury likes teddy bears, and if your D.A. is a bear hunter. Don't lose sight of reasonable doubt, because we don't have a damned thing going with Seth's testimony all by itself."

"You still believe it's wise to put him on the stand?"

"I don't think we have much choice. The jury will want to hear from him, and frankly, I think he'll be a boost after Skelton lays the groundwork."

"I don't know if they're going to buy Skelton's theory."

"They don't have to buy it outright, but Skelton's testimony might blast a nice hole in the wall." Payne leaned his head back and exhaled a plume of smoke. "Smoke screens," he said with a smile. "Shake a juror's mind. Twist it. Bake it. Confuse the hell out of them so they'll doubt their sanity before it's over. The only way I can do that is to scare them to death."

Aaron hastily scribbled a few notes. "I've never been comfortable deceiving a jury."

"It's not deception. You just dodge in and out of shadows. From what I've seen of D.A. Whittaker, this could be fun."

"Whittaker can be a patsy sometimes," Aaron said with a smirk.

"Then we turn the jury on him. Let him stroke himself. His back yard is chock-full of evidence, so let him parade each piece out like a kid showing off new toys."

"Do you think Carswall has reached out to Whittaker?"

"Tough call. All the publicity the trial's getting may have Carswall nervous. Whittaker holds press conferences every other day, it seems - and he always shows up when the TV cameras are on."

Aaron sighed. "I'm not accustomed to this spotlight; it's giving me the hives. Last week a reporter knocked on Gracie's window at eleven o'clock and asked for an interview. Why would they want to interview a fifteen-year-old girl?"

"Her last name is Aaron, that's why. Reporters are idiots; they'll interview your cockroaches if they can. It isn't every day an accused murderer claims little green aliens butchered his boss. The press is selling a lot of ad space with this fiasco, so be prepared for it to get worse."

"I can't believe they're going to televise this thing."

"You'll be famous, partner. And so will Jonathan Carswall. The media loves conspiracies, especially when they can bash the government in the process. Trying Seth in the press just might buy us a hung jury at the very least."

"The Attica UFO Trial . . . the whole world must think we're raving lunatics."

"Let them think it," Payne said.

"But that tabloid story about you having an affair with Mary Reeves? Something like that can't possibly help us."

"Sure it can," Payne laughed. "Morons who read those papers have the I.Q. of lice. In the meantime, it helps make the trial a national spectacle, and that's the last thing Carswall wants."

"It's disgusting."

"Thicken up, big brother. When the jury meets me, it'll be love at first sight. Come show time, we're gonna strike up the band." Payne played an imaginary trombone, "Yaaa-taa-taa!"

Aaron rubbed his eyes again. "Okay, maestro, the tune is fine, but we still have a big problem with the chorus. Linville Reeves officially and irrefutably went to his great reward via a very messy shotgun blast to the head. We have no foundation to challenge the autopsy."

"Maybe, but we have a fat and stupid M.E. to hose. I can't wait to get him on the stand - it'll be a pig roast."

"But Linville, or whoever that poor soul was, is now conveniently a pile of cremated dust. And to think I was the bonehead who helped Linville draw up his will ten years ago. Why would he want his ashes spread out in a corn field?"

"How did you know he was gonna get abducted by aliens?" Payne squirted the doll's eyes at his brother.

Aaron shuffled his notes. "Seth's entire testimony keys on

Linville, and we don't have a shred of evidence to shake the real body out of the trees."

"Not yet," Payne said, lighting another cigarette from the burning stubble of the last. "That's the biggest wall we have to climb, but we have a couple of ringers lurking in the woods. Don't forget, those ashes in the field aren't the remains of the real murder victim. Linville's out there somewhere."

"What do you mean, ringers?"

"Jackson and his sweetheart. They think they're hood-winking us, but I know they're up to something."

"He hasn't said much the last few months, outside of telling us the bizarre tale that Carswall pitched at Sheriff Halfwit."

"Jackson's flying under the radar. He's scared, and I don't blame him, but he's smart, too. Let's just hope he and Carly are as busy as I suspect they are."

Aaron nodded and scanned his notes. "We're still light on witnesses. Your meeting in Rockford tomorrow is critical if we want to tie Clyde Majors' UFO story to the Reeves farm."

"I'll get him," Payne said confidently. "I've met him maybe a half dozen times now. He trusts me a little more each meeting. I'll get him drunk again and he'll bite - I can feel it. He's a straight-shooter - the kind who wouldn't lie if you held a gun to his head."

"I hope you're right."

"I'm always right."

"What about the airline pilot?"

Payne flicked an ash and rubbed his forehead. "He's a tougher cut. The man's ex-military, and he obviously doesn't like lawyers. But I read something in him. Every time he tells me to go to hell, I think he's sending a message; something like - keep digging and maybe you'll finally ask the right question."

"What do you think he knows?"

Payne shrugged with a playful smile. "He flies a commer-cial jet over town that night, and he hangs up every time I ask if he had any unusual experiences. If his answer was no, why doesn't he say so?"

Aaron conceded with a monstrous yawn. "God, Marcus, I'm spent." He dropped his papers on the desk with finality. "If you want to stay here and speak to my walls, you may, but I must go remind my wife she's still married - happily, I hope."

"I surrender."

Aaron leaned back in his chair in exhausted amazement. He managed a weak smile. "Look at us. Who would have expected to see you and me working together? You, a Supreme Court barrister, and me, a humble country lawyer whose fees are often paid in eggs."

Payne chuckled. "You had your chance for the big time years ago. You know you always had a partnership in my firm waiting for you."

"I know," Aaron said with an affectionate nod. "Don't think I wasn't tempted sometimes, but I've never had the skin for your kind of lawyering. Besides, Sybil's a farm girl, and we didn't want Gracie growing up in the city. In all the years I've conducted these late-night vigils, I've never worried about my girls being alone at home." Aaron suddenly stopped, realizing the nerve he just struck. "I didn't mean to say that . . . I'm sorry."

"Don't," Payne said as he crushed the life from his cigarette. He threw a hasty smile. "Anyway, we're stuck now - a small town P.D. and a recovering drunk about to go Prime Time." Payne stood and struck a stately pose. "Your Honor, we intend to prove that our client - yes, that fellow over there with the antennae - was indeed the victim of a wandering pack of space bullies, cosmic bikers you might say, who lend new meaning to the word 'harvest!'"

"Stop," Aaron weakly laughed.

"You'll forgive that Seth may have accidentally stabbed two women over twenty times, of course," Payne continued, stuffing his hand into his shirt. "You'll forget he beat hell out of three cops, snapped an orderly's arm in two, and tried to throw Virgil White out a window. No, little Seth was simply the victim of extraterrestrial circumstance."

Aaron chuckled like a poorly firing engine. "I'm too tired for this."

Payne staggered back to his chair and collapsed. Aaron blotted a tear from his eye. His aching head didn't appreciate the spate of laughter. "Don't forget you have an appointment in Rockford tomorrow . . . today . . . whenever."

Payne didn't hear. Oblong thoughts twisted his eyes to the ceiling, and he suddenly took a walk to a dusty corner in his memory. "Have you ever seen a UFO? Ever have an experience that you couldn't rationally explain?"

"Me? An esteemed member of the legal profession?"

"Have you?"

"No," Aaron said with a hint of disappointment.

Payne still lurked in that corner. "When I was seven or eight I saw something in the sky that to this day I still can't explain. It was a late summer night, and I was up on the roof." He smiled at Aaron. "Hey, it's something I just do, okay? I was up there watching stars - maybe peeking in the neighbor's windows - when I saw a light on the horizon. At first I thought it was a plane, but its movements were erratic. Suddenly, that light streaked in an arc from horizon to horizon. It went so fast that I almost fell off the roof watching it. Then, it was gone." Payne simply sat in silence, staring at the ceiling. "The night of the Reeves murders, I saw something again... lights in the sky. I was pretty toasted at the time, but I think I saw - "

Aaron's head dropped like a rock, his eyes popping. He jerked up so quickly that his glasses jumped from his nose. "Huh? I'm sorry, Marcus; you were on the roof and what?"

Payne threw a weary smile and considered repeating the story. He gave up, the smile still there. "Nothing."

Aaron stood and packed a few papers into his briefcase, but Payne remained, his mind wandering through the haze.

"C'mon, Marcus, get the lead out."

Payne's hypnotic glaze stopped Aaron short. "I've been hearing voices again."

Aaron's spine iced. "I thought they stopped."

Payne's eyebrows flickered. "They did. A few weeks after I dried out; they'd gone, and I thought I had it licked. What's it been - five months we've been on this case? But lately, I've been hearing them again."

Aaron pulled on his heavy overcoat and plucked Payne's coat off the rack. His voice was pensive. "We've been working nonstop since day one, Marcus. You're pushing at a pace you aren't accustomed to. And smoking those damned cigarettes one after another isn't helping, either."

"Yes, Mom." Payne pulled himself to his feet and put his coat on. He followed Aaron out the door. They walked down the long courthouse hallway. The elevator was slow to respond, and it seemed a waste of valuable sleep time to wait for it. Instead, they took the stairs, their feet echoing down the barren stairwell as they reached the second floor. They passed Sheriff White's office and rounded down to the lobby.

"Sometimes," Payne said, "it sounds like Lori's voice; other times, it's a male."

Aaron fumbled with his keys and nervously tried to unlock the front doors. "Marcus, you're tired; you've wreaked havoc on your body with booze and tobacco for more than a year. Thank God I convinced you to move into the hotel, but I wish you'd move in with us and eat Sybil's cooking, and look into Gracie's little blue eyes. You'd feel better in a week, and that troubled head of yours would clear."

"I don't know," Payne said. "I have strange habits. I'd probably scare them to death. Hell, there was only one person on this planet who could put up with me." Payne's voice trailed off. He sadly looked at the floor.

Aaron put his hand on Payne's shoulder. "It's okay, Marcus."

Payne clenched his eyes, but a small tear leaked out. "God in heaven, I miss her," he whispered.

"I know. I know." Aaron struggled with a tear of his own. He pushed it back and summoned the big brother Payne needed right now.

Payne swallowed his grief and sucked in the musty air with a half smile. "I never told you this, but the weekend she died was a time of revelation for us." His eyes slowly wandered the floor. "You were going to be the first to hear we were retiring from law."

"Retiring?" Aaron said. "You were leaving your practice?"

"Yeah," Payne said with a hollow chuckle. "The papers were all drawn up for the firm to buy me out. I'd done it all. There were no more mountains to climb. I have millions, Reed. I didn't have to go out and face juries, judges, or goddam murderers anymore. Lori and I wanted more time together. Can you imagine that? If we'd made the decision a year earlier, we'd have been holed up in a little mountain cabin right now. But I had cases to wrap up – fucking murderers to set free . . ."

Aaron's heart twisted at Payne's rarely exposed vulnerability. "I'm sorry, Marcus. I'm so sorry."

"That was the first announcement. The second was you and Syb were going to become an aunt and uncle." Payne's wet eyes fell on Aaron.

"Oh, my god," Aaron whispered. He could only stand in silence with Payne, who simply stood and stared at the floor.

"Lori told me she was pregnant two days before she died. We were going to celebrate that weekend."

Aaron closed his eyes and valiantly fought his tears. "I don't know what to say, Marcus."

Payne inhaled and pulled a cigarette, deliberately pushing the demons from his back.

"We need to get some sleep."

"One more mountain," Payne replied.

"What?"

"This is the last one, Reed. I'm doing this for you, for Seth, and for Lori. I've spent my career wading in sewers, but suddenly I've found a swan. For once, I have an innocent client who needs me more than I need him. I'm not going to lose this one; after that, I'm finished, providing my government doesn't retire me permanently."

Aaron gently patted his arm. "Come on, I'll drive you to the hotel."

They stepped outside and met the ungracious breath of a frigid norther. "I think I'll walk," Payne said, pulling up his collar.

"It's cold as a hooker's heart out here," Aaron called over his shoulder as he locked the courthouse door. "You sure?"

He turned and found Payne bolting down the steps.

"I'll call you when I'm back from Rockford!" Payne hollered without looking back.

Aaron stood in the cold wind and watched Payne disappear around the corner. Payne never said 'good-bye.' It wasn't a word in his vocabulary . . .

Attica's winters were equally brutal as its summers. Payne hadn't forgotten the weather extremes, but wise natives avoided a night like this. He put his head into the wind and pushed down Main Street, alone with the whistles and clicks of a healthy winter blow. An invisible storm left a smooth sheet of black ice on the sidewalk and street, making for some dicey footing. The traffic lights flashed up and down Main, throwing eerie streaks of yellow and red across the glazed street. It occurred to Payne, if he slipped and broke a leg, he'd no doubt freeze right to the walk.

He reached Tremont, a wide intersecting street, and he glanced in both directions. A childlike smile cracked his red cheeks, and he took off running. He hit his heels in the intersection and glided all the way to the curb, his arms wildly flapping for balance. He hopped once and made a graceful two-point landing on the walk.

A gentle melody rolled over his lips as he folded an arm behind his back and glided down the walk on dress shoes seemingly made for sidewalk skating. He skated another block, still madly humming, and executed a graceful spin in the middle of the next intersection before continuing on. He slid effortlessly by the revolving door of the Oxford Hotel. Inside, a sleepy night clerk glanced up from his magazine, curiously looking at the door. He shook his head and returned to his reading.

Payne glided back into view, this time stopping in the doorway. His eyes suddenly jumped to the clearing sky.

A shooting star . . .

He smirked and made a wish. "Where were you when I needed you?" he whispered a moment later. He slid through the door.

The Oxford had seen better days, that was a certainty, but it was clean. It was a palace as far as Payne was concerned. He blew into his freezing hands.

The night clerk lazily looked up from his magazine. "Hey, Mr. Payne," he said through a yawn.

"Calm down, Tod," Payne said in passing.

"Another late one, huh?" Tod said, still smacking away the yawn.

Payne mumbled and threw a haphazard wave over his shoulder. He bounded up the staircase like a teen-ager. The cold air had energized him. The upstairs corridor was dim, greeting him with the smell of dusty carpets as he unlocked his door.

It was cool in his room, but Payne tossed his coat on the floor. Thin white light dropped from a bare bulb on the ceiling. Payne rubbed his hands together and perused the place. It was modest, but three times larger than his cell at Rusman mansion. The carpet was old with worn trails running from the bed to the bathroom and the television set. A small hotplate sat on the table next to a half-empty coffeepot. Payne found a doughnut where he'd left it this morning. After a hasty inspection, he tried to bite into it with little success. He pounded it on the table, the doughnut banging the wood like a stone. Payne turned and eyed his wastebasket, juking once, and sunk a perfect hook shot. The doughnut rimmed the metal basket with a resounding clang.

After a satisfying visit to the toilet, Payne stripped to his skivvies, flipped off the light, and crawled into his lumpy bed, throwing a tremendous breath into the air. He turned on a small lamp on the nightstand. From the drawer, he grabbed a small tattered paper bag full of memories. He lit a cigarette. A stack of photographs slid out of the bag, and Payne sifted through them. The first was a picture of him and a beautiful woman. They stood on skis at the top of a majestic snowy mountain. The woman's silver-blond hair fell over her shoulders, and her figure was beautifully accented in a powder blue ski bib. She was frozen in laughter at Payne, who stood stoically with a mound of snow piled on his head.

Payne smiled and thumbed through the photos, stopping at a picture of Lori sitting on a sofa with her mother, a woman who could be Lori's twin - just twenty-five years older. Payne admonished himself for forgetting to call Lori's mother as he had planned to do today. Selective amnesia, he secretly admitted, because hearing Mom's hauntingly familiar voice always ripped his heart from its mooring. She still called Payne her 'sunshine-in-law,' and she ordered him to stay in touch, but conversations with her sometimes turned to tears on both ends of the line. She always hung up, saying, "I love ya, Sunshine - I always will."

Payne never told her that Lori was pregnant. He never would.

The next photo was an intimate shot of Payne and Lori. This one was snapped at a Harrisburg restaurant on their tenth wedding anniversary. Payne looked at the camera with a good smile, but Lori's eyes were on him. Her soft arm was draped on his shoulder, and seconds later, her lips would gently touch his cheek.

"This is my favorite," Payne said to no one.

He stared at the picture until Lori kissed him. He suddenly jumped and looked around the room.

"What?" he said.

The room was tiny.

Payne stuffed the pictures back in the bag and put it on the stand. His cigarette died harmlessly on the floor. He dropped an arm over his eyes and didn't move again until dawn . . .

* * *

A single light burned in a small home on Quaker Street. Zack Taylor stood guard at the window in worn pajamas. He looked out into the cold darkness for a moment and then returned to the kitchen table, where he finished his sixth Scotch. He gently puffed the last breath of life from an old pipe - a gift from his father shortly before the old man died.

Shit, he thought, what I wouldn't give for the past.

Taylor tapped the pipe on an ashtray and poured himself another drink. He scrubbed his bare feet back to the window and put his face against the cold glass. Outside, it was still. The only signs of life were great clouds of steam rising from rooftops in the neighborhood. Taylor stood back and saw the glassy image of a man he no longer recognized. All the training, the dedication, the desire - it disappeared over the last few years just like the soft fog he briefly left on the window. Life was once good. Taylor climbed to the job of air controller at Harrisburg International Airport in less than ten years, but it all ended three years past with one hellish mistake that dropped three hundred people out of the sky like a nuclear bomb.

Taylor never enjoyed another moment of peace since that night. Unemployed for two years and living like a tramp, Zack's life was only beginning to suck air. He'd even quit the booze for a while, and Faye and the kids were under his roof again. And now, he thought, after finally landing a job at the airfield, that little fucker, Cameron . . .

He gulped his Scotch, gritting his teeth in anger. He hated Seth Cameron. He hated Jonathan Carswall.

"Damn those bastards," he whispered. "God damn them all . . ."

9

Ken Jackson stood at Seth Cameron's cell door, awaiting a security guard to key the lock. The guard nodded at Jackson and allowed him to pass. Seth, standing alone across the cell, looked at Jackson for a moment and then turned his head back to the heavily screened window. It was cloudy and cold outside with snow expected by afternoon.

"Morning, Seth," Jackson said.

"Mr. Jackson," Seth said, still looking out.

"How you doing?"

Seth shrugged. He turned and sat on his cot. "I guess I'm okay."

Jackson sat on the other end. "I thought I'd drop in and see if you need anything."

"Much obliged. Mr. Payne brings me candy bars and cigarettes. Wish you could bring me some hooch."

Jackson smiled and nodded. "Trial's not far away, Seth. It won't be long now."

"Can't get here quick enough for me." The little man leaned over, his elbows on his knees. His hair was prematurely gray, and it wasn't cut well. He'd started a beard, but it wasn't a good one.

"Payne says he likes your chances with the jury."

"Chances for what?"

"He thinks he can prove you're telling the truth."

Seth stared at the floor. "Nobody's gonna believe me, Mr. Jackson. I ain't even sure I do no more." He lit a cigarette and held it with his thumb and first finger like a cigar. His bony hand had the hint of a tremor as he put the butt to his mouth.

"You won't get anywhere with that attitude, Seth. Payne

and Aaron believe you. I believe you."

"I'm obliged to you for sayin' that, Mr. Jackson, but Mr. Payne and Mr. Aaron is always talking over my head. It's like I ain't even in the room. They act like it's them going on trial instead of me."

"That's the way trials are, Seth - lawyers against lawyers. That's why you want the best one."

Seth tried to nod, but his head didn't work all that well. He took a drag and spat the smoke. "I feel like a pig outside the slaughterhouse."

"Just do what they tell you. They'll get to the truth."

"Yeah? Maybe I ain't so sure I want the truth."

"How's that?"

"Mr. Jackson, I killed Mary and Lisa. I didn't mean to. I couldn't control myself, but that don't make them less dead. I saw what them bastards did to Linville. Proving it don't make life any easier." Seth's voice was shaky. "Linville was the first man I ever knew who didn't treat me like I was a no-count. He trusted me with his farm and his family. All I done in return was lay there and let them bastards kill him and make me light into Mary and Lisa like some kinda wild animal. I tell what happened and I'm gonna look crazy - like I seen ghosts or something."

"You can't change what happened, Seth. But you have to do what's right."

"They made me do it, Mr. Jackson."

"Then don't be afraid to tell the truth."

Seth leaned back against the wall. He closed his eyes and let his cigarette drop on the concrete floor. "I can't get what I done outa my mind. Mary, she treated me like I was one of her own. Lisa, she was just a little high-spirited, but she was gonna turn into a good little girl."

Jackson gazed at Seth with sad eyes.

"Mr. Jackson, you ain't got no reason to come by here all the time and keep company with me. How come you do?"

"I got a personal stake in it, Seth. I won't lie to you. Something happened to me out on that farm, too. Maybe this whole thing is a test to find out just how much courage we both have. Just trust Payne and Aaron. I do."

Seth gazed at Jackson with pitiful gray eyes. "Everybody acts like I'm some kinda snake ready to strike. How come you don't?"

"You're not a snake, that's why," Jackson said.

They sat for a minute, but the conversation was over. Jackson finally stood and told Seth he'd see him later. He called for the guard and slowly walked out as the cell door banged behind him. His footsteps echoed down the long corridor. Before leaving the cellblock, Jackson stopped and looked back. He heard Seth softly weeping. Jackson shook his head and walked out . . .

* * *

The day shift passed without any significant incidents - a victory in itself for any cop. Snow started falling around noon, but never materialized into anything appreciable. It did, however, leave Attica a fresh layer of ice to fight. Jackson yawned as he sat on the bench in front of his locker, contentedly oblivious to the commotion surrounding him. A shift change always turned the locker room into five or ten minutes of chaos.

Jerry Monroe popped Jackson on the back and sat next to him. "You and Carly doing anything tonight?"

"No plans," Jackson said, arching his back and letting out a grunt. "I'm spent from fighting the damn roads all day."

"How about some high class entertainment?" Monroe said as he quickly changed into his sneakers. "'Hedge Clipper Massacre' opens tonight."

Jackson gave Monroe a twisted scowl. "You actually want to see that?"

"Damn. Ruthie said the same thing. Tonight's the opening of Slasher Festival at the Westminster Plaza. You just don't have any appreciation for cinema classics. Come on. It's the end of the week. We could catch the massacre and then take our girls for a beer or two."

"Thanks just the same. I got a rendezvous with a curvy

cop and a bottle of wine. It's sofa time tonight. I will buy you a beer on the way home."

"Can't," Monroe said, closing his locker. "Ruthie said if she has to go to the Slasher Festival, I have to pop for dinner first. Last chance for the hedge clippers?"

"Pass."

Down the row, a locker slammed hard enough to stop the conversation. Jackson and Monroe curiously looked at Officer Kerry Young, who strapped on his weapon. Young's eyes fell when Jackson looked at him. The temperature in the locker room rose, and Monroe warily tried to cool things.

"Hey, Youngster," Monroe said. "S'matter? Get up on the wrong side of the crib?"

Young propped a boot on the bench and strapped it. "Piss off."

"Rookies," Monroe said. "So sensitive."

Jackson's eyes met Young's, this time long enough to speak volumes. The rookie cop turned and headed out.

"That boy's one fine example of an asshole," Jackson said, closing his locker.

"He's still a pebble in your shoe, huh?" Monroe said.

"Amazing some of the trash they let wear a badge these days."

"Aw, he's just disappointed that cops in this town wear uniforms instead of sheets like his daddy used to."

Jackson slung on his leather jacket and followed Monroe out. "Yeah? Well, he'd better take care. His opinion on minority issues is coming back around to the wrong people."

"I wouldn't worry about it," Monroe said as they walked into the cold night. He stopped and took Jackson's arm, whispering, "Rumor has it the next sheriff's gonna find a way to fire his ass. Don't tell anybody, but I hear the next boss man is . . ." He playfully looked around as if he really cared who was listening. " . . .a darkie."

Jackson clamped his big hand over Monroe's face. "Darkie?"

"Fried chicken and watermelon in the cafeteria every day!"

"You're a dog, Monroe," Jackson said, giving his pal a shove. "Go join your fellow intellectuals at the Slasher Festival."

"Woof woof!" Monroe tossed a wave and two-stepped across the ice toward his car.

Jackson chuckled and turned in the other direction, pulling his collar up and plugging his hands into a pair of leather gloves. The snow had turned to freezing rain, and the parking lot was a breeding ground for broken bones. He walked bowlegged, hoping to give himself a wider base, and he cursed himself for parking his sports coupe so far out. Times like this made him realize that protecting a custom paint job from wide-swinging doors wasn't all that important. He opened his car door, but he stopped when he noticed a dark sedan parked down the street.

Attica was a pick-up truck and SUV town – SUVs on icy nights like this, in particular. It wasn't unusual to see the occasional luxury vehicle about, for a few of the older farmers did indulge in city perks now and then, but something about this sedan struck Jackson. He squinted in the dark and noticed, through the darkened windshield, what appeared to be a small flame lighting a cigarette.

Jackson warily climbed into his coupe and was suddenly taken by an almost surreal sight. Scraped into the ice on his windshield was the word NIGER.

He almost laughed. "You can't even spell it right."

Jackson climbed out, ice scraper in hand, and looked at the grammar-challenged graffiti. He shook his head and scraped the ice away. Before he climbed back in, he looked down the street. The dark sedan was gone…

* * *

Clyde Majors wasn't in the habit of going outdoors in this kind of weather unless it was important. He stood in the drive and peered through the falling snow, wondering if it would have been smarter to take that slick attorney's offer of help. Marcus Payne spent the whole afternoon with Clyde, but he was probably back in Attica by now. Old Clyde's ego was pliable enough to allow him to cuss himself for challenging this broken tree limb alone, but the branch had dropped on the main power line and threatened to put the farmhouse into a deep freeze. Had this been last summer, when the weather was hot and clear, the limb would have fallen to the ground; but tonight it draped over the line like a two a.m. drunk on the shoulders of a disgruntled barkeep. It was getting dark and damned cold, but the old farmer knew the limb had to come down. Clyde scowled at the branch, which was too far from the house to reach from a ladder, and far too high to snag from the ground.

Clyde scrubbed his heavy boots through fresh snow and entered the barn, pulling a canvas tarpaulin off his tractor. He fired her up, the engine sparking on the first try. No tractor would dare screw with old Clyde - ten degrees or not. The tractor gutted a plume of blue smoke and pushed outside, rolling toward the tree like a lumbering elephant. Clyde carefully maneuvered the tractor under the tree limb. With luck, he could reach it by crawling up on the engine.

Out beyond the drive in the pale darkness, a dark blue SUV stopped and doused its lights . . .

Clyde cursed the best he knew how as he set the brake and dragged his old knees up on the tractor's engine. He asked God for a little boost, wavering as he gingerly stood. He stretched his arms out for balance and grabbed another limb for security as he tugged at the broken branch. The sky mercilessly spat in his eyes. Clyde defiantly spat back and wrestled the tangled mess, careful to avoid the power line.

Minutes passed, and the cold took the fight from Clyde's arms. It seemed that just when he managed to free one of the limb's many suckers from the wire, another would grab it and hang on for life. Clyde meticulously snapped each offending twig, clenching his teeth in the sandpaper wind. To ease the agony, he thought about the expensive bourbon that city boy lawyer Payne brought to bribe him into testifying at his damned trial . . .

A dark shadow slipped into the seat of the tractor, and a large boot gently pushed in the clutch . . .

Clyde's battle was all but won. He grunted, steam blowing from his nose and mouth. The branch surrendered and let go of the wire, pelting Clyde's face with a pillow of snow.

A gloved hand engaged the gearshift . . .

Clyde called the branch a 'lousy stinking bastard' and threw it to the ground. He shook his head and tried to clear the snow from his eyes as he clumsily turned away from the wind, waving an arm for balance. Suddenly, his foggy eyes told him someone was sitting in the tractor seat. Before Clyde gasped, the tractor violently lurched backward, throwing the old farmer's knees to his chest. He cried out, dropping on the engine and sliding off the front of the tractor. He landed on the right front wheel, crotch-first. Clyde's testicles burst into his intestines. He threw a guttural scream, rolling to the ground in front of the tractor. His mouth sucked in dirt and snow, and he defensively balled himself, trying to pull his ruptured guts away from the beast that was going to kill him.

The tractor belched smoke as it jumped forward and buried Clyde's arm under the right tire. Clyde screamed into the frigid air, his eyes swirling as the big tire backed off and uncovered his twisted arm. He scurried back, his arm dangling backward from the shoulder. The tractor let out a murderous growl and lurched at him with a wicked grin.

The last thing Clyde felt was his spine snapping as the tractor jammed him into the oak tree. He choked on his own blood, trying to suck for air, but his lungs were flat.

The tractor rested on old Clyde, its engine now idling. A pillow of snow sifted through the air as the shadow jumped from the tractor and faded into the night. White snow around Clyde gushed to a mushy red, but the wind would soon cover any trace of life on or near the Clyde Majors farm . . .

* * *

Marc Payne growled as a stream of hot water pelted his head and shoulders. He leaned on the shower wall and let the water flow down his back as the hotel bathroom steamed up like a spa. After a moment, Payne gently slipped to the floor of the tub and relaxed, drowning in pure, wet pleasure. He let the tub fill to the rim, and then turned off the water, draping a wet washcloth over his eyes. He lustily blew out the remnants of his exhaustion.

His cell phone rang through the mist. Without removing the washcloth, he groped for the phone.

"Speak," he said.

Aaron was on the line. "Marcus! I thought maybe you skidded into a ditch! I've been calling for hours! Why didn't you answer?"

"Sorry, Dad, but it took me three hours to get home. I couldn't even see the road. Answering the phone while avoiding ditches didn't seem the best choice."

"Glad you're alive. How did it go with Clyde?"

"The old bastard talked my skinny butt off. He tells me the saga of his life every time we meet."

"Did you have any luck?"

"Jackpot. He agreed to testify."

"Excellent! What changed his mind?"

"Booze and brilliance," Payne chuckled. "I think Clyde's tired of taking a beating by the press. Back when he first reported the UFO and his gutted bull, he was a celebrity. Now his cronies are jabbing him pretty good, and the media's crucifying him. More importantly, I think he's been having a little trouble sleeping since the Reeves murders."

"Do you think he'll come off as a credible witness?"

"I believe him, so the jury will. I'm convinced he saw the same thing Seth saw. Clyde believes there's a cover-up, and wait 'till you hear the priceless gems he laid on me, now that he decided to talk. He didn't trust me until now, but today he showed me some photos he's been hiding. First, there were a few gruesome pictures of the bull, which, by the way, was entirely gutted without a trace of blood anywhere. I asked

Clyde if he didn't think that was a tad odd, and he just shrugged and said 'Yeah, godammit. Don't ya wonder how the hell that happened?'"

"You've got to be kidding!"

Payne laughed. "I have to keep reminding myself that some country folk just never get the old pickup out of first gear. I guess a major financial loss lying there with a hole in its gut was Clyde's only worry. But something else in the photos that caught my eye was the background. There was a large patch of burned weeds in the distance."

"Burned?"

"Remember the burned weeds on Linville's farm?"

"Yes. I didn't think much about it at the time."

"Nor did I until I saw Clyde's pictures. Now, get this: I asked him if he knew how the ground got burned like that, and he said 'I reckon it must have been done by the chopper.'"

Payne let Aaron digest that one. "Wait," Aaron finally said. "What chopper?"

"That was precisely my next question, Counselor!"

"Oh, crap!" Aaron laughed. "Chopper! You mean Carswall paid Clyde a visit?"

"A silver-haired government cocksucker with a pretty badge and a smart mouth, as Clyde put it."

"Oh, this is too good," Aaron said.

"I think Clyde's just naturally a little slow on the draw, because he didn't even call the Rockford sheriff about the bull for at least a day. Even then, he didn't mention the UFO, because he thought the sheriff might put him on a 72-hour mental health hold if he did. So, the sheriff called animal control to remove the bull, and he and Clyde just resolved that lady luck was a bitch that night."

Aaron chuckled. "And you thought small-town lawyering wasn't a challenge."

"I had no clue, big brother," Payne said. "Anyway, Clyde thought he'd let it go, until a couple neighbors asked him if he saw something strange flying around the fields on that night. About that same time, somebody from the local paper heard about the mutilation from the Rockford sheriff, and next thing you know, Clyde's on the front page. Faster than you can say 'extraterrestrial,' Carswall was on Clyde's doorstep. Clyde told him his story, but lucky for us, he didn't mention his neighbors seeing an unusual aircraft in the area that night. He didn't want Carswall harassing them, too."

"Excellent. I'll go after those boys right away. So, obviously Carswall continued the Arrowhead spin?"

"Right. He dipped into his satchel of lies and gave Clyde a tale similar to the one he laid on Sheriff White."

"Ah, the mysterious black helicopter . . ."

"He didn't explain it in quite the fanciful way he told White, but he gave Clyde the same crap about cancerous nuclear waste descending on us. He said the craft was off course because of an inexperienced pilot, and he spiced it with malarkey about bumbling but well-meaning butchery in the name of national security. Clyde was more concerned about losing his bull, so Carswall offered to write him a check for ten grand right on the spot if Clyde would keep his mouth shut and forget the whole thing. Since the Reeves murders hadn't occurred yet, old Clyde didn't see the harm."

"So, why did he come clean now? Isn't he afraid that Carswall will bite?"

"I think the Reeves murders are eating his conscience. And, with a few drinks under his belt, that old boy isn't afraid of anybody."

"So, now we have him on the stand."

"And he's going to plant another seed of doubt," Payne agreed.

"Treacherous games, Marcus," Aaron said with apprehension.

"Don't you just love me?"

"I don't know who scares me more, you or Carswall."

"I have more charm."

"Did anything else come out of your meeting?"

"Clyde promised he'd convince his neighbors to testify. So, how was your day?"

"Well, while you were getting Clyde drunk, I came up with a little gem myself. I uncovered some interesting information regarding a prosecution witness - Zachary Taylor."

"Taylor?" Payne said. "Remind me who he is."

"The controller at Attica airfield. He's part of Whittaker's preemptive strike, remember? Taylor told the Grand Jury there was no air traffic in the vicinity on the night of the murders. Attica's airfield is just one runway and a little tower. These little regional fields don't normally have personnel on duty late at night. If a private plane comes in, the pilot relies on visual contact and a radio beacon. So, I decided to find out why Taylor was out there so late."

"You're not such a bumpkin after all."

Aaron ignored Payne. "I had a talk with an old fellow in town who part-times as a night security guard at the airfield. He confirmed that nobody works the tower after eight o'clock. When I asked him why Taylor might be out there so late, he said it was probably because Taylor was too drunk to find his way home."

Payne sat up in the tub. "Once again?"

"Yeah, too drunk. We know he took the fall for that airline disaster in Harrisburg a few years ago, but the investigation only accused him of negligence - no specifics."

"Until now."

"The guard said Taylor often stays at the airfield when his wife won't let him in the house."

"This is fantastic!"

"I asked the guard if he'd be willing to testify, but he's not sure he wants to get involved."

"The hell he won't testify! Subpoena his ass!"

"Easy, Marcus. Don't forget, this is a small town. Everybody knows everybody, and everybody owes everybody. He may not want to put a shiv in Taylor's back. He might find himself sitting next to Taylor at Rusty's Tavern the next night, you know."

Payne calmed. "Any ideas?"

"My legal aide is digging into Taylor right now. We'll know more about him than he knows about himself. We'll also know more about him than Whittaker. We'll ambush the good D.A."

"Ambush? Is that you talking?"

"I'm a quick study."

Payne slumped back into the warm water with a devilish smile. "Nice work, big brother."

"Thanks. I guess we don't need to get together tonight."

"Not unless you want to bathe with me. I have to make some notes, and then I'm going to bed."

They said goodnight and hung up. Payne stepped out of the tub and towled off. He climbed into his running shorts and walked into the other room, sitting at the table and grabbing a legal pad. But his attention was quickly drawn to a brown paper bag that always seemed to be nearby. He smiled and pulled out the photographs, searching out his favorite - the picture of Lori and him in the restaurant. He jumped when the hotel phone on the table suddenly rang.

"Damn," he grumbled. He considered ignoring it, but relented and answered.

A grisly voice on the line was dark and unfamiliar. "Fucking scum! You get that butcher off and you'll pay!" The phone died in Payne's hand.

He looked at the receiver. "Goodnight," he said, hanging up and looking back at the pictures with little concern.

The phone rang again.

"You'll pay, fucker!" the voice hollered. "You'll get what your wife got! Cut in pieces!"

The line buzzed in Payne's ear. This time the call bothered him. He shook it off and hung up.

The phone rang again.

Payne picked up. "Mom, how many times have I told you - don't call me when I'm working!"

The squeaky voice wavered. "You . . . you fucker!"

"No, no," Payne said. "You brought her; you fuck her." He hung up and smiled triumphantly. He then clicked the line, and in a moment the desk clerk answered. "Hey, Tod," Payne said.

"Hey, Mr. Payne. How ya doin'?"

Payne paused and smiled. "Good, Tod."

"Great. What's up? Ya need some take-out? I can probably

get ya some pizza or something. Or - "

"No, Tod. Just take a deep breath and listen to the sound of my voice. Those calls I just got were cranks."

"Oh, man! I'm sorry! I wouldn't have sent them up if - "

"It's alright, Tod. But I have a job for you. Would you mind screening my calls from now on?"

"You kidding? That'd be cool! So, what if something important comes in? What if the judge wants to talk to you? Or the cops or something?"

"See, that's why I want you to screen them. So - at night when I'm here - only send up a call from Reed Aaron, the sheriff's office, or the President."

"Aaron, the sheriff, and, uh, did you say the President?"

"That's correct. Got it?"

"Woah. Cool."

"Goodnight, Tod. . ."

Payne laughed and hung up. He put the pictures in the bag and leaned back, rubbing his forehead. He looked at his inviting bed and then at the wall across the room, where a dreadful oil painting of apples and a banana always seemed to sneer at him. Obsessive compulsive behavior was not a part of his makeup - God knew from the clothes strewn all over - but Payne was taken by a sudden uncomfortable twitch. The damned painting wasn't straight. He'd stared at the thing with contempt enough times to know it had moved since he last saw it. He got up and straightened the picture.

He sat down again and found another bag, this one containing two forgotten doughnuts from the half-dozen he bought before leaving for Rockford. He fished inside and pulled one out. This time he tried banging it on the desk before breaking a tooth. Payne sighed and took a hook shot, but the stale doughnut bounced across the carpet. Curiously, he looked for the wastebasket, which had somehow moved to the corner.

He froze, and he carefully scanned the room. Irritated, he picked up the phone and clicked the line.

"Tod? It's me again. I told you I didn't want housekeeping in my room."

"Huh?" Tod muttered. "Housekeeping? Yeah, I know."

"But you didn't tell the maid, Tod," Payne said in a singsong voice.

"Yeah, I did, sir. Besides, the cleaning lady has been sick for three days. I been cleaning rooms, and I didn't go into yours. Honest!"

"No?"

"I never go in your room, Mr. Payne!"

"Don't give birth, Tod. My mistake. Pretend this didn't happen. Goodnight." Payne put the phone down and nervously looked at the misplaced basket.

His breath was slow and deliberate. He didn't move. His eyes shifted, and he let his suspicion breathe.

"Tod," he whispered, "somebody's been in here."

Now his cell phone rang, and Payne suspiciously checked the screen before answering. It was Aaron.

"Marcus," Aaron said hollowly. He sounded quite dead on the line.

Payne's brow furrowed. "Reed?"

"Sit down."

"What's with you?"

"I just got a call from Dan Williams. Clyde Majors is dead."

"What!"

"A neighbor found him. It's on the TV news right now. They're saying it looks like an accident. Clyde was run over by his own tractor."

"What the fuck! Accident?" Payne blindly stumbled around his room. "How do you run over yourself? What's he doing on a tractor in a blizzard?"

"The Rockford sheriff says it looks like Clyde was standing on the tractor, messing with some broken tree branches. Somehow, he and the branches all ended up under the god damned thing."

Payne closed his eyes. "I can't talk, Reed. I'll see you tomorrow." He clicked off and sat on the bed, his fists clenched in anger. His room suddenly felt uncomfortable. He glared at the crooked picture and the misplaced wastebasket.

Treacherous games. Carswall's working the mind and body, Payne thought.

He couldn't remove the sight of Clyde Majors from his mind; the old farmer throwing back good booze and slapping his knee every time Payne cracked a good one. He couldn't remove from his mind the look in Clyde's eyes when he told him that testifying at Seth's trial was the right thing to do . . .

10

Zack Taylor slumped in his easy chair. His head wallowed in an eddy of liquor, but he was quite aware of what the television news reported. The local station's announcer updated the death of Clyde Majors, the Rockford farmer who'd gained folk hero status for a time last summer, and a figure sometimes linked to the upcoming Attica 'UFO Trial.' Taylor's erratic heart pounded furiously as he poured another shot.

Faye Taylor pounded down the staircase with daughters Emily and Michelle in tow. The children were bundled in snowsuits, and Faye wore a heavy fur coat. She struggled with a suitcase, while Emily and Michelle toted hastily packed backpacks.

"Go out to the car, kids. It's all warmed up," Faye said.

The girls obeyed, both tossing wary glances at their dad, who appeared pretty calm after screaming at the top of his lungs and hitting Mommy just a few minutes ago. Faye waited for the girls to leave before she turned and stood directly in front of Taylor, her body trembling with rage.

She breathed heavily as she pointed her finger at him. "If those little babies weren't here, the cops would be dragging your sorry ass to jail right now."

Taylor looked up from the TV. He saw an ugly purple welt rising on Faye's cheek. His drunken face screwed into a cry. "I'm sorry. I didn't mean to. I won't do it again . . ."

"Shut up!" Faye snarled. "This is the third time in two years, Zack. Three strikes, you're out."

Zack's face quickly dulled when the tears didn't come. "You're not going to your parents, are you?"

Faye smirked. "I really should, you know? I ought to drag

our two terrified babies in front of my dad. When he told you he'd kill you if you ever hit me again, he meant it."

"Please, just stay. Don't tell him. Don't take my kids away."

"I'm going, Zack. I'd rather be dead than live like this. In fact, I honest-to-god would cut my wrists right now if it wasn't for those babies. I'm not going home, only because I know Dad would beat you to death. Believe me, I'm not doing it for you; I just don't want him paying for your pathetic problems."

"Where are you going? Please don't go." Zack was indeed pathetic.

"I'm going to heal and let the kids spend a week somewhere where there isn't any screaming. I'm going to file for divorce in the meantime. Don't worry, I don't want anything but my babies and my life. You can have the empty check account, the foreclosed mortgage and that half-empty bottle. God knows you worked hard for them." She turned and headed out.

"Faye!" Taylor called, trying to stand. He fell back into the chair when she slammed the door. Zack slouched and took shallow breaths to keep his head from bobbing. Instantly, the whiskey produced what Taylor considered rational thought.

Good, the half-empty bottle said. We can be alone now.

Zack clicked the TV off, remembering something about a news report that seemed important at the time. UFO Trial, that's what the news guy said. Fucking UFO Trial. Somebody just died. He looked at the door and listened to the mini van drive away. At first, he couldn't believe they actually left, but the bottle said to forget it. He clumsily put his chin in his hand.

The phone rang three times before Zack heard it. He picked up, sounding suddenly quite sober.

"Taylor," the voice on the other line said. "Carswall here."

Zack's blood boiled whenever he heard that voice. "We gotta talk."

"This will be our last communication before the trial. I'm calling to be certain you are prepared."

"No, no, no. I want to talk about that guy who got killed

up in Rockford. The one in the news."

"I don't know what you're talking about."

"The farmer who got killed today. Did you kill him?"

"You're drunk."

"You think I don't know what's going on?"

"Listen, Taylor. Be very careful how you talk to me. We have an agreement regarding your testimony. I suggest you focus your attention on your end of the deal."

"Or what? You gonna kill me, too? I got news for you. I don't fucking care if you kill me, you hear? You'd be doing me a favor!"

"Look, Taylor, we have a deal. You don't have to do much for me, and in return, you're going to get your family back on its feet."

"I don't have a family, just like I don't have to listen to your threats! That's 'cause I don't care anymore!"

"But you probably care about Faye and your children."

Zack's eyes pushed open. "You leave them out of it."

"Shame on you to let them leave on a night when the roads are so dangerous."

"You son of a bitch! How did you know -"

"I suggest you pour yourself some coffee and spend the rest of the evening thinking about that. Perhaps screwing three hundred people into the end of a runway is something you can live with, but I wouldn't want to be in your shoes if you caused something to happen to your family tonight."

Zack's heart kicked his chest. He fought for breath, but the whiskey rationed the air.

"You better start reviewing your testimony," Carswall said. "You're wasting precious time talking on the telephone. Have a nice evening."

The receiver spat a monotonic buzz at Zack. He stood with a scream that never left his mouth, and he threw the phone across the room. By the time he passed out on a pile of shattered dishes, the house was entirely wrecked . . .

* * *

Jackson jumped from a light dream as Carly walked in the front door. He stirred in his chair, and, realizing his heart could resume its natural beat, he pulled himself up and snagged Carly with a huge hug.

"Ooh," Carly said, barely dropping her coat in time. She dug inside the warmth of Jackson's big arms, shivering from the cold. "Now that's my idea of a welcome home."

"I was worried about you," Jackson said.

"I'm sorry I took so long. The roads are bad, and I stayed in Harrisburg a lot longer than I should have."

Jackson grabbed her shoulders and looked into her marvelous eyes. "Thanks for calling. If you hadn't, I think I'd be white by now."

Carly laughed curiously. "Did you get anything to eat?"

"I got a pizza warming in the oven. It's probably stale by now."

She hung her coat on the rack. "I don't care - I'm starved."

Carly walked into the kitchen with Jackson nipping her heels like a puppy. She grabbed some dishes while Jackson retrieved the pizza. "I found out some interesting things today, big guy." She perked when Jackson's arms came around her. He planted a soft kiss on her ear that made her nearly drop everything. "Ooh, Officer Jackson. I think you missed me."

Jackson didn't bite her neck hard, but he did bite. "I miss you when you go to the damned bathroom," he whispered.

Carly turned and looked into a pair of sad eyes. "Hey? Are you okay? Hard day?"

"I've had better."

She put a wet kiss on his mouth and playfully shoved him out of the way. "We eat first. I can't reduce you to mush on an empty stomach. Grab a couple of beers, and I'll brighten your day."

Jackson complied and walked out to the table, where Carly had already put a piece of pizza on his plate. She stuffed another in her mouth while Jackson smirked.

Carly defensively tried to speak through a wad of cheese and sausage. "Hey, I said I'm starved!"

"Okay," Jackson said with a coy smile. "You eat twice as much as me and never put on a damned ounce."

"I get a lot of sweaty workouts," Carly said, starting on a second piece.

"So what's the interesting news?"

"I had a great time with my vet friend. She took me around the animal shelter, and I saw the cutest puppy. We really need a dog, Kenny."

"What's the news?"

"She doesn't do much work for the Humane Society anymore, but we took a ride and she introduced me to another vet named Cindy who does. This lady is a firecracker - talks a mile-a-minute - a real crack-up. Cindy was involved in several mutilation investigations, including the one in Rockford, and does she have some killer information. Guess who was right in the middle of each investigation, flashing his badge and threatening everybody."

"Carswall?"

"Bingo. Cindy was able to inspect the mutilated bull from Rockford before Carswall moved in, however. Kenny, she described that bull just like the animals you saw on the Reeves farm. She said it was dissected, and the incisions were more precise than what she could make with a scalpel. And get this: there wasn't a drop of blood in that animal, and there were no jagged rips or tears like a wolf might make; besides, what wolf is dumb enough to attack a bull?"

"I read somewhere that most of these mutilation cases are just a predator attacking an injured animal," Jackson said.

"Right, that's what Cindy says. In some cases that's been proven, but in others the incisions have been too clean - like the Rockford bull. Plus, the farmer insisted his bull was healthy, and a carcass completely drained of all blood is just way too weird."

"Yeah, just like the horse and pig that I saw. So, how did Carswall fit into Rockford?"

"A day or two later he and his goons storm the lab where Cindy and her colleagues were studying the bull. He flashes his badge and demands they turn it over to him. Cindy said there was a lot of bickering with the Humane Society director, but Carswall must have pushed the right buttons, because he got what he wanted. She said Carswall was a real prick."

"She's a good judge of character."

"Wait, this gets better. Now we have the murders here, and the Humane Society again is interested in newspaper reports about the mutilation of a pig on the Reeves farm. They call Virgil White, who immediately refers them to Carswall."

"Out of the frying pan . . ."

"Right. They called Carswall, and he denied the pig even existed - end of story."

"I've got to get this info to Payne. Did you ask Cindy if she would testify?"

"She can't wait," Carly said. "I have one more thing that may help us. Cindy says there's a veterinarian in Harrisburg, an ex-military guy who investigated two cattle mutilation cases a year ago. She had dinner with him once - she says he turned out to be married - but he got drunk and bragged that he conducted the investigation for the government. It may have just been a play to get into her pants, but I think we should check him out."

"We'll have to figure a way to get to him without raising suspicion."

"Cindy says he's a real hound, so I think I have an idea how to do it," Carly said, smiling.

Jackson scowled. "Not sure I wanna hear that one."

Carly finished her beer and closed the pizza box. "So, what screwed up your day?"

Jackson shrugged, almost apologetically. "I don't know. Some asshat scraped the word 'nigger' in the ice on my windshield."

"What? Why, the son of a bitch! Who the hell do they - "

"Easy, girl," Jackson said, always surprised at the cop lurking around what normally looked like a woman more suited to angel's wings.

"I didn't expect that kind of bigotry here."

"If it's any consolation, he misspelled it."

Carly laughed. "Oh, good. For a minute there I was afraid

we were dealing with a literate asshole."

"Lately, I've been catching some strange vibes around the station."

"Who?"

"Kerry Young for one."

"Oh, well he's a dick. That isn't anything new. Every time he says anything to me, his eyes never come off my boobs."

"But his old man was a cop here for years. Rumor is, he was in the Klan a long time back."

"The Klan? In Attica?"

"You're from the city, babe. It's hidden better there; besides, these days they operate more subtly. Klan don't dance around fires in bed sheets much anymore; these days they get elected and dance around Congress in blue suits."

"Kenny, almost half the station is black. I think if a civil war breaks out, we'd have a good chance."

"We?"

Carly shrugged. "I'll be your pale spy."

Jackson laughed. "I'm not playin' here. I don't think you and me are as much a secret as we think. Maybe Young and others don't see things in – you know – black and white."

Carly knocked on Jackson's forehead. "Knock! Knock! This century calling K.J. Who cares? Virgil doesn't have a problem with us. He's busy building that fishing boat of his and planning his retirement. And once you're sheriff, you got the hammer, buddy." Carly gathered the plates and took them into the kitchen. "We have more important things to worry about than a few ignorant rednecks."

Jackson followed her with the empty beer bottles. She quickly cleaned the plates and handed them to him for his half of the domestic deal they cut last summer. He smiled and dried them, still looking at her. "You tired?"

She flashed those incredible eyes.

Jackson opened the refrigerator and pulled out a bottle of wine. He held it tantalizingly in front of her. "I thought we might break this open, put on a fire, and tell each other secrets."

Carly purred and kissed him. "You get the glasses, and I'll get the fire."

"And I'll get to heaven before you," Jackson sang with a jazzy baritone voice.

Carly offered her contagious giggle and danced out of the kitchen.

Jackson took a lot of time with the wine bottle. He had to pry the cork out with a knife, because he'd never invested in a corkscrew. Other than a beer now and then, Jackson was alcohol-incompetent, primarily due to his daddy's endless sermons about letting booze rule a man's life. He finally found a strainer and poured the entire bottle into a bowl to remove the cork debris. He then funneled the vino back into the bottle. After looking at his handiwork, Jackson shook his head and hoped he would never have to rely on bartending as a career.

"Oh, lord help me," he said as he walked into the living room and found Carly lying on two silk pillows by the fire. She was dressed in a black teddy that showed an awful lot.

"I bought this in Harrisburg," she said with a naughty smile. "It doesn't cover too much, does it?"

"I think I'm gonna have a coronary." Jackson felt like he was eighteen, despite being well acquainted with his lady for eight months now. He was beginning to believe Carly might just make him feel eighteen the rest of his life.

"Don't just stand there, big guy, let's have a belt."

Jackson crawled next to her, juggling the bottle and glasses. He poured, and they toasted with a kiss and a belt. "Zing, right to my head," he said.

"It's not the wine," Carly said, trying to dig a hole in his shoulder with her soft chin.

Jackson put his arm around her and watched the fire. He rubbed her soft shoulder, marveling at her milky skin. "Have you ever given it any thought?" he said softly. "You know - you're white, and I'm . . . not."

Carly looked at him dumbly. "Funny thing about falling in love - it blinds one to another's peculiarities."

"Wait a minute. You didn't think about me being black?"

"You *are?*"

Jackson laughed.

"Oh, well, that's it," Carly said. "I'm outta here . . ."

"C'mon – I'm serious. Don't you ever worry about it?"

"As I recall, even though your smile and incredible looks took my breath away the first time we met, you were pretty arrogant. You had that 'Oh, shit, a lady cop' attitude all you guys have."

"What? That's not true. I like lady cops."

"Yeah, those with arms like pipes and a moustache problem."

Jackson laughed again. "I'm gonna respectfully decline to answer that one, Your Honor."

"Yeah, right." She playfully primped up her hair. "Just because I should be a centerfold, you guys think I can't kick butt when I have to."

"Centerfold?" Jackson said. He reared back and checked the uninhibited lace. "Yeah, I guess so. Modest, too. You aren't gonna be a centerfold, are you?"

"Only if you take the pictures," Carly said, melting Jackson with that clear, sexy voice.

"Cut it out. My heart, you know?"

"Why, Officer Jackson, I swear your face is red. I still don't believe you people can do that!"

"Yeah, yeah. And we do sunburn, too. We bleed red, and some of us don't have any rhythm at all."

Carly laughed with him. She sat up and got in his face. Her dark green eyes lit up her silky black hair. "Kenny, I don't care what color anybody is. I wasn't brought up that way. I'm not in love with a black man; I'm in love with a man - one with integrity, compassion, and a big heart."

Jackson was right. The wine made a beeline to his head. At least, he thought that might be what made his brain swirl.

They shared a long kiss, the kind of kiss that never preceded sex. It was a kiss that meant much more than a signal of passion.

Carly slumped back down and excavated his shoulder again. "I'm glad we have that settled, big guy. So, what say we stop discussing racial harmony and drain this wine bottle."

Jackson sighed and absorbed the extraordinary security within him that seemed to grow every time he held her. They poured another drink and sipped, watching the fire dance in the fireplace. The hot crackle of burning wood hypnotized them. Orange and red flames darted in and out, casting soft shadows on the wall and throwing heat into the quiet room.

The spell abruptly shattered with a violent bang on the outside door. Jackson jumped, knocking Carly back. A second bang at the door followed the sound of glass breaking outside.

"Stay down!" Jackson scrambled across the room and peered out the window. He saw nothing outside, but he didn't remain at the window long. Outside, he heard muffled voices. Jackson crawled to the table and grabbed his holster. He drew his weapon and crawled back to Carly. "Where's your piece?"

"In the bedroom," Carly whispered. "I'll get it."

"Wait," Jackson said, putting his hand on her arm. "It may be just a calling card."

"A what?"

"Shh." Jackson slipped back to the window and cocked his ear to the ominous whispers outside. He looked back at Carly. "I think we're getting a message."

"From who?"

"Congress," Jackson whispered.

Everything grew suddenly quiet. Carly darted to the bedroom and retrieved her service weapon. She returned quickly, covered by Jackson's big robe. "What now?" she said.

"They had their fun."

Jackson looked through the curtains and saw nothing but a dark, quiet street. He stepped out onto the porch and found two rocks, one sitting in the ruins of a broken flower pot.

"Oh, now they've done it," Carly said, coming out and kicking the broken pot around. "I just got that on sale for next spring. Somebody just bought himself an ass-kicking."

Jackson smirked and grabbed her weapon. "Okay, deadeye, let's not mix wine and firearms, if you don't mind." He tossed the rocks into the snow and led Carly back inside, but before he locked the door, he looked back down the street, half expecting to see a black sedan . . .

11

ayne's gold watch read two-fifty p.m. He turned up the heater in his rented 4x4, wondering if he had been stood up. The heater fan kicked in, and a breath of warm air took the edge off the chill. Payne crushed his cigarette, hoping he might soon see some evidence his long trip wasn't a bust.

He was parked near a well-constructed airplane hangar that guarded an unpaved airstrip. Rugged foothills surrounded him, spotted by patches of ice, snow, and barren groves. The property was isolated, and Payne might not have found it without a detailed map provided by the man he was to meet here at two-thirty. Payne was grateful he rented the sturdy SUV, for the old Aaron mini van wouldn't have made the cross-country trek to this remote meeting place. The long drive to Harrisburg and subsequent journey to the middle of nowhere left Payne in a sour mood, but he had little choice but to cooperate with Captain Franklin Mitchell's demand to meet at this location. Mitchell made Payne's life an adventure over the last few months, but at last he appeared ready to talk. He could prove a powerful trump card, if Payne's suspicions about him were true.

His ears perked to an ominous sound. He shut off the motor and opened his window. The sky echoed the monotonous beat of helicopter blades whipping the air. Payne stepped out and looked up. Over the rise, a sleek helicopter suddenly broke and rounded the landing strip. It was a vintage army recovery and observation aircraft - a four-seater in mint condition. The husky war bird circled once more and flared in near the hangar, kicking dirt and weeds into swirling plumes. Payne shaded his eyes to watch the chopper land. Its engine fell, and the rotor blades clipped down to a slow and steady rhythm.

The pilot's door flapped open, and a sturdy, graying black man hopped out. A green beret laid smartly on his head, accented by a heavy leather airman's jacket, baggy military trousers and boots. This was casual attire for Frank Mitchell. His stoic, granite shoulders were as square as his attitude. He looked deliberately at Payne and pulled off his sunglasses, tucking them neatly into his flight jacket as he walked up. This was their first face-to-face meeting, and Payne's mental image of Mitchell was uncannily accurate.

"Captain Mitchell," Payne said, extending his hand. "You're late. I was afraid you changed your mind."

Mitchell brushed by. "Park your vehicle in the hangar."

Payne could have called a cadence to the way Mitchell marched to the building. Old habits die hard, he thought. He pulled his rover to the hangar doors as Mitchell played an elaborate electronic security keypad to gain access. The doors swung open, and Payne pulled in. Inside, he saw four small airplanes - all pristine, vintage aircraft - lined neatly in a row. He climbed out and followed Mitchell back outside.

"Nice spread," Payne said. "This is all yours?"

Mitchell locked up, speaking over his shoulder. His heavy voice came from deep inside his chest. "A hundred acres with a spring and two ponds. The aircraft are mine. I built the hangar myself. It's my piece of the planet. I'll build a home and retire here." He turned and glared at Payne. "Unless you get me killed."

Payne curiously watched Mitchell walk to the chopper. "Captain?" he called.

Mitchell stopped and looked back with disdain. "I don't have all day; let's go."

"Can't we talk here?"

"Were you followed?"

"I don't think anybody could have followed me, unless they were in a damned tank."

Mitchell smirked at Payne. "Let's go."

Payne hesitated as Mitchell marched to the chopper. He shrugged and tagged along.

In moments they strapped in, and the chopper lifted with a terrific roar. Payne's stomach dropped to his right knee when Mitchell gunned the chopper to maximum boost. The helicopter reached 120 knots and leaned toward a range of rugged hills to the west. Payne said nothing. He couldn't be heard anyway. He simply watched with childlike fascination as Mitchell directed the craft over the hills and descended into what looked like impossible terrain for a chopper to negotiate. The bird danced not more than twenty feet from the treetops. Payne's stomach was near his foot now. Suddenly, an open patch of land broke underneath, and Mitchell dropped and hooked the chopper to the ground with adroit grace. The skids kissed without so much as a bump, and the engines suddenly cut.

Mitchell ordered Payne out as he hopped from the other side. Payne's legs were mushy, but he gained enough strength to chase Mitchell into the woods. They hiked uphill for fifty yards through tangled brush until a small cabin came into view. It stood on a rocky crest, rustic and with no amenities but a small outhouse in back. Mitchell pounded onto the porch, followed by Payne, who gasped for every breath.

"You smoke?" Mitchell asked, unlocking the cabin door.

"Incessantly," Payne breathed.

"Figures." Mitchell walked in. He rummaged through the dim light and pulled back the burlap curtains from a window. Payne found a small table and a trio of handmade chairs. He gratefully sat and caught his breath. Mitchell fished through a stack of crudely constructed cabinets and found a jug of corn mash. He unscrewed the bottle and took a healthy pull, slamming it on the table once he was satisfied. "Help yourself," he said.

"No thanks," Payne said. "You're not going to drain that jug and expect me to fly back with you?"

"You're welcome to walk back if you want." Mitchell turned a chair around and mounted it. "I'm a treetop flyer, Payne. Been one for forty years." He didn't expect the need to say more in his own behalf. He jerked a green cigar from his flight jacket. The stogie had to be an inch thick. Mitchell pulled a wood match and sparked it with his thumb.

Payne responded with a tug from his cigarette package. "I got the impression you didn't smoke," he said, accepting a light.

Mitchell smirked at Payne's cigarette. "I don't. I savor the gentle nuance of a perfect cheroot. The habit leaves me healthy enough to run uphill, unlike yourself." He torched the cigar and puffed until it took. Mitchell dropped the dying match on the bare table and squinted at Payne. "So, I finally meet the infamous Marcus Andrew Payne."

"In the flesh," Payne said.

"You look better on television."

"Who doesn't?" He heaved the smoke and looked around Mitchell's musty cabin. It reeked of pine and dust. "Nice place you have here. Who's your decorator?"

Mitchell rubbed his thick black chin. He had a sense of humor when he was a young man, but a life in the military had all but extinguished it. "Bought and paid for," he said. "It's a private getaway for contemplative reflection. I bring close associates here for fishing, hunting, and excessive drinking."

Payne nodded. "This, a hundred acres, and all those fancy aircraft - all yours?"

"It's not what I might have accumulated on an attorney's salary, but I can sleep at night, Counselor."

"Don't get me wrong. I envy you - your serenity, Captain."

"Colonel."

"Excuse me?"

"The airline calls me Captain, but my retired military rank is Colonel."

"Can I call you Frank?"

"My friends call me that. You can call me Colonel."

"Give me time; I grow on people."

"So do boils."

Payne gave a patented smile and took another drag. "Very good, Colonel. Mind if I use that one in court sometime?"

Mitchell didn't smile back. He tipped the jug, drank and swallowed hard. "Let's get on with this."

"I appreciate your meeting with me."

"I want you off my back."

"No, I think you have more in mind. You wouldn't go to this much trouble without an agenda."

"Counselor, your agenda is winning your homicide trial, but I wonder if you really know what it's about. You're forcing my hand, but I have no intention of becoming a victim. That's why we're here."

Payne measured Mitchell. "A bold statement coming from a civilian 747 pilot. Out of curiosity, did your distinguished military career include more than skidding along treetops?"

Mitchell leaned back and sucked his cigar. "I retired with brass on my collar, Payne. Let's just say you don't reach my level of experience without gaining knowledge of covert operations."

"Fair enough."

"Your persistent phone calls leave me with no alternative but to deal with you. Show your hand, Counselor."

"To the point," Payne said. "I like that. Okay, Colonel, let's put everything into perspective. Four months ago, I contacted five commercial airline pilots who passed over Attica in the morning hours of the murders. When I asked four of them if they experienced anything unusual during their flights, they all said 'no' without hesitation. You, on the other hand, hung up on me, which is just as good as a lie."

"Is that so?"

"You see, Colonel, I have a gift. Actually, I think of it as a curse, because it makes me quite good at what I do. What some people find out too late is a cold and undeniable fact. Nobody can lie to me. Face-to-face, on the phone, even if I just read someone's words on paper, nobody can lie to me without my knowing it."

"Startling," Mitchell sarcastically said. "How do you manage to pass that gigantic head through doorways?"

"I turn sideways," Payne said with a smile. "But this clandestine get-together proves I'm still batting a thousand."

"Payne, I retired from the military because I'm moving on in years, and I didn't want to waste time training young boys how to avoid augering into a mountain. I was born to fly, and that's how I intend to spend the rest of my life. I'm quite contented ferrying civilians around the world and flying my toys in my spare time. I don't want complications in my life, but you are fast becoming a complication."

Unmoved, Payne blew smoke over Mitchell's head. "Then why not live with your lie and be content? I doubt even I could persuade you to share what's on your mind. I could badger your 'brass' until this trial ends, but I can't force you to give anything up. I don't believe I'm the biggest complication in your life, Colonel."

Mitchell rolled the perfect cheroot between his thumb and first finger, his gaze on Payne quite solid. "You're the point man in this UFO Trial. You say you believe your client's story, and you have the CIB dogging your scent. Obviously, they must share your confidence in the defendant."

"And you know more about the situation than you'd care to?"

"Like I say, Payne, I'm familiar with military intelligence."

"Then something did happen on your flight over Attica? Or, did you just bring me here to get drunk and engage in male bonding?"

Mitchell continued to roll his cigar. He took another drink. "Do you have any idea just who you're screwing with?"

"Why don't you tell me."

"I'm meeting with you because the stakes have just been raised."

"You're talking about Clyde Majors, I'd guess."

"They killed him, Counselor. That shouldn't come as a surprise to you."

"Nothing surprises me, Colonel."

"Then you know they'll kill anyone who is vital to your planting doubt in a jury's mind about this UFO incident. Your client killed two people, Payne. Copping a plea and letting him die peacefully in prison might not revive your career, but this trial is a virtual death warrant for anybody you drag into it, yourself included."

"Let's get something straight, Colonel. Are you more than

a civilian pilot? If you're simply here to threaten me for them, then we have nothing further to discuss."

Mitchell pointed his cigar at Payne. "Don't be stupid, Payne. If I was on a government ordered sanction, do you think you would have been alive more than two seconds after you walked into this cabin? I am a civilian - just like you. In fact, I wish I never gave up the military; then I wouldn't have been flying that night. Thanks to you, I'm a goddam target, too!"

"Thanks to me? Colonel, did I blow the head off some poor homeless patsy and use his body to cover up God knows what?" Payne's eyes pierced Mitchell's. The colonel, for the first time visibly shaken, simply sat back and chewed his cigar furiously. Payne nodded and exhaled smoke. "That's right. Majors wasn't the first on the sanction list. Now, tell me what happened up there."

Mitchell stood and wandered to the window. He madly chewed, his mind drifting back to that hot summer night. "We were descending into Harrisburg at fifteen thousand feet." He puffed and stared into the woods. "You ever hear of a 'bogey?'"

"I have," Payne said, his heart beginning to race. "It's aviator lingo for an unidentified aircraft."

Mitchell nodded. "We were on a normal glide path. The weather was clear; my co-pilot and navigator were bullshitting about this and that. I suddenly saw an incredible burst of energy at two o'clock high. It was a green-white arc that blew by in seconds. I couldn't even speak before it passed."

"Did your crew see it?"

"Negative. We searched for a few minutes."

"How about your passengers?"

Mitchell shook his head. "We only had fifteen or twenty. Nothing was reported; most passengers at that hour are asleep."

"What about ground control?"

"I radioed Flight Services. The controller said he thought he'd seen something on his monitor - some kind of anomaly. He was certain it was nothing. There are no aircraft fast enough to disappear from radar range in one pass. It's theoretically impossible." Mitchell returned and straddled the chair, looking straight into Payne's eyes. "Something was there, Payne."

Payne leaned on his elbows. "But nobody else saw it."

"The crew wasn't looking. I had no choice but to take some shit about needing a urine test."

"You're sure it wasn't just a reflection?"

"It was a bogey," Mitchell said as if he just gave an order.

"You say it was a flash of light. Couldn't that be a hundred different things?"

"I said, a bogey, Payne. An arc light, green and white. The curvature of the glass in relation to the object and other lights in the cabin ruled out a reflection. I've been a pilot since I was thirteen, and I've never seen anything like it. The craft was a delta configuration, and it trailed a pure white exhaust. I estimate it was doing at least mach-four."

Payne took careful stock of Mitchell's eyes. The colonel was not lying. "At that speed, how could you have seen so much detail?"

"My vision is 20-10, Payne. At any given moment when I am in the air, I can give you an estimate of my position within one degree. If it's nighttime and I see just one star, I'll estimate even more accurately. I've piloted every fixed-wing aircraft from a hang glider to the latest supersonic. I tested the space shuttle. I've flown aircraft that don't exist, according to the military. I saw a bogey, Payne."

A long silence followed. Payne smoked his cigarette to death, finally crushing it on the old wooden table. "Did you report it?"

"Report what?"

Payne was in no mood for this. "I see, Colonel. It never happened, right?"

"Counselor, most airline pilots are reluctant to officially declare a bogey unless they're willing to undergo a hell of a lot of scrutiny. Airline presidents are damned careful about who they hire to take passengers to thirty thousand feet in a jet-propelled, pressurized tube."

"No sale, Colonel. Surely, with a fat military pension and your little 'piece of the planet,' you wouldn't starve if the airline decided it didn't want you up there. This boils down to why you will, or will not testify for me."

"What choice do I have? You singled me out. Your phones are tapped - you surely know that, don't you?"

Payne didn't answer.

"Your calls put me squarely in the crossfire of this goddam crusade you're on. Lately, I get the feeling I can't even piss without wondering who's watching me shake my dick. You're forcing me to stand alone whether I like it or not."

"You're lying again, Colonel."

"And you're a son of a bitch!"

"It's part of my job description. Look, I understand your fear, but all you had to do to get yourself off the hook was tell me - and whoever else was listening at the time - that you had no unusual experience on that flight. Instead, you damn near run a tree up my ass, flying me to this little hideaway so you can play games. You don't give a damn about my client or me, so stop wasting my time and tell me what's really on your mind."

Mitchell took a hard draw from his cigar. "I brought you here to ask you to plea your client and cut your losses. I'm accustomed to giving orders, but all I can do with you is make a sincere request."

"Request denied. You're still hedging."

Mitchell watched his cigar throw gentle waves of smoke. He stood again and paced the little cabin, finally stopping at the window. "Several months ago, a small twin-engine plane disappeared around Rockford. Did you know that?"

Payne cautiously pulled out another cigarette. "I heard something. The wreckage was found later, wasn't it?"

"I said it disappeared, Payne. The FAA reported it found wreckage with the pilot's burned body inside. Dental records reportedly matched, the pilot's charred remains were buried, and his widow grieved. Case closed."

"Plain language, Colonel."

Mitchell walked up and leaned on the table. "That aircraft

disappeared, and it was never found, Counselor. Plain enough?"

Payne nodded. "You apparently haven't lost touch with some sensitive sources."

"Apparently," Mitchell said. "Don't forget, Payne, the 'F' in FAA stands for 'Federal.' An air traffic controller in Rockford was in contact with the plane. She claimed the pilot reported an incredibly fast aircraft with unusual lights and markings tailing him just before he vanished. Her story was suppressed. The FAA's official report concluded the pilot became disoriented and was flying upside down. Poor boy just augered in when he thought he was climbing. It was a convenient excuse to explain why he reported seeing strange lights, just in case the air controller went to the press. But whomever this woman was, she knew what kind of plane the pilot was flying. The wrecked aircraft didn't match her description, so she started sticking her nose where it didn't belong."

"Did you say, whomever she was?"

"My guess is she was banging the pilot. She knew enough details about him and his plane to know the puzzle pieces weren't matching. She made a lot of noise, that is, right up until the State Patrol dragged her body out of her mangled car."

Payne smoked without much expression. "I don't suppose your sensitive sources explained the nature of her accident?"

"Funny thing about accidents - they just happen." Mitchell sat again, nervously fingering his cigar. "Something's out there, Payne. It seems any civilian involved with seeing lights in the sky around Attica and Rockford is having trouble staying alive. If Central Intelligence is watching you, then they know about everyone you're questioning. Don't forget, even though I didn't file a report, my two crew members can verify I claimed I saw a bogey that night, if anybody asks. That means I have to be a very careful driver. Understood?"

Payne could only give a conciliatory nod.

"I really didn't think you'd come here and allow me to talk you out of trying your case, so here's my only alternative:

Once I finish telling your jury what I know, I become a missed opportunity. If I can just make it to the stand alive, I can fly my toys until I die an old man, and I don't have to worry about checking my fuel tanks."

"Okay, Colonel, but you're not just saving your own neck. I don't think you particularly care for what's going on, either."

"I spent my career protecting your right to think whatever you want, Counselor. You're damned good at what you do, I'll give you that, but let me tell you something: You're searching for the truth, but you may discover it's something you don't want to know."

Payne sadly nodded. "So I can count on your testimony?"

"You get your witness, and I get you and your deadly friends out of my life."

"I'll make the necessary arrangements, Colonel, and I'll get you on the stand as quickly as possible. For now, I want to hide you."

Mitchell uncharacteristically chuckled. "Wrong."

"Colonel, I can keep you off my witness list for just so long. There will be a period of time when you'll be vulnerable."

"Look, Counselor, right now you have an expected life span about as long as this cigar. I don't want to be anywhere near you until I take the stand. If you die, my problems are over anyway, so I'll take my chances alone. Have a written message hand-delivered to my wife within thirty hours of the time I'm to appear."

Mitchell stood. The meeting was over. He took a pull from the bottle and stashed it before heading for the door. "Let's go before it gets dark. Choppers and trees don't get along well at night."

"Colonel," Payne said as he stood. "For what it's worth, thank you."

"Stow the gratitude. You just put your legal wheels into motion. When this is over, I don't want to hear from you again. You're a dangerous individual . . ."

* * *

Shortly before Captain Mitchell and Payne returned to Mitchell's private airfield, District Attorney Roland Whittaker stepped from a comfortable steam bath back in Attica. He walked into a spacious shower room and cooled himself with a spray of water. The Park Country Club facilities were impeccably clean, luxurious, and expensive. Whittaker came here for a shower and steam almost every day. Despite his regular usage of the steam bath, golf course, swimming pool, and tennis courts, Whittaker never dropped a pound from his middle-aged frame. That was because he dined in the club's restaurant religiously, entertaining politicians, attorneys, and potential campaign contributors almost every day.

His was the good life.

He cajoled in the shower with two bankers, a stockbroker, and the mayor today as he relished the comforting cool water. In here, the naked men were simply old, fat white men. But power, even in the form of wrinkled pink flesh, was recognized and respected.

Whittaker turned off the spray and dried himself, noticing a young man showering at the far end of the room. Perhaps it was a man - perhaps a boy. He was smallish, his blond hair cropped very short. In fact, there was little hair on his lathered body. He soaped himself almost passionately, drawing Whittaker's attention. The man/boy stole a sudden glance, his eyes hauntingly light.

Whittaker nervously turned away and walked into the massage room.

"Afternoon, Mr. Whittaker."

"Hello, Bee," Whittaker said. He rolled onto a large padded table.

Kevin 'Bee' Harden cracked his huge knuckles. Bee's muscular arms bulged from his 'Park C.C.' t-shirt. He was a retired pro football player who once played offensive tackle for A.H.S. during the school's three-year reign as state champions. The star of those memorable teams was a swift running back named Kenny 'Jack Magic' Jackson. Harden earned the name 'Bee' because his blocks stung opponents like a hornet. Bee claims the nickname was given him because he likes 'the honeys.' Since losing his professional football career to five knee surgeries, Bee worked at the club as a personal weight trainer and masseuse. He also serviced several wives in town, one whose husband was a regular customer. Bee didn't care. He slapped his oiled hand on Whittaker's back and started rubbing firmly. "How goes it, boss?"

Whittaker growled with delight. "It goes, Bee, usually all over me."

"I hear ya," Bee said. He commenced the rubdown, knocking an occasional satisfied breath from Whittaker. "By the way, boss, I got a free day tomorrow. Want me to do that oil change on your car?"

"That would be fine," Whittaker said. He turned his head and rested it on his folded arms. "Pick it up at the courthouse. I'll be in the office all day."

"You got it."

"Have my secretary pay you."

"No charge, boss."

Whittaker raised an eye. "Uh-oh."

"You got any other repairs you need done while I'm at it?"

"Okay," Whittaker said. "What are the charges this time?"

Bee kept on rubbing. "Boss, I - uh - got pulled over the other night. I don't know, it was some rookie cop, I guess."

"And?"

"He didn't actually pull me over. He found me parked on the front lawn of the library. He says I was passed out, but I say I was just sleeping. It was a technicality, you know?"

"Isn't this your fifth 'technicality?'"

"Fourth."

"Bee, a driving record like yours lands most people in prison."

"Hey, do you need your car painted?"

"It's six months old," Whittaker said.

"You need to get an older car, Mr. Whittaker."

The D.A. sighed. He then smiled at Bee's perfect hands. "Check the timing. It's running a little rough."

"I'll wash it, too," Bee said. "And the DUI? The ticket says I have to appear next month."

"What DUI?"

"Thanks, boss." Bee nearly put Whittaker into a trance.

It was a feeling. Whittaker couldn't describe it, but the word that most appropriately fit was 'power.' It didn't matter if he could put a person in prison for years, or if he could just exchange a buried drunk driving charge for a nice rubdown. Power was power, and Whittaker adored it. It was far better than sex.

Whittaker opened an eye, his head still resting on his arms. He suddenly caught sight of the hairless young man from the shower room. The boy was skinny, but his body was smooth and not bony. He was still naked, and quite uninhibited. His eerie blue eyes fell on Whittaker as he gracefully stepped into the steam room.

"Bee?" Whittaker said. "Who was that boy? I've never seen him around here."

"Hell, I don't know. I just work here."

Whittaker sat up and cranked his head around a few times. "I need more steam. I'll be back."

"You got it, boss." Bee watched Whittaker drop his towel and enter the steam room. He shrugged and went on about his business . . .

The steam room was hot, but not unbearably so. Whittaker inhaled deeply and sat in the opaque bath. He leaned against the tile wall and tried to see the young man through the steam. He saw nothing, but he could feel him.

In a moment, a gentle voice lilted over the air. "This is so nice."

Whittaker's eyes searched. The voice was flawless. It was the voice of a boy - a very gentle boy. It sounded almost feminine. "Very relaxing," Whittaker responded. "Are you a member here?"

"No."

Whittaker awaited an explanation. He tried another topic. "This is the best time to come here. You generally have the facilities to yourself."

"I like it, Roland. I'd like to come here more."

Whittaker hesitated. There was still too much steam in the

room for him to connect that odd voice with a face. "Do I know you?"

"I don't think so. I've seen your picture in the paper. The UFO Trial, you know?"

"Oh, that," Whittaker said, relaxing.

"You're a very famous man."

"I don't know about that," Whittaker said. "It's fame I could do without."

"I don't think so," the boy said. The small room grew quiet. Whittaker couldn't explain to himself what made this invisible boy so mysterious. The voice drifted through the steam again. "Could I offer you some advice?"

"Advice?"

"Don't let the nigger testify."

Whittaker's heart suddenly raced. "What?"

The invisible, hairless boy let out a girlish giggle. "I'm just a big fan of yours. I want to help you."

"Who are you?"

"The nigger won't help your case, Roland. He'll hurt it. He's lying - that's how niggers are. They're insincere, they lie, and they can be so awfully rough."

The steam pushed Whittaker's blood to his head. His round flesh dripped profusely. "Look, I don't know what you think you're trying to do - "

"I just want to help, Roland," the boy said. "You have a job to do, and the nigger's trying to win the sheriff's job by making you look bad. I don't want that to happen - in fact, I'd do anything to help you. I like you."

"That's enough," Whittaker said. He tried to stand.

"Oh, no," the boy said. His voice squeaked to a whine. "Don't be mean to me. Don't make me beg you. I will beg you if you want."

Whittaker warily stopped and sat back down. Adrenaline pounded in his heart.

"I just don't want you to be hurt, Roland. I want you to be happy - very happy. I can make you happy."

"Look, you, tell me who you are. Who put you up to this?"

The boy giggled, sending an electric tingle to Whittaker's groin. "I'm your friend, Roland."

Whittaker's heart strained in the heat now. "What do you mean?"

"You know, Roland. They say that you are very good to your friends, and I can be good to you."

"Stop this," Whittaker said. He leaned back and shook the water from his head. "Stop teasing me."

"But they say you like to be teased. They told me about everything that you like. Don't you like me?"

"Look, just get - yes - I . . ." He suddenly jumped when a tiny, soft hand touched his shoulder. Instead of pulling back, Whittaker gazed at the hand. The steamy shadow before him was oddly soft and fleshy.

"Don't work with the nigger, Roland. He could find out a lot of things about you."

The boy slowly ran his hand down Whittaker's chest to his abdomen and softly stroked his penis before sucking it. Whittaker closed his eyes and let out a low moan. He then wrapped his hands around the boy's neck and violently pumped, instantly exploding in the child's mouth. He gritted and pumped harder until the boy gagged and tried to pull away. He finally bit down, and Whittaker stifled a cry and let go. The boy pulled back, coughing and spitting, and quickly walked out. Whittaker trembled, his head whirling. He stood and opened the door for a breath of dry air, peering down the corridor. The hairless, naked boy waited at the corner. He playfully looked at himself and then at Whittaker before he turned and disappeared.

Whittaker hid behind the door and glanced at Bee, who read a magazine next to the rubdown table.

"Ready to finish?" Bee asked.

"In a minute," Whittaker said. He retreated to the steam and sat on the tiles. He shook his head, wondering what the hell just happened. The steam was harsh, and Whittaker wanted to come out, but he had to wait a moment. A silent curse fell from his lips as he dropped his head and closed his eyes. The hairless boy had terrified him for a reason he could never understand. However, fear wasn't the only emotion he felt. He couldn't come outside yet, because he still had a rock-hard erection . . .

12

A tumultuous crowd surrounded the Attica court-house. Locals gathered under a blanket of visible steam, huddling for warmth and rubbernecking a scene that resembled a carnival midway. Hawkers roamed about, doing a brisk business in shirts and alien dolls, while reporters engaged in elbow combat for position near the courthouse doors. The wind-chill was hideous this morning, despite intermittent appearances of an impotent sun. A dozen television transmitter vans gathered in the street, attended by technicians, reporters and miles of yellow cable. Many spectators were enthralled by the presence of national television news correspondents. The famous TV talking heads behaved like spoiled movie stars, ignoring the stares and primping for the cameras.

A week passed since the death of Clyde Majors, but the media had injected electricity into his story. It was a perfect jump-start for the Attica UFO Trial, scheduled to commence on the *TV Trials* cable network this morning at nine a.m. The town had been dressing up for its television debut literally before the Reeves bodies were cold. City officials, store owners, and randomly chosen locals had seen themselves on the evening reports and tabloid news programs, or read their own comments in news magazines. Even Rusty Wade, the venerable tavern owner, was cashing in, having talked with a literary agent about hiring a ghostwriter to pen a tell-all book. Three publishers had already bid six-figure advances.

At eight o'clock, the pushing and shoving reached a crescendo as a large black sedan edged through the sea of reporters and gawkers. It stopped in front of the courthouse, and Roland Whittaker stepped out of the passenger's side. A platoon of Attica police officers formed a wedge and cleared a path. The heavy, dark-haired D.A. smiled and waved to the crowd, stopping to sign an autograph and throw a snippet to the hot microphones. His deputy D.A., a mousy kid fresh out of law school, had a look of terror in his eyes as he followed closely on Whittaker's tail. The flare of quartz lights and clicking cameras whirled as the prosecutors quickly entered the courthouse.

Someone hollered that the jury was coming, and the crowd rotated back to the street in a tumbling ball of chaos. A black van whipped by, its tinted windows hiding the jurors inside. Reporters and technicians took off in chase, realizing the jury was going to enter a side door generally used for deliveries. Locals caught up in the excitement ran after the reporters. The van stopped, and a second wave of cops emerged from the side door and formed a gauntlet. The nervous jurors stepped out and quickly walked toward the courthouse. One of the national TV celebrities positioned himself in front of a camera and tried to stage a dramatic on-the-spot report, but he was overrun by the crowd. His toupee flipped into the tidal wave.

He desperately groped for his hair, hollering, "Son of a bitch!" at his open microphone.

The wide-eyed jurors bogged down in the crush, and several cops shoved people out of the way. A few obscene insults took air as the jury finally pushed inside. The crowd rolled about, some of the locals learning a lesson about messing with electronic equipment and their testy operators. The cops searched for a commander, hoping one might radio a request for additional units. Before anything cooled off, someone hollered and pointed down the street. A police car pulled around the corner, leading a blue jail van and a second patrol unit bringing up the rear. The three vehicles stopped behind the jurors' van.

"It's Cameron!" yelled one reporter.

The crowd instantly converged. Six guards from the county jail bolted from the cars, decked in riot gear and armed with assault weapons. They surrounded the van's door and backed the wide-eyed crowd with intimidating glares. More Attica cops pushed through and made a wall. Despite several rude exchanges between journalists and guards, a distinct line was drawn.

The van door slid open, and Sheriff Virgil White stepped out. He cursed at the bevy of people, cameras, microphones, and lights. The sheriff turned and impatiently signaled. Ken Jackson emerged, holding Seth Cameron by one of his shackled arms. In a sudden final attack, the journalists exploded with questions and shouts. Seth leaned into Jackson, startled by the microphones and lights. Jackson reassured him, and they made their push forward.

Behind the crowd of reporters, a raspy voice pierced the cold air. "I hope they fry your ass!"

A rumble of disgust rolled over the crowd as heads turned toward the disembodied voice.

"Fucking butcher!"

"C'mon, K.J.!" White ordered. "Get him inside!"

Jackson took Seth's arm, whispering in his ear, "Don't worry about them, Seth."

White elbowed through the crumbling path, knocking cameras and microphones as he went.

"Hey! Watch it!"

"Mr. Cameron! How do you -"

"Fry, you fucker!"

"Mr. Cameron!"

"Move it! Come on, K.J.!"

"Do you hold to your confession?"

"Mr. Cameron!"

"Does Marcus Payne -"

"- is a fair trial -"

"Butcher!"

Seth's eyes glazed as each step moved him deeper into the mouth of darkness. His gait was clumsy.

"Mr. Cameron!"

"Get out of the way!"

"Fry your ass!"

The path collapsed a few feet from the door. Seth slowed

and ducked.

"Come on, Seth!"

"Did you kill -"

"Fry!"

The crowd engulfed Jackson, White, and Seth. Seth heard nothing. He pulled his cuffed hands to his head and shut his eyes. To his right, two press photographers suddenly broke into a fistfight.

"Get outa my way!"

"Fuck you!"

The combatants rolled into the center of the storm, flailing at each other and setting off a chain reaction that swept a TV cameraman and a smartly dressed, and quite famous woman journalist into the fight. The Famous Woman Journalist started kicking with her expensive high heels.

"Cut it!" White screamed, putting a smart headlock on one of the combatants.

"Son of a bitch! I'll sue you!"

A baton wildly swung into the remaining fighters, landing directly on the Famous Woman Journalist's skull. She dropped like a bag of cement, while two cops moved in and violently restored order amid an ocean of screams.

"Stop!" Seth cried. "Momma! No!"

A pall of silence suddenly fell over the crowd. All eyes turned to Seth, who dropped to his knees. He trembled like a dying bird.

"Move!" White ordered, helping Jackson lift Seth to his feet. They carried him inside, leaving a wake of stunned observers. The reporters quickly separated, leaving the dazed Famous Woman Journalist on the ground. They regrouped in various war camps to file their stories . . .

Across the street, a tall, sandy-haired man leaned against the wall of the AAA Hardware Store. He watched the entire episode from that safe distance. Grinning, he sipped from his flask. Dan Williams put his pipe in his mouth and happily puffed, quite satisfied with himself. He shivered as a cold wind blew up his coat. Willy took one last drink, capped the flask, and stuffed it into his coat pocket. He took inventory of the other pocket to be sure it was full of pens and notepads.

Curtain's up, he thought with a smile. He hitched his collar up and strolled across the street . . .

Marcus Payne pounded down the corridor with Virgil White in his crosshairs. The sheriff and Ken Jackson looked up from outside the defendant's holding cell just before Payne struck.

"What the hell happened out there?" Payne bellowed. His voice boomed off the corridor walls. Reed Aaron followed close behind.

White raised his hands. "Now, ease yourself, Counsel. No harm's been done. We just had a little excitement coming in."

"A little excitement?" Payne said, landing in White's face. "There's a reporter out there with a gash on her head. Another guy has a shiner as big as my fist, and three others are in handcuffs. Is this your idea of police protection?"

White always prided himself on knowing his own limitations, and that included who not to screw with. He didn't use them much anymore, but he wanted to keep his balls right where they are, thank you. "I'm sorry, Counsel. Things got out of hand, and we mishandled it."

"I told you I wanted to accompany Seth!"

"I was ordered to have him here by eight-thirty. I figured you'd meet us."

"You figured wrong." Payne turned to Jackson, ignoring White for a reason. "Is Seth all right?"

Jackson nodded. "He's shook, but he's okay."

Payne brushed by both lawmen and entered the cell, finding Seth seated at a small table by the window. Seth looked decidedly awkward, wearing a cheap brown suit and poorly shined shoes. His tie was thin and tied crookedly. He was no longer handcuffed, and he fidgeted with his roughly clipped fingernails. Aaron and Jackson walked in behind Payne, while White wandered down the hall. He intended to teach his troops the time-honored theory that shit does roll decidedly downhill.

"Seth?" Payne said.

Seth didn't look up.

"Dammit, look at me!"

Seth jumped and turned his head. His eyes were wet. "I'm sorry, Mr. Payne."

"The hell you are! You listen to me, Seth; you have nothing to be sorry for - nothing! From this point on, you don't apologize to anybody for anything. I don't care if you break wind and burn the judge's eyes - you will never speak the words 'I'm sorry' again! I'll kick your ass into next week, you understand?"

Seth lowered his head and nodded.

Payne grabbed Seth's chin. "Get your goddam head up! You don't bow your head to me; don't bow your head to anybody!"

"But I let you down, Mr. Payne. I let 'em get to me."

Jackson caught Aaron's eyes, a bit surprised by this side of Payne he'd never seen. Aaron, however, watched his little brother with great confidence.

"Stand up, Seth," Payne said. "Listen to me. You are Seth Cameron, and you're as good as any son of a bitch in this town. From now on, we are on a stage. Whatever I may say or do, you must not be surprised. We're gonna take on these bastards and spit in their faces! Now straighten that tie and stop whining."

Seth, bolstered by a hit of pure, uncut Marcus Payne, fidgeted with his tie and made a point of holding his head high. Payne put his arm around him and led him out the door, expecting Aaron and Jackson to damn well clear a path for them.

Jackson watched them leave and then looked back at Aaron. "Damn, talk about a game-day attitude."

Aaron walked out, flashing a cautious nod. "He wasn't kidding about not being surprised by anything. Fasten your seat belt, K.J. . . ."

* * *

District Court Judge Kathryn Falco, her graying hair tied back in a tight bun, solemnly seated herself at the bench. Her eyes danced across the crowded courtroom with a certain, unspoken message. Judge Falco could impose her indomitable will with but a fleeting glance. She deliberately gave a nod that signaled her permission for everyone to be seated. It didn't show, but she was nervous. She never dreamed she'd ever face a hired gun like Marcus Payne. He was a judge's worst nightmare, but she resolved to make sure history didn't include her on his long list of victims. When her eyes met his, she regretted looking away so quickly. She knew Reed Aaron was sitting next to Payne, but she didn't look at him. Falco respected Reed, both in the courtroom and out, but her admiration was pale today. It was due undoubtedly to the shadow Payne cast on the entire place. She looked out on the gallery. The spectators were uncomfortably packed together, all staring and waiting for her to speak. Next to the gallery was a makeshift media box - press row - where Judge Falco recognized many TV news stars. Next to them a television camera stared with its imposing red light.

The jury was seated on the opposite side of the room near the witness stand, obstructed from the view of the camera. It was the most protective position that could be arranged.

Juror number one, the elected foreman, was a thirty-one-year-old male bank teller, a squeamish-looking white man, and a closet homosexual who had no intention of ever unlocking that door. Number two was a white male, twenty-three, just out of college. He studied philosophy in school, but he didn't have a clue what to do with his life. Number three was a well-known fellow, age fifty-seven, white, and the owner of a small real estate company in Attica. Number four was a forty-five-year-old white woman, a mother of two who enjoyed her profession of providing a home and mother for her kids. Her husband managed an Attica branch of a large stock brokerage firm in Harrisburg. Five was a white woman, twenty-nine, and a women's apparel sales clerk. It wasn't even remotely apparent yet, but in five years she would suffer from severe paranoid schizophrenia brought on by what she would hear in this trial. Number six was a forty-nine-year-old white construction foreman. He was as big as a tree, but not as smart.

Juror number seven was a white woman, thirty-eight, and an associate professor of anthropology at the junior college. Number eight was a thirty-nine-year-old white farmer. He was a family man who worked eighteen hours a day and believed in the values his daddy and daddy's daddy taught him. Nine was a thirty-year-old woman who worked for the local grocery chain. She was about to become the store's first black woman manager, and she was determined to prove she was worthy. Juror number ten was a bartender, a twenty-seven-year-old black male who hadn't grown up, and probably never would. He was the best-liked person on the jury. Eleven owned a small coffee shop in downtown Attica. He was sixty, white, and had lived here all his life. The final juror was a forty-year-old black woman who taught math at Attica High School. She had earned a dozen honors in fifteen years of teaching at A.H.S. She was the kind of teacher that students fondly recalled at high school reunions. Six alternate jurors were also seated.

Judge Falco quickly ran her eyes past each juror, and then found the prosecutor's table. D.A. Whittaker, for the first time Falco could remember, actually looked like a friend. She found little comfort in that, because they had a history of ugly confrontations. Finally, the judge looked at Seth Cameron. Since the beginning of this terrible business, Seth unnerved Falco for a reason she could not pinpoint. Judge Falco was one of very few people in her position who actually had a life. She was a grandmother and loyal spouse of an honest and decent man for thirty-five years. Their lives together portrayed morals and values quite foreign to the defendant's, a man accused of three hideous murders. This would be the most heinous crime she ever tried, and she didn't look forward to it. She knew what fun was, and, after looking at Seth Cameron, this was definitely not going to be fun.

The bailiff stood like a concrete pillar at the right of the bench, flanked by two Attica police officers. Along the perimeter of the courtroom, ten cops warily scanned the room. Their mood was ugly, for they just spent the last fifteen minutes with the enraged Virgil White.

Falco banged the gavel. "Ladies and gentlemen, before we begin, understand my ground rules. This room is too small, and there are too many of you in here. Therefore, I will say only once that disruptive behavior will not be tolerated. I'm aware of the incident outside this morning, and I find it appalling. This is my first and final warning."

Payne intentionally stifled a yawn.

Falco didn't look at him, but her voice let on that she saw it.

Aaron looked over at Whittaker. The D.A. sat stoically, his large frame stiff and defiant. Aaron's career record against Whittaker was a wash. He had nailed the arrogant attorney many times, but he also had many defeats. Whittaker never hid his game, and today he leaked the confidence of a heavy-weight fighter about to have a workout with the bum of the month. Despite the apprehension he felt facing Payne, he smirked more than usual.

Aaron liked that. He had watched Payne crush high-pow-ered attorneys in cases most lawyers would have lost. Whittaker had never taken on this kind of talent, and Aaron was silently surprised the D.A. looked so cocky.

The game began. Falco removed her reading glasses and addressed Whittaker. "Opening statements, Mr. Prosecutor?"

"Thank you, Your Honor." Whittaker walked to the dais and opened his notes on the stand. He was fifty-two and looked it. He dressed conservatively, and was perfectly groomed. He leaned on an elbow and faced the jury, speaking into the microphone. "Ladies and gentlemen, good morning. My name is Roland Whittaker. I'm the Attica District Attorney. You will hear me referred to as the prosecutor representing the People's case against the defendant."

The jury displayed wide-eyed attention. Their concern was typical of a first-morning jury. Payne carefully sized up each pair of eyes, looking for cracks in which he'd inject his potion.

Whittaker, still leaning on the dais, intentionally flipped through the pages of his notebook. He blew a theatrical sigh. "I have to say, in all my years in this profession, I've seen some pretty terrible things; but this crime transcends all boundaries of rational thinking. This is a trial of first-degree homicide - three counts - so heinous, so despicable in nature that you, dear jurors, may find listening to the details unbearable at times. But listen you must, ladies and gentlemen. I implore you to dig deeply in your souls and trudge with me through this bloody debacle with courage and determination to see that justice is done. Together we must see that the perpetrator of these crimes is punished. You are not here to try only sense-less murder and rape of your neighbors; you are here to try the conscience of a community devastated by hucksters and opportunists who've blemished this town's good name. And it is all due to one man. The defendant, Seth Cameron."

Seth shrank next to Payne. Payne whispered in Seth's ear, and the little man perked. He shyly looked at the jurors. He appeared awkward with his head held so high.

Whittaker continued. "We will prove beyond a reasonable doubt that Seth Cameron did willfully plan and commit three crimes of first-degree murder and two counts of rape, sense-lessly shooting to death his employer, Linville Reeves; raping and stabbing Linville's wife, Mary, and the couple's sixteen-year-old granddaughter, Lisa Reeves. The evidence will show that the defendant admitted his crimes to police officials after the fact. He was forthright in accepting the blame until he fell into the trap of his flamboyant and headline-hungry attorney, a man who makes a living of mocking the judicial process by defending radicals, anarchists, and mobsters. I remind you that we were brought up on small town values and morals. We're unaccustomed to being made into fools by the prepos-terous claims fabricated by defense counsel, whose ulterior motive of personal and professional profit is obvious."

"Your Honor," Payne objected. "I'm looking at my pro-gram here, and it says, 'The People versus Seth Cameron.' If Mr. Aaron and I are on trial, don't you think we should be arrested and booked first?"

"Stay on track, Mr. Whittaker," Judge Falco said.

Whittaker slammed the dais and laughed aloud. "UFO indeed! Space monsters! Ladies and gentlemen, unless you've lived under a rock for twenty years, you're aware that the defendant's legal counsel is notorious for this type of folly. In many cases, he has so muddled trials with misleading and outrageous elements that juries were left hanging in confusion!"

"Your Honor," Payne again interrupted, "can I at least have my phone call? I need a lawyer . . ."

A few chuckles rolled across the room. Falco gaveled. "Mr. Payne, please . . . and Mr. Whittaker, I say this once more, please direct your opening to the case at hand."

Whittaker never broke stride. "I implore you to not allow such an assault on your collective intelligence and consider only the facts. Ignore the dazzling science fiction circus this ringmaster intends to wield before you, and concentrate on the gruesome and undeniable facts we shall present. Seth Cameron, acting alone and with malice aforethought, murdered the Reeves family. We shall present two murder weapons, undeniable medical and forensic evidence linking the defendant to the murders and rapes, and, although it's not our burden to prove a motive, we will show this man was a ticking time bomb just waiting to explode. Simple facts, ladies and gentlemen. No mirrors, no smoke, no space monsters whirling around the sky."

Payne yawned again, his mouth so large it might crack his cheeks. He smiled and put a gentle hand on Seth's shoulder, making sure he distracted the jury. He whispered to the obviously shaken little man. "Remember what I told you, Seth - yelling, screaming, name-calling. It's all a lie." Seth nodded with some confidence.

Whittaker's face, as if on cue, grew ruddy and indignant. He paced before the jury box. "The defendant has been a festering sore on this town's complexion for years. His reputation as a barroom regular is well known, and his history of violence and perversion will be proven to you. We will show you how the defendant was given a chance to lead a clean and decent life by Linville Reeves, a man whose noble family spanned four generations in this community.

"But on one hot summer night, something violent broke out between him and the defendant, and the Reeves family legacy was cruelly wiped out in a single, wicked moment. We will prove that the defendant, acting with full intention and in a fit of lethal rage, went after Linville Reeves with a twelve-gauge shotgun. The defendant chased poor Linville down, caught him out in the very wheat field he had worked all his life, and shot him in the head point-blank. Seth Cameron literally blew Linville Reeves' poor head off! And then he stabbed and raped Mary and Lisa, leaving them naked in a field to die - Lisa with twenty-one knife wounds in her body! In his rage, for a reason we'll probably never know, he even butchered a live farm animal with that knife." Whittaker's glare threw the jurors into a pool of disgust.

"I implore you, dear jurors, to weigh the evidence we present. Listen carefully to our witnesses. Be strong and courageous as you evaluate what, sickening and disturbing as it is, is a very simple case. Sift through the sideshow antics the defense will use to mislead you, and concentrate on the facts. We may never know what motivated the defendant to murder the Reeves family, and it is not required of you or me to establish any theory. We will, however, present reasonable conclusions that logically accompany his terrible act. In the searing heat of that summer night, Seth Cameron completed a lifelong cycle of violence. He murdered Linville for his dominating discipline and demand for perfection, of which the defendant was entirely incapable. He sexually assaulted and killed Mary out of his twisted hatred for his mother, and he brutalized an innocent teen-age girl who represented budding sexuality - something this pathetic man feared and loathed."

Seth stared at the table. Mother? Sexu-what? He shook his head. Payne responded with a gentle hand on Seth's shoulder. Ignore it, Seth said to himself, that's what Payne said to do.

"The Reeves family members are victims, dear jurors. But you and I are victims, too. We are victims not only of the defendant's senseless evil, but victims of the media's mockery of Attica and its citizens. And we are victims of the defendant's attorney, who shunned this decent community for a life in the headlines like the ones you've read all these months. He only came back to this town to perpetuate his fame and fortune at our expense. Please, dear jurors, ignore the circus he brought to town. Cold facts are synonymous with truth." Whittaker struck a stately pose and turned his best side to the TV camera. He reveled in the quiet sounds of pencils scratching in press row as he triumphantly returned to his seat.

Judge Falco looked at Payne. "Mr. Payne?"

Payne stood, and every eye turned to him with anticipation. "Thank you, Your Honor, but the defense will run the elephants and clowns later."

The courtroom rolled with chuckles, stung by Payne's expected charm.

"Order," Falco calmly said. "Mr. Payne, the court would appreciate a straight answer."

"Thank you, Your Honor, we'll reserve opening statements for our portion of the trial."

Judge Falco left Payne's disturbing eyes. "Very well. Call your first witness, Mr. Whittaker."

"The people call Raymond Wade."

The big redheaded barkeep nervously stood and made his way to the witness stand, sitting after he was sworn in. He wore a tan corduroy jacket with a plaid shirt and pink tie. His blue jeans were worn and too small to support his big belly.

"Mr. Wade," Whittaker said, "will you please tell the court who you are and what you do?"

Wade coughed through his thick beard. "Raymond, uh, they all call me 'Rusty' Wade. I got a joint in town."

"Rusty's Tavern?"

"Yeah."

"Specifically, this 'joint,' as you call it, is a bar?"

"Yeah."

"Let's move to the morning in question, Mr. Wade. Did you see the defendant?"

"Yeah, I found him outside my place."

"What time was it?"

"Around eight-thirty. I ain't usually up that early, but I had a beer delivery at nine."

"What was the defendant doing outside of your bar?"

"He was face-first in the road. Scared hell outa me. I thought somebody got run over, but I went up and saw it was Seth. He looked all beat up."

"Mr. Wade, you know the defendant, don't you?"

"Seth? Yeah, he comes in the joint now and then."

"Sir, your tavern not only sells liquor, but has entertainment, does it not?"

"Entertainment?"

"Nude dancing? Strippers?"

"Objection," Reed Aaron said. "Irrelevant."

"Sustained," Falco said.

"What did you do when you found the defendant lying in front of your bar?"

Wade rubbed his beard. "I figured somebody rolled him, so I took him to the police station."

"Thank you," Whittaker said.

Aaron stood at the table. "Mr. Wade, was Seth in your tavern the night before you found him in the road?"

"No. No way."

"In fact, Seth hadn't been in your tavern recently, had he?"

"No. He don't come in during harvest. None of the farmers do."

"Thank you."

Wade looked at Judge Falco, who instructed him to step down.

"The People call Sheriff Virgil White," Whittaker said.

White lumbered up from the back of the courtroom. He swore in and sat on the stand, nervously clearing his throat three times.

"Sheriff, introductions are hardly necessary. Let's put it on record, however. You have been Attica's sheriff for how long?"

White squirmed. He'd been on the witness stand hundreds of times, but he was uncomfortable today. "Twenty-three years," he said.

"With a meticulous record, I'll add."

"Your Honor," Payne said. "If I'm not mistaken, the sheriff has no need for a campaign manager."

Falco's glare popped the random laughter. "Let's just move to the questions."

"Sheriff, would you please tell the jury what happened, beginning at the morning in question."

"It was after roll call, about quarter of nine. The day watch was heading out when Rusty Wade brought Seth in."

"What was his condition?"

"He was beat up - was in his pajamas. He seemed incoherent."

"Did you know the defendant prior to that morning?"

"Yeah, I know Seth."

"How so?"

"We have to lock him up every now and then."

"You've arrested him for drunk and disorderly charges before, haven't you?"

"Objection, irrelevant," Payne called.

"Foundational," Whittaker returned, "it goes to character."

"Sustained. You may answer, Sheriff."

"Uh, yeah, Seth's been locked up for being drunk."

"How many times has he been arrested?"

"I guess we run him in a few times a year," White said. "We usually found him asleep at Rusty's. Locals like him we sometimes offer to drive home, but he always wanted to sleep it off in jail."

"Why did he prefer jail?"

"He'd say he didn't want Linville to see him drunk."

"Did anyone come to bail him out?"

"Linville always came down the next day and picked him up."

"Did Linville Reeves employ the defendant as a farmhand?"

"Yeah."

"Did he ever demonstrate unhappiness with the task of picking Seth up?"

"He wasn't overjoyed, Counsel. Seth didn't go drinking

when there was work to be done, but he had some problems when the work slacked off in the winter."

"And Mr. Reeves was not happy when he came to get the defendant out of jail, was he?"

"No. Linville, he was a teetotaler, not a religious nut or anything, but he wanted Seth to straighten up. He said he had Seth under his wing, and he wanted to help him out."

"Getting back to the morning he was brought in, was he drunk then?"

"We didn't smell nothing on him, but the medical examiner ran a toxicology late that morning. It showed his blood alcohol level was .02."

"Did you observe him drinking that morning?"

"No."

"And so, sometime prior to his entering the courthouse at approximately eight-thirty or nine, he had consumed at least enough alcohol to show a .02 blood alcohol level, correct?"

"Yeah."

"What did you do next?"

"Me and two officers tried to get something outa him, but he wasn't talking much sense."

"What did he say?"

"Something about somebody being dead. Then he mumbled things like, 'I'm dead.'"

"Hearsay, Your Honor. No-no." Payne smiled.

"Goes to show subsequent action," Whittaker said.

"Overruled," Falco said.

"Did he specifically mention the Reeves family?"

"He said something about Linville, but he also said things like, 'momma's dead.' I figured it was best to get him to a hospital, and I told one of my officers to go out to the Reeves farm. I thought maybe Linville might know something."

"What happened then?"

"I tried to help him up, and he just went off."

"Explain what you mean, 'he went off.'"

"Crazy," White said. "He started screaming, and he grabbed me by the throat. He cut off my wind, and I didn't think he was gonna let go. He's a little guy, Counsel, but his hand felt like a vise. It took two cops to pull him offa me. We got him cuffed, and I sent him to the hospital."

"What then?"

"I went to the hospital to see if I could get anything else outa him. One of my boys went out to Linville's. We got a call about the murders on the farm about a half-hour later."

"Describe what you found."

"Mary and Lisa, they were out back of the farm. Lisa's body was nude, and she was stabbed multiple times. Mary, she was nude, too - had a knife in her chest. Linville was out in the field, and we didn't find him until that night."

"Where was Mr. Reeves' body found?"

"He was out about a hundred yards from the other two victims, lying in an overgrowth of weeds."

"Describe the body."

"He was clothed, and he had a head injury consistent with a gunshot wound."

"Sheriff, did you retrieve any weapons at the scene?"

"Yeah. We found a hunting knife in Mary's body, and we found a twelve-gauge shotgun with two shells in it - one unspent and one spent."

Whittaker produced a large hunting knife from an evidence bag. "Sheriff, would you open this bag and identify its contents?"

White complied. "That's the knife we found in Mary."

"Let the record show Sheriff Virgil White identified People's Exhibit number one. It is a stag-handle hunting knife with a polished carbon steel blade, eight inches long." He produced the shotgun, which White unwrapped and identified as the Linville Reeves murder weapon. "Sheriff, were any photographs taken of the murder scene?"

"Yeah."

Whittaker produced twenty photographs, containing grisly shots of the victims. "Sheriff, these photos were all taken by your department?"

White didn't care to look closely. "That's them," he said.

Whittaker spent the next forty-five minutes carefully examining each photograph with White, who identified them and commented on their contents. Each was tagged with an exhibit number and admitted. Payne interrupted with an objection to eleven photographs, attempting to break the jury's concentration on the bloody photos. At the end of the photo evidence admissions, the D.A. picked up the Attica Sheriff's Department homicide investigation reports. "Sheriff, did you check for fingerprints on the murder weapons?"

"Yes. We lifted prints from each."

"Were you able to identify them?"

"We sent them to the Harrisburg police crime lab - they ran a comparison and matched the prints with the defendant's."

"Please check these records and tell us if you agree with the fingerprint verification."

White fumbled through the papers. "Yes, it's correct."

Whittaker tagged and entered the reports. "What else did you find on the murder scene?"

"There was a dead pig. It was butchered up pretty bad."

Again, Whittaker produced photos, and White verified them before they were entered. "Now, Sheriff, did you have any more discussion with the defendant regarding the Reeves murders?"

"Yeah."

"Please tell the jury what was discussed."

"He said he killed them," White said bluntly.

"Where did this conversation take place?"

"Like I said, he mentioned something about it at the court-house. I went over to the hospital that afternoon, and he said he killed them."

"Did you advise the defendant of his right to legal counsel before he made this admission of guilt?"

"He was advised of his rights at the hospital, and again when I talked to him the second time. He said he didn't want a lawyer."

"What was your response to his declining counsel?"

"What I was thinking was, it's not a good idea. Under the circumstances, Seth wasn't thinking too straight to be making a statement. I figured he should have a lawyer looking out for him."

"But he did admit he killed the Reeves family?"

White swallowed two or three times before he answered. "Yeah, he said it."

"Sheriff, the defendant waived right to counsel. Legally, you could have obtained his confession. Why didn't you?"

"I just didn't think Seth should make a formal confession until the P.D. was there. I wanted to be sure I went by the book. If Seth confessed, I wanted him to have counsel present, and I wanted him to be thinking straight."

"However, he did make an informal admission of guilt to you at that time, correct?"

"Yeah."

"What happened then?"

White's anus itched furiously as he scooted in his chair. "He was strapped down because of the way he jumped me earlier, so I guess I was off my guard. But damned if he didn't rip out of those straps and clout me again."

"This was a second vicious attack on you, is that right?"

"Yeah." White's face reddened. "He nearly threw me right out the window this time. I took ninety stitches in my hands and scalp. We had one hell of a fight. One of my cops was out in the hall when I got jumped. He came in, and Seth pounded on him pretty hard, too."

"Who else was involved in this altercation?"

"Seth's doctor, and a hospital orderly. Seth busted that kid's arm right in front of my eyes. I never seen anything like it. We finally got on top of him, but the doctor had to drug him before he let up."

"Based on the incidents of that day, we're you convinced that the defendant was violent and clearly dangerous?"

White sighed. "I'd say that was an understatement, Counsel. He sure was unhappy with me. I still got scars to prove it."

"When did he see the public defender?"

"The next morning."

"And, after Mr. Aaron spoke with Seth, did you try to obtain a confession?"

"Mr. Aaron wanted to talk with Seth alone first. After that, no confession, no nothing; end of interview. Next thing I know, the newspaper runs this UFO story, and I look like a moron."

"And so, Sheriff, you allowed the defendant to consult Mr. Aaron, and then he suddenly changed his story, didn't he?"

"Now, now," Payne objected, "Counsel is leading the witness."

"Sustained."

"Nothing further. Thank you, Sheriff," Whittaker said.

"Mr. Payne, do you wish to cross-examine?" Judge Falco asked.

"I'd like that - thank you," Payne said.

He stood, again knocking the wind out of the courtroom. During much of Whittaker's presentation of evidence, the gallery, jury, and media shuffled and whispered; but, when Payne stood up, a mystical hush crushed the place. Not only did Judge Falco notice it, but Whittaker did as well.

"Good morning to the jury." Payne smiled and the jurors responded. "Morning, Sheriff White, it's a pleasure to meet you."

White's eyebrows tensed. "Counsel," he nodded dumbly, as if he hadn't been reamed by Payne just an hour ago.

"You're a good-sized fellow, aren't you?"

White unconsciously sucked his belly in. "I guess so."

"Your Honor, may I approach the witness?"

"You may."

Payne walked up and poked White's stomach. White lurched and halfheartedly pushed Payne's hand away. "What're you doing?"

Payne pulled back, curiously inspecting White's body. He stood back and rubbed his chin. "Two-fifty," he finally said.

"What?" White said.

"I'm trying to guess your weight. It's a hobby of mine. I say you weigh two-fifty. Am I right?"

"Two forty-eight," White said.

Payne looked at the jury and waved a gesture that said, 'not bad, huh?' He stalked the witness stand and leaned on the railing in front of White. "My client almost tossed you out the window?"

"Yeah," White said, for some reason feeling very stupid.

"Seth? Seth Cameron? The defendant? That little fellow with the ugly tie over there?"

"Yeah." White's voice was defensive.

Payne pushed himself off the railing and glided to the jury box. Every head in the place followed him. At the defense table, Reed Aaron held his breath.

"Interesting," Payne said. "And on that morning when Seth came in, he grabbed you by the throat, and two officers had to pull him off?"

"Yeah, that's what I said, Counsel."

"Are either of those officers in the courtroom right now?"

White looked around. "Yeah, one is."

"Point him out, will you?"

White didn't point. "Officer Jackson back there."

Payne swiveled, quickly finding Jackson, who stood by the back doors. "Him?"

"Yeah."

"Your Honor, may we have Officer Ken Jackson approach for a sec?"

"Go ahead."

"Step up here, Officer Ken Jackson," Payne said. Jackson walked to the front, and Payne eyed him. He tilted his head back as if he was looking at the top of a tree. Several people laughed. "Good lord, you don't miss many meals, do you? What do you say, Officer? Two-thirty-five?"

Jackson nodded. "Yes, sir."

Payne clapped his hands and looked to the jury for approval. Most were smiling. Payne walked back to White. "So, little Seth, who weighs one-twenty-one - I already knew that - not only whipped you, but it took Officer Ken Jackson here and another cop to pry him off of you? Is that what you want us to believe, Sheriff?"

"Objection," Whittaker said. "Argumentative."

"Sustained."

"All I know is, he had me," White said.

"I'm no physicist, Sheriff, but I'd say that's pretty remark-able."

"It happened, Counsel."

"Stop," Judge Falco ordered. "The objection is sustained, Mr. Payne. Move on to your next question."

"Thank you, Your Honor," Payne said. "Sheriff, I wonder if there may be a reason why Seth got so strong. Maybe a gallon of adrenaline, you think?"

"Objection!" Whittaker stood. "Your Honor. Counsel is badgering the witness. Sheriff White was indeed attacked, and we can present offer of proof, if necessary."

"Sustained," Judge Falco simply said. "Mr. Payne, please move on."

"On we go," Payne said. Jackson returned to the back of the courtroom, having been successfully introduced to the jury by Payne. "Sheriff, what's the legal blood-alcohol level for drunk driving in this state?" Payne continued.

"Ya gotta be at .08."

"So, the defendant's .02 blood-alcohol level that was measured the morning after the Reeves murders wouldn't even be enough to get him arrested for a DUI, correct?"

"Right."

Payne walked to the evidence table and picked up the photographs of the murder scene, thumbing through each one carefully. He stopped and handed one to White. "Sheriff, describe what you see in this photo, marked 'People's 15.'"

White scratched his head. "Looks like Mary Reeves' body."

"Take a closer look, Sheriff. Look at the background."

"I don't know what you want me to see."

"The field back there - what's that brown area out beyond the body?"

"I don't know."

"Looks like the ground is scorched. Maybe burned?"

"Speculation," Whittaker said.

"I'll rephrase, Your Honor. What is that brown area out there?"

White hesitated. "I'm not sure."

"You're not?"

"I wasn't concerned about the ground."

"You weren't concerned? Sheriff White, is it not common practice in a homicide investigation to scour every inch of a murder scene?"

"Every inch of what we suspect is part of the murder. I have to make decisions about what to rule out; otherwise, I'd end up bringing the whole farm in. The burned grass didn't amount to anything."

"Hold it. I thought you said you weren't sure what that brown patch was."

"Well, yeah . . ."

"You just called it burned grass, did you not?"

"Yeah."

"Then, which is it? Do you remember? Don't you remember? Burned grass? Not burned?"

"I remember now - it was burned."

"And you weren't concerned about the burned ground, right?"

"Sometimes farmers burn off portions of land to clear out brush."

"But you don't know that Linville Reeves burned the ground himself, do you?"

"No," White said.

"So, who decided that the burned patch of ground had nothing to do with the murders?"

White paused for a moment before speaking. "It didn't have anything to do with the murders, Counsel."

"Please answer my question. Who decided it was not important?"

"Who?"

"I asked you."

"We decided that - "

"We? Who was out on the farm during the initial hours of the investigation?"

"Me and the medical examiner, and several of my officers."

"Who else?"

White's eyes shifted. "There were a few government agents."

"Government agents? What kind of government agents?"

"They're with the C.I.B."

"What are their names?"

"Uh - one was named Carswall."

Payne leaned close to White. "Who is Jonathan Carswall, Sheriff?"

Payne saw a blue implosion behind White's eyes. "Carswall?"

"Jonathan Carswall."

White cleared his throat. His tongue was suddenly very dry.

"J-O-N-A-T-H-"

"I know!" White said. "He was in charge of the agents."

"Jonathan Carswall was in the courthouse the morning Seth was brought in - before you discovered the Reeves murder scene, isn't that correct, Sheriff?"

"Yeah."

"Do you know why he was there?"

"He wanted to talk to me about something, but the commotion with Seth interrupted us."

"You just testified that he was also at the homicide scene. Did he arrive there before you?"

"Yeah."

"Did you instruct him to go out there?"

"No."

"Did he tell you he was going out there?"

"No."

"So, Jonathan Carswall, agent for the Central Intelligence Bureau, went to the Reeves farm on his own and saw the bodies before you did, didn't he?"

White nodded.

"Sheriff, the court reporter can't draw a nod."

"Yeah, he saw the bodies." White's anus caught fire.

"Are you uncomfortable? You need a pillow or something?"

"No."

"You testified that you sent an officer to the Reeves farm after Mr. Cameron was brought into the courthouse. Who was that officer?"

"Officer Jackson."

"Officer Ken Jackson? That big guy who was just up here a minute ago?"

"Yeah." White wanted to punch Payne for his condescending tone.

"If you know, who was the first to discover the bodies - Officer Jackson or Special Agent Carswall?"

"Jackson found them."

"Officer Ken Jackson found the bodies, and Jonathan Carswall, special agent for the Central Intelligence Bureau, arrived on the scene sometime after that, correct?"

"Yeah, that's right."

"Okay, so you arrive at the farm, and you find Officer Ken Jackson and Jonathan Carswall, secret agent for the Central Intelligence Bureau - "

"Objection!"

Judge Falco put her hand up to Whittaker, knowing what was coming. "Mr. Payne . . ."

"Okay," Payne said. "Special agent for the Central Intelligence Bureau. We'll find out about the secret part soon enough."

"Your Honor!" Whittaker said.

"Mr. Payne - enough. The jury will disregard Counsel's comment."

"Thank you, Your Honor," Payne said. "Sheriff White, you arrived and found Jonathan Carswall running the investigation, didn't you?"

"Objection," Whittaker chimed in. "Leading, and misstates the sheriff's testimony."

"Sustained."

"Okay, Sheriff," Payne said. "When an officer discovers a crime, it's proper procedure for him to secure the scene until his superiors arrive, isn't it?"

"Yeah."

"Particularly with such a serious crime as homicide, preserving the integrity of the chain of custody is essential, would you agree?"

"Yeah, that's right."

"Please explain 'chain of custody' to the jury."

White unconsciously cleared his throat. "Well, evidence in a crime is discovered and preserved by police, collected from the scene by medical or police forensic personnel, and then later inspected and tested either locally or at special crime labs. Anyone who comes in contact with that evidence is considered part of the chain."

"So, everyone in that chain must be authorized to handle the evidence, otherwise it could open the door to contamination, alteration, removal or destruction of that vital evidence, correct?"

"Yeah, Counsel."

"Have you ever been involved in an investigation where evidence was found inadmissible in court, due to someone in the chain mishandling it?"

"It's happened," White said.

"That's why you put barricades and yellow tape around a crime scene, right? You want to protect evidence and restrict the scene to authorized police and forensic personnel, correct?"

"Right."

"So, when a crime is committed in your jurisdiction, you are responsible for determining who may or may not enter the scene and handle evidence, correct?"

"Yeah."

"When Agent Carswall entered the Reeves crime scene, he was not acting under your authority, was he?"

"Uh . . . I guess . . . no, he wasn't official . . ."

"Was Officer Jackson or Agent Carswall in charge of the Reeves murder scene when you arrived?"

"At that time Carswall was in charge."

Payne abruptly stopped and let White dangle in front of the jury for an uncomfortable moment. He knew the question they wanted to hear, but he wasn't about to satisfy them yet. "Okay, Sheriff. Now let's go back a moment to when Agent Carswall came in to speak to you at the courthouse. Why was he there?"

"He was investigating cattle mutilation incidents in the area."

"Hold it!" Payne said. "Cattle mutilation incidents?"

"Objection. Hearsay."

"Overruled. The witness answered the question," Falco said.

Payne wandered toward the jury box. "You mean dissected cows out in the middle of nowhere, and devil cults, and UFOs, and all that weird stuff? Agent Carswall was investigating that?"

"Yeah."

"And then, it is your testimony that you were interrupted when Mr. Cameron arrived. After that, Agent Carswall went to the Reeves farm, and for some reason he took charge of the crime scene, correct?"

"He just took charge until I got there," White said.

"But Officer Jackson arrived on the scene first. Do you know why he wasn't in charge?"

"Carswall said that Jackson was kinda shook-up from seeing the bodies, so he took over."

"Did Officer Jackson appear shook-up to you?"

White didn't look to the back of the courtroom, but he could feel Jackson's angry eyes on him. "I know that Jackson was close friends with Linville and Mary."

"Did Officer Jackson's demeanor give you any reason to believe he was unable to do his duty?"

White couldn't hold the betrayal. "When I got there, he was okay."

"It's fair to say, then, that Officer Jackson didn't appear shook-up to you, correct?"

"Look, I said he was okay by the time I got there."

"And so," Payne continued, "acting essentially in the capacity of a civilian, Agent Carswall took over and circumvented proper procedure, didn't he?"

"I don't see him as a civilian."

"Nonetheless, Agent Carswall altered proper procedure when he took charge of the crime scene. Consequently, it was your responsibility to find out if he had touched any evidence, correct?"

"Yeah."

"Did you ever consider that Agent Carswall might have contaminated the crime scene?"

"No."

"Did you question him to be certain he didn't alter or remove any evidence?"

"No."

"What if one of Mr. Reeves' neighbors had been out there? Would you have asked him if he had touched anything?"

"Well, sure . . ."

"Then why didn't you ask Mr. Carswall the same question?"

"He's a government agent. I figured he was a professional who knew how to protect the evidence."

"I see." Payne wandered through another long silence. He walked to the evidence table and grabbed a photo. "I'm interested in Agent Carswall's claim that he was investigating animal mutilations. Take a look at this picture of the butchered pig, Sheriff. Did Carswall say anything to make you conclude he was there to examine the carcass?"

"Uh . . . no."

"It's a mutilated animal. He told you he was investigating mutilated animals. But he was more interested in the murders, wasn't he?"

"We all were, Counsel."

"You know, I see something interesting here." Payne moved in on White again. "This poor animal is cut up badly, but I don't see much blood, do you?"

White nervously looked at the photo. "The picture's pretty grainy."

"Of course," Payne said. "You were right there, though, so you probably saw a lot of blood on the carcass, correct?" White didn't answer. "Sheriff? Was there a lot of blood on and around the pig?"

"I didn't spend much time examining it, Counsel."

"You didn't examine the pig at all, did you, Sheriff?"

"Hey, I had two butchered women to worry about."

"In his opening statements, the Prosecutor accused Mr. Cameron of slaughtering the pig. Did you find any evidence to prove Seth did this?"

"Look, the two homicide victims were more important to me."

"Was there any blood evidence on Mr. Cameron that might suggest he was responsible for killing the animal?"

"Uh, I didn't focus on looking for pig blood on him, if that's what you mean."

"If he butchered that pig, it's reasonable to assume he might have the animal's blood on him, isn't it?"

"Like I said, I was more concerned about the Reeves family," White said.

"Fair enough," Payne said. "You have no physical evidence to tie Mr. Cameron to the slaughtered pig, do you?"

"No!"

"Let's move on. Did Special Agent Carswall participate in the murder investigation?"

"He gave us a hand."

"Wasn't this a matter for local authorities?"

"Yeah, but like I said, he offered to help. He said he was an experienced homicide investigator."

"Okay, Sheriff. The photos show a barn on the farm, correct?"

"Yeah."

"What did you find in the barn?"

"Nothing."

"Did you search it?"

"It was searched before I got there."

"So you didn't search it?"

"It was already searched."

"Jonathan Carswall searched the barn, didn't he, Sheriff?"

"Yeah."

"Special Agent Jonathan Carswall, who offered to 'lend a hand,' as you put it, had searched the barn. He was already lending a hand before you arrived on the crime scene, wasn't he, Sheriff?"

"Objection! Leading!"

"Overruled," Falco said. "You may answer, Sheriff."

"He said they searched the grounds, in case the perpetrator was still on site. It made sense to me."

"I see what looks like a chicken house in this photo, correct?"

White squirmed. "Yeah."

"Did you search it?"

"They searched it. They found some hens killed by the heat."

"They, meaning Special Agent Jonathan Carswall and his agents?"

"Yeah, Counsel."

"And, they also conducted this search before you arrived, correct?"

"Like I said - they helped us out."

"So," Payne said, "if any of these agents had tampered with, or removed evidence, you wouldn't know because you never questioned them, isn't that right?"

"Objection," Whittaker said. "This is inflammatory and speculative!"

"Foundational, Your Honor," Payne said.

Falco pondered for a moment. "It better be, Mr. Payne," she said. "I'll overrule for now, but rephrase the question."

Payne turned to White. "You cannot testify to any degree of certainty that you know the CIB agents did not alter or remove evidence from the Reeves murder scene, can you?"

White heaved an audible sigh. "No."

Payne fired again. "What did you do with the pig carcass?"

"Your Honor," Whittaker said. "Are we trying the murder of a pig or the Reeves family? This is irrelevant!"

"To the contrary," Payne said, "the dead animal has been established as evidence in this crime. My question is entirely relevant."

"I'll allow it," Judge Falco said.

"Thank you, Your Honor. Sheriff, what did you do with the dead pig?"

"The feds removed it."

"Special Agent Carswall took the carcass?"

"Yeah."

"Okay, Sheriff, let's just cut to the bone here. You have no idea why Special Agent Carswall happened to be out on the Reeves farm that morning, do you?"

"Calls for speculation," Whittaker objected.

"Overruled," Falco said.

"No - he's right," Payne said. "You can only speculate as to why Agent Carswall happened to show up at the Reeves farm that morning. You don't really know the reason, do you, Sheriff White?"

"No," White said.

"Let's move on to the murder victims. The body that was identified as Linville Reeves wasn't discovered until late that night, is that your testimony?"

"Yeah."

"Who found the body that was identified as Linville Reeves?"

White's eyes shifted. His answer was weak. "Mr. Carswall assisted with the search."

"I didn't ask who assisted. I asked who found the body."

"Carswall and his agents."

"Special Agent Carswall, who initially claimed he was investigating cattle mutilation incidents, was now in charge of searching for Linville Reeves?"

"Yeah."

"Did any officer from the Attica Sheriff's Department participate in the search and recovery of the body that was later identified as Linville Reeves?"

"Three of my officers were out there," White said.

"Three Attica police officers guarded the farm perimeter, but the CIB searched for a body, isn't that correct?"

"Uh – yeah."

"If you know, please name any Attica police officer who might have directly participated in the search and recovery of the body that night."

White helplessly looked down. "I . . . don't know of any."

"The chain of custody was now completely under the control of the C.I.B., wasn't it?"

"Look, I was in charge of the investigation!"

"That isn't my question, Sheriff. The CIB produced a headless body, claiming it was Linville Reeves. The chain of custody was not under your control, was it?"

"Okay - no, but I was in charge!"

"You were? You weren't with Agent Carswall during that search and recovery, were you?"

"No."

"Where were you?"

"At the hospital, questioning the suspect."

"Okay, let's look at that. You testified that Seth confessed to the crimes when you spoke with him that evening?"

"Yeah."

"You told the court he said, 'I killed them,' correct?"

"Yeah, Counsel."

"Did you ask how he killed them?"

"No. How it was done was pretty obvious. He wasn't too with it to explain much."

"Was he sedated?"

"Yeah."

"Wigged out? Incoherent? Didn't know what he was saying?"

"Calls for speculation as to state of mind, Your Honor."

"Withdrawn. He said he killed 'them.' Them. Did he say, 'I killed Mary?' 'I killed Linville?' 'I killed Lisa?' 'I killed a pint?' Did he specify who he killed, or was it just, 'them,' Sheriff?"

"He said, 'I killed them,' Counsel. He wasn't specific, and, yeah, he was pretty wigged out for me to trust what he was saying. At that time, I had two victims and two murder weapons with Seth's prints on them. When he said he killed them, I didn't think he was talking about flies."

"'Them,' meaning Mary and Lisa? At the time, you didn't know if Linville was dead or not, correct?"

"No, not then."

"So, at that point, you could not yet assume that Linville was included with 'them,' could you?"

White tried to pull his foot from his mouth. His mind was in a stir. "He said he killed them."

"Did he specify each victim by name?"

"I killed 'them.'"

"Who? Mary and Lisa - are they them?"

"Your Honor, Counsel is deliberately trying to confuse the witness."

"He doesn't need my help, Your Honor," Payne said.

"Mr. Payne, that's inappropriate," Falco said. "The objection is sustained."

"Sheriff, did Seth Cameron ever tell you that he killed Mary, Lisa, and Linville Reeves?" Payne asked.

"He said, 'them!'"

"That's not the question, Sheriff. Did he ever tell you that he killed Mary, Lisa, and Linville Reeves? Did he ever say their names?"

White blew a sigh. He rubbed his ass in the chair and finally said, "No."

"Thank you, Sheriff. I have no more questions," Payne said. He abruptly walked back to his table and sat next to Seth and Aaron.

White was excused. He extracted himself from the witness stand and slowly lumbered away, looking like a punch-drunk heavyweight who just took the worst pounding of his life . . .

13

Dr. George Baker's jacket came off before he took the stand. Although the temperature outside was fifteen degrees, Baker leaked visible rings of sweat under his arms. He connected both murder weapons to corresponding wounds on the bodies, and he estimated the time of Mary and Lisa's deaths between one and four a.m. Because Linville's body wasn't immediately found, Baker estimated time of death within 24 hours of the body's discovery. He also identified bloodstains found on Seth's pajamas as consistent with the blood types of both Mary and Lisa Reeves. Similar blood samples were found on two tattered women's nightgowns found near the female victims. Autopsy reports were then entered and reviewed, and D.A. Whittaker enhanced the horror through introduction of evidence of sexual assault on the women:

"There was visible evidence of vaginal penetration on both female victims," Baker said. "There was no semen present, but there were blood traces and bruising, indicating violent penetration - possibly with some kind of blunt instrument . . ."

Baker's lengthy and graphic testimony compounded the jury's mental image of a sick and brutal perpetrator. The selected autopsy photos evoked strong revulsion from the jurors, and Payne went immediately to work to diffuse their emotions on cross-examination.

Payne stood, and Baker's armpits gushed again. "Good morning, Dr. Baker. It's a pleasure to meet you."

Baker nodded and looked at Payne's endearing smile. "Morning."

"Doc, what time did you arrive at the Reeves farm that morning?"

Baker checked his notes. "I got a call from the dispatcher at nine-forty-five. I got there at ten-thirty."

"Who was there when you arrived?"

"Virgil, uh, Sheriff White, four or five officers and para-medics, and a man named Carswall, who had two men with him."

"Jonathan Carswall, Special Agent for the Central Intelligence Bureau?"

"Mr. Payne," Judge Falco interrupted, "I believe the jury is now well aware of Mr. Carswall's full title - and your overt reminders."

Payne waved to Falco and continued. "Did Jonathan Carswall identify himself to you, Dr. Baker?"

"Sheriff White introduced us."

"Did Agent Carswall tell you why he was there?"

"No."

"Do you know why Agent Carswall was there?"

"Objection," Whittaker said, "calls for speculation."

"Withdrawn," Payne said. "Doc, did you speak with Agent Carswall?"

"Not much at the murder scene; I started processing the bodies, and he talked to Sheriff White."

"Did Officer Ken Jackson accompany you to where the bodies were?"

"Jackson? No," Baker said.

"Who walked you through the crime scene?"

"Sheriff White."

"Anyone else?"

"Carswall."

"Was Officer Jackson allowed to come?"

"No."

"Did you hear Agent Carswall specifically order Officer Jackson to stay away from the victims?"

"Uh, yeah - he did - "

"Did Officer Jackson ever go to the area where the bodies were, while you were present?"

"No."

"Okay, sir," Payne said. "I'd like to ask you about the

clothing you examined. You found blood on Mr. Cameron's pajamas that was consistent with the blood types of Lisa and Mary Reeves, correct?"

"Correct."

"If there was animal blood on Mr. Cameron's clothing, would you have been able to distinguish it from Mary and Lisa's blood, even if all three blood types were mixed together?"

"Animal blood? Uh - yeah, but - "

"And you found no animal blood on Mr. Cameron's paja-mas, did you?"

"No."

"What about the knife? You found it in Mary's body, so if the same knife was used to slash the pig, then the animal must have been killed prior to Mary's death, is that a fair conclu-sion?"

"Yeah."

"Were you able to discern if any animal blood was mixed into Mary's body at the knife wound?"

"Uh, I didn't check her for that."

"Interesting," Payne said. "Now, Dr. Baker, you identified the victims to this court, and you testified that you performed autopsies on them, as shown in these photographs. Would you mind explaining autopsy procedure, and why it is neces-sary to a murder investigation?"

"A medical-legal autopsy is required to discover cause of death, identify wounds and their cause, and to assist in esti-mating time of death, among other things. I examine the head, chest and abdominal cavity by exposing them and removing the internal organs. They gotta be individually weighed, examined, and sectioned."

"I'd first like to ask you about your examination of Mary and Lisa. You testified to the bruising of the vaginal area on both women. Your testimony continued, and I quote, 'indicat-ing violent penetration - possibly with some kind of blunt instrument.' You also testified that there was no semen pres-ent, correct?"

"Yes."

"Would you agree that there is a difference between the act of rape, and sexually abusing someone by a means other than forced sexual intercourse?"

"Yes."

"Your testimony about a blunt instrument implies that the women were sexually abused but not necessarily raped; is that a fair inference?"

"Yeah, the trauma could have been caused by penile penetration, but it would have to have been a pretty violent act."

"But, the use of a blunt instrument, as you called it, and the lack of semen could indicate the women were sexually abused with some kind of object, but not raped, correct?"

"The lack of semen doesn't necessarily rule out rape."

"You specifically said 'some kind of blunt instrument.' If the evidence was conclusive, you would have no hesitation testifying that the women were victims of forced sexual intercourse, wouldn't you?"

"Yeah."

"What? You would hesitate?"

"No!" Baker was rattled now. "No, I wouldn't hesitate . . . I mean - "

"So, you conclude the evidence indicates some kind of sexual abuse, but you cannot conclude that either woman was actually raped, can you?"

"No."

"Alright, Doctor Baker. Let's move on to the medical-legal autopsy on the body identified as Linville Reeves. There was no head to examine, was there?"

"There wasn't much left."

"Please elaborate on the nature of his gunshot wound."

"He was struck at close range in an upward trajectory of about ten degrees, directly into his face."

"How close?"

"I'd say about one foot or less."

"On what do you base your estimate?"

"General physics. When a gun fires, explosive gas expands and propels the bullet - or in this case - steel shot. The gasses expand out the barrel, and when someone is shot at close range, the expanding gasses can do as much damage as the bullet or buckshot. That's why the upper torso looked like it did - explosive energy penetrated around the chin, expanded upward into the cranial vault and forced the skull to explode. The destruction of the head and the presence of steel shot pellets was consistent with a shotgun discharge."

"When you tested Mr. Cameron's clothing, you only found Mary and Lisa's blood on it, didn't you?"

"Right."

"In your opinion, if Mr. Cameron shot Mr. Reeves, is it unusual that no blood splattered on him?"

"It is a little unusual, but I can't say that it's impossible. The blood, skull fragments, and brain tissue would have exploded away from the weapon and the shooter," Baker said.

Payne stalked Baker. "Now, at autopsy, the condition of the male body probably made visual identification of the victim difficult, didn't it?"

"Huh? Yeah, it would."

"What method did you use to identify the headless body as Linville Reeves?"

"He was already identified."

"By whom?"

"I guess I should say, we already knew who it was."

Payne looked at the photograph of the corpse. "I don't see a face here, Dr. Baker. How did you determine that this corpse was Linville Reeves?"

Baker rolled fifty pounds of stomach to the left as the gallery disgustedly mumbled. "There wasn't any doubt about who it was."

"No doubt at all? Did you identify the body through dental records?"

"His teeth were destroyed."

"Were there any noticeable old scars unrelated to the wounds inflicted by the shotgun?"

"Scars? Uh, none that I recall."

"On his arms? How about scars on his legs or feet?"

"No. I didn't note any scars."

"Okay. How about a blood match? What was the blood

type, Doctor?"

"Type O."

"Pretty common, isn't it?"

"Yeah."

"Did you identify the body by comparing the blood type of this corpse to Linville's medical records?"

"Uh, no. Look, I - uh - wasn't asked to identify the body."

"You weren't? Are you saying you're never called to assist the police department in identifying a corpse?"

"Not never - I didn't mean to say it's not my job. Sometimes it is, but I didn't have to identify anybody in this case - "

"You weren't asked to confirm the identity of any of the three victims, were you?"

"No."

"Dr. Baker, isn't positive identification of the victim necessary in a medical-legal autopsy when the body is rendered unrecognizable like this?"

Baker wiped his brow. "Yeah - usually, but - "

"Then, how was this corpse positively identified as the body of Linville Reeves?"

"They told me it was him! I mean - they found him out on the Reeves farm."

"They? Who are they?"

Baker squirmed and wiped. "Sheriff White and Carswall."

"Doctor Baker, who was present when you performed the medical-legal autopsy on the male victim?"

"I always do the autopsies."

"I didn't ask that. Were you alone when you performed the autopsy on the body identified as Linville Reeves?"

Baker shifted his stomach again. "No."

"Who was with you?"

"Who?"

"I asked you."

"The crime photographer . . . uh, a medical technician assistant . . . and Mr. Carswall."

Payne stopped gawking at the photo and looked at Baker. "Special Agent Carswall was present at the autopsy?"

"Yeah."

"Why was he there?"

"He wanted to observe."

"Is it normal practice to allow non medical personnel to watch a medical-legal autopsy?"

"Uh, no . . ."

"Because a medical-legal autopsy is a vital function of the Coroner to gather evidence in the investigation of a capital crime, isn't it, Dr. Baker?"

"Yeah, but – "

"Did Jonathan Carswall ask permission to observe the autopsy?"

"Permission?"

"Or did he demand that you let him observe?"

Baker's eyes shifted and he rolled his blubber back to the right. "He, uh, just said he wanted to watch."

"Did he participate in the autopsy, or direct you in any way?"

"No."

"Did he observe the autopsies on Lisa and Mary Reeves?"

"No."

"Okay, Dr. Baker. Getting back to the identification question - based upon your expertise as a forensic pathologist, can you say to a scientific certainty that the male victim you examined in this case was Linville Reeves?"

"Yeah, it was."

"Upon what scientific evidence do you base your conclusion?"

"Well - I mean - it was him . . ."

"Scientific evidence, Dr. Baker. Upon what physical or scientific evidence gathered during the autopsy did you base your conclusion that the male victim was indeed Linville Reeves?"

"I guess I don't - "

"You don't have any evidence, do you, Dr. Baker?"

"Well, no."

"Because you didn't perform any tests to confirm the identity of the body, correct?"

"It wasn't necessary."

"It wasn't necessary, was it, Doctor? You assumed this was Linville Reeves, because Sheriff White and Special Agent Carswall told you it was him, correct?"

"It was pretty obvious who it was, Mr. Payne."

"Obvious? A headless corpse?"

"Argumentative, Your Honor!" Whittaker called.

"Sustained."

"What did you do with the bodies after they were released from the investigation?"

"I sent them to the funeral home."

"Do you know if they were buried?"

"They were cremated."

"Doctor, if the sheriff had asked you to identify the male victim, you have the expertise to do that, don't you?"

"Yeah - I could, but - "

"A DNA test is often used to identify victims or perpetrators in crime investigations, isn't it?"

"Yes."

"You could have taken tissue samples and sent them to a DNA crime lab for a more thorough investigation into the identity of the male corpse that Agent Carswall produced, isn't that right?"

"Yeah, a – uh – a DNA test maybe – "

"It's possible that a DNA test might have established to a scientific certainty that the corpse Agent Carswall produced was indeed Linville Reeves, correct?"

"Yes."

"Consequently, that DNA test might have proved to a scientific certainty that the corpse Agent Carswall produced wasn't Linville Reeves, isn't that right?"

"Yes!" Baker said.

"But it wasn't your call, was it? You acted simply on the information provided to you by Agent Carswall and Sheriff White - that this was Mr. Reeves, end of story, right?"

"Uh - yeah. That's right."

"Doctor Baker, I ask you again: Based on your scientific expertise and not on what you were told or what you assumed, can you say to a scientific certainty that the male body you performed the autopsy on was Linville Reeves?"

Baker's eyes bounced off the jury and dropped to the floor. "No."

"Thank you, Dr. Baker." Payne looked at the jury as he returned to his seat.

"Redirect, Your Honor?" Whittaker said, quickly standing.

Judge Falco nodded. "Go ahead, Counsel."

"Dr. Baker, you processed three bodies, and you performed medical-legal autopsies on them, correct?"

"Yes."

"Linville, Mary, and Lisa Reeves, correct?"

"Yes."

"In your professional opinion, is there any doubt in your mind about the identity of Linville Reeves' body?"

Baker dug his finger into the top of his collar. "Uh, no."

"Thank you."

Payne smiled at Aaron and whispered, "Get a mop. Our jury's bleeding all over the place . . ."

*　*　*

Judge Falco recessed proceedings just before four p.m. The jury was sequestered to a local hotel, and reporters rushed to file their reports. After White and Baker, the prosecution witnesses were police and hospital staff. Whittaker's only other witness of consequence was a teen-age girlfriend of Lisa Reeves. She gave a tearful account of Seth Cameron's relationship with the Reeves family, and his sexually menacing behavior around Lisa. She claimed Seth once enticed her and Lisa into a strange game that involved kissing whenever someone lost a hand of cards. Seth, she claimed, fondled both of them.

Rather than attacking the direct with hearsay objections, Payne deftly impeached the girl's testimony on cross-examination, and he poisoned the jury's sympathy for her. He tricked the teen-ager into admitting the alleged sex game was a case of two mischievous girls making a fool out of a drunken man. The witness even admitted to performing a moderate striptease that Seth clumsily tried to stop. The girl broke into tears, having been caught in numerous lies, and Payne smugly walked away from her beaten and bloody corpse. Whittaker, bailing water helplessly, was impotent on redirect. By evening, the media would tell the world that the prosecution lost opening day by a landslide . . .

The Aaron dinner table was brisk with activity. Reed picked at his food, while Payne bolted everything in sight. Sybil and Gracie Aaron tried to talk about anything but the Cameron trial, but it seemed Payne and Aaron had only one thing on their minds.

They finished dessert, and Gracie slipped out quickly to catch Daddy on the TV news. Sybil made the rounds with the coffeepot as Payne leaned back, exhausted from eating.

He affectionately rubbed her arm as she poured him a cup. "Syb, you are not only the most gorgeous woman on this planet, but you could cook for the gods."

"Oh, but I do," Sybil said. She was only two months younger than Aaron, but, at fifty, she could pass for fifteen years less. She was in remarkable shape, thanks to aerobics, careful dieting, and a husband who still took her breath away. Men both young and old always took a second glance at Sybil, and many wondered aloud how an 'old coot' like Reed Aaron snared such a perfect woman. Sybil was the consummate mom, wife, and philanthropist. She had a hand in every charity and civic club in town. Reed called her a 'professional citizen.'

Sybil and Reed had been madly in love since they were caught smooching behind the barn at age eight. They attended grade school, high school, college, and law school together. In fact, they couldn't recall a time when they were ever interested in anyone else, and they could count on one hand the times when one had a cross word for the other. After law school, Sybil and Reed spent a year litigating pro bono spousal abuse cases through various Harrisburg women's shelters. They then opened a private practice together in Attica. Sybil loved lawyering, but she insisted it wasn't a life sentence. Gracie was born ten years later, and Sybil started the career she had always wanted - Mom and Ruler of the Roost. She never regretted leaving law to anchor a stable home for her family. Reed joined the Public Defender's Office that same year. Reed and Sybil Aaron chiseled out a reputation as the best known and liked citizens in Attica; and true to form, little Gracie was the most popular and brightest student at Attica High.

Marc Payne wasn't impressed by many things, but the Aaron family astounded him. As much as he loved them, however, he sometimes had to hide his bittersweet jealousy.

Aaron wiped his mouth and kept the prime topic of conversation going. "Whittaker just didn't behave the way I expected, Marcus."

Payne lit a cigarette and sipped his coffee. "He's an arrogant chap. You were right about that."

"But he's uptight. The grand gestures and Holy One attitude are there, but something's different about him."

Payne grinned. "You've probably never seen him with such a soundly kicked ass."

Aaron laughed. "Do you have any idea how badly I've wanted to make him squirm like that? It took my baby brother to do what I've been trying for years. I loved it when you threw Jackson at the jury."

Payne agreed. "We gotta make every juror wonder why Whittaker won't touch him."

"Jackson said Whittaker only interviewed him once - last week - and he never asked any specifics about the bodies."

"D.A. Whittaker just may be feeling the subtle prod of Jonathan Carswall, Special Agent for the - "

"Easy, Counselor," Aaron laughed. "I'm not a juror, remember?"

"I wish you were. So, do you think Carswall has reached out to Whittaker?"

"I don't know. Screwing with the D.A. is a risky proposition, even for Mr. Special Agent."

"Perhaps, if he's just fishing; but there are several ways to turn a screw. I'm talking about backing Whittaker into a corner."

"What do you mean?"

"It's pretty standard stuff. If I want you to jump through my hoop, I dig into your closet and find something you don't want anybody to see. You know, you boff your secretary, you call phone sex numbers, maybe you bungee jump naked. What are Whittaker's quirks?"

"Other than narcissism and severe anal retentiveness? Not much. He's a right-handed conservative down to his wingtips. He's not a drinker, doesn't chase around; he's a country club lizard; service clubs - I think he's a church elder. You know - good politics."

"Any family?"

"His wife died of breast cancer ten years ago, and I haven't seen him with steady company since. He has a grown daughter who lives out of town. He owns some real estate, and he likes to crow about market upticks. There are rumors about a political run."

"How about Judge Falco? Any connections that Carswall could exploit?"

"Kathryn? Not a chance in a million. I've known her twenty years, and she's the complete package with heavy political connections. No, Carswall's too smart to touch her."

"She's scared of me," Payne said bluntly.

"So what? I'm scared of you. She's just out of the blocks on a highly publicized trial. Nobody around here is accustomed to a TV camera and a press row in the courtroom. We ordinarily look around and find Dan Williams napping by the back door."

"I agree that Falco is too dangerous to approach, but don't assume it unreasonable to suspect Carswall could get to Whittaker. I sense vulnerability in the good D.A."

Aaron nodded and suspiciously looked around the room. "What our friend Captain Mitchell told you about being watched never quite leaves my mind. Every so-often I find myself looking into my toothpaste tube for a microphone."

Payne chuckled. "You read too many spy novels. Don't forget, they're dealing with me, and I've had so many wire-taps that I could open an electronics superstore. Although Carswall thinks the Constitution has an amendment in there just for him, I can pitch a bitch about illegal wires and make it stick. They already broke into my hotel room once, and I went straight to the press with it. The last thing he needs is more publicity, so he's hatched more covert ways to intimidate us."

"How's that?" Aaron said.

"This bastard's a prime hitter for an agency that operates outside any jurisdiction - even the goddam President. They're military-based, and military-minded. They win by destroying the hearts and minds of the enemy."

"And we're the enemy . . ."

"Winner-take-all, big brother. Don't get me wrong, I still sweep our sensitive conversation places – like this dining room - and we have to make empty small talk on the phone, but the feds are aiming for the crotch. They're using psycho-logical terrorism to undermine us. It's more efficient than try-ing to glean out our trial strategy through endless hours of risky electronic surveillance."

"Psychological terrorism?"

"Phone calls in the middle of the night - redneck voices on the other end, digging at me about Lori's death. Carswall found out about my head problems, so he's priming the pump. And Jackson is an easy target. They call him 'nigger,' and they toss stones at his house. They know he has a little chip on his shoulder, so they amplify his paranoia and screw his mind." Payne took a long drag from his cigarette and shared a contemplative stare with Aaron.

Aaron sighed and shook his head. "God, Marcus. I pay taxes for this?"

Payne smirked. "Grow up, big brother . . ."

Gracie Aaron bounced into the dining room, breaking the spell. "Stop it!" she ordered. She wrapped her arms around Payne's throat and snatched his cigarette. "Come on! Spit it out!"

Payne choked and laughed at the same time, smoke exploding from his nose. "Help!" he cried. "Crazy teen-ager at six o'clock!"

"No smoking! This is a smokeless home!" Gracie let go of his throat and planted a wet kiss on his cheek. She came around and posed like a teen model. "Now, stop talking shop and tell me how bee-youteeful I look in my new dress!"

Payne theatrically gasped. "Who is this stunning creature?"

Gracie giggled, spinning like a doll on a music box.

"It's cut too low," Aaron grumbled.

"Oh, Daddy! Get with the times!"

"Yeah, Daddy," Payne said. "Sweet Thing, you're too beautiful to look at."

Sweet Thing. Gracie's heart always jumped when Payne called her that. It was a nickname he gave her when she was three.

Gracie was a carbon copy of Sybil. Her auburn hair was the same, and their figures were identical. Her dress accented new curves the fifteen-year-old didn't have a few months ago.

"Do you really like it, Doc?"

Payne, too, had a nickname - 'Doc.' "I love it, but not as much as I love who's in it."

Gracie giggled and gave Doc a big hug. Lori Payne had given him the Doc nickname many years ago. It referred to an old doctor he unsuccessfully defended for malpractice. The old sawbones was a lecherous fool who fondled a patient with his bony, arthritic hands. During the trial, Payne and Lori shared a lot of private laughter over his nasty client. Payne gave birth to a sick routine of sneaking up on Lori, his hands hideously curled, growling, "I must examine your glands!" It ignited a shiver up Lori's spine and sent her screaming through the house with the perverted 'Doc' on her tail. Of course, Gracie never got the same treatment, but the nickname stuck.

Payne pulled Gracie on his lap and returned her kiss. "What's the occasion?"

"I'm going to my first school social in a couple of weeks. It's gonna be at night and have a live band with these five wicked-looking guys in it!"

"I have an old baseball bat you can take with you."

Aaron gave a daddy's whimper and put his face in his hands.

She giggled again. "You should come and dance with me, Doc. Everybody at school talks about you. You could be my celebrity date!"

"Me? You don't want to dance with an old guy like me."

"You're not old. Daddy's old."

Aaron sighed through his hands.

"He's a fossil," Payne said.

Gracie couldn't stop giggling. Doc made her giggle.

Payne put on a contemplative face. "Say, if I'm not mistaken, you have a birthday coming up soon."

"Cut it out!" Gracie protested. "It's two weeks from tomorrow, and you know it."

"Yes, I do remember that. Sweet sixteen. What's your favorite color?"

"Blue," Gracie said suspiciously.

"Marcus," Aaron said, warily looking through his fingers.

"And, just out of curiosity," Payne said, "do you like chrome or wire wheels?"

"Doc!"

"Marcus!" Aaron cried.

"It's an innocent question."

"No!" Aaron said.

"Oh, Daddy! Oh, Doc!"

Sybil heard the conversation from the kitchen. She walked into the dining room, laughing. "Marc, you're gonna give the fossil a heart attack."

"I just want to know how a beautiful lady in a new dress is going to get around town, that's all," Payne said.

"No, no, no . . ." Aaron's face disappeared into his hands again.

"Doc! A car? Really? I love you!" Gracie almost broke Payne's neck. "Oh, please, Daddy? Pleeeeeese?"

"Two Aaron women on wheels?" Aaron mumbled. "Marcus, just take a gun and shoot me."

"I aced Driver's Ed., Daddy," Gracie indignantly said.

Payne whispered in Gracie's ear. "Sweet Thing, what you do is plant a seed and let it grow. Daddy's awful worn out from planting right now. Let's just let the idea simmer."

Gracie whined as if the battle was already lost.

"We'll talk about it," Aaron said, scowling at Payne.

"But -"

"We'll talk!" Aaron's voice was convincing this time . . .

* * *

A telephone rang through the cool, lonely darkness of Payne's hotel room.

He crashed to the floor, a bodiless scream penetrating the walls of his slumber. He rolled about, his mind groping for some mental high ground - some foothold in the dark. Bits and pieces of understanding slipped through the cracks of his mind, and questions were answered here and there. The phone rang again. A weary grumble rolled from his throat as he pulled himself up and found the lamp switch. He clicked the light on and found reality. His cell phone was adamant, but he wondered if he should answer. The readout on the screen simply said "caller unknown." A similar call came in earlier when he walked into his room. No one on the other end of the line then, but Payne suspected it was the little mind carpenter trying to screw another bolt of guilt into his brain. Finally, he answered.

His voice was a bark - an unfriendly one at that. "What?"

The line was quiet.

"Are you going to talk, or shall we breathe in code?"

Still, nothing.

"I'll say this for ya, Jonny; your vocabulary is improving." Payne turned his phone off.

He blew a breath and draped an arm over his eyes. Although he wasn't certain, he thought he had a nightmare - something about Lori, lights and a bodiless voice.

Payne considered going downstairs to see if Tod might have a bottle stashed somewhere. After a second thought, he settled for smoking six cigarettes, one after another . . .

14

Jackson stood at the back of the courtroom with his muscular arms folded across his chest. He chatted briefly with Dan Williams before taking his post at the doors. Judge Falco sat with a cursory nod to the jurors, and everyone situated. Payne looked particularly slick for the camera this morning, and Aaron made a nice contrast with his simple, country gentleman elegance. Cameron sat between them, wearing the same brown suit he wore yesterday. The general atmosphere in the courtroom was decidedly different than opening day, due to the strong, no tolerance display of force by the police. Spectators and reporters behaved cautiously, as if they feared they might get a baton over the head for any minor indiscretion. Virgil White still smarted from the emasculation Marcus Payne performed on him yesterday. He was decidedly out of sorts, and consequently, his officers were testy.

Judge Falco's eyes unconsciously darted to the TV camera as she called court to order and instructed Whittaker to proceed.

"The People call Jonathan Carswall," Whittaker said.

Payne winked at Aaron as Carswall took the stand amid a notable murmur in the gallery. Many strained for a look at the government man who became a mystery media star overnight. Carswall was impressive, his silver hair brushed straight back to his collar, and his fifty-year-old frame hard and lean. Most of the men found him rugged and suited to his persona; the women (and one male juror) found him grimly handsome. Many noted his dark eyes. They weren't just black. They were inky and quite solid.

Whittaker took his place at the dais. "Will you please state your name and occupation."

"Jonathan Carswall, Special Agent, Central Intelligence Bureau." A smattering of laughter rolled across the room. Payne took advantage by turning from his seat and acknowledging it with a smile.

"Order," Falco said. The laughter died as if struck by a bullet.

"Mr. Carswall," Whittaker began, "in fairness to you, your name came up in yesterday's session. Were your ears burning?"

"No."

Whittaker dropped the smile and returned to his script. "Sir, I would like to ask some questions regarding your agency's role in the Reeves homicide investigation. Let me start by asking, where were you at 8:30 on the morning in question?"

Carswall transformed into a rather stiff but charming man. He rolled a chalky smile at the jurors and they smiled back. "I was in the Attica courthouse."

"For what purpose?"

"To speak with the sheriff."

"And what did you discuss with Sheriff White?"

"I was in charge of a survey team on assignment to investigate an alleged UFO sighting in Rockford, reported several days prior to that morning. My purpose was to ask the sheriff if he had received any such reports in his jurisdiction."

"Was that the only subject of your inquiry?"

"No. I asked if he had received any recent reports of suspicious disappearance or death of livestock."

"Why is the CIB interested in that?"

"These so-called cattle mutilation incidents are not our primary concern; however, from a military security standpoint, all UFO reports require a routine check no matter how frivolous the alleged sightings may be. The Rockford incident included an animal death, necessitating my question about livestock."

"Did you visit with Sheriff White?"

"Briefly. I met him at his office on the second floor, but we were interrupted."

"What happened next?"

"I followed the sheriff downstairs, where several officers were confronting a man; the defendant. He suddenly attacked all three, and they wrestled to the floor. They put him in custody, and the sheriff ordered one officer to investigate the Reeves farm; he then went to the hospital."

"What did you do then?"

Carswall feigned perfect embarrassment. "Well, I have to say I've been an ambulance chaser since childhood. I also have a background in the Military Police. I found myself caught up in the excitement. So, out of personal and professional curiosity, I decided to follow the officer out to the farm."

"Were you alone?"

"No. Two of my deputy investigators were waiting for me outside, and they joined me."

"And why were they there?"

"They met me in Attica that morning to file field contact reports. After visiting Sheriff White, I planned to review their findings and then dismiss them to new assignments."

"So, what happened when you arrived at the Reeves farm?"

"We noted the officer's patrol car was empty - he was out on the premises. Shortly, he wandered back in visible distress. I rushed to offer assistance and found him terribly shaken. I identified myself and asked him what happened, but he just sat down in his vehicle, quite incapacitated. It was hot, and I suspected he might be suffering from heat exhaustion or shock."

Jackson, still standing in the rear, shook with anger. He received a stupid smile from Payne.

"What did you do?"

Carswall continued, never looking to the back of the courtroom. "I decided the officer was incapable of performing his duty. He mumbled that someone had been murdered, so I told him to radio for help. My deputies and I searched the grounds, and we discovered two dead women and a butchered pig."

"What did you do then?"

"I ordered my men to carefully search the various structures - a house, barn and a hen house - primarily to look for more victims and a possible perpetrator."

"Did you assume command of the crime scene, Mr. Carswall?"

"At that time, I felt it necessary for our safety. The officer was unable to make a decision. I had no choice but to search and secure the area until a capable authority arrived."

"Did such an authority arrive?"

"Yes. Sheriff White."

"And, sir, did you give orders to the sheriff and direct the homicide investigation?"

Carswall appeared mildly surprised. "Direct? Of course not. When Sheriff White arrived, I identified myself and apprised him of the situation. The Medical Examiner arrived several minutes later, and I walked them through the crime scene. I certainly did not direct anyone; I have experience in homicide investigation, and so I offered help, which the sheriff accepted."

"At any time when you were at the scene of the crime, did you or your agents ever touch any evidence?"

"I'm a trained investigator, and I'm fully aware of proper crime investigation procedure. I didn't touch anything until Sheriff White arrived, and only under his direction did I or my agents come in contact with evidence or victims."

"Did you ever manipulate, alter, or remove anything that was determined to be evidence by the sheriff?"

"Absolutely not."

Whittaker triumphantly looked at the jury, but their response was less than comforting. He turned back to Carswall. "Sir, did you ask to observe the autopsy on Mr. Reeves?"

"Yes, I did."

"Why?"

Carswall shrugged. "Ambulance chaser again. Frankly, the case fascinated me."

"Did you observe the autopsies on the females?"

"No. I was fascinated, but one autopsy was enough for me."

"Okay, Mr. Carswall. Now, with due respect to the victims, I want to turn for just a moment to the pig you found out there. You mentioned 'cattle mutilations,' as they are sometimes called. How do they relate to the CIB investigating UFOs, specifically, this incident in Rockford?"

"In a few alleged UFO sightings, dead farm animals were discovered nearby. These rare incidents have spawned many folk tales and legends, but the government has never substantiated any UFO sighting, and cattle mutilations have always been easily explained. The Rockford incident was one such hybrid."

"You say cattle mutilations are easily explained?"

"Yes. The alleged mutilations are simply the work of predators; on rare occasions, cultists are responsible."

"Please explain what you mean by predators and cultists."

"Nomadic cults associated with devil worship have been known to perform rituals involving animal sacrifice - killing them, cutting off parts of the carcass, drinking the blood and so on. They secretly practice in remote areas to keep their illegal activities hidden from authorities. The results can be very grisly.

"And, when I speak of predators, I refer to predatory animals, like wildcats or wolves. Weak or ill animals attract predators. A pack of wolves can thoroughly gut an animal in a short period of time, leaving behind mostly bones and very little blood. It can be startling to find an animal stripped clean like that, particularly if the carcass lies in the sun for a time, but predatory kills are common and natural occurrences."

"But how do UFO sightings fit in?"

"I believe it's romantic folklore. Years ago, there was an incident not far from here in which a rancher thought he saw unusual lights in the sky. At dawn he found a dead horse in his pasture. He called his local paper, claiming a UFO was related to the killing, and an imaginative reporter seized the opportunity for a tabloid headline. The media milked this so-called mystery, despite the official conclusion that the horse was weakened by disease and had clearly been attacked by predators - most likely wolves. The press apparently felt that UFOs sell newspapers, wolves don't. But, to answer your question, there is no evidence that connects UFO reports to cattle mutilations. In fact, both are simply fodder for campfire stories." Carswall smiled, and the jury looked satisfied.

"What was your conclusion in the Rockford case?"

"A Mr. Clyde Majors claimed he saw bright lights over his farm, and he found a dead bull on the premises the next morning. He believed the death was connected to his alleged sighting. The local press found out and concocted a mutilation/UFO tale, I suspect due to Mr. Majors' - shall I say 'fondness?' - for colorful conversation and drink. I interviewed Mr. Majors, and I inspected the remains of the bull a few days later at a veterinary clinic operated by the Humane Society in Harrisburg. Its leg was broken, suggesting vulnerability, and the carcass was clearly ripped and torn by predators. As for the UFO, there was no substantiation of aircraft activity in that vicinity."

"Returning to the Reeves farm, did you see any similarity in the dead pig, compared to the Rockford bull?"

"No, the pig's wounds looked more like slashing. We transported the animal to our facility in Harrisburg for a thorough examination, and it was determined that the wounds on the pig were most likely caused by a knife. The two incidents are dissimilar."

"Were you aware that the defendant told a newspaper reporter that a UFO landed on the farm?"

"After I read it in the paper."

"You never heard about it before then?"

"No."

"Did you investigate the defendant's claim?"

"Yes, we checked the local airfield and luckily found that someone was on duty during the morning hours in question. The tower is equipped with radar."

"What did you find out?"

"There was no local air traffic between one a.m. and seven a.m., other than five commercial overflights at high altitudes."

"If there had been an aircraft over the Reeves farm that night, could the air controller recognize it as something extraordinary?"

"At that late hour, and in this remote region, a low-flying aircraft might be remembered by someone monitoring a radar screen. It wouldn't have necessarily been seen as 'extraordinary,' as you put it, but the controller recalled no local traffic at all."

"Mr. Carswall, my last question is simple. At any time, from the moment you walked into the Attica courthouse that morning until now, have you directed any portion of the Reeves homicide investigation?"

"No."

"Thank you." Whittaker sat.

"Counsel?" Judge Falco said to the defense.

Payne took the dais quickly. He tossed his grin. "Mr. Carswall, good morning. It's a pleasure to meet you - although, for some reason, I have the feeling we've met before."

Carswall's smile was gone. "I don't think so."

Payne glided in front of the witness stand. "Sir, you say your job at the Central Intelligence Bureau is to investigate UFOs and mutilated livestock?"

"It's a living," Carswall said to the jury.

"You testified that you were going to meet with the agents who accompanied you that morning, and then dismiss them to other assignments. However, after the Reeves murders were discovered, you and those agents remained and participated in the investigation. My question is this: why did you take such an interest in this case to the point of abandoning your investigation of UFO and livestock mutilation incidents?"

"The sheriff was grateful for my offer of assistance, as his department doesn't have a lot of experience in a crime like this. I immediately contacted my superiors, and I requested that they allow us to spend a day or two and help out."

"So, you and your men searched for and recovered a male body on the Reeves farm late that night, correct?"

"Yes."

"Did any Attica police officers assist you in the search?"

"Their assistance was better directed at guarding the Reeves farm perimeter, which was inundated with quite a few sightseers from town that evening."

"So, your answer is, no, there were no Attica police officers present at the site, where you found the male body."

"That's correct."

"Okay," Payne said. "Now, you investigated a UFO sighting that accompanied this bull mutilation in Rockford, correct?"

"Yes."

"You spoke with Mr. Clyde Majors about his seeing a large aircraft, sporting metallic green lights; it was capable of incredibly rapid acceleration, correct?"

"Objection," Whittaker said. "Assumes facts not in evidence."

"Sustained. Rephrase the question."

"Clyde Majors saw a UFO, correct?"

"He claimed he saw lights over his farm that night. But there was no UFO."

"No? Clyde Majors was quoted in his local paper as saying he saw a large, fast aircraft the night before he found his prize bull dissected."

"Hearsay," Whittaker objected.

Payne suddenly turned to the jury box. "I guess we could ask Clyde, but he was killed a few days ago."

"Objection!" Whittaker stood. "Mr. Payne is clearly trying to imply that the accidental death of - "

"Accident?" Payne said. "A tractor ran over him in a blinding snowstorm! Your Honor, I object to Counsel's use of the word 'accidental.'"

"Objection!"

"Order!" Falco called. "Counsel, approach the bench!"

Payne calmed and walked to the bench, his smile dripping in Whittaker's path. Falco angrily moved away from her microphone and stepped to the side bench. "Mr. Payne, you are pushing me, and nobody pushes me. I will not tolerate this in my court. Try me, and I will slap you with contempt."

"He should be cited now, Your Honor; and I want sanctions," Whittaker said.

"Watch your step, Mr. Payne," Falco said. "I know what you're up to, sir, so tread carefully. Do we understand each other?"

Payne's eyes sliced through her. "We do now, Your Honor." He didn't smile again until he turned to the jury. His face curled, and he put his finger to his lips like a scolded child. The jurors simply sat in confusion over Payne's unexpected broadside.

Judge Falco, still angry at the chill that Payne put on her spine, looked at the jury. "Mr. Payne's comments about the death of Mr. Majors assumes facts not introduced as evidence and are irrelevant to this case. They shall be stricken from the record, and I admonish the jury to disregard them."

Whittaker's face was crimson. He slapped the table as he sat.

"Okay," Payne said, "where were we? Yes, Rockford. Mr. Majors sighted a UFO and then found a dissected bull in his field. You investigated this incident, correct?"

"Your use of the word 'dissected' is inappropriate."

"Is it? Mr. Majors said it looked like the bull had been dissected - clean incisions, its brain removed . . ."

"Objection. Hearsay."

"Sustained. Mr. Payne, this is my second warning. The jury will disregard Mr. Payne's last statement."

"No hearsay, now, Mr. Carswall," Payne said. "Was the bull dissected?"

"The animal was ravaged by predatory animals."

"A bull? Ravaged by a coyote? A very brave and husky coyote, wouldn't you say?"

"The carcass was too damaged to determine what type of animal attacked, but a pack of larger wolves are more likely. The bull had a broken leg. It was probably helpless."

"What type of wolf is indigenous to this area, Mr. Carswall?"

"Irrelevant," Whittaker said.

"Withdrawn. You say there was no UFO in Rockford?"

"We found no evidence of an aircraft in the area."

"You told Mr. Majors there was a military helicopter in the area that night, didn't you?"

"I had no such conversation with Mr. Majors."

"And he can't tell us now, can he?"

"Argumentative!" Whittaker said.

"Mr. Payne," Falco warned, "tread carefully."

"Treading, Your Honor," Payne said. "Mr. Carswall, are you aware that it's a crime to lie on the witness stand, even if you are a secret agent for the Central Intelligence Bureau?"

"Objection! Counsel is badgering the witness!"

"Sustained. Mr. Payne - "

"No more questions," Payne said.

* * *

Zack Taylor sat next to the back door. He was next up. His sweating palms drew two damp circles on the knees of his trousers. Judge Falco called a fifteen-minute recess that went for twenty, and Taylor watched every tick on his wristwatch.

Whittaker quietly conversed with the A.D.A. In his stomach was a barbed wad of apprehension, the second such time he felt this way since going to school to study Payne's Law. Payne was charming the jury and shredding witnesses like cheap dime store dolls. The D.A. knew his evidence was poison, based on the testimony of White, Carswall, and the autopsy reports, but Payne used curved mirrors to make the jury sway. The A.D.A. cautioned Whittaker about calling Zack Taylor to back up Carswall. In light of Payne's recklessness, he suggested Taylor might be slaughtered; let Carswall's testimony stand and let's move on.

Judge Falco returned to the bench before Whittaker gave the question any further thought. He approached the dais. "The People call Zachary Taylor."

Taylor's heart fluttered as he stood. He unconsciously rubbed his hands on his trousers and walked to the stand.

After swearing in, he looked at Whittaker, who fumbled through his notes. Zack believed every eye was on him.

"Please identify yourself to the court, sir, and tell us your occupation?"

Taylor's voice was thin. "Zachary Taylor. I work at the Attica airfield."

"Mr. Taylor, you are an air traffic controller?"

"Yes."

"You were employed at the airfield on the date of the Reeves family murders, correct?"

"Yes, sir." Taylor wiped his hands.

"Were you working in the tower that night?"

Taylor unconsciously glanced at Carswall, who stood near the doors. He focused on the memorized testimony he'd practiced for months. "I was there from midnight to eight a.m."

"And so, you were in the tower during the time frame that the medical examiner has established as the specific time period when the victims were killed, yes?"

"I was."

"Did you monitor the radar screen during that time?"

"Yes."

"Outside of high-altitude commercial flights, did you see any local air traffic in the vicinity of Attica?"

"I saw no local traffic between one a.m. and seven a.m."

"Mr. Taylor, if there had been any low-flying aircraft over Attica between one and three a.m., would you have seen it?"

"I would probably have remembered it. I don't."

"Thank you," Whittaker said, holding his breath.

"Good afternoon, Mr. Taylor," Payne said. He walked to the dais and calmly adjusted the microphone. "It's a pleasure to meet you." Taylor didn't respond. Payne flipped through a small notebook. "Taylor. Air traffic controller. Attica airfield. That's a small airfield, isn't it, Mr. Taylor?"

"Yes."

"In fact, no commercial airlines land at that airfield, do they?"

"No."

"The airfield serves just local private planes, isn't that right?"

"Yeah."

"What are your assigned working hours there?"

"I was there from midnight to eight a.m."

"That's not what I asked. What are your assigned working hours at the Attica airfield?"

"I, uh, work the evening shift."

"Darn," Payne said, laughing. "I'm not much of a communicator, I guess. What I want to know is, what are your assigned working hours at the Attica airfield?"

Taylor wiped his knees. "Noon to eight," he softly said.

"Whoops, there go my ears now. Did you say noon to eight?"

"Yes."

"Noon? Eight p.m.?"

"Yes."

"You testified that you were there from midnight to eight a.m., correct?"

"I was."

"I guess, since there was no local air traffic, we can rule out a huge workload requiring your presence all night." Payne's gentle smile gave Taylor no comfort. The attorney stood silently at the dais. The shark was circling. He deliberately changed his habit of walking about just to give Taylor one more thing to think about. He shuffled and pretended to be mentally assembling his next question while he scribbled circles on his notebook. Through this seventy-second ruse, Payne simply allowed Taylor to squirm.

"Mr. Taylor," Payne finally, mercifully said, "what were the hours of operation at the Attica tower that night?"

Taylor cleared his throat. "Uh, the hours? It depends on the season."

"Here I go again," Payne said in mock frustration, "asking questions you don't seem to understand. I'll try again. What were the hours of operation at the Attica tower that night?"

"Hours. That depends."

"How late are you open?"

"Seven a.m. to eight p.m.," Taylor said, looking down.

Whittaker silently cursed. He felt like he was watching a

three-alarm blaze with a garden hose in his hand.

"Sir, help us out here. If the airfield closes at eight o'clock, does that mean airplanes can't land there after hours?"

"Uh – no. If a private aircraft wants to land, the pilot can key a code to the tower that activates lights on the runway, and he adheres to visual flight rules when coming in."

"Part of visual flight rules includes the pilot being aware of his airspace, transmitting a call on his radio to alert other pilots, and watching for other aircraft when he wants to land, correct?"

"That's right."

"Yes," Payne said. "And, of course, the Attica area is so sparsely populated that on the rare occasion of a pilot wishing to land late at night, there is simply no need to keep an air traffic controller on duty, isn't that right?"

"Yes."

Payne scratched his head. "Mr. Taylor, your shift is noon to eight p.m. In fact, the tower is only open until eight p.m., but you just testified that you were there from midnight to eight a.m. Are you absolutely certain you were there at those hours?"

"Yes, I was there."

"Workaholic? Locked in? Why were you there if the tower closed at eight p.m.?"

"I . . . just didn't feel like going home."

Payne ran his waiting game again. He scribbled circles and shuffled paper, this time for sixty-one seconds. Taylor dabbed a bead of sweat from his brow, and the jury swallowed him whole.

Reed Aaron was simply awed by this master manipulation. He wondered how anyone could command something as banal as silence. The entire courtroom, including Judge Falco, was hypnotized by this magician, who displayed yet another character in an attaché full of personalities.

Payne broke the quiet air. "You worked from noon to eight, and, deciding you didn't want to go home, you stayed in the tower until eight the next morning. Is that right, Mr. Taylor?"

"Yes," Taylor said. He tried to swallow.

Payne took a step and counted to thirty before his next question. "You just happened to stay there all night - the very night three people were murdered - and you diligently monitored air traffic for twenty hours?"

"Argumentative," Whittaker said.

"Sustained."

"The airfield was closed," Payne said. "So you weren't actually working as a controller, were you, Mr. Taylor?"

"Uh, not officially, I guess. But-"

"Do you *always* stay in the tower all night?" Payne asked.

"No, sir."

"But you were there on this particular night?"

"Look," Taylor finally said, taking the bait. "Last summer I was having troubles at home. My wife and I weren't getting along. I spent the night there because I wasn't welcome at home."

Payne went into hibernation again. Two minutes. His notepad was black with scribbles. The jurors grew impatient. "I realize you're embarrassed to share this, Mr. Taylor," Payne said, "but you testified that you monitored the radar, and that you saw no low-flying aircraft during the hours crucial to the murders of the Reeves family. I can't help but wonder if you really were monitoring air traffic that long. Give me a ballpark figure of how long during twenty hours in that tower were you watching the radar screen - taking careful note that during these critical hours, there was absolutely nothing to watch."

"How long?"

"I asked you."

"I guess I checked it now and then."

"Did you sleep during this twenty-hour vigil?"

"Did I sleep?"

"I asked you."

"I, uh, guess I dozed."

"You guess," Payne said. "Mr. Taylor, how long have you been an air traffic controller?"

"About thirteen years."

"Have you always worked at the Attica tower?"

"No."

"Where else have you worked?"

Taylor swallowed. "Harrisburg International."

Payne's smile faded. "Why did you leave that job to come to an airfield as small as Attica's?"

Whittaker, garden hose firmly in hand, stood. "Your Honor, Mr. Taylor's work history is irrelevant."

"Oh, I disagree," Payne said. "Your Honor, my client claims an unidentified aircraft had a significant role in the deaths of the Reeves family. This witness refutes that claim with testimony based upon implied professional skill to alertly make radar identifications. However, now he 'guesses' he dozed at his post from time to time, and he admits he was in that tower for twenty hours due to a squabble at home. Mr. Taylor's work history is clearly relevant and foundational to both his reliability as an expert and to the credibility of his testimony."

Judge Falco didn't hesitate. "I'll allow the question."

"Why did you leave your job in Harrisburg?" Payne said.

"I was fired."

"Why?"

Taylor's eyes were moist. "I was blamed for a crash."

"A Midwest Airlines flight, Mr. Taylor? The crash several years ago that we all remember, is that what you're referring to?"

"Yes."

"Are you the air traffic controller whom the Transportation Safety Board blamed for the incident?"

"I cleared it for landing on an occupied runway," Taylor said. "The plane came in and hit a commuter that was taxiing to the terminal."

"I see. You were fired after the investigation, weren't you?"

"Yes."

"What was the basis for your termination?"

"The official report found me personally responsible for not knowing the runway was occupied."

"Did you just make a terrible mistake, or did the investigation turn up other reasons for your clearing that plane to land on an occupied runway?"

Taylor took a deep breath. "The safety board found me negligent."

"Do you 'guess' you dozed off then, too?"

"Objection!"

"I was intoxicated."

The room dropped at Zack's admission. Whittaker stood to object again.

"Overruled." Falco's stare froze the D.A.

Payne didn't say anything. He just looked at Taylor while the jury tried to ingest what they just heard. Whittaker closed his eyes and heaved a sigh.

"Intoxicated?" Payne said.

"Yeah, I was goddam drunk."

"Mr. Taylor, please refrain from obscenities," Falco said.

"Drunk," Payne quickly said, not allowing the judge to break Taylor's fall. "Did this fact appear in the board's report?"

"No."

"I'm confused, sir. You admit to being intoxicated; however, it was not documented in the report. Why, if you know?"

"Maybe this is the first time anybody in the general public has heard the truth."

"Excuse me, sir?"

"I'm a government employee," Zack said, his eyes brimming. "Controllers are under a lot of pressure. Believe me, I'm not the first controller to be caught drunk in the tower - just the first one to kill three hundred and six people. That's not news that would give airline passengers much confidence. I made a deal, okay? The board officially dismissed me for negligence. I avoided criminal prosecution in exchange for keeping my mouth shut. The deal kept me out of jail, and out of the papers."

"I see. But, how did you manage to return to the profession?"

"I didn't have a criminal record. I was trained to do one

thing, and I had a family to support. They gave me a second chance. I spent a year in rehab, and then I was assigned to Attica as part of my probation. They said I'd never work anything larger than a place like Attica, but at least I could work somewhere. I had to take weekly drug and alcohol screens for a while, and then I was left alone to put my life back together."

"Were you taking drug tests on the night in question?"

Taylor shook his head. "The testing stopped a few months before. I thought things were getting back to normal for me, and so did they."

"And now you work at the Attica airfield, in charge of regional air traffic. On the night of the Reeves murders, you spent at least twelve hours in the tower before you carefully monitored radar from one a.m. to seven a.m. The only reason you were there was because you weren't welcome at home. Were things back to normal, Mr. Taylor?"

"I . . . guess not."

"Were you drinking that night?"

Taylor hesitated. He thought about his wife and children, who were out there somewhere under Carswall's watchful eye. "No."

"I remind you, Mr. Taylor, you're under oath. Did you consume any liquor or drugs that day or night?"

"No."

"Was it your primary concern to constantly monitor a blank radar screen all night?"

"I watched it."

"Have you taken a drink since your therapy?"

Taylor nervously looked around the courtroom. He prayed no one in the jury had ever been inside Rusty's Tavern. "No."

"Did you sleep in that tower all night?"

Taylor hesitated. "No," he said, thinking again of Carswall.

"Twenty hours without sleep? I don't think watching a supposedly empty radar screen all night would be high on your list of priorities!"

"Objection! Argumentative, Your Honor!"

"Withdrawn," Payne calmly said. "Mr. Taylor, has anyone coerced you to testify that you saw nothing that night?"

Falco interrupted. "Counsel, I trust this is foundational?"

"Indeed. Answer the question, Mr. Taylor."

Taylor closed his eyes. "No."

"Other than the prosecutor and my associate, Mr. Aaron, has anyone else talked to you about your testimony here today?"

Taylor stared at the floor. "No."

"Did Sheriff White ever question you about your observations at the Attica airfield that night?"

"No."

"Mr. Taylor, have you ever been questioned about this by a government agent by the name of Jonathan Carswall?"

Taylor barely whispered, "No."

"I'm sorry, can you speak up and repeat your answer so we can hear you?"

"No!"

"Your Honor, in light of Mr. Taylor's revelations, I request he be subject to recall."

"Very well," Falco said.

"No more questions at this time." Payne quickly walked away.

"I'd like to redirect," Whittaker said.

"Go ahead," Judge Falco said.

Whittaker weakly stood at his table. "Mr. Taylor, did you at any time drink alcohol on the day or night in question?"

Taylor could only look at his lap. "No."

"And you are certain that you saw no local air traffic?"

"Yeah."

"Thank you."

Judge Falco excused Taylor with the admonition that he may be recalled to the stand. She then called for a lunch recess.

Payne put his arm on Seth's chair and nodded first at him, and then at Reed Aaron. "Down in flames," Payne said with cruel satisfaction. Aaron agreed, his stomach churning. Payne patted Cameron on the back. "Reasonable doubt, Seth. We won that round big."

Cameron hollowly looked at Payne. His saddened voice was a whisper. "You busted that man's soul."

Payne looked at Seth, taken back. He glanced at Taylor, who quickly left the stand. Zack passed the jury as if he was running a gauntlet. He shoved through the standing crowd. Payne put his hand on Cameron's arm. "It's a hard life, Seth..."

* * *

Jonathan Carswall sat in his car near the intersection of Main and River streets. A spiteful wind whipped the gray day, shoving dead leaves into the streets and bullying pedestrians up and down the sidewalk. Carswall punched in numbers on his cell phone, and then heard Baytree's familiar voice on the line.

"Good day," Carswall said, "this is Eric Sinclair. I would like to confirm the balance in my account."

"Proceed," Baytree replied.

"I'm afraid I might be overdrawn. The number is 0911 . . . dash . . . 0911."

"Yes, sir," Baytree replied, "would you care to request credit to cover the balance?"

"Yes."

"For what amount?"

"The maximum," Carswall said.

"To confirm - you are requesting the maximum amount to be credited to your account?"

"That's affirmative."

A momentary silence dulled the line. Baytree came back on. "Thank you, sir. Your request has been authorized."

"I understand. Thank you." Carswall clicked off and tossed his black eyes to and fro as the passing citizens went about their day. He checked himself in the mirror and meticulously smoothed his silver hair . . .

15

D.A. Whittaker still reeled from watching Payne punch daylight through Zack Taylor this morning. After lunch, he called a Reeves neighbor to the stand, and then the president of Farmer's First Saving Bank, a personal friend of Linville. It was a weak attempt of character assassination, and Payne effectively disrupted the testimonies until the jury lost interest. The witnesses tried to paint Seth as a helpless drinker and a constant thorn in Linville Reeves' side. After Taylor's self-destruction this morning, Whittaker's crumbling credibility rendered these witnesses impotent. They only suggested Seth had alcohol problems, and that he argued with Linville from time to time, but nothing in their testimonies provided bricks for the foundation of a heinous murder. Payne commented to Aaron that Whittaker was plainly trying to plant a motive in the jury's mind.

"Considering the hard evidence he has," Payne said, "Whittaker is almost trying to be stupid . . ."

At lunch, Payne and Aaron agreed they should fire additional shots at Carswall's credibility by calling Clyde Majors' neighbors to the stand. The two farmers saw something in the sky when Majors' bull was killed, and they were still willing to testify despite Clyde's 'accident.' Payne told Aaron he was surprised Whittaker tried so diligently to refute the UFO issue when his physical evidence was so strong. It opened up new windows of opportunity, and Payne relished adding the UFO arrows to his quiver . . .

Dr. Terence Bundy took the stand. Whittaker continued questioning witnesses from the safety of his podium. "Dr.

Bundy, would you please tell the court your profession?"

Bundy, a thin, scholarly white man in his late sixties nodded. "I'm a Doctor of Psychiatry. I've been Chief of the Psychiatric Unit at Southmore General Hospital in Attica for thirty-three years."

"Are you acquainted with the defendant?"

"Yes."

"What is your relationship to him?"

"He was a patient of mine years ago, and I testified at his competency hearing."

"How long have you known him?"

"I first met him when he was about eight or nine."

"Is that when he was your patient?"

"Yes."

"And how was he referred to you?"

"The county sent him to me after the death of his mother."

"Why?"

"Mrs. Cameron was murdered - a very traumatic experience for the young boy. The court placed him in Southmore General for treatment. I was called to provide psychotherapy for him."

"What were the circumstances of this murder?"

"It was very grisly. Mrs. Cameron was killed by a drifter who lived with her at the time. A violent argument apparently escalated, and the man shot her to death and then killed himself. Seth witnessed both deaths."

"What type of weapon did the drifter use to kill Mrs. Cameron?"

"A shotgun."

"Why were you called to administer psychotherapy?"

"Mr. Cameron suffered from catatonic shock. It is a rare condition that sometimes strikes victims of severe trauma. The phenomenon of catalepsy is not well understood. The symptoms vary, but the victim tends to mentally 'shut down,' if you will."

"And Mr. Cameron - then a child - suffered from this condition?"

"Yes. He was found hiding under a bed at the crime scene.

His breath was shallow, and his heart rate was slow. We could manipulate his body position, but he was unresponsive to voices."

"How long did he remain this way?"

"Three weeks. He slowly began to respond to my voice, and he eventually emerged after several months of therapy. He had little recollection of the experience; or, little he cared to tell."

"What do you mean by that?"

"I tried to help him adjust to the trauma. He never directly referred to the murder, but he expressed great anger toward his mother and her killer."

"Why was he angry at his mother?"

"A child at that age has very little control of his environment. I'm afraid many depraved things went on in their home, and Mrs. Cameron did nothing to stop it."

"Such as?"

"Melissa Cameron was a convicted prostitute and drug addict, and her murderer, Pearly Scott, had served time in prison for solicitation, child abuse, and child prostitution. Seth alluded to such abuse."

Whittaker directed himself to the jury. "Doctor, considering the circumstances of the defendant's home life, was this the cause for his hatred of Melissa Cameron?"

"Objection. Leading question, Your Honor, and calling for a conclusion," Payne said.

"Sustained."

"Doctor, did you observe any lasting emotional damage in the young boy?" Whittaker said.

Bundy sighed. "The sordid life of his mother and the association with her murderer undoubtedly harmed him."

"Did you help the boy?"

"Not enough."

"How so?"

"This was thirty years ago, Mr. Whittaker, and Attica was even smaller than it is now. This situation was the source of great shock and embarrassment to the people who lived here. Seth lived in many foster homes through his teen-age years, but he was virtually an outcast."

"Did you continue to treat him as he grew up?"

"Legally, I had no responsibility for him after he was discharged from the hospital. However, I took the liberty of following his progress."

"Did he make progress?"

"Not a great deal. He was unruly in school, and he got into trouble frequently. As he matured, he stopped getting into scrapes, but he dropped out of high school and couldn't hold a job for very long."

"Did you have any contact with him while he was working for Linville Reeves?"

"Not professionally," Bundy said. "I've seen Seth now and then over the years. Each time we visited, he was employed at menial jobs. I was acquainted with Mr. Reeves through our church, and it was at my urging that Linville hire Seth. Linville had back trouble at the time, and he needed help around the farm."

"Did you believe the defendant might fit the bill?"

"One thing I knew about Seth was that he worked hard when he wanted to. He once mentioned an interest in farming, and I thought this was a chance to get experience. I also believed the Reeves family might offer some permanence in his life."

"Doctor, did Mr. Reeves ever express any regrets for hiring the defendant?"

"If he had any trouble, he never expressed it to me. Seth, on the other hand, once mentioned he was afraid Linville was unhappy with him. He said they often argued about his drinking. I think Seth wanted to please Linville like a son wants to please a father. At his age, this was difficult."

"Doctor, given the defendant's history - growing up with a prostitute; possibly being sexually abused; witnessing a brutal murder - all due to controlling figures in his life - is there a potential of violence against a perceived authority?"

Dr. Bundy gave a sincere shrug. "Psychiatry is an inexact science, Mr. Whittaker. A pattern of violent abuse exists in Seth's life, and it's my experience that this type of pattern may manifest itself in the victim if he does not receive extensive therapy."

"Doctor, the defendant brutally attacked Sheriff White and others, and is accused of a triple homicide. Based upon your expertise, do you believe that behavior like this could be such a manifestation?"

Doctor Bundy hesitated, never looking at Cameron. "The potential is there."

"Thank you."

Payne walked around the dais and stood in front of Dr. Bundy. Apprehension now seemed to drip over the room every time Payne turned on the switch. His eyes glowed at the old doctor. "Good afternoon, Dr. Bundy. It's a pleasure to meet you."

Bundy smiled cautiously. "Good afternoon."

"You said psychiatry is an inexact science?"

"Yes."

"God knows," Payne mumbled, "that's what my shrinks tell me."

The jury and gallery laughed with Payne. "Order," Judge Falco said.

Payne still smiled, and Dr. Bundy didn't notice the cannon pointed at him. "A doctor takes an oath when he earns his medical degree, doesn't he, Dr. Bundy? He or she commits to the confidentiality of a patient's medical record, correct?"

Bundy paled. "Yes."

"Did you forget your oath when you told everyone about Seth Cameron's medical history, Doctor?"

"Of course not."

"No? You just told us he was crazy enough to murder three farmers."

"I most certainly said no such thing."

"Objection. Misstates the testimony, Your Honor," Whittaker said.

"Sustained."

Payne dug a finger in his ear. "I could have sworn that's what I heard. Did you not, in fact, reveal confidential patient info?"

Dr. Bundy was visibly stunned by Payne's inference. "I only answered questions that pertained to the public history of his life."

"You just said he was crazy enough to kill."

"Objection!"

"Withdrawn. Do you think Seth could kill someone, Doctor?"

"I'm saying - no, I didn't say that."

"Then you don't know what you're saying? Which is it, Doctor?"

"Wait," Dr. Bundy said. He was still shaking from the ambush. "I merely answered the prosecutor's questions."

"And he asked if you thought all those terrible things that happened to Seth as a child might make him go on a violent rampage thirty years later. You said, and I quote, 'The potential is there.'"

Dr. Bundy felt naked. "I meant, yes, in theory, he is capable."

"Theory? Seth is accused of murder, and you're saying he might have done it in theory? Theory. Conjecture. Speculation. Hypothesis. Assumption. Wild guess. Check your thesaurus, Dr. Bundy. That's a pretty ambiguous word to use when you're passing judgment on a man's life!"

"Objection. Argumentative."

"Sustained."

"Which is it, Doctor, a theory or just your opinion?" Payne said.

"I am not saying I believe Mr. Cameron killed those people."

"Ah, you're not? You don't believe he did it?"

"Calls for a conclusion," Whittaker said.

"I agree; withdrawn," Payne said. "If we're talking theory, Dr. Bundy, then let's consider that Seth Cameron just might have benefited from living with the Reeves family. Maybe having Linville Reeves busting Seth's chops for drinking was something Seth respected. Maybe you succeeded in your attempt to get Seth that permanence and love he never had before. Doctor Bundy, aren't these theories worth tossing out?"

"Calls for speculation," Whittaker said.

"Theories and speculation are the foundation of Dr. Bundy's testimony, Your Honor."

"I'll allow it. You may answer," Falco said.

Bundy, clearly rattled, was all but cooked and ready to be devoured. "Yes, those theories are valid."

"After suggesting to Mr. Reeves that he take Seth into his home, did you ever bolt from your bed in the middle of the night and say, 'My god, I've set a murderer loose on that poor family?'"

"Of course not."

"If you had any suspicion this man was a potential killer, would you have told Linville Reeves to hire him?"

"No!"

"In all the years you've known Seth Cameron, did you ever know of him harming anyone?"

"I can't say I have."

"That's a problem, isn't it, Doctor Bundy? Let me use your words, sir." Payne strolled to the table and plucked a report from Reed Aaron, who calmly held the document up on cue. "I have a transcript of your testimony at Seth Cameron's competency hearing, in which you stated: 'Mr. Cameron's attack on Sheriff White is inconsistent with his behavioral history. I'm frankly at a loss to explain this anomaly. He's been docile and without aggressive emotion for thirty years now.'" Payne tossed the document back to Aaron. "Doctor, was that your testimony at the competency hearing?"

"Yes, I said that."

"Are you changing your testimony now?"

"Perhaps I implied I believed he committed these crimes, but that was not what I meant. I simply meant to say that violence is possible."

"Possible? You said before that he isn't aggressive. Which is it, Doctor?"

Bundy squirmed. "Let me say I was surprised by his behavior."

Payne tossed the ruthless glare of a thug kicking his opponent into the asphalt. "Falling back on the old inexact science excuse, Dr. Bundy?"

"Argumentative!" Whittaker called.

"Sustained. Mr. Payne, a little discretion, if you will?"

Payne never looked at the judge. "Would you say it is unusual for a man, who has been a docile, nonviolent person all his life, to suddenly become violent?"

"Yes," Bundy sighed.

"Then how do you explain his attack on Sheriff White?"

"I simply don't have the answer."

"Doctor, is it possible for violent behavior to be caused by a neurological, rather than psychiatric disorder?"

Still reeling, Bundy was open to anything that might get him off the hot seat. "Yes."

"I'm talking about a brain injury, drug ingestion - maybe a chemical imbalance, Doctor. Could those things cause a healthy patient to suddenly behave erratically - even violently?"

"I am aware of no brain injury to Mr. Cameron."

"I didn't ask that."

"Yes, the things you suggest could cause erratic behavior in a patient."

"So, since you're so happy to give us one theory, should we not consider a vast array of theories for Seth's attack on Sheriff White?"

"Objection," Whittaker weakly said, "speculative."

"I'll say again, Your Honor, speculation is the foundation for the doctor's entire testimony," Payne argued. "He opened that door, so I'm just walking in to take a look around."

"I'll allow the question, but don't stray too far, Counsel," Falco said.

"There are many possible reasons for his behavior, correct, Dr. Bundy?"

"Yes, there could be other reasons."

"But, because you practice an inexact science, you shouldn't anchor yourself to any hard conclusions, should you?"

"No."

"In fact, you're just qualified to testify that Seth is sane and competent to stand trial, correct?"

"Yes."

"Thank you." Payne returned to his table.

Whittaker cut his losses and passed on redirect. Doctor Bundy was dismissed. He quickly retreated, avoiding Whittaker's eyes.

A passive lull shrouded the room as D.A. Whittaker collected himself. It took him several moments to finally stand and address the court. "Your Honor, the People rest."

Other than the furious scratching of pencils in press row, everyone in the courtroom quietly sat and waited for the next move. It was as if a curtain fell on a play that didn't appear to be over, and everyone was waiting for the next act. Judge Falco didn't look up, but she scribbled notes with great diligence. She finally responded with authority.

"I believe we'll take an afternoon recess until tomorrow when the Defense will begin its portion of the trial," she said. "I want to remind the jury that you must not discuss this trial or formulate any opinions until the matter is submitted to you. We'll recess until nine a.m." She quickly departed.

The weary participants and observers packed up and began their exodus from the courtroom. The media made its dash, but Dan Williams lingered and approached Payne, who'd given Seth a few reassuring whispers before the bailiff escorted him out the side door.

"Any comments, Counselor?" Williams asked.

"That's the worst suit I've ever seen," Payne said as he loaded his briefcase. Reed Aaron chuckled.

Williams grinned broadly and swept a hand through his sandy hair. "I can't print speculation," he smirked. "Do you think Whittaker finally decided to stop shooting himself in the foot?"

Payne gave a sarcastic nod. "Did he do that?"

"I'll ask the questions here. Spill the truth, Counselor."

"Okay. Don't buy off the rack."

Williams never could lose that grin. It was cemented to his cocky face. He pulled out his pipe and fired it up, sucking smoke like a helpless junkie. "How much cold cash would you take for a printable comment pertaining to this trial?"

Aaron stepped in. "You don't have that much money. By the way, there's a no smoking sign right behind you." He sniffed cautiously and turned to find Payne lighting a cigarette.

Payne shrugged.

"Come on, boys," Williams said. "Toss a bone to your old pal. I want to get on national TV and be somebody."

"No comment," Payne said as he followed Aaron to the door.

Williams still grinned, but that didn't necessarily mean he was happy. Secretly, he would drain his savings for a one-on-one with Payne, but he also was a realist. Besides, he had a better idea about who to follow for a bone right now, and he needed to get going - fast.

Willy jumped at a not-so gentle hand on his shoulder.

Sheriff White glared. He puffed madly on his cigar, pointing at the no smoking sign. "Put it out," he growled.

Willy checked White's cigar, and then looked at his pipe like a child. He grinned and put it in his pocket. "Never a problem from humble me, Constable," he said. He darted from the courtroom before he went up in flames . . .

* * *

Carly stood quietly at a receptionist desk and glanced around the empty room. She wore a sweater she had once accidentally shrunk in the washer. It made her look very preppy before she ruined it, and she hadn't put it on since. The sweater left her cute little 'inny' belly button exposed, and it hugged her breasts so tightly that she didn't dare take a deep breath. She wore a leather skirt and black hose, and wore enough perfume to make the smell in this veterinary clinic pleasant. Her eyes were shaded blue, her lipstick was red, and her jet black hair was curled and very big. As women go, Carly left no question what she was, but right now she looked more like the kind of lady Ken Jackson would arrest rather than love. Playing this role reminded her of her undercover days in Harrisburg before she opted for an easier life in Attica.

Easier? She gave that a healthy second thought . . .

She looked around the office. The front counter had a few spay and neuter brochures scattered about. On the back wall were several horse posters and one comical photo of a pig sitting at an elegant dinner table with a big napkin around his neck. Below the picture were the words: Swine & Dine.

Carly tapped a bell on the counter.

She heard stirring in the back room, and in a moment a pleasant looking man in his early fifties rounded the corner. He almost gasped when he saw Carly, but he caught himself in time. Surprise turned to lecherous charm as the vet slowly approached the counter. "Can I help you?" he asked, his voice implying he was capable of helping her with more than spaying her cat.

"Are you Dr. Lee?" Her smile and perfume ran a surge of hot blood through the man's scrotum.

"Yes, thank God," he said, returning the fire.

She held out her hand. "Carol Hill, Food and Drug Administration."

The doctor's charm dissolved. He was expecting to hear her say something more in line with, 'Bambi's Mobile Massage.'

"My pleasure. Forgive me for being a bit startled. I've never had a visit from the F.D.A. Is something wrong?"

"Not at all," Carly said with her killer smile. "Just a spot inspection. Actually, I have a new supervisor. Whenever that happens, we spend a week checking physicians and veterinarians for unlocked drug cabinets until the boss gets tired of reports. So, we threw a dart on the directory, and you won." She didn't let go of his hand right away.

"Lucky me," Dr. Lee said. He was indeed a handsome man, Carly thought, but she could see through the horny, married, always available charm she'd heard about from her friend at the Humane Society. Dr. Lee walked around the counter and locked the front door, turning with an innocent smile. "I was just about to close. I hope you don't mind. It's inevitable that somebody wants a rabies shot just when I'm trying to get out of here."

"I understand," Carly said. She hated doing it, but she gave him another smile - a special one she usually saved for Kenny. "This will just take a few minutes. I hope you're not annoyed."

"Who could be annoyed by such a pretty face?"

Carly gave a stupid giggle and fished in her purse for a pen and what looked like a very official form. "I need to take a quick look around your clinic, and then I'll be out of your hair."

"No problem," he said, leading her to the back. With a little luck, he thought, you'll be running your elbows through my hair.

They walked down the hallway into a large room that contained several rows of roomy cages occupied by dogs and cats. Carly stopped in front of Dr. Lee and deliberately bent over. She squealed at a little puppy that snoozed on his back, bombed by anesthetic. "Oh, he's so cute!"

Dr. Lee's eyes went right to Carly's leathered bottom. His overactive hormones begged him to cut loose and put it to her now while she was squealing. However, it was far too early for that kind of attack. "All the medications are kept over here." He pointed at three locked cabinets. "I guess you can see I keep a tidy house."

She came up smiling and turned so she was very close. "I sure can," she said. "I just had to verify your drug cabinets are properly secured - and they are." Her eyes held on just long enough to tell the doctor she was falling under his spell. She finally glanced at a closed door to the right. "What's in there?"

Dr. Lee's train of thought derailed. He pulled his eyes from her chest and glanced at the door, crafting a sublime response. "There? That's where I operate." He truly believed he was doing very well.

Carly raised her brows at him, secretly trying not to get sick. "Oh, may I see?"

"Sure." Dr. Lee walked to the door, wondering if he dare suggest a boff on the old operating table. They walked into the large surgical suite, which was as impeccably clean as any hospital operating room. On the far end were two large doors.

The room was divided in the middle by a partition. On one side was a small table, and on the other was a larger table connected to a hydraulic lift.

"Oh," Carly said, "you treat large animals, too?"

"Yes," Dr. Lee said, his chest puffed with hormones, "most city vets do just domestics, but I handle both."

"You know, with one glance, I don't think I need to waste any more of your time."

"Waste my time?" Dr. Lee said, almost drooling. "This is the nicest time I've had in years!"

"Oh, you," Carly said, tantalizing him with a wink as she walked back out. She continued back to the hallway. Dr. Lee prayed for the little wag of her bottom. Carly moved quickly, making the horny doctor chase her to the reception room. Her eyes took quick inventory of the file cabinets near his office door. She turned, and he almost ran her over. "Well, nice meeting you."

"Nicer for me," he said. He set the phony charm into motion. "You know, this is so unlike me, but I don't suppose, well, with it being quitting time and all, that you might be free for a drink?"

Carly put on an exquisitely executed shy smile. "Oh? I don't know."

Lee's face flushed perfectly. "Oh, look at me. I'm sorry for doing that. As beautiful as you are, you must have a hundred men pestering you."

Carly laughed and grabbed his arm. "You're sweet, and I'm flattered."

Bingo, Dr. Lee thought, spread your thighs, bitch, you're mine. "I'm thinking about a terrific restaurant downtown, and how nice it would be if I didn't have to eat alone."

Carly pulled the trigger. "It sounds awfully nice." Her eyes peeled his skin. "And I am hungry. Can I meet you there?"

"No, I can take you," Dr. Lee said. "Look, I need about ten minutes to wash the dog fuzz off. Let me go into my office and clean up. I'll call for a reservation. Okay?"

"Sounds delicious," Carly said.

"I'll be right back. Make yourself at home." Dr. Lee pathetically winked as he walked into his office and closed the door. He clenched his fist and mouthed the word 'yes!' as he whipped off his lab coat and shirt. He made a beeline to the bathroom to scrub down, have a quick shave and toss three or four blasts of whiskey to get the motor running. But first, he opened his cabinet and stuffed six condoms in his pocket.

Outside, Carly rifled through his file cabinet. What a sucker, she thought, this will be easier than I planned! She moved stealthily through each drawer like a bandit, not certain what she was looking for, but determined to explore. The file cabinets contained 'patient' records. In the bottom drawer was a heavy book, bound by a strap locked with a metal buckle.

Interesting, Carly thought.

With little time to pick the lock, Carly instead pried the edges of the book to peek in. The pages looked like ledgers of some kind. She poked her long fingernails into the pages and looked for a word, a number, or any kind of clue to reveal what was important enough to be locked up. She finally got a glimpse of a memorandum with the words, 'Crane Lodge Mortuary' on the top. Her brow furrowed. 'Mortuary?' She wrestled with the book, running a nail along the edge of the paper to keep her place. Her finger carefully worked around to the bottom as she gave a little grunt to arc the pages. As if someone just poured a bucket of ice water down her back, her mouth dropped when she caught a signature at the bottom of the page. 'J. Carswall.'

She warily perked to the footsteps inside Dr. Lee's office. Carly nearly dropped the book. Her heart stopped as she clutched it to her chest just in time. She swallowed hard and placed the book back in the cabinet drawer, clenching her teeth as she eased it shut. Again, her spine curled when she heard Dr. Lee on the phone behind his door.

"Waldo?" he said. "Dr. Lee here. I need a table for two in the dark."

Carly, teeth still clenched, tiptoed to the front door and grabbed the handle. Her eyes popped. Locked! She looked back to the hallway and heard Dr. Lee.

"We'll be there in ten minutes."

Damn! Carly messed with the lock, cursing her fake fingernails. The office door opened. She finally unlatched the door and slipped outside. Jackson was parked down the block. Carly kicked off her high heels, picked them up, and bolted down the frozen sidewalk, knocking a half-second off Jack Magic's state high school record in the hundred-meter dash.

"Go!" Carly hollered, leaping into the sports car.

"What the hell?" Jackson said as he watched the love of his life dive face-first into his crotch.

She clumsily reached back and slammed the door, hugging Jackson's thighs and putting a considerable strain on his important parts. "Pull out! Burn rubber, Kenny! Go!"

Jackson fired the engine and backed into the busy street. "Honey, if we get pulled over, how's a black boy gonna explain a white hooker nibbling his fly in traffic?"

"Shut up and blow, Kenny! I don't want that creep to see me!"

Jackson shut up and blew. They passed the vet clinic, and Jackson saw Dr. Lee standing in the doorway with a very sick look on his face. Lee glanced at the big black guy in the coupe for moment and then stepped out, his head swiveling back and forth. The little sports car razzed the stood-up doctor as Jackson wrapped around the corner and zipped into the falling darkness.

"Are we clear?" Carly asked. Her head still pressed Jackson's crotch.

"Not yet. He may follow. You better stay down there until we get back to Attica. Feel free to entertain yourself, baby, I got a pocketful of cash."

Carly went limp. She sat up, her frizzy hair dropping over her eyes. Her face was smeared with gaudy red lipstick. In fact, she looked ready for the Big Top. "You're a funny guy."

Mindful of the road, Jackson took one look at her and exploded into laughter that quickly evaporated to tears. "Oh, man, how come I never have my video camera when I really need it?"

She slapped his arm and tried to pull her leather skirt down. Her hair looked as if a bomb went off under her ears. The tight sweater had inched up past her tiny bra, nearly choking her poor breasts. "Go ahead, big guy, this really is funny. Har har!"

Jackson pounded the steering wheel and tried to wipe his tears. "You shoulda seen yourself ripping down the street. You were bouncing right outa that sweater!"

"Har har." She wriggled in the leather skirt. Finally, she spewed a word Jackson rarely heard her use, and she pulled the damned thing off and rolled her black pantyhose to her ankles. Through his tears, Jackson saw her conservative 'nice girl' underwear.

"What? No crotchless black lace?"

"Shut up. Where are my jeans? Where's my coat? I'm freezing." She knew her clothes were in the paper bag at her feet. It just felt good to imply he was hiding them. She nearly strangled as she wrestled the sweater from her neck and quickly pulled on her jeans and a bulky sweater, spitting at her bothersome hair the whole time. She finally stopped and glared at Jackson. "Come on, watch the road . . ."

They sped down the interstate, a road sign indicating thirty miles to Attica. The car, as well as Carly's mood, was toasty now for sixty miles. Her clothes fit snugly, and the war paint was thoroughly removed from her face. She even discovered what Kenny thought was so funny, and she laughed with him for a mile or two. After the yuks died, she told him about her visit with lecherous Dr. Lee and the memo she'd found in his file cabinet. They tossed a few ideas around without getting anywhere, and then settled for a few minutes of quiet brainstorming. The last five miles were devoted to some nice jazz on the radio.

Carly watched the darkened landscape do a slow dance outside. She took a deep breath and used her hands like an orchestra leader. "Okay, Crane Lodge Mortuary and Carswall's signature on the memo. What's the connection?"

"Probably standard Carswall procedure. Stab 'em, then

slab 'em," Jackson said.

Carly smirked. "Okay, let me see if I got all this. A veterinarian, whom my friend says is tied to the cattle mutilations, has a letter from a federal goon, signed on a letterhead from a mortuary. What do we have?"

"We obviously got us a mortuary to check out."

"This isn't the best time to tell you that I hate mortuaries."

"They're not on my short list, either, but I'd say it's a damned good place to go snooping."

"In a mortuary?" Carly said with a sour wriggle in her mouth.

"Aren't you a tad curious what may be in there?"

"I know what's in a mortuary. Dead people. You want to snoop around dead people? Given a choice, I think I'd prefer lying naked on an ant hill for two hours."

"I'll bet Carswall could arrange it."

Carly rubbed her arms. "Mortuaries. Yuk."

"Carly, like you say, that's where the dead folks live, and we're looking for one."

"Do you think Reeves might be stashed there?"

"Think about it. Carswall's been scouring the state for these mutilation incidents. We know he snatched Linville and the animal carcasses from at least two farms. Bodies aren't easy to tote around – people tend to notice if you have a dead bull in your back seat. So, it makes sense he would stash them locally in a secured place."

"But Crane Lodge Mortuary? I mean, wouldn't you get a little weirded out if your mother was in a mortuary with a pig?"

Jackson laughed. "Yeah, I guess. But this is old Jonny Carswall in charge here. Those documents you saw obviously ties him to this place, so it can't be your average pump-and-bury mortuary. It's probably a government set-up of some kind. It's a perfect place to keep stiffs on ice."

Carly cringed. "So you want to sneak into a mortuary to prove how smart you are?"

"I want to see what we can dig up."

"Oh, bad." Carly allowed a nervous laugh. "All my life -

thirty-one years - I've looked for a handsome stud to give me love and babies. So what happens? I get one who wants to sneak around a mortuary."

"I'm funny that way . . ."

* * *

The last leg of the trip was slowed by dangerous ice patches on the two-lane Attica cutoff. The road stretched for twelve dark miles of open range. Carly, a hopeless backseat driver, pointed out every ice slick and told Jackson to slow down each time. He imagined she was probably a real joy on a traffic stop. Nine miles from Attica, the radio broke for news at the top of the hour. The national headlines were bland and dreary, but the local news made Carly perk and turn up the volume.

The radio announcer's voice was low and melodic: "In Attica, District Attorney Roland Whittaker rested the State's case against Seth Cameron this afternoon in the sensational Attica UFO Murder Trial. The D.A.'s extensive presentation included evidence against Cameron, accused of slaying an Attica family last summer. Cameron's attorney, Marcus Payne, will begin defense arguments tomorrow morning with the highly anticipated 'UFO Defense,' in which the thirty-eight-year-old farm worker claims he was forced to kill two family members by inhabitants of an unidentified flying object, while the third victim was murdered by the UFO occupants." The announcer's voice trailed off skeptically.

Jackson shook his head and looked at Carly. "We gotta be nuts," he whispered.

"Shh." Carly turned the radio up.

The announcer continued. "In a related story, a prosecution witness in the UFO Trial was found dead late this afternoon on a remote country road near Attica."

"What?" Jackson cried.

"Attica police say thirty-six-year-old Zachary Taylor was found in his car with a single gunshot wound to the head. Police found a gun on the seat next to Taylor. Attica Sheriff's

Department officials say a preliminary investigation suggests suicide, but will turn the case over to the county Medical Examiner's office. Taylor testified for the prosecution at the UFO Trial this morning . . ."

"Woah," Carly said.

Jackson turned the radio off and stared at the icy road. "I guess we don't have to ask Payne how things went after we left."

"Suicide right after testifying?" Carly said.

"Yeah, suicide," Jackson said.

Carly didn't like the feeling in her stomach. "You don't sound too sure."

"These feds are stone-cold, Carly," Jackson said. "That's two witnesses down now . . ."

Neither one of them said it, but they both were thinking about Carswall. They also were thinking about the little stunt they just pulled in Harrisburg.

"Turn up the heat," Carly said with a sudden chill.

"We gotta be careful about letting on what we found tonight, babe. Marc made it clear that Carswall and his boys are watching and listening. They're playing mind games with us. Payne says it's a scare tactic, but they're upping the ante. There's no way those two died by accident."

"Yeah, I'd say two dead witnesses is a pretty clear message."

"We can't let anybody know what happened at that vet's office."

"Don't you think Payne might be able to help?"

"We can't be sure any conversation with him isn't going right to Carswall. He's hip to it all, and he gives me little signals when we can't talk freely, but we gotta be sure that anything we say to Marc is private - real private."

"Do you think we were watched today?"

"I don't know," Jackson said. "We darted through enough alleys and back streets to lose any tail." He looked in his mirror. "There are two cars behind us a mile or so. One pulled out of the gas station back at the interstate exit, and the other is behind him . . ."

The little car purred down Highway 30, six miles from Attica. Town lights twinkled on the horizon, and several taller buildings downtown jutted into the clear black sky. The last storm centered in this region, and the last few days gave just enough sunshine to melt the road in patches. A healthy layer of sand made the highway easy to negotiate, but Carly still reminded Jackson of his speed.

The river overpass rose ahead. Jackson squinted over the headlights. The bridge was dark and unoccupied, and all the streetlights were out. As the overpass approached, Jackson felt an unexpected smoothness under his tires, unlike the hardened ice and sand he'd felt just seconds earlier. The bridge gently lifted the car, Jackson still warily holding a wheel that seemed oddly light. A pair of bright truck head-lights approached from the other end of the bridge. Yellow running lights ran along the top of the semi tractor. Jackson flashed his brights on and off - the universal message: 'Hey, fool, turn off the goddam brights . . .'

Suddenly, the semi drifted across the double yellow line.

"Shit!" Jackson cried, hitting the brakes. "Brace!"

The car drifted wildly out of control. Its tires gave no cry as they helplessly slid across the yellow line on sheer black ice. Carly was belted in, and she ducked low, covering her head and face. The sports car spun and careened backwards on the bridge. Jackson tried to turn with the skid, but the car was unresponsive. He quickly ducked, aware that the semi was about to climb right over them. They revolved in a perfect 360-degree spin and bounced like a pinball off the opposite guardrail. The murderous truck, now fully in the oncoming lane, swerved back, and Jackson's little car miraculously dodged through the gap.

The truck cleared them, but they didn't know it yet. The car started another spin and made 187 degrees before bounc-ing off the other guardrail, which reversed the spin and took them forty feet sideways down the other side of the overpass. Carly's head whipped violently to her window. She gasped as her eyes watched the road slowing in front of her. Jackson blinked blood from his eyes, clutching the wheel and wondering if he was dead. The car finally stopped sliding, and the two sat like trembling birds.

"Baby," Jackson said, his breath tossing the words like little stones. His hand shook too hard to find her leg. "Are you okay?"

"I don't know yet . . ."

The overpass stopped spinning in Jackson's head, and he finally took command of his senses. He reached for Carly, but she intercepted him. They collided in a terrified embrace over the gearshift.

Carly wasn't a crier. She wept when both her father and brother died, and she wept once when she found a three-year-old girl beaten to death by a drunken father, but the tears ripped out of her now. Jackson wept, too, but it wasn't love sprinkling his eyes. They held the embrace for more than two minutes as the terror washed out of the car.

Carly pulled back and looked into Jackson's bobbing eyes. "Kenny, you're cut!"

Jackson drunkenly put his hand to a gash above his eye. It was small, but it spat a lot of blood. "I'm okay," he breathed.

"Oh, damn," Carly whined. She bent over and blew the rest of her tears on her jeans.

"What, honey? Are you okay?"

"Oh, Kenny, I peed my pants!"

In the midst of the most terrifying experience of his life, Jackson spurted a tiny laugh as he covered Carly. "It's okay, baby. We're wet, but we're alive."

Carly sucked her tears like a drugged-out vacuum cleaner. She threw back the shock like a veteran cop.

Jackson turned his head to her window. Ahead, the road was dark. He swiveled to his window, expecting to find a jackknifed tractor trailer sprawled across the bridge, yet there was nothing but a tiny pinpoint of red lights running away in the darkness.

"What the hell? The bastard didn't stop?"

He shakily opened the door and rolled a rubber leg onto the pavement. As he stepped out, both legs darted out from under him. He hit the pavement with his chest and almost bit a fender.

Carly leaned over on his seat and peered out. "Are you okay?"

"Compared to what?" Jackson angrily mumbled. He fought to stand, but his boots couldn't grab the icy blacktop. Finally, Jackson hung on the car door and pulled himself up, looking like a punch-drunk heavyweight. His feet danced madly on the ice. Carly started to climb out his side. "Stay in the car, girl, you could break your damned neck out here."

Jackson clumsily edged around the front of the car. He looked back up the highway, but the truck was out of sight. No cars were coming from either direction. He inspected his car and found an ugly gash on the right front fender. Jackson slipped again and sprawled over the hood, fighting to get his feet back under himself. He went down to his knees for more control and looked at Carly's side of the car, grunting when he found the right front tire was flat. Considering the severity of the crash, his car was still relatively intact.

Carly watched Jackson five-step back around the front of the car. He looked like he was walking a thin wire. He made it to the door and stood for a moment, staring at the road. Carly leaned back over. "What are you doing?" she said.

"Look at this," Jackson said, propping himself on the door. She squirmed over the gearshift and squinted toward where he pointed. "Look at these tracks in the road."

Carly saw what appeared to be heavy tracks in the oncoming lane, no doubt made by the truck that nearly ended her dream of a handsome stud and babies. She contemplated several puzzle pieces. Piece number one: the tracks looked heavy and pocked. In fact, through the black ice on the road, the big truck tires had not only easily bit into the asphalt, they dug holes in it. Piece number two: Why was the bridge so damned slick?

Jackson didn't say anything. He fell back inside the car. The wound over his brow stopped bleeding, thanks to the freezing wind. His face, however, looked like it had a red-brown crack running from his eye to his neck. Carly pulled a tissue, unceremoniously spat in it, and cleaned him up while he suspiciously peered out the windshield at the frozen river below. "That truck had chains," he said.

"Yeah," Carly said as she wiped his face clean. "And he didn't stop."

"Pretty strange, huh?" Jackson said.

"And when we drove across this bridge this morning, there were just a couple patches of ice."

"Yeah," Jackson said. "It was damned near dry. But tonight it's got a sheet of black ice on it from end to end."

"The highway department doesn't water the bridges, Kenny. I know these things."

Jackson peered down the road with suspicion. Quickly, he turned the key, and the engine sputtered. After he turned it over a few more times, the motor finally fired up.

"What are you doing?"

"We're getting the hell outa here."

"On a flat tire?"

"Do you want to stick around and wait for that truck driver to come back and help us change it?"

"Step on it," Carly said.

Jackson clutched and pointed the crippled car toward town. The flat tire, humping and bouncing all the way, actually gave them some traction. They slid down to the end of the bridge, where the road miraculously turned back to sand and roughed ice patches. The ride home nearly loosened their teeth, but they never considered stopping . . .

16

Payne peered down the empty street. Tod, the hotel night clerk, insisted a woman had asked him to waken Payne and send him out here. Payne's eyes suddenly caught sight of Jackson standing at the mouth of a darkened alley.

"K.J.?" Payne said as he cautiously approached. Carly emerged from behind Jackson. "What's up?"

Jackson pulled Payne into the alley. "Marc, we can't stay long. Somebody just tried to kill us out on the bridge."

"What!" Payne checked the gash on Jackson's head. "Are you two okay?"

"We were set up - a semi damn near swallowed us. It wasn't an accident, either."

"What were you doing out there?"

Jackson gave Payne a dumb look. "Sightseeing."

Payne knew this line of questioning would go nowhere. "Alright, I get it. Thank God you're okay."

"Yeah, for now," Carly said.

Payne blew a ring of smoke and shook his head. He looked into Carly's bright, young eyes, and then at Jackson. "They won't miss you next time . . ."

"Stop right there, Marc," Jackson said. "I know what you're thinking."

"Do you?" Payne snapped. "Then you know what I'm gonna say."

Jackson's eyes burned. "No way, man . . ."

"I run this show, Jackson, not you!" Payne said.

"And I'm telling you, no goddam way! We're not gonna bail out now!"

Payne glided back and forth, puffing madly and stalking Jackson with his eyes. "I got a body count going, K.J. . . . . Two

. . . goddam two are dead now!" His voice trembled.

"I know," Jackson said, "we heard about Taylor."

"He died to save his children . . ." Payne's glide turned to a nervous pace. His cigarette spewed ashes as he puffed. "But I put the barrel in his mouth. His hands were tied behind his back on that stand, and I butt-raped him!"

Jackson looked at Carly. His concerned eyes told her this was not any Marcus Payne he'd met yet.

Payne continued. "I'm not a goddam lawyer anymore. Who the hell put me in charge of this? I'm not a goddam lawyer! I have a conscience now, you understand me?"

Jackson grabbed Payne's arm and stopped his pace. "Marc, take it easy . . ."

Payne grabbed Jackson's arm and held him tight. "I told you when we met - I like you." His touch grew affectionate as he moved his hand up to Jackson's shoulder. He looked at Carly. "You're both under my skin now. If I get you killed, the barrel goes in my mouth next."

"Marc!" Jackson ordered. He grabbed Payne's shoulders and brought him back to the ground. "It's okay, man . . . it's okay . . . "

Payne nodded. "It's okay - yeah." Payne eased himself. The raging fire slowly flickered out, and a more familiar Marcus Payne emerged.

"You didn't get your witnesses killed," Jackson said. "If anybody's to blame, it's me. If I'd have kept my mouth shut, Aaron would have pled Seth to life with three squares and a roof over his head, and none of this would have happened."

"Wrong," Payne said, now very much in control. He let go of Jackson. "We know who's to blame. And I'm gonna eat that sonofabitch alive!" Payne put one hand on Carly's shoulder and the other on Jackson's.

Carly's hand moved to Payne like a magnet. She hardly knew him, so she'd never be able to explain it, but her heart cried out to grab this man and never let go.

"Look," Payne said, "whatever you're up to, watch your-selves. The rules are changing fast."

"We're on something, Marc," Jackson said, "that's all I can

say for now."

Payne nodded. "Don't leave me hanging too long."

"Just buy us some time," Jackson said. "You may get yourself a surprise witness."

Payne looked right through both of them. He touched Carly's face and then burned Jackson with a glare. "Just don't forget what I told you, K.J."

Carly and Jackson watched Payne walk back to the hotel. "What did he mean by that?" Carly asked.

Jackson sighed. "Past history . . ."

* * *

Marcus Payne stood before the jury with that magical smile curling his lips. Everyone in the courtroom sat in quiet reverence befitting royalty. Roland Whittaker watched intently, trying to hide his apprehension. He nervously picked at a button on his jacket, occasionally glancing at the jury.

Seth Cameron sat next to Reed Aaron, who had an arm draped over the back of Seth's chair. Reed didn't look like he was holding his breath, but he was. He was the only person, outside of a few veterans in press row, who knew that Payne had not yet revealed even a fraction of the insanity he could splash on a jury.

Payne walked the length of the jury box, personally handing his smile to each juror without a word. One hundred and twenty-two seconds of silence. He knew the exact time it takes a jury to simmer.

"Good morning, ladies and gentlemen," Payne said with infectious charm. "It's a pleasure to meet you." By now the jurors laughed every time he said that. "I guess you know me, but for those of you who doze, my name is Marc Payne. I'm honored to represent Seth Cameron. I'm also the one getting in trouble with this very honorable judge, who's certainly earning her pay." The jury beamed at Judge Falco. "I just can't seem to get through a trial without upsetting people like the prosecutor here."

Whittaker folded his arms and looked at his notes.

"Mr. Whittaker seems to think I'm here to sell trinkets and UFO shirts." Payne pulled out his space alien doll and squirted its eyes at them. The jurors didn't laugh, but most of them nodded in recognition. "Cute, isn't it?" Payne said, squeezing the doll. "Hawkers are making a fortune off this kind of junk." A sudden black fire blew into Payne's eyes. He turned and hatefully threw the doll against the wall. It came apart and scattered, knocking the breath from the jury. Falco considered an admonishment, but her breath was gone, too. Payne sneered. "But I don't think it's too awfully funny, do you?"

Payne stalked the box, throwing fear into the jurors' eyes. "Three of your neighbors were brutalized last summer, ladies and gentlemen. A decent man, woman, and teen-age girl were murdered, and opportunistic leeches out there are making a profit from it. They're mocking this entire town in its most tragic moment. No, I don't think it's funny, and I'm not amused that Seth Cameron is taking the blame!"

He backed away and strolled to Cameron and Aaron.

"Ladies and gentlemen, for those of you who have not had the pleasure, this handsome devil here is Mr. Reed Aaron. Reed is your Public Defender - he's one of your neighbors. And next to him, it's my pleasure to introduce Mr. Seth Cameron. He's your neighbor, too. I imagine some of you have seen him around town, maybe in church, at the market; and maybe a few of you've tipped a cold one with him now and then.

"For those of you who don't know him, by God you will. He's one of you, ladies and gentlemen - not a cold-blooded murderer - not a mentally deranged butcher. He's scratched out thirty-eight years of a hard life with nothing but his bare hands - getting by honestly, just like you. The only thing that makes him different from you right now is he's wrongfully accused of three counts of first-degree murder and two counts of sexual assault. First-degree murder, folks, that's a premeditated and willful act. That's murder Seth had to conceive and carry out with malice aforethought. If the prosecutor presents enough evidence to eliminate any doubt he did it, you must convict him. And if you convict him, the D.A. is going to make you decide if this state will execute him. His life is in your hands, ladies and gentlemen."

Payne looked at Seth for a moment and everyone looked with him. He scratched his head and walked back to the jury box. "It's not funny, is it? What makes this tragedy worse is that Seth isn't guilty of premeditated murder. To convict this man, you have to believe that Seth Cameron is guilty to a moral certainty and beyond a reasonable doubt. I promise I'm going to rip your minds with reasonable doubt; and I'm going to throw moral certainty in the dumper. Seth Cameron is not guilty of premeditated murder. And you know what? I'm gonna prove it to you."

The jurors sat remarkably still, each and every eye on the magician.

"Buckle up, ladies and gentlemen," Payne continued. "Over the next few days, Mr. Aaron and I will present a most remarkable mystery of which not only the Reeves family members were victims, but Seth Cameron as well. You have a tough job ahead of you, folks, because you must decide if he willfully participated in these homicides - I'll say it again - willfully - because that's the primary requirement of conviction. I remind you again that you must acquit Seth if you have the slightest doubt of his guilt.

"I will prove to you that something happened out on that farm last summer that perhaps no one will ever understand. Remember last summer? Lord, it was hot. The hottest summer in Attica's history. One hundred degrees or higher for twenty-nine consecutive days. Five elderly folks died. Crops burned. Livestock died. Ponds dried up. And on one of those sultry nights, blasted by wind and dust, Seth Cameron and the Linville Reeves family fell into a nightmare; a nightmare so hideous and beyond the realm of logic that you may find yourself looking over your own shoulders. He's going to tell you the same story you read in the papers, because that is what happened, folks. He will tell you about an aircraft landing out there, and its two occupants attacking him and the Reeves family. He will tell you of the unspeakable harvest that ensued. It happened, ladies and gentlemen, and I want you to think about something while you consider this mystery: But for the grace of God, it might have happened to you.

"All I ask is that you open your minds, as Reed Aaron and I have. Give careful consideration to the possibility that something extraordinary happened out in that dusty wheat field that's been covered up in a conspiracy perpetrated by your own government. It turned Seth Cameron's life into a living hell in which we all now reside. Yes, Mary and little Lisa Reeves were brutally stabbed to death. And you know something? Seth may have stabbed them. But he was not in physical control of his mind or his body."

A rumbling of nervous voices rolled over the courtroom. "Quiet, please," Judge Falco said.

"The Prosecution wants to deny it," Payne said. "The Sheriff's Department does deny it. They want to believe there was no aircraft flying around our countryside that night. They want to believe the spate of cattle mutilations during that time is unrelated to the murders. Why? I've asked myself that question a thousand times since this happened. Why do they want to believe Seth did it? I know the answer: Fear. For one reason - or another - they're afraid of the truth.

"Ladies and gentlemen, some kind of aircraft landed out there. Some thing attacked the Reeves family and Seth Cameron. Some thing possessed Seth to grow uncharacteristically violent. Some thing - not Seth Cameron - in fact killed Linville Reeves. And when it was over, an agent for the Central Intelligence Bureau just happened to show up and commandeer the homicide investigation. Why did a government agency usurp the sheriff's authority? Why did the police officer that first arrived on the crime scene get pushed aside? What is the government trying to hide? I'll produce witnesses who will answer these questions. Somebody's covering up the truth, and I'm gonna prove it to you.

"Rely on your sense of reason, folks. Listen to the facts, and don't tell yourself some things are impossible until you ask yourself what might be possible. When you answer that question, remember that you can convict Seth Cameron of the charges only if you believe to a moral certainty he planned and executed the crimes; only if you have no reasonable doubt of his guilt. Thank you and good luck."

Payne returned to his seat and loitered for forty-nine seconds before approaching the dais. "The Defense calls Dr. Cindy Luciano."

A smartly dressed woman in her late twenties confidently walked to the stand and was sworn in. She ignited a fire two feet in front of her. Her skin was olive and her hair reddish brown; her business suit conservatively kept the wolves' eyes in check. Like everyone else, Payne's smile hypnotized her.

"Good morning, Dr. Luciano."

"Hello."

"What is your profession?"

She coughed into her small fist and began. "I'm a Doctor of Veterinary Medicine - I own a clinic in Harrisburg - and I also do volunteer work for the Humane Society."

"Are you familiar with the case of a dead sow found on the Reeves farm last summer?"

"Yes. The Humane Society is concerned with all of the animal mutilation incidents in this region."

"All of them? How many cases have you investigated?"

"This year, there were five that we know of in this state."

"How many were reported in the vicinity of Attica?"

"Four, all around the same time last summer."

"Do these incidents include the Reeves farm?"

"Yes."

"Where were the others?"

"We investigated the mutilation of a bull in Rockford."

"What case was that?"

"The Clyde Majors farm. And three weeks prior to Majors, we checked out the mutilation of a horse and two calves on a farm sixty miles south of here. A week after the Reeves incident, we investigated the mutilation of a bull elk, also near Rockford."

"Let's begin with the bull on the Majors farm."

"Your Honor," Whittaker said. "Objection - irrelevant."

"Foundational, Your Honor," Payne said. "The Majors

incident and CIB-investigated cattle mutilations in this state are a matter of record in this trial."

"Continue, Mr. Payne," Judge Falco said. "Hush, Mr. Whittaker."

"Tell me about the Majors bull, Dr. Luciano," Payne said.

Cindy's eyes flared. It was a sign only her boyfriend could recognize as a signal that she was about to explode with rapid-fire dialogue. "When the story hit the news, I went to Rockford and contacted Mr. Majors. We investigate this kind of thing with an interest in how an animal died. We look for signs of negligence or cruelty. You'd be surprised how many people beat an animal for no reason."

"Did Mr. Majors cooperate?"

"Oh, yes," she said with a pretty laugh. "He loved to talk. In fact, he told us the story he told the papers about a large aircraft with a bright light hovering over his farm the previous night. He waited until dawn, and then went out to look around. That's when he found the bull."

"Did you examine the animal?"

"Yes. In fact, Mr. Majors consented to our taking it back to Harrisburg for a thorough examination."

"What was the bull's condition?"

"It was a pretty strange sight. One side of its facial area was cleanly removed, as well as its eye, ear and brain. The other side of the face was untouched. It had a large incision from its throat to mid torso, and its stomach and heart were removed. Its anus and testicles were also gone."

"You use the word 'incision,' Dr. Luciano?"

"Yes. That carcass looked as if a skilled surgeon had operated with precise instruments - possibly a laser. The organs were cleanly incised, and the carcass didn't have an ounce of blood in it. In fact, we didn't find a trace of blood anywhere. The ground around the carcass was dry and dusty without any discoloration. A bull has a lot of blood in its body, but we didn't find a trace."

"Based on your expertise, how was this done, if you know?"

Cindy smiled and tried to keep from laughing. "Sorry, but

I have absolutely no idea how the animal could have such precise incisions like that, and less idea where the blood went. But this isn't the first time I've seen something like this."

"When have you seen it before?"

"I mentioned the other farm where the horse and two calves were found? They were dissected the same way."

"Doctor, are you familiar with the term 'predator,' in the context of the animal world?"

"Yes."

"Based on your knowledge, is it your opinion the bull was attacked by a predator?"

"No. A predatory animal rips and tears a carcass. I saw incisions, Mr. Payne. That bull was definitely not attacked by a predator."

"What was the condition of the bull's legs?"

"There was no damage."

"Did you inspect the legs for broken bones?"

"We x-rayed the entire carcass. His legs weren't damaged."

"I see." Payne strolled away from the dais and looked at the jurors. "Doctor, in the course of your investigation of the Majors incident, did you find anything else unusual in the vicinity of the bull's carcass?"

"Yes. I saw a large area of burned grass and weeds about fifty yards away. It was burned in a perfect circle."

"Why do you consider this unusual?"

"I've seen circular patches of burned ground on other cattle mutilation sites. In fact, I saw a patch of burned ground on the farm where we investigated the dead horse and calves."

"Did you ask Mr. Majors if he knew how the ground got burned?"

"Yes."

"Objection," Whittaker said, "hearsay."

"Overruled," Falco said. "Let's hear the next question."

Payne smiled at Whittaker. "Based on Mr. Majors' answer, what did you conclude?"

Cindy furrowed her brow as if to say, 'Why don't you lawyers ever ask a straight question?' "I concluded that he didn't know."

Payne walked to the evidence table and picked up the prosecution photo of Mary Reeves' body. He handed the picture to Cindy. "Look at the background of the photo, Doctor. Does that brown area in the distance look like what you saw on the other farms?"

She grimaced and tried to block out the body. "Yes. There's a burned area like the others I've seen." She shoved the photo back to Payne.

"Okay, Doctor." Payne waved the photo at the jury before he put it back on the table. "What did you do with the bull's carcass?"

"It was confiscated."

Payne stopped and turned hard. "What do you mean, confiscated?"

"A man claiming he was with the government came to the clinic in Harrisburg where we examined the bull, and he took it."

"Do you remember his name?"

"Jonathan Carswall."

"Do you know Jonathan Carswall?"

"Oh, boy, do I."

"Did he explain why he wanted the bull?"

"He didn't explain, and he didn't ask. He demanded. The other animals were also confiscated."

"What others?"

"Remember the horse and the calves I mentioned? That event happened several miles from the owner's farmhouse. That farmer had no idea what happened, and he hadn't seen or heard anything unusual the night before. He called the sheriff, who called a local veterinarian. The vet notified us because of the nature of the animals' deaths. In this particular case, we were confronted by Mr. Carswall and his people right out there on the farm."

"He showed up out there?" Payne looked at the jury.

"Yes, and he threatened to arrest us if we didn't leave."

"What did you do to twiddle his crank?"

"He . . ." Cindy paused and tried to cut off a laugh. "He

accused us of interfering with a federal investigation."

"Did you ask the nature of his investigation?"

"They escorted us away before he was kind enough to explain. He also said it wasn't a good idea for us to snoop around any more cattle mutilation incidents."

"Doctor, did Special Agent Carswall threaten you or any of your team?"

"I can't say it was a threat, but he and his goons gave me the impression my medical license might not be worth much if I didn't shut up."

"Objection," Whittaker called. "This is highly prejudicial. The witness testified she wasn't threatened - her personal inference is unfair and inadmissible."

"Sustained," Judge Falco said. "Dr. Luciano's last answer is stricken, and the jury will disregard."

"Okay," Payne said, "let's go back to the incident on the Reeves farm. You said you investigated the reported mutilation of the sow?"

"We were way behind in that race, but the Humane Society director did call the Attica police to ask for permission to inspect the animal. The sheriff referred us to Mr. Carswall. I, who am a glutton for abuse, contacted Mr. Carswall."

"Your Honor!" Whittaker protested.

Falco waved him off. "Dr. Luciano, the court would appreciate it if you simply answer Mr. Payne's questions without the side comments."

Dr. Luciano shrugged. "I thought I did."

Payne jumped in. "Doctor, based on Mr. Carswall's response to your telephone inquiry, what did you do?"

"What did I do? I decided I'd be smart to mind my own business, and I told him I am not a bitch. Being a veterinarian, I didn't appreciate that . . ."

A few people in the gallery chuckled.

"Dr. Luciano," Falco said, "I'll say again, please just answer the questions."

Payne let the gallery settle. "Doctor, you testified that you also investigated the death of an elk?"

"Yes, a bull elk found by hunters at Echo Lake near

Rockford. It was also taken by Mr. Carswall before we could investigate."

"Did you obtain any information regarding either the Reeves sow or the elk?"

"No. In fact, Mr. Carswall denied they existed."

"Pardon me?"

"He said the report of a mutilated animal on the Reeves farm was false. And, even though the State Patrol confirmed a bull elk was slit open and its insides were gone, they told us - holy cow - we had to call Jonathan Carswall to get more information."

"The State Patrol filed a report about the dead elk?"

"They probably don't exist anymore, either."

"Doctor," Judge Falco interrupted. "This is my last warning. If you continue to make these unnecessary comments, I'll be forced to find you in contempt. The last comment is stricken, and the jury will disregard."

"Sorry," Dr. Luciano grumbled. "Okay, yes, the State Patrol filed a report."

Payne smiled at her. "Dr. Luciano, is it your testimony that Mr. Carswall told you there was no dead sow found on the Reeves farm?"

"Yes."

"Thank you. No more questions." Payne walked back to the defense table.

"Great lead-off," Aaron whispered.

"Falco's ready to eat somebody, and look who's stepping to the table." Payne watched Whittaker slowly move to the dais. "I just hope you're right about how Whittaker will handle this."

"Trust me, Marcus," Aaron said with a grin. "He's a classic barefoot-and-pregnant chauvinist."

Roland Whittaker hitched his pants for no reason. "Dr. Luciano. You're a vet, yes?"

"I'm a Doctor of Veterinary Medicine."

"Small animals? Large animals?"

"I treat companion animals at my clinic."

"Kitties? Puppies? Little parakeets? You don't treat horses, cattle, elephants, or anything like that, do you?"

"I rode an elephant at the circus once," Cindy said. The snickers broke at the bang of Judge Falco's gavel, and Cindy continued. "Yes, my practice is limited to small animals . . ."

"You testified that you examined these large animals - a horse, calves, a bull. You spay kittens, but you claim an expertise in surgery on a bull. That confuses me, Dr. Luciano, I - "

"I'm sorry you're confused. Maybe you should lie down."

"Dr. Luciano," Judge Falco said.

Cindy snapped a glare at Falco. "He said he was confused, Your Honor. That wasn't a question."

"Let the prosecutor finish," Falco said.

Whittaker looked like an aristocrat confronting a bowling alley waitress. "Dr. Luciano, my question is this: How does a vet, who treats only small animals, have the proper expertise to testify that this bull had so-called surgery performed on it?"

"Like this: I'm a doctor who treats small animals, and I'm experienced enough to testify that the bull had surgery performed on it. Still confused?"

"Dr. Luciano," Judge Falco said, "do you understand what contempt of court means?"

"Yes, I do. I don't have any contempt for the court, but he's showing contempt for my professional skills. Don't I have the right to defend myself?"

"Doctor," Falco said with a frustrated sigh. "You're not on trial, here. Please, I don't want to cite you, but I'm ordering you to give a simple answer to Mr. Whittaker's questions."

"I did, Your Honor . . ."

"Your Honor," Whittaker interrupted, "may I make a point here? This is a murder trial." He turned to the jury for help. "We're trying the deaths of the Reeves family, not a pig!"

"Counsel is testifying, Your Honor," Payne objected.

"Ask your next question, Counsel," Falco snapped.

Whittaker bristled. "This witness is testifying about the death of a bull - an incident totally unrelated to this trial! Three people were murdered, and we're wasting the court's time talking about animals?"

Before Payne could object, Cindy jumped in. "Maybe you're forgetting something, Mr. Whittaker. You're an animal, too."

"That's enough!" Falco said. "Counsel, if you're just going to make a speech without any further questions, I suggest -"

"I have no questions for this witness." Whittaker waved Cindy off and stomped back to his seat.

"You're excused, Dr. Luciano," Falco gratefully barked.

Payne and Aaron chuckled with the gallery. Payne put his arm around Seth, who didn't have a clue what was going on...

* * *

Payne sat in a big overstuffed chair by Aaron's desk, giving up on a dry hamburger he'd picked up at the cafeteria. He gulped a lime soda and chewed on the ice as he reached for his favorite photograph. Lori Payne. She sat at the dinner table with her arm around Marc; she was about to kiss him.

"I'm trying, Lors," he whispered.

"What?" Aaron said, walking in unannounced.

"Dammit to hell!"

Aaron circled the desk and sat with a curious look on his face. "Sorry to sneak up on you. Who were you talking to?"

Payne sighed and flashed the photo at Reed. "Ghosts."

Aaron's stomach fluttered as Payne tucked the photo back in his pocket. He returned to the thought he'd brought in with him. "Uh, I'm glad you're sitting."

Payne stopped drinking and spat the ice back in his cup. "What?"

"Captain Mitchell just turned up."

"Good," Payne said. "I told you he would. Is he outside? I want to talk to him before he goes on." He blanched at Aaron's sad eyes. "What . . ."

"He's dead, Marc."

Payne could only throw an incredulous stare at Reed. "You can't tell me this. You goddam can't . . ."

"He was found floating in Ortin Creek up near Kington."

"That's a hundred miles from here."

"I just spoke with his wife. She called the Harrisburg cops yesterday after she couldn't reach him on his cell phone. She knew where he was hiding out, and they traced him to the Kington morgue. He's been there a week, tagged as a John Doe. Somebody found him dressed out in fishing gear, but no I.D. They figure he slipped, banged his head on a rock and drowned."

Payne pounded his cup on Aaron's desk and put a two-finger squeeze on his forehead. "God dammit, Reed. God dammit!" He closed his eyes and continued rubbing his head. "That son of a bitch was too smart to get killed. We're putting the kiss of death on everybody." Payne angrily looked at Aaron. "He cooperated because I put him in Carswall's crosshairs. He knew he was dead if he didn't get on the stand as soon as possible. Thanks to me - oh, god dammit . . ."

"Thanks to us, Marcus." Aaron was unconvincing.

Payne shook his head and slumped back, still remembering that honorable pilot chewing a big stogie and swilling whiskey in his mountain retreat.

Aaron took Payne's soft drink and dribbled some on his chin. "I wish Mitchell was all the bad news I got just now."

"You gotta be kidding."

"After hearing about Mitchell, I got a bad feeling about the others we've tangled in this web. I put in some calls to Rockford, just to reassure myself that we have any witnesses left." Aaron stopped and sighed.

"I don't know if I want to hear this," Payne said.

"Clyde Majors' neighbor, Edgar Bower - the guy who said he heard Clyde's UFO that night? He's not home."

"Not home?"

"Anymore."

"What the hell are you talking about?"

"His line is disconnected. I called the sheriff to find out if he knew anything. He says Edgar's house is empty - and I mean empty. No furniture. No farm vehicles. Nothing."

"The sheriff doesn't know where he went?"

Aaron shook his head. "Edgar was a widower just like

Clyde, and he doesn't have any family in town. He's just gone, Marc. Nobody knows where. So, I called Sam Lewis, the other neighbor who heard something that night. Guess what?"

"He's gone, too?"

"No. He's home, but his memory just failed. He said, 'I don't remember hearing nuttin' that night. You can go ahead and goddam put me on the stand, and I'll tell the goddam jury I didn't hear nuttin'. He also told me to go to hell if I want."

Payne angrily sighed. "I don't blame him. The message is clear."

"Yeah, when Carswall's the messenger."

"I'm concerned about the message he sent K.J. and Carly last night."

"Perhaps we should insist they let us put them in protective custody."

"I would, but K.J. won't have any part of it. He says they may have something big."

"Marcus, if we get them killed . . ."

"Don't say it. I hear it enough in my nightmares. But I'm inclined to let them go. They're experienced cops, and they know their trail is hot."

"But Captain Mitchell was a damn soldier, and they got him!"

"I know - I don't like it any more than you, but if Jackson and Carly are sniffing out a bomb, it may be Seth's only shot."

Aaron sighed in agreement. "Whatever happened to the good old days of chicken thieves and drunk drivers?"

"What good old days?" Payne said.

"I wish I could pack up and go buy a pig farm somewhere."

"You'd probably get a UFO in your back yard."

Reed checked his watch. "We have to go back to work. I guess the best we can do is push contempt this afternoon and make a big splash about Frank Mitchell."

"Push contempt? Big Brother, I think I've taught you too much."

Aaron nodded with a shrug. "You and my government..."

17

ayne opened the afternoon session by informing the jury of the death of his scheduled witness. He knocked the breath out of the court with carefully structured innuendo that skated lightly across the thin ice of contempt. Subsequently, D.A. Whittaker exploded and at one point had to be restrained. Judge Falco called a recess and hauled both attorneys over the carpet in her chambers.

The chambers session ended with obligatory threats aimed primarily at Payne. The judge then paneled each juror for reactions to Payne's antics. Falco reassembled everyone and tried to get the trial back on an even keel, deciding none of the jury members believed they had been biased in any way. Through all of the chaos, Reed Aaron tried to keep Seth Cameron focused. "Remember," Aaron said, "don't be surprised by anything Marc says or does."

Aaron then had to remind himself . . .

In all, Payne successfully disrupted two hours of court time and twisted the jurors' minds like rubber bands in the process. Several now looked as if they could snap any time.

Payne called Dr. Sydney Skelton to the stand. Dr. Skelton was a gentle, gray-haired black man who smelled of a smooth pipe tobacco. His wiry body athletically glided to the stand with the vigor of someone half his age. He draped his right leg over his left while identifying himself as a neurologist and member of the Board of Regents at Hilliard Paul University School of Medicine in Harrisburg.

Payne smiled and produced a magazine clipping. "Dr. Skelton, I'm reading an article from the National Journal of Medicine: 'Dr. Sydney Skelton was this year's recipient of the

Edgar Scythe Award for his tireless work and accomplish-ments in neurological laser microsurgery and research devel-opment in the treatment of brain diseases and disorders.' Doctor Skelton, you are the same Sydney Skelton to whom this article refers, correct?"

"Yes."

"Would you please tell us a little more about your qualifi-cations and experience?"

"Of course," Skelton said. "I hold a medical degree from Hilliard Paul University, where I also received my neurologi-cal training. Over my thirty-year career, I've consulted at more than two hundred hospitals worldwide, and I've pub-lished over three thousand articles. I'm Chief of Staff at the St. Anthony's Hospital Department of Neurology in Harrisburg, which, if you'll excuse my bias, has the finest resident teach-ing program in the world."

"Your Honor," Whittaker interrupted, "for the sake of time, the People stipulate to the credentials of the witness."

"Mr. Payne?" Falco said.

"Very well," Payne said. "Dr. Skelton, is it safe to call you an expert in neurology and the broad field of brain function disorders?"

"Very safe," Skelton said with a confident smile.

"Sir, did you examine Mr. Cameron three months ago?"

"I did."

"Doctor, we've been talking ourselves stupid the last few days about Seth Cameron. The court has heard theories about Seth's psychological makeup and how it might relate to his motive for murder. Are you aware of his sudden, unexpected violent attacks on the sheriff last summer?"

"Yes."

"Did your examination differ from a psychiatrist's?"

"Yes, my examination of Mr. Cameron was neurological rather than psychiatric."

"To quickly move to the point, Doctor, might Seth's unprovoked violent behavior of this degree and haste suggest the possibility of other causes besides mental illness?"

"Yes, I would consider other possibilities based upon my

examination of Mr. Cameron."

"Before we get to that, give us some insight on your research into brain disorders as they relate to violent behavior."

"The reasons for violent behavior of this nature - explosive, uncharacteristic, sudden - are very elusive. Exploring a patient's psychological history, his childhood, his emotional constitution and so on is, of course, a logical diagnostic course for a psychiatrist. If the patient displayed a propensity for such behavior over a long period of time, this may very well be the best approach to a diagnosis. However, the appearance of sudden, brutal behavior in someone without a history of violence is not necessarily consistent with mental disease in my opinion."

"Okay, Doc," Payne said with a friendly scold, "you have a rich and impressive medical vocabulary, but you're losing me."

"Nature of the beast," Skelton said apologetically. "I'll stop talking like I'm addressing a medical convention. Simply stated, my course of examination is intended to explore the possibility of violent behavior that's caused by a physiologic, rather than psychological deviation."

Payne raised his hand. "So, you would look for a physical abnormality in the brain?"

"Yes. I don't rule out the patient's mental history, but sometimes a sudden violent shift in personality may be symptomatic of a brain injury or disease. This is not to say that every barroom brawl or unexpected punch in the nose is symptomatic of a mental disease or a neurological anomaly. I'm talking about random and unprovoked violence by someone who has displayed no previous disposition to such behavior."

"How would you characterize a person who snaps and commits a violent act?"

"Yes, some people certainly do 'snap,' as you say, but a psychological breakdown usually follows a history of emotional stress that deteriorates to this unfortunate resolution."

"What about someone who experienced abuse as a child?"

"A person may be aggressive because he has been exposed to violence all his life, but you shouldn't assume this as true in all cases. There are violent people who don't fall in the category of mental deviation or learned response."

"Doctor, I'm intrigued by your work in neurological disorders; would you tell us a little more?"

"Certainly," Skelton said. He was happy to talk about himself anywhere, anytime. "I've devoted most of my career to researching behavioral patterns in relation to pathologically altered states of the brain. I've studied many prison inmates with a predisposition to violence, and inmates who are diagnosed criminally insane. I'm particularly interested in the connection between their behavior and the physical condition of their brains."

"What exactly is the nature of this electric shock therapy we hear about?"

"Irrelevant," Whittaker objected.

"Foundational, Your Honor," Payne calmly said.

"Overruled," said Judge Falco.

"Again, Doctor," Payne said, "electric shock therapy?"

"The clinical term for it is Electroconvulsive Therapy, or ECT; it's been used for years in the psychiatric community, primarily for the treatment of severe depression. Its common - and I'd say more accurate term - is 'shock therapy,' which involves the administration of drugs and electricity to induce coma or seizures."

"Is it an accepted practice?"

"No, it's not standard by any means. It's used when a depressed patient doesn't respond to any other treatment - a last resort, if you will. ECT involves the passage of one hundred and fifty volts of DC current by two electrodes placed between the patient's temples. It causes loss of consciousness and convulsions, and is administered on a regular schedule for up to a month or so. It's prohibitively effective in reducing symptoms of what is called 'involutional melancholia' in some patients who haven't responded to drugs or psychotherapy. The treatment isn't widely used anymore due to advances in the development of antipsychotic drugs, and because of isolated abuse in mental hospitals."

"Abuse? Please explain."

"I've seen incidents where poorly trained or misguided mental hospital employees administered ECT as punishment or control of unruly patients."

"What about side effects to this treatment?"

"The resulting convulsions can cause injuries like bone fractures, broken teeth, dislocated shoulders - and ECT can induce cardiac arrhythmia and cause memory loss or intellectual impairment."

"You say the treatment is used on sufferers of depression; what about its use on volatile and aggressive patients?"

"That would make a bad idea worse, in my opinion. ECT is even more unstable as a treatment for anxiety, because of the adverse side effects."

"So, would a patient in a severe state of anxiety be put at risk if his brain was electrically stimulated?"

"Personally, I disapprove of the treatment under any circumstances. Passing electrical current through the brain is dangerous, even under strict clinical control. Administering ECT to a patient suffering from anxiety is like throwing gas on a fire."

"Doctor, are you saying then that passing electrical current to the brain could stimulate an aggressive, violent reaction from someone who is already emotionally agitated?"

"It could. It's my opinion that ECT's unpredictability produces more problems than it solves."

"How can electricity stimulate violent emotions, Doctor?"

"By disrupting what you might call the natural circuitry of the nervous system."

"Would you explain what you mean by 'natural circuitry?'"

"There's an electrical-chemical message process that takes place in the nervous system. You might say the brain is like a computer, but not like your PC at home, which employs the movement of electrons through metal conductors and semiconductors. The nervous system functions more efficiently by the movement of ions in a liquid environment. The brain's primary nerve cells, called 'neurons,' are in charge of all the central nervous system's characteristic action. These cells conduct nerve messages, receive sensory input, and dictate behavioral responses. An emotion is a reaction to a corresponding stimulus, and by that definition, anger is really no different from the emotions of elation, love, fear, lust and so on. Each individual's learned experience determines how he will respond to a stimulus - in the case of an anger response, that stimulus may be some type of provocation."

"Can you give us an example?"

"Oh, let's say you call me a pompous intellectual."

"Dr. Skelton, you are a pompous intellectual!"

Skelton smiled with the jurors. "Your provocation injures my pompous ego, and an impulse fires to the area of my brain that stimulates anger. Other neuron responses make my heart rate jump and my blood pressure rise. Adrenaline is released, and I'm now prepared for some type of confrontation."

"I didn't realize insulting you could be so complicated," Payne said.

"Mind you, this takes place in mere seconds. Now, I am angry, and I make a cognitive decision how to respond. I was raised not to react violently, but perhaps in the heat of the moment my ego pushes me to pop you on the nose. I would more than likely then regret my action. However, I would probably control my temper and simply say, 'Mr. Payne, I may be pompous, but lawyers are so far beneath my intellectual strata that I consider your childish provocation an indication of your net ignorance.'"

Payne stepped back. "I think I'd prefer a punch in the nose."

"We are role playing with great exaggeration, of course," Dr. Skelton chuckled. "If I did throw a harmless punch and then suffer embarrassment for losing my cool, my response is uncharacteristic but not completely beyond reason. But if I pulled a gun and shot you six times, this is a major deviation from my historical behavioral pattern. I should react according to my learned values, providing my brain is functioning normally."

"And so, Doctor, a sudden, uncharacteristic violent act might be due to a problem with the brain itself, correct?"

"Yes, that is possible."

"How does this work?"

"Well, for example, a physical malfunction in the temporal lobe of the brain may induce psychomotor epilepsy, causing impedance of conscious thought and the ability to rationalize and decipher consequences. My research has followed the pathologic routes of criminal violence compared to functions of the healthy mind. In test studies of prison inmates, a violent criminal's history can sometimes be traced to abnormal brain function instead of an environment that failed to teach him right from wrong."

Payne wandered the witness stand. "Let's go back to an earlier point - the physics of the nervous system's electrical conductivity. How could you electrically induce a physical response?"

"The concept is relatively simple. An electrical impulse is generated to stimulate a nerve center by electrodes implanted in the brain. Conversely, aggressive seizures might be prevented with electrical stimuli to specific nerve centers of the brain."

"Didn't you say ECT is not recommended for violent subjects?"

"Yes, but my example isn't ECT. This illustration supposes the application of extremely low-voltage stimuli that will not produce a seizure."

"Electrodes. Stimuli." Payne helplessly shrugged. "You make it sound like we're all wired for sound. Explain how this works, and remember, I'm just a lawyer, so try to keep it simple."

"Let's go back to considering the brain a sophisticated computer processor. Similar to electronic signals transmitting through a PC, you have electrical signals transmitting in your body."

"I have electricity in me?"

"Not like the current you use to plug in your computer. I won't bore everyone with a physics lecture on the difference between electrons in a metallic conduit and ion movement through a liquid medium like the body, but I'll use the computer analogy to simplify. So, here we have this circuit board - the brain, pathways along which neurons receive and chemically process messages, and the spinal cord conduit through which the messages travel. If you strike your thumb with a hammer, neurotransmitters fire instantly along larger nerve fibers to a receiving neuron, and your thumb throbs. The same applies to other senses through neurotransmitters along various sized nerve fibers. Your empty stomach transmits a message of hunger; your dry mouth transmits the message of thirst; emotionally, you feel love, anger, fear, happiness, sexual arousal. Some responses are a result of outside provocation that stimulates the appropriate receiving neuron. Every motion, thought, and perception is a result of this electrical and chemical process."

"What about something involuntary, like my heartbeat?"

"The very same. Your brain is, to stay with the computer analogy, 'programmed' to maintain your heartbeat. My descriptions here are elementary for the benefit of explanation. The brain is complex. Fully understanding itself is an ongoing pursuit."

Payne stopped and rubbed his chin. "Interesting way of putting it, Doc. So let me try to at least understand one point. Could an electrical impulse cause me to react irrationally violent?"

"I couldn't just 'push a button' to induce a violent reaction, but a rogue electrical impulse in the temporal lobe could, theoretically, induce aggression."

"What if I were confused - perhaps frightened or drunk? If an outside electrical transmission 'scrambled my circuits' and induced this message of anger, would I be more likely to respond violently, if you know?"

"Yes, that leads us back to electroconvulsive therapy and why the treatment is not effective in patients suffering from anxiety. It's obvious to say electricity can be lethal - we all know that - but there's a scientific reason to explain it. The simple version is this: The body is a poor conductor. Just think of a time when you've felt a minor electrical shock - perhaps just a harmless static shock when you touched a light switch. You feel a burning sensation, and your entire body feels an uneasy and painful disruption. Electricity disrupts the nervous system, even in non-lethal doses."

Payne nodded. "You are an expert in microsurgery, correct?"

"Yes."

"Could some kind of wireless electrode be implanted in the brain - a mechanism that might stimulate nerve centers by means of a remote transmitter?"

"In theory, yes, but no such device exists to my knowledge."

"If there was such a device, however, do you possess the technology and surgical skill to implant it?"

"Yes, implanting a device you describe is possible, but the neurological and psychological complications are numerous."

"What are they?"

"Well," Dr. Skelton said with a challenged sigh, "let's say, hypothetically, I implant a microreceiver in a violent patient's brain in order to block or intercept an impulse that triggers aggression. The device would have to be precisely placed, for one thing. For another, it would have to be driven by a computer with the capability to decipher which nerves to stimulate and when. Because it was receiving transmissions from a remote source, other impulses might interfere, resulting in hundreds of dire consequences."

"In other words, this technology might make the patient react in a number of ways you could not predict?"

"Indeed. It could be fatal."

"Your Honor," Whittaker said. "This science lesson is fascinating - truly fascinating. What's the point?"

"I assume you are heading somewhere with this witness, Mr. Payne," Judge Falco said.

"Just pulling into the garage right now, Your Honor," Payne said.

Falco simply gestured for Payne to continue.

"Dr. Skelton, you conducted a neurological evaluation of

Seth Cameron with prosecution representatives present, correct?"

"Yes."

"Would you describe your findings?"

"Yes. It was a rather startling examination. Mr. Cameron
told me the details of his experience the night of the murders.
I was skeptical but interested in a claim he made regarding a
reference he made to something, as he put it, 'shot into my
head.' I conducted a neurological examination, with x-rays
and CT scan. We have a state-of-the-art computer imaging
process at St. Anthony's Hospital, which enhances CT scan
imaging. It literally slices layers of the brain, and gives us a
color pixelated view of microscopic tissue. I discovered an
anomaly deep in Mr. Cameron's temporal lobe - toward the
back near the cerebellum - the region of the brain that controls
motor function."

"Describe what you mean by 'anomaly.'"

"An irregularity. It is a tiny spot, solid, and very unnatural."

"Could it be a tumor?"

"No. It's inconsistent with a tumor. As I said, it is solid and
more consistent with a foreign object of some kind."

"Are you saying it's something that penetrated his brain?"

"I'm saying it is possible. There was microscopic evidence
of a tissue disturbance path which concerned me."

"A path?"

"Yes, it appeared like a path - just like a bullet would leave
a path. It was microscopic, but any lesion in the brain, large or
tiny, warrants concern about permanent damage."

"Could permanent damage - this lesion you mention in
Seth Cameron's temporal lobe - be considered a possible reason for his uncharacteristic violent behavior after the Reeves
murders?"

"It's hard to diagnose or predict the results of brain damage, but I would begin at that lesion, if I were conducting a
thorough case study."

"One last question, Doctor. Based upon your expertise
and your neurological examination of Seth Cameron, is it

your opinion that a foreign object passed into his brain?"

"I can only testify that there is an object present, but I can't say conclusively what it is or how it got there without extracting the brain and examining the tissue."

"Thank you. I have no more questions."

Whittaker jumped to the dais, clutching his notes. "Doctor, am I to understand the defendant has a foreign object in his head?"

"It appears so."

"You say you found a 'spot.' And you speculate that it is responsible for the defendant murdering three people?"

"This misstates the testimony, Your Honor," Payne objected.

"Sustained."

Whittaker nervously tapped the dais. "Doctor, since you offer speculation that this spot could be something shot into the defendant's head, do you concede this 'anomaly' could be just one of many possibilities? Maybe a mole? Maybe a natural imperfection? Maybe your computer has a glitch in it?"

"All of your examples were considered and scientifically ruled out."

"But to be certain this is a solid foreign object, you should remove it and have a look before you testify to what it is, don't you think?"

"Removing it is impossible. As I said, the brain must be extracted to do that."

"Then your little spot will remain the subject of speculation, correct, Doctor?"

"Yes."

"Doctor, how many times did you examine the defendant?"

"Just the one time."

"No follow-up? No further examinations into this mysterious spot?"

"No."

"Did you examine the defendant for the purpose of treating him?"

"No."

"Did you examine him just for the purpose of giving this testimony for the defense?"

"I examined him at Mr. Payne's request."

"Did he pay you for this examination?"

"I was compensated for my time, and the hospital tests were billed to the Public Defender's Office."

"How much were you paid to come here to testify?"

"Irrelevant," Aaron said.

"Sustained."

"Were you paid to come to Attica and testify, Dr. Skelton?"

"My expenses were covered, Mr. Whittaker."

"You were employed, in other words."

"Argumentative," Payne called.

"Sustained."

"No more questions."

Doctor Skelton was dismissed, and Payne quickly moved to the dais. "The Defense calls Officer Ken Jackson."

Jackson lingered by the back door. Carly stood by a side window. Her job was to keep her eyes glued on the gallery, but she couldn't help glancing at Jackson, who walked to the stand and swore in.

Payne fooled around with his papers while the jury had a chance to size up the witness. Jackson's physical presence and outward confidence were formidable components to his reliability as a witness, and Payne wanted those ingredients to spice the stew for a minute. Payne, Aaron, and Jackson had orchestrated and rehearsed this important moment to perfection. Payne planned a hot introduction to his star witness, Seth Cameron, by twisting the jurors' minds around the highly credible Jackson. Payne's earlier escapades chewed the clock perfectly, and the hour was late. With a few well-crafted questions, Payne planned to leave the jurors staring out their hotel windows all night.

Jackson looked over the courtroom. He saw familiar faces, but some didn't look as friendly as they used to. As always, Jonathan Carswall wasn't present.

"Good afternoon, Officer Jackson," Payne said. "How long have you been an officer for the Attica Sheriff's

Department?"

"Going on eleven years, sir."

"I refer to sheriff's department records, indicating you are a field training officer, is that correct?"

"Yes, sir. I've been an FTO for eight years now."

"Officer, during your distinguished career, ASD records show you received five official commendations for exemplary conduct and demeanor, and a Superior Tactics and Response award for safely ending a hostage-taking incident three years ago, in which you convinced a mentally disturbed, suicidal man to release his wife and young child and surrender himself, is this correct?"

"It is."

"You have also been named Attica Sheriff's Department Officer of the Year for the last four consecutive years, correct?"

"Yes, sir."

"Sir, on the morning in question, Sheriff White testified that you were present at the Attica courthouse when Rusty Wade brought Seth Cameron in, is that correct?"

"It is."

"Did you know Seth prior to that day?"

"Yes, sir."

"Wade claimed he found Seth wandering outside his tavern, incoherent and beaten. Is that your recollection of Seth's condition?"

"Yes, sir. I would add that Mr. Cameron was wearing pajamas that had what appeared to be bloodstains on them. He seemed to be in pain, so I pulled up his shirt and saw deep bruising around his ribs. I pointed this out to Sheriff White."

"Did Seth say anything?"

"He said, 'I ain't dead yet,' and 'we gotta stop them before they kill us all.'"

"They? Did he say who 'they' were?"

"No, sir."

"Did anyone else hear him say that?"

"Yes, Officer Jerry Monroe, Sheriff White, and someone I later learned was a federal agent named Carswall."

"Was that Agent Jonathan Carswall, from the Central

Intelligence Bureau?"

"Yes, sir, he was with Sheriff White that morning, and he stood by while we talked to Seth."

"Seth said he wasn't dead yet. What did you make of that?"

"At first I believe we all thought it might be related to a barroom brawl that broke out at Rusty's Tavern the night before, but Rusty Wade said Mr. Cameron hadn't been there – that he found him outside the bar that morning. Also, Mr. Cameron was wearing pajamas, which didn't make sense. So, Sheriff White asked Seth who hurt him, and Seth said it again: 'I ain't dead yet' – but he then said, 'Linville,' and he broke down and cried. That suddenly changed things."

"Did he say anything else?"

"I asked him what about Linville, and he then said 'they killed Momma.'"

"You knew who he referred to when he said Linville, correct?"

"Yes, sir. I knew Mr. Reeves – all three of us did – and we all knew Seth worked at the Reeves farm just a few miles from Rusty's Tavern."

"Officer Jackson, at any time in your presence that morning, did Seth Cameron say he killed anyone?"

"No, sir."

"Sheriff White testified that Seth attacked him. Did you witness this?"

"Yes, sir."

"Describe this attack."

"It came from nowhere. One moment, Mr. Cameron was docile and barely coherent, and then suddenly, he jumped at Sheriff White and tried to choke him out."

"What did you do?"

"Monroe and I tried to pull him off, but he knocked both of us back."

"Officer Jackson, earlier in this trial, I kidded you about your size, but now I must ask: My client is much smaller than you, and I assume in your job you've been in a few scrapes from time to time. Is it your testimony that Seth Cameron knocked you and another officer back?"

"He knocked Monroe to the floor, and he nearly knocked me out with a shot to my jaw. It's the hardest punch I've taken in my life."

"What happened then?"

"After the stars cleared from my head, I wobbled back with Monroe and tried to pull Seth off of Sheriff White. It took another three officers piling on before we managed to subdue and handcuff him."

"Have you ever been in an altercation with my client before this?"

"No, sir."

"Ever arrested him, or had any official contact with Seth?"

"Never arrested him, but I did drive him home to the Reeves farm one time when I found him walking alone on Highway 84."

"In an official capacity?"

"If you mean, was I on duty, yes."

"Do you often give civilians a ride home?"

"Yes, if it's in their best interest."

"It's alright, Officer Jackson. The obvious question – why did you determine giving him a ride home was in his best interest?"

"He appeared intoxicated. He wasn't driving, and I didn't consider him to be a danger to anyone but himself, so giving a citizen a short ride home is more in his best interest than locking him up."

"Is this policy?"

"It's a small town, Mr. Payne. You probably won't find it written down anywhere, but if a citizen's best interest is better served by driving him home safely rather than carting him off to jail, the Attica Sheriff's Department unwritten policy is to be a good neighbor."

"Has it ever been your experience that Seth Cameron displayed any violent behavior?"

"No, sir."

"Alright. So, on the morning Seth suddenly makes this uncharacteristic attack on Sheriff White, you detained and handcuffed him. What happened next?"

"He calmed down a bit, but he kept saying he couldn't help himself because 'they' were inside his head, and I recall him asking us to kill him before he killed somebody."

"Again, did he ever specify who 'they' were?"

"No, sir."

"What happened then?"

"Sheriff White ordered Officer Monroe to take Mr. Cameron to the hospital to get treatment for his wounds, and he told me to go to the Reeves farm to check on the welfare of Linville Reeves and his family."

"Were you the first officer to arrive at the Reeves crime scene?"

"Yes, sir."

"I'd like for you to tell the jury exactly what happened from the time you left the courthouse."

Jackson's voice was solid. "I drove out on County 84 to the farm. When I arrived, everything appeared to be very quiet, but I was suspicious that something was wrong."

"Because of what happened at the courthouse?"

"Of course, but also finding a quiet farm at harvest time is unusual."

"Describe the entire farm as you found it."

"I remember seeing hundreds of birds all over the place. It was strange - I've never seen anything like it."

"How so?"

"They were perched all over the place. They were in the trees, on the fences, on the roofs of the farmhouse and barn. When I got out of the car, they all at once took off in a frenzy. There was something else, too. The Reeves family had a big dog named Jake. I've been to the farm many times, and big Jake always came out to see who was stopping by."

"Did Jake come out to meet you?"

"He's gone, Mr. Payne. He's never turned up."

"Okay. What happened next?"

"I went to the farmhouse. Seth's pickup truck was parked in front. I knocked on the door a couple of times, but I got no answer. The door was unlocked, so I opened it and called out before I went in - I was an old friend of the Reeves family, and they would have known me. The house was empty."

"What did you find inside?"

"The electricity was out. All the clocks in the house were stopped at two-fourteen. The living room and kitchen were undisturbed. Linville and Mary's bed had a single sheet thrown to the floor, and the curtains were open. A guestroom was undisturbed, but Lisa Reeves' bedroom was just like the master - curtains open, sheet thrown back. After I was sure nobody was in the house, I went back outside."

"Everything, Officer Jackson," Payne said like a tour guide. "Remember everything you saw, and everything you thought."

"It was hot that morning. When I went back outside, I picked up a bad smell."

"What kind of smell?"

"There were two distinct odors. The first was a smell of something burnt. When I reached the corner, I found the electrical junction box melted to the side of the house."

"Melted?"

"I'm surprised it didn't set the place on fire."

"Officer Jackson, the police report makes no mention of a melted junction box. Do you know why?"

"No," Jackson said. "A few days later I checked, and the box had been replaced. The side of the house was repainted."

"Are you aware of any official acknowledgement or explanation of this box?"

"No, sir."

"What did you do next?"

"I investigated the other odor. It's a smell cops know the minute they pick it up - death. There's no other smell like it. I also remember hundreds of flies buzzing around. I looked over the grounds and followed the buzzing, figuring I'd find where the smell came from. I walked out to the barn, and I opened the doors."

Payne allowed the proper silence. "What was in the barn?"

"I found a dead horse."

"Officer Jackson, there is no mention of a dead horse in the police report. Are you certain this is what you saw?"

"There was a dead horse in the barn."

"Describe it."

Jackson looked directly at the jurors. "It was cut open from its throat to its gut. Its internal organs were gone. I saw no blood in or around the carcass."

"What did you do then?"

"I walked outside. The first thought that went through my mind was the bull mutilation in Rockford the week before. I walked about thirty yards to the chicken houses and checked them. Because the electricity was out, the fans inside weren't working. Nearly every chicken was either dead or near death from the heat, but I found three chickens on the floor that were dissected like the horse in the barn."

"Officer Jackson, again, the police report doesn't include this information. I must ask if you are certain you saw the dissected chickens you described?"

"I am absolutely certain."

"What did you do next?"

"I continued to scan the area, and my attention was drawn to some buzzards in the pig pens. There was a dead sow lying there with wounds like the other dissected animals had."

"The police report states that only this one dead animal was found. Do you disagree with the report, Officer Jackson?"

"Yes, sir. The police report is incorrect," Jackson said.

Every member of the jury panel listened intently. They watched Jackson from a gray mist of confusion.

"Please describe the condition of this dead sow," Payne said.

"I could see from my vantage point that it was dissected similarly as the other animals I observed. The body cavity was open and empty, and much of the skin was peeled away from its face. I saw no blood on or around the animal."

"What did you do next?"

"I walked back in the direction of the farmhouse. There was a small cabin behind the house where Seth Cameron lived, so that seemed the next logical place to search."

Payne scanned the jurors. They looked helplessly lost. "Did you go there?"

Jackson unconsciously wiped his mouth. "No. I suddenly caught sight of more buzzards in a field beyond the cabin, maybe fifty to seventy-five yards away. I looked in the field, and I saw bodies."

"Did you approach them?"

"Yes."

"How many bodies did you find?"

"Three."

A few whispers sprinkled the courtroom. Payne looked at the perplexed jury. "At this point, Officer Jackson, I will ask you to offer a simple yes or no answer to my questions. Did you clearly see the bodies?"

"Yes."

"Did you see wounds on the bodies?"

"Yes."

"Mary Reeves' nude body was reportedly stabbed in the chest with a knife still protruding from her body. Did you recognize one body as that of Mary Reeves, and is this how you found her?"

"Yes."

"Lisa Reeves was reportedly nude and stabbed twenty-one times. Did you recognize one body as that of Lisa Reeves, and was it in this condition?"

"Yes."

"Is it your testimony that you found a third body in the field, at the same time you found the other two?"

"Yes."

Payne stalked Jackson, feeling the heat in the jury box. He waited briefly. "Did you recognize the third body?"

"Yes. I recognized it as the body of Linville Reeves."

"Quiet, please," Judge Falco had to order.

"Officer Jackson," Payne said, "the official police report states that the body of Linville Reeves was not discovered until later that night. Do you disagree with the report?"

"Yes, sir. The police report is incorrect."

"Okay," Payne said. "Linville Reeves was reportedly shot

by a single shotgun blast to the head. Was this the condition of the body as you saw it?"

"No."

"The Medical Examiner's autopsy report states Linville Reeves died from a single shotgun blast to the head. Do you disagree with this report?"

"Yes, sir. That was not the condition of Mr. Reeves' body."

"Officer Jackson, please tell the court the condition of his body, as you found it."

"Mr. Reeves was lying face-up, his body was nude. His testicles and penis were cut off and were not visible on or around the body."

The gallery erupted. "Order!" Judge Falco said. She gaveled twice to quell the noise. "If any spectator speaks again, I'll clear the courtroom!"

Jackson ignored the judge and continued. "There was no blood on or around the body. I saw a clean incision near his abdomen, and it ran to his throat, similar to the incision I saw on the horse in the barn. Because I'm no doctor, I can't identify what organs were removed from his body, but I clearly saw that the inside of his chest cavity was empty. Beginning at his eyebrows, an incision ran the circumference of his head. Both of his eyes were removed, and the top of his skull was cut off, but I did recognize him to be Linville Reeves. His brain was not visible to me in or around his body." Jackson abruptly stopped.

A cloud of gasps and sickened cries had peppered Jackson's description, but Judge Falco was too stunned to carry out her previous threat. Payne mercilessly allowed everyone to stew in the carnage for thirty-three seconds, and the room finally settled on its own.

Payne looked at the jury with an ashen face as if he might vomit any second. Many jurors passed ashen and had advanced to green. Payne turned back to Jackson and spoke. "When you took the stand, Officer Jackson, you swore to tell this court the truth under penalty of perjury, do you understand that?"

"I am fully aware of my legal responsibility to this court."

Payne breathed deeply with the jurors. At the defense table, Seth Cameron stared at his hands, begging himself not to cry. He knew he wasn't the smartest guy in the world, but he was smart enough to know Officer Jackson just slit his own throat for him. Reed Aaron's chin was propped in the webbing of his fingers. Not only was he amazed by how Jackson just leveled the place with unbelievable courage, he was also frightened by how Marcus almost crumbled.

"What did you do next?" Payne said, his voice gunning with power.

"I threw up," Jackson said. "I'm a cop, and I've seen some bad things on the job, but these people were my friends - very close friends. I got sick, but I recovered and tended to my duty. I ran back to the car to call for help."

"What happened next?"

"I started to call my dispatcher, but I was suddenly confronted by the man I saw at the courthouse earlier. I drew my weapon and ordered him to put his hands on the car. Three murders had been committed, and I had no intention of being the fourth. I searched him and found a semiautomatic weapon on him. He then identified himself as Agent Jonathan Carswall and produced a badge representing the Central Intelligence Bureau."

"Officer Jackson, were you in command of your senses at that moment?"

"Yes, sir. I was fully aware of the danger I might be in if the perpetrator was still there."

"Were you incoherent and incapable of telling Agent Carswall what happened?"

"No, sir."

"But you did testify that you got sick. Was there any time that you might not have had your wits about you?"

"No, sir. I got sick when I saw Linville Reeves's dissected corpse, but I'm trained to deal with my emotions, and I never 'lost my wits' - whatever the hell that means – and I strongly deny any accusation that I did."

A few jurors appeared sympathetic to Jackson's comment.

"Did Agent Carswall explain why he was there?"

"He asked me what happened, and I believe I said I had a butcher shop, or words to that effect. And then he asked me if this was another cattle mutilation."

"Cattle mutilation?" Payne said. "Had you mentioned the dead animals at that point?"

"No, sir."

"What was your response?"

"I told him that there were dead animals out there, but I then specifically told him that three people had been murdered. When I said that, he said he was commandeering the investigation. He ordered me to call for Sheriff White and the M.E. Then he waved to his car, which was at the farm entrance, and two more agents drove in and came out. They proceeded to the murder scene, carrying several large aluminum cases. I called my dispatcher."

"Officer Jackson, the murder scene was your responsibility. Did you question Agent Carswall's authority to commandeer the investigation?"

"Yes, sir. He said that the situation out there was, in his exact words, a matter of national security. He asked me to cooperate, as there was no time to explain."

"And you cooperated?" Payne said.

"Yes, sir."

"How long were these agents with the bodies before backup arrived?"

"Twenty minutes."

"During that time, did you join them?"

"I am sorry to say, no. Agent Carswall ordered me to guard the entrance to the farm."

"While you waited for help, did you see any activity around the farm?"

"I saw Carswall's two agents near the barn and the chicken houses. I assumed they found the animals. There was a lot of activity around the barn, but the open doors blocked my view."

"You say that help arrived in twenty minutes?"

"Yes. Another officer was first, followed by Sheriff White. Dr. Baker arrived several minutes later. Agent Carswall met

White and Baker out front. After a few words were exchanged, Sheriff White took orders from him."

"You say a few words were exchanged?"

"Agent Carswall continued to insist that he was in control of the investigation. He ordered Sheriff White to seal off the area, because he was concerned about the media. Then he took Sheriff White and Dr. Baker to the murder site."

"Did you go with them?"

"I was not allowed to go back."

"On whose authority?"

"Agent Carswall specifically ordered me to stay behind when he took Sheriff White and Dr. Baker to the bodies."

"Did you tell Sheriff White about what you found?"

"Not there, because I assumed Linville was still in the field. I met Sheriff White back in the courthouse later that day, and that's when I learned that Linville was supposedly missing. I told him what I saw. Agent Carswall then joined the meeting, and Sheriff White confronted him."

"What happened?"

"Agent Carswall insisted the body had not been found. He suggested I'd gotten too much sun and was hallucinating."

"Officer Jackson, when you are the first officer to discover a crime scene, are you required to file a report?"

"Yes."

"And are you usually called then to testify about your report, if that crime comes to trial?"

"Yes."

"Only one police report was submitted as evidence in this case, and it is signed by Sheriff White. Did you participate in writing this report?"

"No."

"Did you ever file a report?"

"No. Agent Carswall ordered me not to. He said he would do it."

"Did you press the issue of Linville Reeves then?"

"No. At that time I felt like I was being hung out to dry, so I backed off. Later, when the body turned up with a shotgun wound, I knew I was in trouble if I stuck to my story."

"What do you mean?"

"I received a phone call from Agent Carswall the night after Linville's body was supposedly discovered. From our conversation, I believed my life was in danger if I chose to pursue the matter."

"Is it your testimony that Jonathan Carswall threatened you?"

"Yes, sir."

"Officer Jackson, did you see the body of Linville Reeves in the Attica morgue?"

"I went to the morgue and Dr. Baker showed me a body that was tagged with the name 'Linville Reeves,' but it wasn't him."

"Officer Jackson, the body officially identified as Linville Reeves had no head. Can you offer any evidence to support your claim that the body wasn't Linville Reeves?"

"Yes, I can. I worked as a farm hand for Mr. Reeves when I was in high school. I saw him accidentally cut his left foot with an axe. He didn't have it stitched, and that deep wound left a large scar. I saw no scar on either foot of the body in the morgue."

"Objection - hearsay, speculative and assumes facts not in evidence," Whittaker said.

"Well," Judge Falco sighed, "I'll go with hearsay. Sustained."

Payne checked his watch. "I have no more questions for this witness, Your Honor."

Judge Falco nervously looked at Whittaker, who sat at his table like a statue. "Do you want to cross-examine, Counsel?"

Whittaker barely moved. He paused and drew a blank. "No questions, Your Honor . . ."

* * *

A stately brass clock on Roland Whittaker's desk read 12:49 a.m. The D.A. sat for two hours in the same spot without moving. On his desk was a picture of Anna Whittaker, Roland's deceased wife. She was three years older than him, and that always bothered her. The picture revealed a worn woman with a thin smile. Whittaker stared at her and shook his head. Next to Anna was a photo of Elizabeth Whittaker, his only daughter, decked out in her high school graduation cap and gown. She sported the same tired smile as her mother. Little Betsy, Whittaker thought. He hadn't heard from her in four years. Whittaker deposited two hundred thousand dollars in her bank account the day she left for college. That's all she would accept from him, she said, nothing more - I never want to see you again. She was probably due to graduate.

Over the last two hours, Whittaker thought about Betsy. He thought about the day she left. At eighteen, she showed more courage than he believed he could muster in a lifetime. She told him what he did to her ten years ago was wrong, and she hated him for it. She never told her mother what happened, but Whittaker secretly suspected Anna knew. He only did it one time, but once was enough. He stole his eight-year-old daughter's virginity to please his own dark urges, and indeed, Betsy would hate her father for the rest of her life. The money he gave her wasn't blackmail. In fact, he begged her to take it. He wanted to believe he gave back something to help her cope with the damage he did.

Whittaker breathed hard and rubbed his exhausted eyes. He'd prayed for years that the blackened guts of his life would never surface and keep him out of Congress. Everything was neatly tucked away - until now. He unfolded a small, handwritten letter and read it for the ninth time:

Dear Future Senator Whittaker,

It would be fatal to your proposed career if this video ever fell into the wrong hands. Protect it with your life, for my friends and I will gladly vote for you if you ever make the ballot. I have a copy. It's locked away, so don't worry. We want you to win. In fact, a little birdy tells me it's guaranteed, providing Seth Cameron doesn't survive his trial.

Lots of love . . .

The note wasn't signed, but Whittaker had an idea of who wrote it. His mind turned to a naked, hairless boy surrounded by steam.

Whittaker folded the note and put his cigarette lighter to it. It fell in the ashtray and died in flames. He opened his computer and hit the PLAY button. He'd watched the video three times, but for some reason, he wanted to watch again. The screen flickered without the sound on, and Whittaker watched himself lying naked and handcuffed to a tattered motel bed. Two naked eleven-year-old altar boys snuggled next to him, and they took turns giving him a great amount of pleasure. Surrounding the bed was a trio of men, all in their fifties. One was Herman H. Golding, a Harrisburg district judge and one-time vice presidential candidate. Golding wore a fluffy orange boa around his neck and was dressed in a bright red gown. His black stockings covered two stumpy, hairy legs. The judge was painted like a hooker, and he watched Whittaker and his boyfriends with a lipsticked smile while he urinated on one of the children.

The second man was Father Morris Cleaver, chaplain at Archbishop Lanning Elementary School in Harrisburg, who provided the altar boys. He wore black lace undies and a strapless bra, and he began to masturbate over Whittaker's face. A flowing black wig draped his shoulders. The third participant was a naked Senator Carl Donahue, who mounted the other little boy from behind.

Whittaker blankly watched the video and unzipped his pants . . .

18

Carly thumbed through her cell phone while sipping a cup of strong coffee. It was ten a.m., and the station was hopping, as usual. She impatiently flipped through the search pages, occasionally backing up and then going forward again.

Harrisburg mortuaries. Crane Lodge. There was no listing. She was absolutely sure of the name she saw on that memo, but no Crane Lodge Mortuary. New plan - she returned to the first listing, Atwood and Sons, and called, turning her head so she wouldn't be heard.

"Yes, I wonder if you can help me. I'm calling from out of town. My uncle just passed away in Harrisburg. I'm told he's at a mortuary called Crane Lodge, but I did a search and can't find it. Have you heard of it?" She listened to the terse reply and sighed. "Thank you."

She called the next name - same story, same reply. By the tenth call, she feared this was a dead end, so to speak. She decided to try just a few more.

An oily-voiced man perked to her question. "Oh, yes. Crane Lodge. That's not far from here."

"Yes?"

"It used to be Whispering Woods, but I heard they had tax problems and the government seized the property late last summer. The new mortuary is called Crane Lodge."

Bells went off in Carly's head. "Seized last summer, huh?"

"Yes. It's a lovely site - just across the street from Cherry Hill Cemetery."

"Lovely," Carly said, rolling her eyes at the icky voice on the other end of the line. "Do you know the address?"

"Yes, it's about twenty-fifth and Cherry Drive."

"Thank you."

"Please accept my condolences."

"What?"

"Your uncle."

"My uncle? Oh, yes - Uncle Fred. He's dead. Thank you."

"Should anyone else unfortunately pass, please keep us in mind."

"I'll do that." Carly clicked off and stared at her phone...

* * *

Court didn't start until three-thirty p.m. Juror number 3 awoke in the middle of the night with chest pains. A Southmore General Hospital ER doctor found out number 3 had eaten the hotel's famed spicy calzone and decided his stomach - not his heart - was complaining. The juror was discharged at noon, and he insisted he could put in some time today. Payne wasn't pleased, for he wanted the entire day to begin Seth Cameron's testimony. He didn't know if an hour with Seth would ensure weekend nightmares for the jury. D.A. Whittaker seized the opportunity and filed a series of empty motions through which Judge Falco had to sift, eating up all but an hour of solid jury time. It was Whittaker's first, albeit minor, victory. Stalling the jurors today hopefully diluted the poison of Jackson's testimony yesterday.

Seth sat aboard the witness stand like a sacrificial lamb on the block. From the moment Payne called him, the gallery rolled with quiet conversation. The jurors looked weary. Many dutifully turned the pages of their notebooks, while others simply watched the star of the show take his seat. Seth wore the same suit, but he had a nicer shirt and tie that Payne bought him last night. His hair was trimmed and slicked back, and his beard was neatly trimmed.

Payne's demeanor changed yet again. He was now like a mother bear protecting her cub. "Good afternoon, Seth," he said.

"Afternoon," Seth replied. He'd spent enough days here to be accustomed to the eyes that constantly held him.

"Well, Seth, we're finally here, aren't we?"

"Yes, sir." Seth nodded, remembering that Payne said to keep his head up and his eyes on him or the jury: 'Don't look at the judge, don't look at the prosecutor, don't look at the crowd. Look only at me or the jury, and look at them a lot.'

"We can't hear!" Roland Whittaker boomed.

Seth jumped slightly. As ordered, however, he kept his eyes on Payne.

Judge Falco glared at Whittaker and then turned to Seth. "Mr. Cameron, would you speak a little louder into the microphone?"

Payne winked and nodded. "Perhaps you might sit a little closer to it."

"Now we can't hear Mr. Payne!" Whittaker boomed.

"Oh, I'll fix that," Payne said, turning. He walked to Whittaker, leaned into the D.A.'s face, and hollered, "I told him not to worry, because the prosecutor's gonna try to upset him with cheap tricks like this!"

"Mr. Payne!" Judge Falco ordered.

"Can you hear me now?" Payne hollered again, still leaning into Whittaker.

Whittaker lurched back, stunned at Payne's 'stop fucking with me' glare. Whittaker could only look to Falco for help, but her shock was evident, too. Payne backed into the nervous titters of the crowd. He winked at Judge Falco and calmly returned to the dais.

If anyone in the jury was bored, they weren't now.

Falco swung her gavel like a saber. "Counsel, that was entirely inappropriate! If you think you can turn my courtroom into a nightclub, think again!"

"I'm testing the acoustics, Your Honor - the prosecutor is having trouble hearing."

"I will cite you, and by God put you in jail for another outburst like that!" Falco's disbelief at this goddam pirate dripped over the bench. "Do you understand me?"

Payne theatrically bowed to the judge, but he never apologized. He looked at Seth, who mentally searched his memorized list of Payne's orders and landed on: 'Don't be surprised by anything I say or do.' Payne smiled, and Seth faintly returned it. For some reason, he felt more at ease, for most of the gallery eyes were wide and glued to Payne.

Reed Aaron gritted his teeth and looked at Dan Williams in press row. Willy laughed into his hand and traded glances with his newspaper pals. He silently wished that Payne were a woman, because he was helplessly in love right now.

"All right, Seth," Payne said, "loud and clear so everybody can hear you. Right?"

Seth unconsciously put his mouth on the microphone and boomed, "Yes, sir."

Payne looked back at the disassembled Whittaker, as if to ask, 'Can you hear now, asshole?' Whittaker looked down and scribbled on his notepad. Payne turned back to Seth. "My questions are going to take some time to answer, Seth. You know how I like to show off, so if I talk too fast, or I say something you don't understand, be sure to ask me to repeat myself, okay?"

"Yes, sir."

"The first thing I want to ask is a pretty simple question. You've sworn to tell the truth, so let's cut right down to it. Seth Cameron, did you willfully plan, and under your own power and control, kill Mary, Lisa, and Linville Reeves?"

"No, sir, I didn't."

These were hardly explosive words like the kind Jackson used yesterday, but the gallery felt obligated to offer some whispers. The conversation faded before Judge Falco had to gavel.

"Seth, do you know how they died?"

"Yes, sir, I do."

Payne glided from the dais. "Your Honor, may I approach the witness from time to time?"

Judge Falco gave him a wary nod. "You may."

Payne drifted, folding his arms. "Let's take a little walk back, Seth. A day or two ago, you heard a doctor testify about a terrible incident that took place when you were a boy. Do you remember the murder of your mother?"

"I can't say I recollect it all - just bits of it."

"Do you hate your mother?"

"Momma? I couldn't hate her. Nowadays I understand what was goin' on back then."

"Do you ever feel anger for her?"

"No, sir. I loved Momma - still do."

"How about anger for the man who killed her?"

"Sure."

"Have you ever been so mad at her killer that you wanted to strike out at somebody - maybe get some revenge?"

Seth shrugged. "Ain't no point in that. He's been dead a long time. I figure God's gettin' all the revenge he needs done to him."

"Okay. Now I want to ask you about the Reeves murders. How long did you know Linville Reeves and his family?"

Seth wiped his nose. "Personal? Almost six years. Before that, I'd seen him enough around town to trade hellos."

"How did you get the job as his hired hand?"

"I was a mechanic at the filling station down by the inter-state. He come up one day when I was gassing his truck, and he asked if I knew anything about farming. I said I wasn't too smart about it, but I had a good back. So, he offered me a job."

"Did you enjoy working on the Reeves farm?"

"Yes, sir. Who wouldn't? It was the nicest spread in the county. I got my own little cabin, three meals a day, and I got some real good folks who treated me like I was somebody."

"Did you get along with them?"

"Yes, sir."

"What was it like living there?"

"We used to laugh and talk around the dinner table, and we'd watch TV or rent movies for nighttime. They got me interested in their church, and Linville took me to grange meetings so I could learn about the farm business. Me and Linville, we'd sit out on the front porch come summertime and tell jokes, or talk about the crops, or maybe just fun a bit about town gossip." Seth sadly looked down.

"So, for almost six years, you lived and worked with the Reeves family. Did you ever have arguments?"

Seth shrugged. "Little here and there, but nothing serious.

Now, Mary, she ain't never said a cross word in her life. She had a real good temperament. Only time she ever got cross was for my table manners, or when I tracked mud onto her clean floor and whatnot."

"Did you ever argue with Linville?"

"Well, if he was ever crossways with me, he let me know and I said 'yes, sir.' He was my boss, and I respected it. He wanted things done just right, and he wouldn't hesitate to say if you wasn't doing something his way." Seth's face grew a little red. "He didn't like me drinking, neither."

"Did you ever fight over your drinking?"

"Fight? Oh, no. We wasn't fightin' men. Linville didn't believe in putting a hand to nobody unless he was protecting him or his kin. I just got a lecture when I let the booze get the best of me. He'd say, 'Seth, God don't want you being a booze hound. Booze makes ya worthless, and you're a damn sight better than that.' Uh, sorry, I didn't mean to cuss."

Payne glared at Seth. Don't ever say you're sorry, his eyes said. "How did you and Lisa Reeves get along?"

"Lisa was one of them giggly little girls. She had a hard time because she lost her momma and daddy in a car wreck when she was a baby. One minute she was giggling, and the next, she'd get kinda owly and uppity with her grandparents. Me and Lisa wasn't too close, because she and her little friends liked to make fun of me. You know, they was just kids."

"Did you ever get mad at Lisa for teasing you?"

"Naw. I been teased by worse. She was just a little kid with sadness in her heart. I know all about being a little kid without no momma or daddy."

Payne nodded, not surprised this hardened little guy worked the jury well. "Seth, this is where it's going to get tough. I want you to take your time and start from the beginning of that terrible night last summer. To begin with, I wonder if you might explain something to the court."

"Yes, sir."

"When you were arrested, you told Sheriff White, 'I killed them.' Do you remember saying that?"

Seth sighed. "Some of it, Mr. Payne, but I was real messed

up and scared about what happened. I was tied down in that hospital bed, and everybody acted like I was three ways to crazy. They shot me with dope, and by the time Sheriff White came calling, I just said I done it because I didn't figure nobody'd believe me if I told the truth."

"Why did you attack him?"

"I swear to ya, I had no control over that. All of a sudden, I was on him, but I couldn't help myself. That's the God's honest truth, Mr. Payne."

"All right, Seth. The last few days, you've heard everybody else talk about what happened out there - "

"Officer Jackson told the truth, Mr. Payne," Seth interrupted.

"Objection," Whittaker called.

"Sustained," Falco said. "The answer is stricken and the jury will disregard the last comment. Mr. Cameron, please just answer the questions you are asked."

"I'm sor - " Seth cleared his throat. "Yes, ma'am."

"Okay, Seth," Payne said. "For now, let's just forget about what everyone else has said. I want you to start with what you and the Reeves family did that evening. Tell us everything that happened."

Seth leaned back and threaded his wrinkled fingers together. "Me and the folks had supper. Was about nine-thirty that we went in to watch TV."

"Did you work the farm that day?"

"Oh, yeah. We worked from sunup to sundown, all of us. We sat down for a half-hour of TV before bed, but everybody was nodding off before the first commercial. I said my goodnights and went out to my cabin to hit the sack."

"Did you drink any alcohol?"

"Yeah, I had a belt of whiskey. Working all them hours puts a lot of aches in a body. I just slugged one or two to get a jump on sleep. I wasn't drunked up by it, Mr. Payne. I had to be up with the sun the next morning to put in another day in that damn heat. Uh, I didn't mean to cuss."

"What happened next?"

"I was so spent that my lights was out as quick as my head

hit the pilla. Then, real late, old Jake wakes me up."

"Jake, the dog?"

"Yeah. I rolled over, figuring he cornered a skunk or something, but he just keeps barking. So, I got up and looked out the window. About then, I seen Linville looking out his bedroom window, and he tells Jake to shut up. But Jake just keeps barking."

"Do you know what time it was?"

"Yeah, I looked at my clock, and it was two straight up."

"What happened next?"

"I looked out, and I was squinting so I could see Jake. As mad as he was, I thought maybe something was after the chickens. Finally, I see old Jake out between the barn and the house. He's just sitting there, barking and staring at the sky. Next thing, out comes Linville in his shorts and undershirt. He comes up to Jake and crouches down next to him. Jake's still barking, and they both is looking up in the sky. I was curious as all get-out. Then, I suddenlike hear a strange noise up in the air."

"Describe the noise."

"It was kinda like a whistle at first. Then it gets louder. I tried to look up where Linville and Jake was looking, but I couldn't see from my window. Then, Linville jumps up and runs for the house like something was on his tail. In a minute, he comes back out with his twelve-gauge."

"His shotgun?"

"Yeah. Then he slumps back down near old Jake, and he starts looking at the sky again. I figure I better get out there. I was in my pajamas, but with Linville totin' that twelve-gauge, I lost track of my thinkin' and headed out there without putting my clothes on. I run out my door, and I done stopped in my tracks."

"What stopped you?"

"Fear for one thing. Fright for another."

The courtroom popped with chuckles.

"What scared you?"

"Up in the sky, there was this real bright light, and it was sweeping back and forth like it was looking for something."

"Was it a plane or a helicopter?"

"It wasn't no plane, because it was flying slow and making quick turns and stopping right in the air. And it was't no helicopter. Didn't have no blades chopping."

"What happened then?"

"That big light is still sweeping left and right. It lit up the fields like it was daylight. Then, real slow, this thing starts coming down, and my heart is beating like it was gonna bust. The thing makes this sudden screaming noise like its engines was slowing it down. That was enough for me, so I bolted over to Linville and Jake like a scalded chicken. By the time I got to them, they was running for the barn, so I went with 'em. We rounded the back, where we was outa sight of that thing, and we plastered ourselves against the side of the barn and peeked around the corner. Jake was growlin' like crazy."

"Where were Mary and Lisa?"

"They was at Linville and Mary's bedroom window. I was looking at them when, suddenlike, the fuse box on the house exploded. It blew, and all the lights went out."

"The box exploded?"

"Yeah, right when that big old thing was landing. Me and Linville's hair kinda frizzed up, and you could smell the 'lectricity."

"Smell electricity?"

"Yeah. You know, like when something sparks and you smell the air burn from the 'lectricity? That's what it smelled like. That fuse box went off like a bomb, spewing sparks and fire."

"What happened next?"

"Linville was all riled up, and he yells at Mary to lock the doors and call 911. But Mary yells back that the phone is dead. They didn't have no cell phone, so we was in big trouble. So he puts two shells in his twelve-gauge, and he looks at me square and he says, 'Seth, boy, you gotta jump in your truck and drive down to the neighbor's and call for the sheriff.'"

"Where was Linville's truck?"

"In town. His transmission was busted."

"What did you do?"

"I didn't wanna leave them there, but Linville, he yells at me to move and don't argue. So, I jump and run for my truck, and he goes out toward that thing with his twelve-gauge. About halfway to my truck, I stop, because I hear Linville cry out real bad. I turned around, and I see him standing there. He was just standing, and he dropped his gun because that big ship had a light trained right on him. It wasn't on the ground yet, but it hit him with that searchlight, and he was shaking and quivering. Then the light went on about its business, still searching around. I ran out to Linville to see if he's okay. He was on his knees and rubbing and beating on himself like he had something on him. He said that old light burned his skin, and he felt like he was on fire.

"So, we crouched there, because that thing was about to land. It dropped behind my cabin, maybe a hundred yards out in the field. At the same time, that noise stops dead. I mean dead, Mr. Payne - like they just turned it off. All we heard was this real strange humming sound, and a kinda blue-green light glowed over the roof of my cabin. We was real scared. We'd heard about that UFO in Rockford and the bull that got cut up. This here was trouble, and we knew it. Linville, he says to go on to the truck and get help. He'd try to hold them off. I run to the truck and get in. I always leave the keys in it, but when I tried to turn her over, nothing. The battery was dead. I had this old fishing knife in the truck, so I whipped it out and go back to Linville.

"He'd worked his way over to my cabin, and he was peeking around the corner. I came up and told him about the truck, so he said, 'Seth, boy, then it's just you and me that's gotta protect my girls.' We looked out in that field, and we see this thing; it was big as a house, Mr. Payne. It had blue lights running along the top of it."

"What kind of aircraft was it?"

"I ain't seen nothing like it. It didn't have no wings. It was standin' on these long metal legs, four in all. On the legs was this kinda square body that tapered off to a triangle tail. It made this humming sound, and then something started happening." Seth, wide-eyed, drew a bead of sweat on his forehead.

"What happened, Seth?"

"One side of it opened up."

"Your Honor," Whittaker interrupted, "may I approach?"

Judge Falco felt a bit small in her chair. She looked first at Cameron, Payne, and then Whittaker. "Step up."

Payne, Aaron, and Whittaker walked to Falco. Seth, having no one to look at, remembered Payne's instructions and eerily stared at the jury. As the conversation began at the bench, Seth stared at each juror, and each suffered a terrible chill.

Whittaker half-whispered to Falco. "Your Honor, with due respect to the eloquent Mr. Cameron, I must protest. Counsel is deliberately encouraging the defendant to make a mockery of these proceedings."

Reed Aaron stepped in. "Is Counsel challenging the ruling in Seth's competency hearing?"

Judge Falco measured the lawyers. "Mr. Aaron, Mr. Payne, it's the duty of the court to afford your client a fair and thoughtful hearing of his testimony, but you have to admit this is extraordinarily suspicious."

"I admit nothing," Payne said.

Aaron kept going. "Your Honor, our client is entitled to testify. It's his choice to open himself to cross-examination. What's extraordinary is the prosecution trying to hinder due process."

Judge Falco looked at Aaron. "Mr. Aaron, you may be perhaps the only lawyer I know who has earned the benefit of my doubts. Mr. Payne, you, on the other hand, have a twenty-year rap sheet of highly questionable tactics. You also have a reputation for playing games with juries, lawyers, judges, and the media. Because Mr. Aaron holds some kind of warped, misguided affection for you, I'm willing to give you some latitude. However, if you intend to gain more from your client's testimony than his acquittal, I'll personally see you strung upside down and naked in the courthouse yard and whipped until dead. Do I make myself clear?"

Payne popped a genuine grin he rarely used in court. "As clear as the falling rain, Your Honor."

Falco eased back as an awful spider crawled down her spine. A draw, she thought, that's the best I can do with this bastard.

She checked the court clock as she swept her hands at them, indicating she wanted these bugs to go away. "This has been a grueling week for everyone," she addressed the court. "It's late, and I believe a weekend respite will do everyone some good. This court shall recess until nine a.m. at the first of the week."

She retreated to her chambers . . .

19

Crane Lodge Mortuary sat in the center of stylish Willow Lakes, a high-end suburb of Harrisburg. Cherry Hill Cemetery was across the street - the final stop for Harrisburg's Rich and Famously Dead. The affluent bone yard looked more like a country club golf course with some wicked headstone hazards. Crane Lodge was a beautiful, three-story structure with sculpturesque bushes, lush green lawns, old oak trees, and white pillars lining the front entrance. Jackson and Carly sat in a rented black limousine, Jackson in the front, Carly in back.

Carly looked out the tinted windows. "Looks ghoulish enough."

"If it is a front," Jackson said, "it's a good one. Carswall doesn't seem to have budget problems. You ready?"

Carly put a lace hanky to her face and whimpered.

"Let's do it." Jackson hopped out, decked in a smart chauffeur's uniform. He moved lively around the limo and opened Carly's door. She stepped out, dressed appropriately in black.

"Thank you, Leroy," Carly said.

"You's welcome missa," Jackson said. "I got the car all afternoon, so maybe you'd like to give 'ol Leroy a roll in the back seat when we done?"

"Oh, Leroy, yes, yes."

They didn't laugh. They didn't even smile. They were grieving. Jackson walked poor, anguished Carly to the front doors and led her into the foyer. The smell of freshly cut flowers followed them into the main lobby. No one was at the front desk.

"Perfect," Jackson whispered, "I won't have to bullshit

through this if I can get to that directory on the desk." He moved like a robber in the night, taking the book and checking the list of names.

A soothing voice dripped over them. "May I help you?"

Carly whined and dumped a hard cry into her hanky.

Jackson dropped the roster back on the desk and gently patted Carly's hand. He nodded at a wormish but elegantly dressed man. "Ms. Dainbridge is here to visit Elvin Carter. I can't find his name in the book."

"Carter?" the man said. He swished to the desk and adeptly perused the directory. "Ah, here; slumber chamber twenty-nine. That's upstairs. I am afraid we close in ten minutes."

Carly whimpered.

Jackson kept patting. "We had to drive most of the day. Ms. Dainbridge was very close to Mr. Carter." He gave the little fairy a subtle wink.

It didn't take long for the director to recall Mr. Carter. His family dropped forty grand on the upcoming funeral. Mrs. Carter made all the arrangements for a man she said was her one-and-only for over fifty years. "Of course," the man said. "I'll show you to the chamber. Please take as much time as you wish."

"We won't be long," Carly cried. "I just want to say good-bye to Binky."

The man's eyes popped as he turned and led them to the stairs. Say good-bye to Binky the Wonderhorse, he thought, right at closing so Mrs. Carter won't find out and spit on Elvin's grave.

Jackson noticed another staircase leading to the basement. The steps were cordoned off by a red velvet rope. On it was a polite sign: 'NO PUBLIC ACCESS, THANK YOU.' Jackson and Carly followed the man upstairs. Leroy gave Ms. Dainbridge a naughty grin, and she discreetly elbowed him in the ribs. The upstairs lobby was sterile and smelled sickly sweet. The director led them to slumber chamber twenty-nine and opened the door. He entered and flipped on the light. As he came out, he threw a sympathetic smile to Ms. Dainbridge, who was just busting out of the dress that 'Binky' probably bought her.

"I'll be downstairs if you need anything."

"Than-kyew," Carly sobbed. She walked in, and Jackson turned his back to guard the door. The man went down the stairs, wiping off his mortician's grin. When he was gone, Jackson quickly entered the room and found Carly clutching her mouth with her back to the late Elvin Carter. Elvin reclined in a coffin across the room, enjoying a dreamless sleep. He was whiter than any white man Jackson had ever seen - and older than dirt.

"Excuse us, Elvin," Jackson muttered. He pulled Carly outside.

The lobby was still, except for organ music that seemed to come from the walls. Carly found a padded bench near Elvin's door.

"Okay, big guy, this was your idea. I'll sit here and go into my act if he comes back."

"Ten-four, Dainbridge. If he asks, tell him I went to take a leak." He turned, but stopped and looked back at Carly. "Don't go back in there."

"Shut up and go."

Jackson moved down the long corridor. He didn't like it, but he thought it might be wise to open a door here and there. Each room was dark, but he felt an ominous presence inside. Nothing in these rooms but legitimate stiffs, he thought without any surprise. If this place was a front, then the real operation was churning somewhere in its bowels.

He took one final look at Carly, who crossed her legs and nervously looked around like she was waiting for a bus. Carefully, he stepped down the carpeted staircase, stopping at the landing and peering down to the lobby. Nobody was around.

He peeked downstairs and quickly stepped over the velvet rope, looking as far ahead as each step would allow.

The basement was cool, and thankfully, the organ music faded. He entered a hallway flanked by barren concrete walls. The smell here was medicinal. To his left, the hall led to a right turn. Just ahead was a metal door with a small window. Jackson stood to the side and slowly moved his head to the window.

Inside, he saw a brightly lit tiled room. Two steel gurneys sat near one wall. Directly across the room was another door. Six 3x3 stainless steel doors lined the inner wall. Each door had a latch handle. Jackson looked both ways and stepped in. This is the morgue, he thought, no doubt about it. He approached the first compartment. He took a deep breath and opened it, finding a waxy head with gray hair and glazed eyes. Jackson gritted his teeth and rolled out the steel gurney.

An old woman; very naked, very dead. Crane Lodge Cold Stiff Storage, Jackson thought - okay, Leroy, keep moving, this was your idea. He rolled the corpse back into the refrigerated cabinet and escaped to the hall. I'm still in the front - this is too clean, he thought. They wouldn't hide their secrets here.

He inched to the corner and looked down the next hallway. Quickly, he walked the corridor, stopping at a door labeled UTILITY. He peeked inside and found a huge boiler trapped in a web of pipes. A locked door stood on the far side of the room. Jackson came back out and walked to the end of the hall. He found one last door. This one had no sign on it. Jackson threw a glance over his shoulder, turned the doorknob, and the door squeaked open. His eyes rounded a large garage. Crane Lodge Stiff Delivery, he thought. Two large garage doors were locked, and on the right were swinging double doors.

Jackson wandered the garage for a moment and then slowly pushed the double doors to peek through the slit. It looked like an embalming lab. He opened the doors and saw a sink and a metal tub. Along the wall was a large counter loaded with chemicals, tubes, and embalming instruments. Jackson opened the doors wider and his eyes followed the counter, which led to a pair of elevator doors. He entered, his eyes still moving until they stopped on a cold male corpse that looked like someone had dropped it into a garbage disposal.

"Hey!"

Jackson jumped at a big black woman standing over the

mangled body. She wore a white lab coat, and her hands were full of tubes and probes. Shit, Jackson thought, what now, Leroy?

"Lordy mighty!" Jackson hollered with a stiff southern dialect, his eyes bugging at the wrecked corpse. "Oh, where in the world am I?"

"What are you doing?" the huge woman barked. "You're not supposed to be in here!" She dropped her tools on the body and waddled around the gurney. She swept her fat hands at him.

"I'm lost, ma'am! Oh, lordy, lookie that!" Jackson looked as if he was going to either cry or vomit.

The fat lady stepped in front of Jackson, still brushing. "That's what driving drunk does to ya. Well, turn around and stop looking at him, honey . . . come on." She had a gentle touch for such a behemoth. She spun Jackson around and led him to the garage.

Jackson held his heart and panted. "Lordy, lordy, that was a sight! Oh, lordy!"

"It's okay," the lady said, patting him on the head. "Now, just what do I have here?"

Jackson shook. "I'm a driver, ma'am. I brought my boss lady here to visit a, uh, a passed on person. And, lordy, I'm lost ma'am."

"You must've come down the stairs. The sign up there says you aren't supposed to come down here. Can't you read, boy?"

Jackson looked as if his manly pride just took a shot. "Uh, no ma'am. I can't read."

His sad eyes disarmed the woman. She was a momma, and a dang good one. "I'm sorry, honey, no reason to worry about that. But you just saw why you shouldn't be down here."

"Oh, yes ma'am. Lordy, what a sight!"

"But there was a rope across the stairs. What're you doing crawling over it?"

"I'm sorry ma'am. But I'm kinda desperate."

"Desperate?"

Leroy was entirely embarrassed. "I been searching high and low for a gentlemen's room. This is a real emergency."

"Oh, honey!" The woman's laugh sounded like shotgun blasts. "Go back upstairs to the main lobby. Take a right past the front desk, and you'll find one just down a hall. Go on, now."

Jackson waddled down the hall with his knees together. "I can't thank you enough, ma'am. I'm sorry I run into you. Lordy, I can't say how sorry."

"Go on," the lady said, still laughing.

Jackson pigeon-walked down the hall. The fat lady chortled a little more and shook her head as she returned to her corpse. When Jackson rounded the corner, he slyly looked back and congratulated himself. Good boy, Leroy.

He'd seen enough for now and decided to find Ms. Dainbridge. Before going up, he noticed a half-window on the wall that had a simple bolt lock with no alarm attached. It looked out on the back parking lot from a deep aluminum window well. Jackson shut the window and left it unlocked, hoping the latch might go unnoticed . . .

Ms. Dainbridge and Leroy nodded at the mortuary director as they left. Poor Ms. Dainbridge was still weeping into her hanky as they walked to the black limo in front. The director watched her round bottom wave good-bye. He indignantly shook his head.

"Little slut," he whispered . . .

* * *

Shortly after nine-thirty p.m., two shadows danced along the back walls of Crane Lodge. The temperature dipped to twenty-three, and Jackson and Carly weren't properly dressed, but their tight black clothing and black sneakers hid them in the night. The parking lot was empty, except for three hearses parked at the far end. The bandits ran along the wall until they reached the basement window. Carly crouched while Jackson hopped into the window well.

"Hope this sucker's still open," he whispered. He smiled when the door swung into the basement. Quickly, Jackson slid in and landed on the floor without a sound. He turned and found Carly coming in right behind him. She dropped down, and they stood face-to-face in the dark, clutching each other. "You ready?" Jackson said.

"I'm good," Carly whispered. "Let's get this over with."

Jackson pulled a penlight from his pocket and gently shut the window. They hesitated a moment to adjust their eyes to the cavernous darkness, and then Jackson flicked the tiny beam of light onto the floor. "Stay close," he said, taking careful steps.

"Where else am I gonna go?" Carly said, following close.

They rounded the dark hallway, Jackson pointing the beam of light ten feet ahead. The light found the utility door and pierced the end of the dark corridor. Carly's throat was tight. She hated death and anything related to it. A chemical smell in the air turned her stomach. They reached the door to the garage.

"Hope it isn't locked," she whispered.

Jackson turned the knob, and the door clicked open. "How much security do you need in a mortuary? What kind of sick bastard would break in here?"

"Right," Carly breathed, following him into the garage.

Jackson pointed the light at the double doors, and they pushed into the embalming lab. As the doors shut, Jackson realized that Carly wasn't holding him anymore. He turned in the darkness and pointed the light at the swinging doors. He came back around and the light landed on Carly's face not three inches from his own.

"Damn!" he said, almost breaking a whisper. "You want to give me a heart attack?"

"Sorry. Are you sure there are no windows in here?"

"Pretty," Jackson said.

"Pretty?"

"There's gotta be a light switch around here somewhere."

"Pretty sure doesn't get it! If there's a window, we'll tell the world we're in here. Kenny?"

A sudden electrical buzz popped, and the lab burst into light. Carly froze and jammed her teeth together. Her eyes found the big room. No windows. She glared at Jackson.

He smiled. "Now I'm real sure."

They looked around, Jackson grateful that the steel gurney was now unoccupied. Carly moved about, finding the sink and steel tub.

"Yuck-o," she said knowingly, "who would take a bath in here?"

"Guess," Jackson said. He rummaged around, while Carly was less deliberate in her search. Jackson found a desk and began nosing through papers. He opened the drawers, but found nothing unusual. His next stop was a file cabinet beside the desk. Jackson rifled through the first drawer of folders, finding nothing but names and information about the guests of Crane Lodge. The other drawers contained nothing but nothing.

Carly checked the lab counter and turned her lip at the embalming instruments and chemicals. "How could anybody do this for a living?"

"You always got work," Jackson mumbled, still snooping around. "There's nothing here."

"This place looks like a real, honest-to-goodness mortuary, big guy."

"If they're holding Linville here, he's gotta be in some other place where only the feds go." He propped his arms on his hips, scanning the room carefully until he found the elevator.

Carly saw it too. "Where does that go?"

"Well, you pump up the stiff, and then it goes upstairs, I guess." He stared at the doors. "Wonder if there's a downstairs."

Carly sighed. "I really hate this, Kenny."

Jackson pressed the elevator call button and the doors quietly opened. The car was long and narrow, built for a gurney and similar in size to the refrigerated chamber he saw this afternoon in the other room. It was tall enough for an extra passenger to fit in, if anybody wanted to. Jackson poked his head in and found a control panel.

"Yep, there's an 'up' and a 'down' button," he said.

"I was afraid of that."

Jackson sucked in the chemical air and crouched into the elevator. "There's room enough for both of us, but let me go first. If I send this back empty, come on down. If I come back up and run out of here screaming, be sure to follow me."

Carly didn't smile. "Don't take your time."

Jackson hit the 'down' button, and the doors closed him into uneasy darkness. "Woah. No light in here!"

He heard Carly's voice pulling up and away from him. "How many dead people need a light in an elevator?"

Jackson crouched and prepared to spring out for a reason he didn't know. The ride seemed to take forever. He flipped on the penlight, thinking it might chase off the willies. Wrong...

The air grew colder as he descended. Finally, the car bumped to a stop and the doors opened. He stepped into a black hole, tossing the light beam around as he searched for a light switch. The elevator doors suddenly closed and the car growled to life. It went back up, obeying Carly's impatient call. Oh well, Jackson thought. The room felt like a walk-in freezer. Jackson groped and found a light switch. The light popped on.

Three naked, frozen corpses lay before him on cold gurneys. They stared at the ceiling and didn't wake up when Jackson gasped. One of them was the man whom the fat black lady was gluing back together earlier. Jackson's brain fell onto the floor, and he quickly tried to retrieve it as the elevator arrived. The doors slid open and Carly popped out, claustrophobia strangling her spine. She saw the bodies before Jackson could turn her around.

"Dammit! Oh, shit!" Carly cried. She propped her hand on the elevator door, making sure it didn't close. "That's it, we're outa here!" She scrambled back inside.

Jackson flipped the light off, but he didn't get in.

"Come on, Kenny! I hate this!"

"Do you think I'm in love here?"

"Get in!"

"I don't know if it'll take both of us."

"You want me to go back up and leave you here?"

Jackson climbed in without hesitation. The doors shut, and they were in the dark again.

"How come we're not moving?" Carly said.

"Just a minute." Jackson fumbled for his flashlight and finally trained it on the control panel. He reached for the 'up' button, but suddenly stopped with a second thought.

"Tick tock," Carly impatiently said. "This is starting to really creep me out."

"Hold on." Jackson curiously looked at the two buttons. He knew he might get slugged for this, but he tried the 'down' button. The car lurched downward.

"Kenny! What'd you do?"

"I just wondered if there was another floor. Looks like."

"Oh, great. Perfect."

The car took much longer to descend, apparently dropping them into a deeper room. They finally hit bottom, and the doors opened. Jackson struggled out with Carly glued to his back. "If this room is the same, there should be a light switch on the left," Jackson said.

"If this room is the same, I'm gonna kill you and leave you here."

They fumbled through the darkness and Jackson finally found the switch. Three bare light bulbs popped on the ceiling in a neat row, revealing a large sterile room. A fit of relief fell over them when they found no frozen corpses - or zombies with clubs in their hands. Instead, they saw a room lined with steel doors on both sides. One wall had three rows of six doors each. They were small and very much like the compartments Jackson had found upstairs. On the other wall were four large, floor-length doors. Every door had a steel handle with a lock built in it. At the end of the room were a desk and a file cabinet, flanked by two empty gurneys. Another heavy steel door stood guard, secured by a handled latch.

"Here we go," Jackson said, walking to the end of the room. Carly trailed closely. He opened the door and found a stairway going up. "Hold this open and I'll see where these stairs go."

"Don't take your time."

Jackson took the stairs two at a time. He rounded the landing and made the second flight as quickly. Downstairs, Carly nervously looked back at the lockers and tapped her foot. She refused to let her imagination loose. She perked when Jackson bounded back down.

"There's a landing up there with two doors. One is locked from the outside, and the other opens to that utility room upstairs where we started."

"Where do you suppose the locked door leads?"

"With our luck? Probably into another dimension." Jackson walked to the bare desk. He tried every drawer, but they were locked. He went to the file cabinet. Locked. He boldly moved to one of the locker doors and yanked the handle. Locked.

"Well," he said, "we've found something that somebody doesn't want us to see."

"Excuse me if I'm not overjoyed," Carly said, trying the desk drawer herself.

Jackson joined her, reaching into his pocket. He pulled out a tool that Carly recognized. She got out of his way and watched Jackson pick the desk lock in seconds. "Ain't dealing with no dumb country boy cop," he muttered.

In the top drawer were several pencils, pens, notepads - nothing unusual. Carly rifled through the side drawers and found a black ledger book. On the first page, the heading read, 'SACRAMENT; G-5 EYES ONLY.'

"Jackpot," Carly said, handing the book to Jackson.

He sat on the desk and flipped through the pages, which were written in code. "Looks like computer programming language."

Carly looked over Jackson's shoulder as he carefully checked each page. He shook his head. "I can't make anything out of this."

"Hold it," Carly said, reaching in to flip back a page. "Did I see what I think I saw?" She ran her finger down a row of four-digit numbers, each with a word next to it: 1900James. 1187Saunders. 1908Walker. 1531Pike. She stopped and pointed at 1227Reeves.

"Making progress," Jackson said. "Good catch, babe."

"Yeah, but what did I catch?"

"I don't know yet." He opened the bottom drawer and his eyes widened. "Bingo." He pulled a key ring with three keys.

"I hate this."

Jackson shrugged. "We're this far . . ."

They walked to the smaller doors and inspected closely. Carly saw it first. "Look," she said, pointing to a four-digit number written with a felt marker next to the handle.

Jackson glanced at Carly with a smile.

"This isn't gonna be fun, is it?" Carly said.

"Let's find out. Look for 1227." He walked to the far end of the room, and Carly began at the nearest locker. The search was slow but profitable.

"Kenny," Carly hollowly said. Jackson found her by a locker near the center. He came up quickly and looked. "1227," Carly said.

Jackson felt her eyes on him as he selected a key. He tried the lock, but the key didn't fit. The second did. "I don't think there's gonna be any need for introductions . . ."

He turned the lock and the door clicked. Carly stepped back, covering her mouth as Jackson reached in and pulled out the stretcher.

The frozen, empty eye sockets of Linville Reeves glared at them.

"Oh, my god!" Carly cried.

Jackson, his eyes burning, clenched his teeth and tried to swallow. "God dammit, it's you, you bastard! I'm not crazy. It's you. It's you!"

Carly grabbed Kenny and held him close. She buried her face in his shoulder, unable to look any longer.

Jackson stared at this vision that had taken residence in his mind for months. A tear dropped to his mouth. "All this time," he grunted, "I thought maybe I was just losing my god-dam mind."

Carly stepped in front of Jackson and hatefully slammed the stretcher back into the cabinet. She pounded the door shut and took Jackson by the shoulders. "You were right all along, Kenny, you hear me? I believed you."

Jackson nodded. He wrapped an arm around her shoulder and pulled her into him. "Yeah, you did."

Carly pulled back. "We gotta get out of here and tell somebody."

"No," Jackson said. "I lost this son of a bitch once, and it ain't gonna happen again."

"What?"

"We're taking him with us."

"You gotta be kidding."

"I'm gonna kick Virgil's door in and drop Linville in his lap . . ."

"Drive him back to Attica? Are you out of your mind? I'm not riding with that thing on my lap! Let's call the Harrisburg cops. This place will be buzzing in ten minutes."

Jackson opened the locker door. "He's going with us!"

Carly stepped back and watched Jackson roll out that hideous corpse again. He blindly grabbed its emaciated shoulders, but stopped when he found it frozen to the stretcher. He tugged a few more times, but it was useless. He finally looked at Carly.

"Are ya finished?" Carly said.

Jackson shook some sense back into his own head. "How do we get him out of here?"

"I have friends in this town, knucklehead," Carly said. "Let's get the hell out of here and make a call."

Jackson held his hands out as if he didn't want them anymore.

Carly suddenly froze and curiously looked around. "Wait a minute . . ."

"What?"

"There are numbers on all of these lockers."

Jackson, still short of breath, gave her a sour look. "Oh, man. Do you think - "

"I don't even want to tell you what I'm thinking."

Jackson shoved Linville back in the fridge and took the key out of the door. He jammed it into another numbered locker and pulled it open. "Hold your breath," he said, rolling the stretcher out. "Holy shit . . ."

A frozen woman, or what was left of her, was on her back. Her incisions were similar to those on Linville's body. The top of her head was gone. Her internal organs were gone. Her vagina was nothing but a gaping hole, and her reproductive organs were cleanly excised . . .

A black four-door sedan slowly cruised the rear parking lot. Its heavy spotlight meandered along the back of Crane Lodge. It danced across the bricks, past the window well, over to the door.

The car lurched to a stop. The gears cranked, and the sedan popped into reverse. It backed quickly, and the spotlight fell on the window well again. The light burned on the window for almost a minute before the driver's door opened. A heavyset man in a hooded parka walked over and crouched. He cocked his head from side to side until a freezing wind picked up and made the window bounce. The big man climbed into the well and pushed the window open.

"Shit!"

He climbed out and ran back to the car, plucking his handset radio transmitter.

He spoke deliberately. "Red Crane, control one-oh-one."

The radio crackled. "Red Crane."

He checked his watch. "Security breach, twenty-one-fifty. Rear window, east corner; over."

"Red Crane, clear. Stand by . . ."

"The place is full of them," Jackson breathed, his head swirling. They stood back and looked at a fifth dissected corpse.

"I don't need to see any more," Carly said, closing the body back into its cabinet. "Kenny, what are you doing?"

Jackson tried the lock on the first big door across from the smaller lockers. "I want to know what's in here." The first key unlocked this door. It opened, and a rush of frozen air slapped his face. He squinted and reached inside to search for a switch. The light popped on.

Carly stood on her toes and peeked over his shoulder. The 'oh, my gods' were becoming passé. Inside the walk-in were three frozen calves stacked on top of each other. Next to them was a bull elk, and beside the elk were sheep stacked six deep. The animals were all dissected.

Jackson clicked off the light and shut the door. He looked at Carly and surprised himself with an exasperated laugh. "It's a goddam nightmare . . ."

A harsh BANG! made them both jump. It echoed down the stairwell and through the closed door by the desk. Jackson's eyes met Carly's as they heard heavy footsteps coming down the stairs.

Jackson whispered, "Go down to the elevator and stand there. When he opens the door, let him see you. I'll nail him."

Carly nodded and ran the length of the room. Jackson backed to the wall by the door. The footsteps stopped outside, and Jackson heard a heavy voice behind the door.

"Red Crane, breach discovered. Noise in Sacrament room. I'm investigating."

"Red Crane, clear. Back-up's on the way."

Jackson cursed at the mechanical radio pop outside. This was gonna be a tough night.

A deep voice pierced the door. "Hello in there!"

Jackson's eyes widened. He looked at Carly, who gave him a 'what now?' shrug. Jackson waved her off.

"You want to come out now. Of all the people on their way, I'm the nicest. We can do this easy, or hard - it's up to you."

Jackson didn't breathe. The door slowly gave, its hinges squeaking. A huge man in a parka stepped in, his wet brown eyes falling on Carly. He pointed his weapon at her. "Well, who are - " He let out a cry as Jackson palmed his temple with a lethal blow. The man staggered and dropped his gun, but he didn't go out. He regained his balance, eyes rolling, and backed to the wall. With a guttural growl, he came back at Jackson and swung drunkenly. Jackson dodged him and peppered his thick head with three stiff blows. The goon hit the floor for good.

Jackson dragged him away from the door. He closed it and quickly dragged the desk in front. With a thick grunt, he hoisted the file cabinet and dropped it on the desk. Not much of a deterrent, but enough to slow whoever was coming down the stairs now. He quickly searched for Red Crane's gun, but it was nowhere in sight. The footsteps outside grew louder.

Jackson eyed the three light bulbs lined along the ten-foot ceiling. He took one step back and exploded in a run, leaping and slapping the first bulb dead. The bulb popped, and showered sparks and glass as Jackson landed on the run. The second bulb burst, and Jackson hit the floor hard and stumbled to his knees. He backpedaled and leapt again, killing the last bulb with a swat. The room disappeared, and Jackson staggered into Carly's arms.

They turned in the darkness and heard a mechanical voice crackle outside the door. "Red Crane? . . . Red Crane? . . . come in . . ."

A second, more real voice broke. "This is Blue Crane. I'm on the Sacrament stairwell. Red Crane isn't here. There's a weapon here on the floor."

"Red Crane was there. He's not responding now," said the mechanical voice.

"I'm going in. Send back-up to the lab elevators."

Yet a third voice now came on. "This is Green Crane. I'm at the lobby door."

"Green Crane, get in and cover the elevators in the basement lab. We have intruders in the Sacrament room!"

"Clear."

Carly flattened her back against the wall as the elevator doors closed. She listened as the car slowly ascended. The 'Sacrament room,' as these creeps called it, had just stepped up a few notches on the fright scale. Across the darkness, the door slowly opened, spitting light through the desk/file cabinet barrier. Carly could only see a large shadow on the other side, but its voice was huge.

"Blue Crane, we have a positive breech! Green Crane, haul ass to those elevators!"

"Clear."

Carly closed her eyes and wondered if she was about to commit suicide. "Hurry, Charlie! Get in the elevator!" she hollered.

The man outside attacked the heavy cabinet, throwing several body blocks before it fell with a wet thud. He crawled over, stopping when he found Red Crane on the floor. He fumbled for the light switch, cursing loudly when the lights didn't come on.

"Hurry! Where's the elevator?" Carly hollered, still not quite believing she said it.

"Hold where you are!" Blue Crane ordered. He pulled his weapon and moved in slowly. "You can't escape. Walk toward me and put your hands in the air. Now!"

Carly heard the elevator lurch upstairs. She stepped into a dark corner and held her breath.

"Lady, whoever you are," Blue Crane said, walking slowly, "you know I'm not a cop. I'll cut a deal with you, but if I have to come down there, I will kill you."

"Go to the right," Carly whispered loudly.

Blue Crane stopped. He cautiously spoke into his radio. "Blue Crane, I have at least two in the Sacrament room."

"Somebody's in the elevator," Green Crane responded.

"Cut the power."

"I can't cut it down here. The breaker is up in the lobby," Green Crane said.

The elevator began to descend, straining from the weight.

"Blue Crane? What's going on down there? Talk to me."

"Stand by," Blue Crane said. He gripped his 9mm semi-automatic, aiming it in the general direction of the elevator. He took a careful step forward, his feet crunching a pile of broken glass. Carly swung wildly at the noise in the darkness and struck Blue Crane on the neck. He instinctively flung both elbows, one finding Carly's forehead. She staggered and felt two huge arms smother her. She couldn't see him, but he couldn't see her either. The gun dropped to the floor as she managed to dig her long nails into his cheek. He heaved, pushing hot, ugly breath into her eyes. The bear hug tightened around her chest. Carly couldn't breathe. She forced her claws to his eyes, but she thought her spine might snap at any second.

Instinct. Training. Carly sucked in and brought her knee up, ramming his testicles to his throat. Blue Crane yowled like a slaughtered pig, spitting blood and mucus into her face. His grip died, and he doubled to the floor. Carly waddled back, broken glass ripping into her arms as she skidded across the floor. She fixed her eyes on the black wall, where she prayed she'd reach the elevator doors that opened nearby. She found her feet and ran toward the sound.

"Get in!" Jackson hollered through the darkness.

Blue Crane, his guts dripping out of his mouth, tried to stand and find the elevator.

"Move!" Jackson cried.

Blue Crane was on his feet now, but he couldn't straighten himself. He rumbled after the sound of shuffling at the elevator, but he was too late to catch the doors. They shut just as he slammed against them. The elevator growled again, heading up. Blue Crane screamed an obscenity as he half-crawled through the darkness.

His voice squeaked into the radio. "They're coming to you! Unload the minute that fucking door opens!"

"I'm waiting for 'em," Green Crane calmly responded.

Blue Crane ran, still doubled over, and pounded up the stairs. Rage bit his temples as he took the stairs by threes. He wanted to beat the elevator so he could enjoy pumping a few rounds into the bitch that emasculated him. The stairwell doors flung open into the boiler room, and Blue Crane hobbled into the hallway, bouncing on the wall and pinballing down the corridor. He crashed into the garage and made the turn into the embalming lab, his gun drawn. Green Crane stood in front of the doors, holding his weapon with both hands. He didn't look at Blue Crane's shredded face. He was ready to start capping when the elevator doors opened.

"I'm gonna kill 'em twice!" Blue Crane said, aiming at the doors.

The elevator opened, and they fired. Neither cared about aiming, because the targets inside were helplessly trapped. The elevator car exploded into a cloud of bullets, skin and bone.

"Hold your fire, goddamit!" Green Crane said. He grabbed Blue Crane's arm.

Inside the car, two frozen, naked corpses were now twice dead.

"Son of a bitch!" Green Crane hollered. He shoved Blue Crane out of the way, leaving his half-man partner to look at the Crane Lodge Mortuary guests, whose loved ones were going to have a lot of questions. Green Crane pounded out of the lab, hollering into his radio. "Control! We got at least two, maybe three outside. Scramble! I need backup - now! . . ."

Carly and Jackson had given Blue Crane a five-second lead before tailing him up the stairs. They cut through the lobby and out the front door, now sprinting across the vast Crane Lodge lawn. Jackson's sports car was parked two hundred yards away on the opposite side of Cherry Hill Cemetery. Leaving the car there seemed the logical thing to do when this bizarre stunt began, but now it didn't seem too smart. The shortest route was through the cemetery.

They slipped through the trees and sculpted bushes, and darted across Cherry Drive. A pair of lights hit them in the middle of the street. A sedan squealed from two blocks away, gunning directly for them. A second car rounded the corner from the opposite direction, its horn honking wildly. Jackson followed Carly into the dark cemetery, quickly glancing back as the two cars passed each other. The dark sedan skidded to a stop, but the other car, a beat-up red foreign job, ripped on down Cherry Drive. A man jumped from the sedan's passenger side and pulled his weapon. He bounded after Jackson and Carly, and the sedan took off.

They ran hard, dodging gravestones and trees. The sound of heavy footsteps echoed in pursuit. A sudden crack of gunfire popped the bark off a tree nearby. Jackson's football grace was matched by Carly, step-for-step. She wasn't as fast as he was, but she was just as scared. A second shot glanced off a concrete headstone as Jackson and Carly disappeared down a hill and into a welcome grove of trees. They zigzagged through the verdure, their assailant still behind and out of sight. Jackson's car was visible now, but still at a deadly distance. Ahead were hundreds of gravestones standing like rigid soldiers. Jackson and Carly dodged in an out, trying to keep each other in sight.

The ground suddenly disappeared under Jackson's feet. He grunted as he tumbled headlong into a fresh grave. Carly heard Kenny fall, but she couldn't see him in the terrible darkness. She stopped and looked back, a wad of fear rolling down her throat.

"Kenny?" she whispered.

The heavy footsteps came hard.

"Run, baby!" Jackson's pained voice called.

Carly took off in terror. Jackson clawed and scratched at the black hole. The ground was cold and slick, and he fell back. He finally hoisted a leg over the lip of the grave and rolled out, instinctively ducking in anticipation of a gunshot. In a millisecond, the agent pounded up. Jackson met him with his shoulder, and the two tumbled to the ground. Stunned, the agent pulled away and reprogrammed his mind. Jackson jumped him before he put it together, striking the agent's chest and knocking his breath into the air. He pounded out three quick rib shots, but caught a palm in the nose. It forced him back and twisted his sight. The agent kicked Jackson in the jaw and scrambled back on his ass and up to his feet. Jackson backed off and tried to organize his legs as the agent assumed a martial arts stance. They stalked each other, both wounded but aware this would be fatal for one. The agent made a quick leg whip and caught Jackson on the side of his head. He charged, but Jackson dodged and the agent rolled away. They stalked again.

"So you're the fucking hero," the agent growled. "This is gonna be fun . . ."

A sudden, skull-cracking CLANG! knocked the agent's eyes to the back of his head. His head split open, and he died before he hit the ground.

Jackson staggered back and watched the man's skull spit brains and red goo. He found Carly, who held a heavy spade in her hands. She could hardly breathe.

"Come on!" Jackson said . . .

They reached the outer edge of the cemetery in less than ten seconds. A large marble mausoleum covered them from the eyes of anyone on the street. Indeed, there was someone out there. The black sedan parked across from Jackson's car, and an agent, even larger than the one they'd just left at the grave, got out and warily searched. He stroked the trigger of his gun and scanned the cemetery.

He heard sudden rustling near the marble building. He jumped and aimed that direction. Carly appeared, her hands held high.

"Freeze right there, bitch!" he ordered - the last words he'd ever speak. Jackson arose from behind him and buried the spade in the agent's head.

Jackson flung the shovel in the street and darted for the car. Carly piled in as Jackson fired the engine. Another dark sedan whipped around the corner.

"Get down!" Jackson yelled. He floored it, and they ducked as they passed the sedan. A rapid-fire spray of bullets shattered the front and back windows. Jackson sped down the street, checking the mirror. The sedan wildly spun around and gave chase. They blew a red light at the next intersection, clearing in time to avoid a red foreign job, which soundly broadsided the sedan as it entered the crossing.

"God damn! I don't believe it!" Jackson cried. Carly looked back in time to see the sedan drunkenly weave and plow through a telephone pole.

"Somebody hit him!" Carly said.

"It was that other bastard – the one in front of the mortuary!"

Jackson's eyes remained on the mirror as he pushed the

sports car to seventy. If a Harrisburg cop wanted to stop him, he'd have to catch him first. They couldn't trust anyone now. They reached the interstate, pounding the blacktop at over ninety and disappearing into the darkness alone . . .

The black sedan was demolished, and the furious agent had to kick his door open to get out. He left his gun on the seat and two-stepped along the sidewalk, holding his bleeding forehead and spitting teeth.

The driver of the red car wandered up. "Are you okay?"

The goon shook blood from his head. "You son of a bitch!"

"Me? Hey, you ran the light!"

"Asshole." The agent stupidly sat on the ground.

"Hey, this is your fault, so pull out your insurance card, pal. I'm gonna call the cops." The driver sat down in his smashed car with a grin. He grabbed his phone, and at the same time fished for his pipe.

Wish I could have a damned drink, but that's probably not such a hot idea right now, Dan Williams thought, still grinning – and trembling . . .

20

Marcus Payne confidently measured each doomed bowling pin. He gently raised the ball to eye level. "Take no prisoners," he said.

Three steps, one fluid movement, elbow straight, follow through, into the pocket . . .

Boom!

The pins exploded.

"Three in a row!" Gracie Aaron cried. She quickly scribbled a third 'X' on Payne's scorecard and jumped up for a victory hug. "We skunked 'em, Doc!"

"Of course," Payne said, trading three consecutive high-fives with Gracie and hugging her once for good measure. Reed and Sybil Aaron sat together behind the scorer's table. Sybil laughed as she pulled off her bowling shoes. Aaron pouted and sipped a lukewarm beer he'd nursed for three hours.

Gracie wiggled and danced back to the table. "Let's see. Wow, Doc! Two-sixty!" Payne sighed and polished his fingernails on his shirt. Gracie continued her calculations. "And me, uh, one-fifty-yes!" She pumped her fist. "And now, our worthy opponents. Ma, you got, uh, one-thirty-nine. Way to go, Ma!"

Sybil Aaron stood and bowed to Marc's applause. "Thank you. Thank you."

"Daddy, you got one-eleven." Gracie blurted a lovable giggle. "That was your best game of the night! Yay, Daddy!"

"Stupid ball," Reed Aaron mumbled. "If I hadn't gotten this darned blister on my thumb . . ."

"Boooo!" Gracie waved at Aaron. "Denial! Denial! Ugly apes eat sour grapes!"

"Sustained," Sybil said, patting her partner's leg.

"I couldn't throw the damned ball straight," Aaron grumbled. He pulled off his shoes.

Sybil sat and wrapped a loving arm around Reed. "Let's face it. We got licked."

"Fair and square, Daddy!" Gracie hopped up and planted a wet one on Aaron's cheek.

Daddy melted. "Show a little mercy for your old man. I could write you out of the will, you know."

Gracie started to reply, but she stopped and looked at Payne pensively. "You're a lawyer. Can he do that?"

"He's ornery enough," Payne said.

"But you could adopt me and write me into your will!"

"I'll have the papers drawn up in the morning," Aaron said.

"Daddy!"

"She's all yours, Marcus. The makeup, the hair sprays, the prom dresses, college, medical school, and the insurance on that hot rod you plan to buy her - all yours."

Gracie looked at Payne like a lost soul. "He just gave me away because I beat him in bowling. Will you take me?"

"I don't know," Payne said. "Can you type?"

"Nobody loves me!" Gracie faked a cry that turned to a squeal when Payne grabbed her and tickled mercilessly.

"I don't love you much," Payne laughed.

"Stop! Oh, stop! Stop!"

Payne let go, and they all had a good laugh. It was a laugh everyone needed. Payne and Aaron hadn't laughed much these last few months; and Gracie and Sybil didn't laugh much when Reed was uptight. In fact, although the trial was reaching a critical stage, everyone felt like life was on the verge of normalcy. Payne had all but moved in with them now, and he planned to stay awhile to take stock of his life and make some decisions.

Payne draped one leg over the other and put his arm around Gracie. They watched Reed fuss with his shoes. "How about a cone?"

"Woah, strawberry-yes! I'll get 'em. Money. Money." She

held her hand out and snapped her fingers. "Come on, dude."

"Dude?" Aaron said.

Gracie indignantly smiled. "Daddy, everybody who's anybody is a dude."

"So long as they're fifteen," Aaron scolded. "You know I don't want you speaking to adults that way, not even Uncle Marc."

Gracie ducked and looked at Payne for help, but Doc wasn't going to step in for the defense - not when her father's the judge. She gulped and politely nodded to Doc. "May I please have some money for ice cream, Mr. Payne - Sir?"

"Delighted, madam." Payne winked and slapped a ten in her hand, and she took orders. Reed declined, and Sybil opted for a cola. They watched Gracie bound up the stairs, her ponytail hopping like a spring.

Sybil still had her arm around Reed. "Marc, that little girl worships you, you know that?"

Payne smiled and gave a loving nod. "She has a weak spot for beat-up old fellows - just like her mom. You two should be proud of yourselves. She's going to make a nice adult someday."

"Well, thank you, kind stranger," Sybil said.

"If we can just survive her teens," Aaron mumbled, still bent over his shoes. "Five hours on the phone every night; nonstop talk about that car; a dozen boys hanging around day and night. And the mood swings - my god. We should have had a son."

"Oh, come on, Daddy," Sybil said.

Aaron finally got his shoes tied. He sat back, heaving a titanic sigh. "I don't believe how tired I am. What in the world possessed you to take us bowling tonight?"

"Just a lark," Payne said with a shrug. "It's been a tough week. I thought we could all use a break."

"Amen," Sybil said.

Gracie popped back down the stairs with a cola in one hand and two cones balanced in the other. In her mouth were napkins, straws and change for the ten.

Aaron watched, milking the 'old man' routine for all it

was worth. "Isn't anybody but me tired?"

"Let's bowl just one more line," Gracie said.

"God, no. It's almost one a.m.," Aaron whined.

"We better cart your father home," Sybil said.

"Party poop."

"Give your old man a break, honey," Payne said. "He's ancient." As he stood, his back gave a mean pop. "Ow!"

Gracie laughed at Doc and Daddy, who both looked like statues trying to find their feet. "Your Honor," she said to Sybil, "I think the defense better rest!"

Payne smirked as he put on his coat. "Reed, drop me at the hotel tonight."

"Aw, Doc, you're not going to stay there, are you?"

"Yeah, tonight, Sweet Thing."

"But you were going to take me and my girlfriends ice skating tomorrow."

"And ice we shall skate," Payne said. "I have a few of my legal books and this-n-thats at the hotel. I need them for a little homework tonight. We'll skate our hearts out tomorrow, I promise."

"Then you'll take me for a driving lesson in Daddy's car, right?"

"It's inked on my agenda," Payne said, crossing his heart.

"You better."

Aaron sighed again . . .

An eerie calmness consumed the Aaron mini van on the ride to the Oxford Hotel. So quiet. Reed thought about nothing but falling into bed. No Cameron. No trial. Sex? If Sybil was interested - which she always was - he'd give it his best shot. In fact, that sex thought was beginning to give him a second wind, for Sybil was sneaking a feel in the darkness of the front seat.

In the back, Gracie dozed fast like a manic puppy, her head floating down on Payne's shoulder. Marcus wrapped an arm around her, suddenly hurting inside. It made him long for Lori - and for the child he could have embraced in a future that now would never be. He stroked Gracie's hair, making a silent wish that the horrors and hardships that crept the corners of this world would never find his little Sweet Thing. Payne peered out the window and watched the cold night fly by, catching an occasional glimpse of himself in the glass. For an instant, he saw Lori.

Aaron pulled up to the Oxford. Payne tried not to disturb Gracie, but she perked. "We home?" she mumbled.

"Not quite, Sweet Thing. Just at the hotel."

"Aw, Doc, get your silly books and come home with us."

"You'll be stuck with me long enough." Payne put a little kiss on the top of her head, and he affectionately rubbed Sybil's shoulder. "Goodnight you two."

"See you tomorrow, Marcus," Reed said.

Payne started to get out, but Gracie grabbed his hand. "Hey! Ya love me?"

"More than strawberry ice cream."

"You better."

"Have your skates sharpened by nine." He put a kiss on his finger and stuck it to her nose.

Payne stepped out into the cold and tossed a wave at the mini van. The empty feeling returned as he watched them drive down the street. His melancholy smile faded and he shook the jealousy from his head. He turned and almost slipped on the icy sidewalk. With a shrug, he gave a little hum and skated through the revolving doors.

Tod was propped in his chair, sound asleep behind the registration desk. A book was sprawled face-down on his chest. Payne approached and cocked his head, reading the title of Tod's book: 'Applied Astrophysics.'

"Astrophysics? Tod?" he said. "I should have been consulting you all along."

He leaned over the counter and got close to Tod's ear.

"Can I get a room!"

Tod's legs shot up, and the chair rolled out from under him. He collapsed to the floor, his feet coming back to rest on the counter. Tod's perplexed eyes wandered. "What the hell?"

Payne's smile crept over the counter. "Did you lose something, Tod?"

"Oh - hey, Mr. Payne."

"Nice night out . . . a little cold."

"Uh-huh."

"You aren't hurt, are you?"

"No, sir. Didn't expect you tonight. Need a key?"

"Have one," Payne said. "I'll square my bill and be out tomorrow. I want to give you a little something extra for being a good landlord - and an easy mark."

Tod hadn't moved yet. "Oh, not necessary, Mr. Payne. You're the best resident I ever had."

Payne pulled out his wallet and laid five one hundred-dollar bills on the counter. "Here, maybe this'll help get you started in astrophysics school."

"Holy cripes! What the fuc - shit - I mean - I can't take this kinda dough!"

"Okay." Payne slid the money back his way, and Tod's face dropped. Payne smiled. "Wait a minute. You can take it, and you will. But you have to promise you'll never change your mind and go to law school."

"Thanks, Mr. Payne!"

"Thanks for being my straight-man."

"Huh?"

"Never mind."

"It's sure been a pleasure having you stay here. You're the first celebrity I've ever known!"

"Tod, I think I'm starting to catch diabetes. See you later."

"Goodnight, Mr. Payne." Tod was still under the counter. "By the way . . . you're on the nose with the trial."

Payne marveled at how life sometimes tossed a ray of delight his way. He headed for the stairs, looking back. Tod was still on the floor, and he was apparently going to stay down until he figured out how he got there.

Up the stairs. Payne found each step higher than the last. The final one felt like a ten-foot wall. He walked down the hall and keyed the lock to his door. He stepped in his dark room.

Payne gasped at the face of a huge black man, who clamped a paw over his mouth. Two seconds - but it seemed like two years that Payne waited to die. After that, his assailant turned into Kenny Jackson. Payne had to pinch hard to keep his trousers dry.

Jackson, his big hand still clamped on Payne's mouth, put a finger to his lips. Payne tried his best to nod. He also prayed his heart would stop tap dancing across his ribs. Jackson gently let go, and Payne then noticed Carly sitting on his bed. They looked like commandos in their black getups. Jackson pointed at the door, and Payne walked into the hallway, still clutching his heart.

Carly followed Jackson out.

Payne breathed hard. "You scared the fuck out of- "

"Shut up," Jackson whispered, escorting Payne down the hall to a broom closet. He shoved him inside, Carly on their heels.

Payne, completely perplexed, watched Carly flip on the closet light and close the door.

"I'm sorry I scared you," Jackson whispered.

"Scared me? I think I just had a miscarriage!"

"Keep your voice down," Jackson said.

Payne stepped back and gave them a hard look. Carly had a nasty bruise over her left eye, and Jackson's face was swollen. "God damn, what happened this time?"

"Where have you been?" Jackson said.

"Out with the Aarons. In fact, I'm living with them now. I just came back here tonight to - what the hell happened to you?"

"Marc," Carly whispered, "we found Linville."

Payne looked at Carly as if he hadn't really heard her. He then looked at Jackson, who could only nod.

"We found him in a Harrisburg mortuary," Jackson said.

"You saw him? You actually saw him?"

"Oh, yeah, we saw him," Carly said.

"He's on ice, Marc, dissected just like I found him last summer."

"And he wasn't alone," Carly said.

Payne stopped. Confusion flooded his eyes. "What do you mean?"

"The place was full of 'em," Jackson said. "We saw a couple of men, a woman, even a little kid - all dissected just like Linville. It's a goddam chamber of horrors."

Payne leaned against the wall. "What in God's name is going on?"

"God doesn't have anything to do with it," Carly whispered, her voice trembling.

"A morgue full of them?" Payne said, still astonished. He cocked an eye at Carly's purple bruise.

"We got caught," Carly snapped. "We're lucky to be alive."

Jackson agreed. "We had to fight our way out. I don't think two or three federal employees are breathing anymore."

"You killed them? Holy shit," Payne said. He tried to organize his thoughts.

"They're probably clearing Linville and the rest of those bodies out right now," Carly said.

"Yeah," Jackson said, "while the rest of them are heading for Attica. They gotta know we came to you."

"In other words," Payne said, "we are in deep sewage."

"Nobody's safe," Carly said.

"Wait," Payne said. "When did this happen?"

"Couple of hours ago," Jackson said.

"Oh, god," Payne said. "Those bastards know everything. They must know I moved into Aaron's place. If they figure you'll come to me, they may be waiting over there!"

"Damn!" Jackson cried. Payne was ahead of him. He bounded out of the closet with Jackson and Carly in pursuit...

Jackson's coupe screamed down Constitution Avenue, the freezing wind ripping through his bullet-riddled windshield. Carly sat on Payne's lap in the passenger's seat. Payne frantically punched in Aaron's number on Jackson's cell phone.

"Son of a bitch – no signal!" Payne said.

"Keep trying," Carly said, pulling Jackson's CB microphone from the dash. She called the Attica dispatcher on emergency channel nine.

"Dispatch! This is Officer Farrel!"

A man's voice crackled over the speaker. "Dispatch.

Carly? What are you doing on this - "

"This is an emergency," Carly interrupted. "We need backup at the Aaron house." She turned to Payne and asked the address.

"Twenty-nine Brentwood Circle!"

Carly turned back to the mike. "Twenty-nine Brentwood Circle, code ten!"

"Code ten, copy," the dispatcher said. "What's going on?"

She knew the quickest way to draw some of the lazier cops out of the coffee shops. "Officer down!"

Jackson whirled the coupe onto Quaker Street and opened it up, breaking sixty down the two-mile stretch. The Aaron house was outside of town in Brentwood Estates.

"Marc, there's a piece in the glove box!" Jackson said.

Payne gave up on the cell phone and reached into the box, pulling out a holstered .38 caliber revolver.

"You ever use a gun?" Jackson hollered.

"Only in my dreams," Payne said.

The street was dry and easy to negotiate at this hour. Evans Avenue came up quickly, and Jackson made the turn too fast. The car drifted with a squeal, but it suddenly grabbed the road and powered south on Evans for a quarter mile. Brentwood Estates popped up on the horizon. Jackson downshifted and ripped Brentwood Drive with ease. He caught some gravel on the next turn, throwing the car onto the sidewalk. Jackson whipped the wheel and bounced them back down. The Aaron house was at the top of a steep hill thick with trees. The car skidded up to the property line.

Carly jumped out first. She drew her weapon and circled to the left. Payne put the .38 in his coat pocket and ran up the long drive, while Jackson slid to the right and found a grove of trees for cover.

"Be careful!" Carly hollered at Payne. "You don't know what you're walking into!"

Payne ignored her. He ran until the front door came into view. The porch light suddenly popped on and Payne slowed. He felt himself crouch when the door swung open. Jackson edged to Payne's right, and Carly remained off to the left near some bushes. Distant sirens screamed at the night.

Gracie Aaron stepped out on the porch and squinted at Payne. "Doc? Is that you?"

Payne and Jackson carefully studied her. It was so quiet. Sheriff White's civilian car drifted around the corner with a squeal. He was coming home from a poker game when he heard the call on his scanner. White sped up the street and stopped near Jackson's car.

"Doc?" Gracie hollered. She wore a long sweatshirt with no shoes. "What're you doing?"

"Sweet Thing, where are your folks?"

"Huh? Ma's in bed. Daddy's downstairs. What's going on?"

"Let's get them out of there," Jackson said.

White ran up to Carly, curiously surveying the scene. A patrol car rounded the corner, wailing madly with its over-heads flashing. As Carly started to explain, Payne hollered to Gracie. "Honey, I know this sounds crazy, but don't go back in the house. Come on out here."

"What?" She shyly pulled her sweatshirt over her knees. "Doc, I don't have anything on under this. I can't -"

"Don't argue with me!" Payne said. "Where is your dad?"

Gracie didn't know what to do. She danced on the cold concrete. "He's messing around with the furnace. We smelled gas, and he's checking the pilot -"

Her body suddenly catapulted, engulfed in a thundering white-blue ball of bricks, glass, and fire. Payne and Jackson went down as a wave of debris rolled over them and swallowed Carly and White. The blast blew the roof, sending a torrent of bricks and wood over the neighborhood. Payne was knocked wholly stupid. He saw Jackson on his knees, shaking his senses back to order. On the lawn, Sheriff White limped toward Gracie. Her body was twisted in a thick bush forty feet away. Payne tried to cry out, but his throat was full of smoke. He gasped as the sheriff picked Gracie up and carried her down to the street.

A terrified scream pierced the flames. Payne turned. It was Sybil. Jackson got to his feet just in time to see Payne sprint toward the inferno. He hollered for Marc to stop, but the attorney was gone. Jackson heard another scream inside. He sucked for air, and then followed Payne into the house.

An officer cried for help over the radio, ordering fire and rescue, code ten! Hurry, goddamit! He then ran to Sheriff White, who carried Gracie in his huge arms. They gently put her down on the walk. She wasn't breathing. The officer quickly began mouth-to-mouth as White fell back in excruciating pain. Another scream from the house pumped him. He looked up and saw Carly drunkenly running to the side of the house, where Sybil Aaron desperately hung out the bedroom window. The pain disappeared, and White sucked it up the hill. He reached the window just as Carly tried to pull Sybil out.

"Reed!" she desperately cried. "Gracie! Where is she?"

"She's out!" White said, pulling Sybil away from Carly and letting her fall on his shoulders. He turned and humped it back down the hill as three patrol cars littered the road.

Neighbors appeared from everywhere. A man in boxer shorts plodded barefoot through the snow with a blanket in his hands. He offered it as White tried to lay Sybil down without hurting her. Carly frantically looked at the officer tending to Gracie.

"Where's Kenny?" She looked back at the house.

The officer kneeling over Gracie stopped for a quick breath. "Him and somebody else went inside!"

"Oh, god!" Carly cried. She ran up the hill.

"Don't go up there, goddamit!" White yelled.

Carly didn't look back.

White gritted his teeth as Carly climbed the hill. He lowered his head for a moment and mustered some air. "Well, Virgil," he coughed, "here we go again."

"Hold it, Virg!" an officer called. "Fire's coming! Let rescue go in!"

"No time!" White sputtered. He pumped his knees and trailed Carly with surprising speed.

The front of the house was now engulfed. The heat there was lethal. Carly ran to the side windows, where she found the kitchen area not yet burning. She shielded her face and called toward the window. "Kenny! Kenny! Marc!"

White caught up with her. "You can't go in there!"

"Watch me!"

"Aw, dammit," White said. "Get the hell back." He rummaged through a small garden beneath the window, looking for a rock. Instead, he found a decorative wheelbarrow. He threw a hefty grunt, hoisted it on his shoulders and let it fly. It smashed through the window, and a blanket of smoke belched out. Carly tried to pull herself in, but White's big hand caught her and dragged her back.

"Let go of me!" Carly demanded.

"You got three big men in there! You could end up killing them and yourself! No offense, Officer, but you're too goddam small!"

"I can't just stand here and wait for them to burn up!"

"So, give me a goddam boost already!" He put his hand on her shoulder and stepped into her cupped hands. In a second, he rolled through the window.

The front yard became a sea of emergency vehicles and equipment. Engine 95 rolled in from the Brentwood station, followed by two ambulances and a pumper. The captain ordered a second alarm before his truck stopped.

Carly backed away from the heat, first looking at the paramedics, who feverishly worked on Gracie and Sybil. She looked back at the fire, her feet sinking into the mushy ground. Black smoke mushroomed into the sky, and now only half of the home was still standing.

The pumper crashed through a small wooden fence and rolled up the hill, its long ladder arm bending up at the elbow. A tiny soldier stood in the bucket, aiming his hose at the house as a thick stream of water burst out. Two firefighters plodded up the long hill in asbestos fire suits and gas masks. They hoisted their tanks and large axes, searching for an entryway. A sudden, desperate call pricked Carly's ears. Jackson appeared at the kitchen window.

"This way!" she screamed, running hard. The firefighters weren't nearly as graceful. Carly ran up just in time to see

Jackson fall to the ground.

He got up quickly, turning to the window when Carly reached him. Inside, Reed Aaron rolled over the sill. He limply dropped into Jackson's arms. At the window now, Marc Payne coughed and spit as he made his escape. The firefighters took Aaron out of Jackson's arms and carried him down the hill. Jackson and Carly broke Payne's fall.

"Virgil's still inside!"

"What!" Jackson said, looking back at the window. He turned to Payne, whose head was spinning wildly out of control. "Did you see him?"

Payne couldn't speak. Instead, he shook his head.

"It's cooked inside!" Jackson said.

"God, no!" Carly said.

As Jackson reluctantly turned back to the window, he heard a huge voice - the one that had struck fear in his heart for years.

"Somebody help me, goddamit!"

Through the smoke, a huge shaggy white dog appeared with two big arms around it. The mutt, dizzy from the smoke, squirmed and fought White all the way. White let him go, and the dog hit the ground running. Jackson ran to the window and tried to help the sheriff out, but got a healthy shove for his trouble. White pulled away and staggered down the hill. Jackson, Carly, and Payne leaned on each other and followed.

They stumbled to the command center, where they met an army of paramedics and firefighters. Carly's knees finally buckled. She spat black soot and mucus from her throat as Jackson grabbed her. White preferred to be sick all by himself. Jackson held Carly for a minute and then angrily stepped over to White. He took the sheriff's arm and spun him around.

"Get away from me, K.J.!" White hollered.

"Oh, so you got a problem with me, Virgil?"

"I ain't got nothing with you anymore!"

"You think I screwed you? Look at this, Virgil! Look at it! Your goddam fed hero is killing everybody in sight!"

"Let go of me!"

"We found Linville, you son of a bitch! We found him!"

White pulled away from Jackson's lethal stare. "What the hell are you talking about?"

"You don't know, Virgil?" Jackson growled.

Smoke bubbled at the base of White's gut. He couldn't speak. His empty eyes watched Jackson turn away and stagger back to Carly.

Payne watched them load his big brother into an ambulance. Aaron was motionless on the stretcher, a cervical collar on his neck. A paramedic attached IV lines, while a second frantically took instructions over the radio. Payne turned away as the ambulance screamed into the night. He limped to Gracie, who was being placed into another ambulance. Payne didn't want to look. He climbed in and sat on the bench next to her, dropping his head into his hands.

A raspy voice, soft and weak, fell on him. "Doc?"

Payne's head popped. He found Gracie's clouded eyes. "Sweet Thing!" Payne cried. "I'm here, honey, I'm here . . ."

21

Payne squeezed Aaron's hand and whispered softly. "Syb and Gracie are alive. They had a rough go, but they'll make it. We need you, big brother, so don't goddam die on us, you hear?"

Aaron's teary eyes followed Payne. His breath was slow, rhythmically following the gentle blips on the heart monitor. Thankfully, he breathed on his own, but Payne found little solace in that. His gut wrenched at the hideous skull tongs bolted to Aaron's head.

His voice was wet and druggy. "Take care . . . my girls."

"I'm watching our backs, I promise."

Aaron blinked away the tears.

"Mr. Payne? You'd better let him rest."

Payne turned and met a nurse's sympathetic smile. She thought she might be looking at a soldier fresh from combat - not that gorgeous man-babe attorney she'd been watching every day on *TV Trials*. Payne gingerly came about, his arms and hands buried in bandages.

He limped out of intensive care, holding his ribs as he stepped down the sterile corridor. In the visitor's waiting room, he waded through a wasteland of garbage - coffee cups, paper bags, notebook paper. The press hung out here until Sheriff White ordered the hospital cleared of anything resembling a reporter. Payne sat with a pained growl and lit a cigarette.

In a moment, Ken Jackson peered in. His face was swollen and his hair and eyebrows singed. "Marc? How's Reed?"

Payne waved him inside. "He's out of surgery - and stable. He's got some burns and a broken lumbar vertebrae - too early to tell if his spinal cord is damaged. They won't know for a few days."

Jackson limped on a badly bruised knee. He winced when he sat. "How about you?"

Payne shrugged. "A few cracked ribs . . . a concussion. I'll live - maybe." He took a hard pull on his cigarette.

Jackson rubbed his tired eyes. "I'm sorry, man. I'm so goddam sorry. If we'd just gotten Linville out of there without -"

"Stop," Payne said. "You gave it a hell of a try."

Jackson made a fist. "I swear to God, Marc, if Carswall was standing here right now I'd blow his goddam head off and gladly do the time."

"He'd probably catch the bullet in his teeth and spit it back."

Jackson gave up on his anger and rubbed the formidable knot on his knee. "How are Reed's wife and daughter?"

"That news is better," Payne said, exhaling the smoke. "Syb's in a lot of pain. Both legs are broken - cuts, concussion. She'll be okay." Payne felt a ball of tears welling in the back of his eyes. "Gracie - she's beat to hell . . . a concussion, broken jaw, both arms, a leg . . . they say she's lucky." Payne dropped his face into his hands.

Jackson put his hand on Payne's sore arm. "It's not your fault, Marc."

Payne coughed and let the anger dry his eyes. "Where's Carly?"

"Sleeping upstairs in a private room. She couldn't hold her head up anymore. We're afraid to go home."

"She's not alone, is she?"

"Jerry Monroe's with her - got his goddam gun drawn, locked and loaded. So, what do we do now?"

"Let's talk upstairs. I'll buy you a cup of coffee."

They stood and walked into the corridor, running head-long into Dan Williams. Willy talked fast before Jackson could throw him out, and in a minute, he went to the cafeteria with them . . .

Payne sipped his coffee, wincing in pain. Broken ribs, he was learning, afford no possible comfort. Jackson could barely hold a coffee cup in his swollen hand.

Williams puffed his pipe and managed a sympathetic grin. "You two look like dog dungy."

"It was a bad night," Jackson snapped.

"Of course," Williams said. "I am sorry. Thank God nobody was killed."

Payne lit a cigarette. He tried to sip his coffee again. "You said you have something to discuss?"

"Indeed."

Jackson didn't look up from his coffee. "So discuss."

"The investigators are sifting through Aaron's house, and the talk is they think it was a natural gas explosion. That old furnace apparently sprang a leak, and whammo!"

"That ain't exactly front-page news, Willy," Jackson said.

"No. What I wanted to tell you, is that I don't believe this disaster was an accident. I'm sure you two don't, either."

"What makes you think that?" Payne cautiously said.

"I was, uh, out of town until late last night, but I learned you all were rushing like wild men - and woman - to the Aaron house just before the explosion."

"So?" Jackson said.

Willy puffed and grinned. "Sounds like you knew something was amiss. My guess is Mr. Carswall tried to blow you all into next week because you found Linville Reeves' dissected body in that mortuary last night."

Jackson abruptly stopped drinking and looked at Payne.

Williams' grin had a wicked curl. "Just an assumption based on how you and your girl bolted out of there in a hail of gunfire."

Payne allowed a soft chuckle.

Williams kept puffing and pulled a pint of whiskey to brace his coffee. He sipped, savoring the tang. "Ah, breakfast of champions."

"Wait a minute," Jackson said. "The red car . . . son of a bitch; that was you?"

Willy grinned. "You think the department might see clear to buy me some new wheels? After all, I saved your butts in a spectacular act of heroism."

Jackson huffed a laugh and spoke to Payne. "This moron

broadsided the bastard who tried to kill us in Harrisburg."

"No, Mr. Payne, I saved their lives," Willy proclaimed.

"So, how long have you been following us?" Jackson asked.

"Since the day we went to the Medical Examiner's office and you introduced me to that deceased imposter."

"You mean you knew?" Jackson asked.

"I had a pretty good suspicion when you and Aaron lingered over that mess. I'll admit I was considering a good cookie-blow myself, but I had enough of my senses left to know you weren't marveling over the gentle nuance of a shotgun blast. Anywho, my interest grew even more after you and your girlfriend visited the Harrisburg veterinary clinic."

"How the hell did you know that?" Jackson said. "You were in the courtroom when we left."

"Jackson," Williams smirked, "do you think I'm a fool? . . . uh - don't answer that . . . I'm a firm believer in the powers of C.Y.A. I've had a few flunkies from the paper tailing you whenever I can't. For one thing, it gives Carswall other targets, and for another, my editor has a nasty habit of expecting stories to be filed every day. I broke a few speeding laws trying to get to Harrisburg that evening, but I got a call and heard you were on your way home. I spotted you on the road and gave you a lead before I turned around. I have to say, I nearly swallowed my tongue when I saw that truck try to squash you out on the bridge."

"You were behind us?" Jackson asked.

"I was about a mile or so behind," Williams said. "That semi blew by me in a big hurry."

"Thanks a hell of a lot for coming to help us."

"Hey, you were okay."

"We almost died!"

"Look, after I saw that the truck missed you, I turned around and tried to catch him and get a plate number. Then, I suddenly wondered if I was certifiably insane. You know, they might have killed me just for sport. So, I backed off."

Payne smiled at Willy's logic, but Jackson wasn't amused.

Willy shrugged. "Come on, Jackson. I may be a snoop, but

I'm a perfect coward. In fact, I thought that fed was going to ice me after I wrecked his pretty car last night."

Jackson mellowed. "I guess I ought to thank you."

"Thank me with an exclusive."

"Easy there, Scoop," Payne said. "Has it occurred to you that hanging around us right now may be hazardous to your health?"

"You lawyers have a nasty way with words."

"Wait, Marc," Jackson said. "Why can't he print our story? If we go public about finding Linville, it might protect us."

"Stop the press," Williams said. "You don't have a body."

"I saw it."

"Hey, I've seen three-eyed muskrats run along my ceiling - on two separate occasions - but you have to produce some evidence. Unfortunately, they've surely moved Linville's body by now."

"Would more bodies help?" Payne asked.

"Excuse me, Counselor, how's that?"

"We found a dozen dissected people and animals at Crane Lodge," Jackson said.

Williams stopped puffing. "You can't be serious."

"As a sucking chest wound."

"Good god grief," he whispered. His faced paled.

"What's wrong, Willy?" Jackson chided. "No smartass comeback? Aren't you having fun anymore? Reed Aaron and his family were damned near blown to pieces. The feds have killed three witnesses and some poor wino who had the bad luck of resembling Linville Reeves!"

"Take it easy, K.J.," Payne said.

"Take it easy, my black butt! Marc, we're all walking around with targets on our back!"

"Officer Jackson," Williams said, "for better or worse, I'm on your side."

"Oh, that's a real comfort!" Jackson blurted, waving Willy off.

Payne lit another cigarette, giving up on the coffee. "Okay, let's just calm down and think about this. Willy, how much of this saga have you documented?"

Willy's grin returned. "What do you think, Counselor?"

"I'd say everything is in a computer somewhere."

"Several computers, in fact. I've also given disks to a few trusted pals. If I'm pushed off a bridge, they have instructions to open the files and pass them on to the wire services. It might never fly, no pun intended, but the feds would have a nasty media mess to clean up." He spoke loudly to the ceiling. "Did you hear that, Carswall?"

"Your paranoia aside," Payne said, "you do have a hole card."

"Yeah, but what about us?" Jackson said.

Payne smoked. "Look, Willy, we can't produce Linville now, but Jackson and Carly still have a story to tell; and they have credibility. They're making unsubstantiated claims, but as long as they come forward, your ass is covered."

"I guess you're right," Willy said. "Yeah - we print it, and Carswall can't risk going after us . . ."

Payne turned to Jackson. "Look, K.J., if you and Carly go public, you go right on trial with Seth."

"Oh yeah, like I didn't do that on the stand already?" Jackson said. "Willy, write your story."

Williams relit his pipe. The smoke came out with a pensive sigh. "Have either of you wondered - is whatever's going on around here something we really want to know?"

Neither Payne, nor Jackson answered . . .

* * *

Judge Kathryn Falco opened her chamber door and politely nodded at Marcus Payne. Payne limped in with a small folder under one arm. Falco welcomed him in, and he sat in a large leather chair next to Roland Whittaker. The attorneys exchanged cold greetings, Whittaker uncomfortable with Payne's eyes. The judge circled her desk and sat, her hands tightly laced together.

"How are Reed and his family, Mr. Payne?"

Marc barely nodded. "Reed's doctor expressed optimism this morning. There's some feeling in his legs now."

"That's encouraging after just one week, isn't it?" Falco said.

"Maybe, Your Honor."

"Sybil and Gracie?" she asked.

"Sybil's improving. She has a lot of courage. Gracie, on the other hand, doesn't understand all of this, but who does? I appreciate your concern."

"Anything I can do, Mr. Payne," Falco said.

Payne nodded.

"I'm sorry, too," Whittaker said. "It was a tragic accident."

"Was it?" Payne said with a glare.

Payne's volatility unnerved Falco. She quickly opened her files and changed the subject. "Down to business, I'm afraid. I'll start by saying this week has been extraordinary. In fact, this entire month is one I'd just as soon forget. The statements officers Jackson and Farrel made about their alleged discovery of dissected bodies and animals is remarkable; but my inquiry hasn't turned up anything to substantiate their allegations."

"As I warned it wouldn't, Your Honor," Payne said.

Judge Falco agreed with a nod. "Beginning with this Crane Lodge Mortuary - there is no record of any such facility. Harrisburg County records show that Whispering Woods was seized by the I.R.S. seven months ago. Although we did get a confirmation of Crane Lodge from this other funeral director Officer Farrel talked to, the I.R.S. claims the building has been vacant and locked up tight."

"What about my inquiry into the death of Mr. Elvin Carter - or any reports of missing cadavers?"

Falco gnashed her teeth. "Mr. Carter died ten days ago. His death certificate shows he was processed at another mortuary. As for missing deceased persons in Harrisburg, there are no reports."

"Mr. Carter was a retired Inspector General for the Labor Department, wasn't he?" Payne sarcastically said. "A government agency, if I'm not mistaken?"

Falco sighed. "Mr. Payne, I know where you'd like to go with that, but -"

"Have you contacted Mr. Carter's family to ask what

funeral home received his body?"

"The wheels turn slowly," Falco said with resignation. "I've run into a lot of red tape in this investigation."

"Did you check out this so-called vacant building – Crane Lodge?" Payne asked.

"It took considerable doing for the Harrisburg District Attorney's office to show probable cause, but with my help they obtained a search warrant. The furnishings, equipment, even the light fixtures have been removed. The building is an empty shell."

"Does the report include a description that matches the extensive floor plan Officer Jackson drew for you?"

"It does," Falco said.

"A basement embalming lab, an elevator that leads to a second holding room, and a third lower level with walk-in freezers?"

Judge Falco closed the file. "Yes, Mr. Payne. The building was empty, but the officer's description precisely matched."

"How would Officer Jackson know the locked-up building's layout? Unless, of course, he was indeed prowling around there on the night that Reed Aaron's house later mysteriously blew up."

"I object to that implication, Mr. Payne," Whittaker interrupted. "A natural gas leak is hardly a mystery."

Payne ignored Whittaker. "This is also the same night that Jackson and Farrel were attacked by several gunmen right in front of this vacant building – a fact substantiated by an eyewitness, Dan Williams."

"Your Honor; I object."

"Take it easy, Roland," Judge Falco said, "we're not in court."

"Fine," Whittaker said. "Then I'll say Mr. Payne is blowing smoke to lay grounds for a god damned mistrial."

"Roland," Falco said again. "We're not in court, but you are addressing officers of the court. I will gladly cite you for contempt if you try to turn this into a pissing match."

Whittaker quieted, his mind constantly slipping back to a video floating in somebody's digital cloud. "I apologize, Judge."

"As you should," Falco said. She sat back in her chair and contemplated Payne's unbelievable presence. "Mr. Payne, rumor had it you quit the business. I wish you had."

"Me too, Your Honor. But somebody asked me to step to the plate one last time. He's now in the hospital with a metal halo screwed to his skull."

"I'm still in a quandary over your motive here," Falco said.

"Your Honor, Jackson and Farrel confessed to breaking and entering a mortuary that the government claims doesn't exist. You have a statement from Dan Williams that he saw them run from this nonexistent mortuary under fire. You have both an Attica and Harrisburg police report, confirming at least thirty bullet holes in Jackson's car. Williams states he was involved in a traffic accident with one of their assailants. The accident report is now missing, despite affidavits from the two Harrisburg police officers that responded. My motive is to suggest someone is tampering with this trial."

Falco closed her eyes and took off her reading glasses. She breathed a frustrated sigh and rubbed her eyes. "I don't believe this is happening, Mr. Payne. Is this the way all of your trials go?"

"If you don't believe it, read the *Sentinel*. Turn your cable news channels on every night. Williams has been busy."

"I don't suppose you had anything to do with that?" Whittaker said.

"Pardon me for saying," Payne said, "but both of you are now in this. You, and the Harrisburg D.A.'s Office, and the Harrisburg Police Department, and anybody else who can read. If you haven't figured it out yet, here's the deal: I just bought a very expensive life insurance policy."

"This is absurd," Whittaker said. "Forgive me, Your Honor, but Counsel is denigrating the court with nonsense even a supermarket tabloid wouldn't touch. I resent being made into a fool."

"You don't need my help," Payne said.

"Mr. Payne, please," Judge Falco interrupted. "Frankly, you must admit Jackson and Farrel's claim of dissected bodies in the mortuary is certainly the kind of publicized fodder that could lead to a mistrial."

"Judge, you may not believe this, but I don't want a mistrial. I'm winning, whether Mr. Whittaker likes it or not. The problem is, some of us may not live to see my client acquitted. You have to admit there've been quite a few 'accidents' involving the principals in this case."

"Granted," Falco said. "But numerous dissected bodies hidden away in a mortuary? Who are these people? They wouldn't just disappear without someone missing them."

Payne tossed his folder on Falco's desk.

She curiously looked. "What's this?"

"Missing persons reports," Payne said.

Falco curiously thumbed through the documents.

"In addition to Linville Reeves," Payne said, "Jackson and Farrel found two men, a child and a woman. Item one: A Rockford missing persons report filed by Mrs. Rodney Saunders several weeks after the Reeves murders. Her husband, known as 'Spider' Saunders, disappeared while camping in woods near Rockford. He has never been found. Spider was last seen with a friend, Alvin Pike. Pike also vanished the same week as Saunders. Saunders' abandoned truck was found near Echo Lake, the area where the State Patrol discovered a dissected elk mentioned by my witness, Dr. Luciano. This is the incident Jonathan Carswall investigated and later denied.

"Item two: Corey James, age seven, was camping with his parents and disappeared near Barrow Bluffs. Corey wandered away late at night and has never been found. Five miles from the campsite where Corey disappeared is the Robert Osmund farm. This is where Dr. Luciano was chased off by Jonathan Carswall - the ranch where she observed a dissected horse and two calves.

"Item three: Susan Walker, an Arapaho National Forest ranger, disappeared in the mountains one week prior to the Reeves murders. She left behind an invalid mother and a fiancée whom she was going to marry three weeks later. It's unlikely she would run away from home. Just eight miles away in the town of Fremont, two citizens reported unusual lights in the sky on the last day Ms. Walker was seen alive. I researched those witnesses. One has since died - found in the woods with a bullet in his head. The sheriff concluded he was the victim of a hunter's stray bullet, but the shooter was never found. The second witness died in an automobile accident a week after the UFO sighting."

Judge Falco intently read the missing persons reports. She finally put the folder down. "I'll admit this is shocking, Mr. Payne, but this information cannot be introduced into the Cameron trial. Frankly, I don't know what you want from me."

"I already have what I want, Your Honor. You're my premium on that insurance policy. You're right - I have no hard evidence of tampering, but you have a file full of coincidences to investigate if Jackson, Farrel - or I get killed."

"Your Honor, don't fall for this grandstanding," Whittaker said.

"Sorry to burst your bubble, Mr. Prosecutor," Payne said, "but I'm not fighting you in court. I'm fighting your friend Carswall."

"Here we go. Again, the mysterious Jonathan Carswall, creeping about in the night with his space ships and his buzz saw!"

"Stop it, Roland," Falco said. She stood and paced the room while Payne calculated the seconds of silence. The judge inspected her 'ego wall' for a moment, wishing those damned certificates bore someone else's name. She came back and sat down. "Mr. Payne, I'll admit this information is disturbing. If this were some legal sleight-of-hand, it's hard to believe the officers and this Williams character would jeopardize their careers for you. Frankly, I'm beginning to suspect there is something going on, but I am not a witness for the defense. I can't walk in the court and throw my hands in the air - 'ladies and gentlemen, your government is hiding something, so I'll just dismiss the charges.' Your key is that body you claim was found. You must offer something - anything, Mr. Payne - that proves its existence if you expect the house of cards to fall."

"But Linville Reeves was cremated, wasn't he, Your Honor?" Payne said with malice. "A damned homicide victim cremated! I know you people live in the sticks, but doesn't anyone around here have any regard for proper procedure in a criminal investigation? So much for an exhumation motion, and, so much for proof, but I assure you this jury won't enter deliberations without that little tidbit stuck in their collective craw!"

"This is bullshit!" Whittaker said.

"Roland, shut up!" Falco barked. "This meeting is over, gentlemen. The jury has been locked up for seven days. They are undoubtedly apprehensive and eager to get on with this trial. Mr. Payne, the court is aware of your concerns and will take the matter under advisement. In the meantime, you will conduct your defense according to the canons of the court. I don't want any games."

"It's always a game, Your Honor, you know that," Payne said.

"Perhaps," she sighed, "but I make the rules. The jury must not learn about Mr. Aaron's accident, or any of the incidents discussed here. They only know this disruption was due to matters not concerning them. If you imply anything else, I will carry out my previous threat of hanging you in the courtyard. Do you understand?"

"By the way," Payne said as he stood, "if you lose that file, you can call WCBC. Rumor is somebody leaked it to them this morning."

"Good day, Mr. Payne," Falco hollowly said.

Payne left quickly, but Whittaker meandered out. He still had visions of thirteen-year-olds in his head. When the door closed, Judge Falco could breathe again. She stared at Payne's file for ten more minutes . . .

22

The court reporter read the court transcript aloud, instructed by Judge Falco to review Seth Cameron's testimony up to the point where court recessed a week ago. The jury spent most of the down time individually in their rooms, or together watching movies. Many suffered from cabin fever. The mood in the gallery wasn't much better. The usual spectators were back, mixed with first-timers who watched Seth Cameron's opening testimony on TV. The journalists in press row looked like refugees from a border war. Attica bars did a year's worth of sales the last week, thanks to the media. Rusty Wade used the time to enhance tavern receipts with sales of his book.

As the court reporter continued to slug through Seth's strange testimony, Payne leaned back and winked at Cameron, who dutifully watched from the witness stand. The empty chair by Payne's side reminded Seth of the hole in his heart.

Jackson and Carly sat nearby, suspended from duty pending investigation of their startling admission to breaking into Crane Lodge Mortuary. No charges had been filed, however, because officially, there is no legal charge for breaking and entering a building that does not exist.

Dan Williams pulled a swig from his flask to the chagrin of a few hung-over reporters sitting by him. The *Sentinel* was out on a limb printing Willy's stories, but circulation was up 30 percent, online subscriptions had doubled, and advertisers were now in a bidding war for space. It made a mighty strong limb. Williams watched Jonathan Carswall walk into the courtroom. He nudged his fellow scribes, who all perked and started writing excitedly. This was a rare appearance for the black-eyed gentlemen with the silver hair.

Payne noticed Carswall, too. He made a point of waving so everyone would see. Carswall never looked at Payne. He appeared unconcerned that every eye in the place landed on him at the same time. Payne looked at Judge Falco, who also checked out Carswall. Her eyes then dropped to Payne's thin smile. Secretly, in some strange-minded way, she admired him. She occasionally glanced at Roland Whittaker - yet another enigma. Falco thought she knew Roland well, but even he was behaving oddly. If she ever saw the video in which the D.A. and his friends unwittingly starred, she'd pack her bags and become a hermit the remainder of her years.

Falco nodded as the transcript was completed. Out of control, she thought, I'm no more running this show than I am able to fly in Cameron's space ship. "You may proceed, Mr. Payne."

Payne slowly stood, his ribs protesting. His unexplained bruises nudged the curiosity of a few jurors. "Seth, let's pick up where we left off. You and Linville Reeves were hiding by your cabin. You had your knife, and Linville had his shotgun. The aircraft landed in the field, and you saw a door open. Please continue."

Seth gave a nod. "Yes, sir. Me and Linville, we scrunched down and peeked out. Inside the thing, it was real bright, and we seen these shadows moving around. Then, something moves to the door. It was hard to see exactly what it was until he comes down this stairway thing. Right behind him was another one. They come down, and they stop."

"You say 'him?' Was this someone like yourself?"

"Not exactly. I mean, they had two legs and two arms and all, but they wasn't like nobody I ever seen."

"Describe them."

"They was bigger than us - taller and wider. They had arms and legs like I said, but they looked kinda cumbersome."

"Did they have faces?"

"They was wearing helmets with dark shields, so I never saw their faces. They had silver suits on, and there was big packs on their backs that had hoses running to their helmets."

"What you're describing sounds like space suits our

astronauts wear. Have you ever seen pictures of astronauts, Seth?"

"Yeah, I seen 'em on TV, but they didn't look like that exactly. Their helmets was kinda oblong, and their bodies was wide and bulky."

"Were there any insignias or symbols on their suits?"

"Yeah. They had a dark blue patch on their shoulders that had writing on it."

"Writing? Like numbers, or letters?"

"No. It was symbols I didn't understand."

"Seth, forgive me for asking, but you can read, can't you?"

"Yes, sir, but this wasn't no words. Like I say, they was real strange symbols."

"Okay, go on."

"They carried these big lights, and they flashed them around like they was looking for something. All a sudden, old Jake lets out a bark, and he tears out after 'em."

"Did Jake attack them?"

"I think he had it in mind. I got the idea they was scared of him. But one of 'em raises his light and trains it on Jake, and something real strange happens next. That light flashed real bright, and old Jake lets out a yelp and falls right in his tracks."

"Did they kill him?"

"He looked dead, but after what happened to us later, I think maybe they just stunned him. Leastwise, I never seen him again."

"What next?"

"We're scared as hell now. I told Linville maybe we oughta go back to the house, get the girls and run like hell. But Linville, he said we gotta protect his family and his farm. I didn't think it was too smart, but if I took off, Linville woulda stayed right there, so I stayed.

"The other one comes back outa that ship, and they go on looking around. They shined their lights at the house. That was it for Linville. He was gonna stand his ground right there before they got any closer. He hitches up his twelve-gauge and walks out in the open and confronts 'em head-on. He points the gun at 'em, and he hollers, 'You stop right there, boys!'"

"Did you step out, too?"

"I didn't have no gun, Mr. Payne. I just stayed there by the corner and said my prayers."

"What happened next?"

"They stopped kinda sudden. Old Linville, he had two shots, and he was gonna blast 'em, I'm sure of it. He goes on yelling at 'em, but they didn't back down. One of 'em raised his light, and Linville hitches up, ready to shoot at the same time. But the light hits Linville, and he drops his twelve-gauge. He falls on the ground, screamin' in pain, and his body starts a-shaking like all get-out."

"Was he shot?"

"No. He was squirming like maybe he was 'lectrocuted. His throat was strained, but he hollert, 'Run Seth! Get outa here!' But I couldn't just leave Linville laying there. I was still hiding in the dark, and these two things come up real fast. From what I already seen, I figured to be a goner myself, but I gripped my old knife and thought maybe I could stick at least one of 'em. I jumped out and scared hell outa them, swinging that old knife every which-way. But I didn't hit nothing, and one of 'em knocks me down. I rolled, and I see Linville's twelve-gauge, so I grabbed it and hitched it up to blast at 'em. Next thing I know, that light hits me, and I fall back and shoot straight up in the air."

"Did you hit anything?"

"No, sir. I just blasted once inta the sky, and then I dropped the rifle, 'cause I was burning up inside."

"What happened to you?"

"That light was 'lectrocuting me. I thought it was gonna kill me. My arms and legs felt like they was on fire, and my heart was jumping. The more I tried to fight, the worse it got. Linville hollers at me to try and relax like he was doing. When I did, it still hurt, but it wasn't as bad. We both just laid real still, and these things, they come and stand right over us like they was studying us. One of 'em reached down and started poking at me. The other kept his light on us. Then the one that was poking me picks up Linville's twelve-gauge, and he starts to studying it. The damn fool looks right down the barrel, and I prayed the gun would go off. But then he dropped it. Then, he picks up my knife and studies it.

"Then," Cameron said, his voice cracking, "while the other one was poking and messing with Linville, the other one knelt down aside me. He pulls out this thing that looks like a gun maybe. He puts it aside my head, and I figure I'm done for. But I hear this pop, and my head felt like it busts into a million pieces. I don't see nothing but lights and flashes for a minute. When I look up - my head hurting real bad - I see him still holding that gun. He shot something into my head, Mr. Payne. I know everybody thinks I'm crazy, but I swear it's the truth. They shot something into my head."

"Okay," Payne said. The jurors floated in a stupefied haze, their eyes devouring Seth. "What happened next?"

"My head was throbbing something awful. Then, they shoot Linville in the head like they done me, and he grunts out with his eyes closed, just like I done. Next thing, they turn off the light, and that burning feeling goes away. I figure maybe I can run, but when I tried, my whole body burns real bad, and I fell back. Then I couldn't feel nothing but that throb in my head."

"Did you and Linville say anything to each other?"

"After we both got hit in the head with that thing, I really don't recollect us being able to say nothin' more. My brains was telling me to move, but I couldn't feel nothin' but this tingly pain all over - my mouth and throat was numb, and my legs was just like old dead tree stumps. I'm layin' on the ground, planted in the dirt."

"What happened next?"

"I couldn't move my head much, and all I really saw good was Linville laying next to me. One of them things goes back towards their ship and out of sight. The other one gets down and commences to rip Linville's bedclothes off. Then I hear both Mary and Lisa screaming from somewheres around the house, and the thing stands up and points that light in their direction. I know what musta happened next, cause they stops a-screaming. Then that thing walks towards them and out of my sight." Cameron buried his head in his hands and rubbed furiously.

Payne rounded the tormented jury and watched a few eyes. He liked what he saw. "Okay, Seth, take your time. What happened then?"

Cameron took a deep breath and looked back at Payne. "Me and Linville was head-first in the weeds a-lookin' at one another - both of us trying to say something, but nothing coming out. Then I kinda swiveled my eyes about, and I seen that thing drag Mary up to us and drop her alongside Linville. It's plain that she's feeling that 'lectricity, cause she's real panicky and in awful pain. Then, that thing goes away, and in a minute he drags poor Lisa up next to us. From what I seen, it looks like maybe she's passed out or just froze-up with fear, cause she's real limp."

Cameron's breaths grew shorter as he spoke. "Then, my eyes come up and see the other thing come back from where their ship was. He's carrying this big gadget about the size of a suitcase, made outta what looks like metal. He sets it down next to us, and both them things commence to open it. One of 'em pulls out what looks like some kinda instrument, while the other grabs ahold of Linville's head. Then . . . then . . . they snap this big blade from the end of that hose . . . and one of 'em . . . one of 'em goes up and stabs it right into Linville's neck . . ."

Falco gaveled at the disgusted gasps and whispers.

"He was gagging and spitting, and his eyes just glazed up. I know he musta died real quick, and I hear this gadget of theirs make some kinda sucking noise, and that hose pumps up. I swear to God, I reckon they was sucking the blood outa him. . ."

"Order," Falco said, quelling more gasps.

Seth lost his awareness of the courtroom. His eyes were in that horrible place. He dropped his head and wept.

The judge sadly looked at Cameron as she spoke. "Your client needs some time. We'll recess for an hour." She gaveled and quickly escaped to her chambers. . .

* * *

Payne retreated to Reed Aaron's office, resisting the urge to throw a few punches at the reporters along the way. The journalists chased him, flinging questions like stones. Payne rushed in, throwing his back to the door and heaving breaths. His eyes remained closed as he fumbled with his cigarette. He pulled the butt to his lips and sucked mercilessly, closing his eyes and taking a long drag.

"Smoking killed my father . . ."

Payne jumped and almost ducked, his eyes popping at Carly Farrel, who sat at Aaron's desk. "Carly," Payne breathed, "do you get some kind of wicked pleasure - scaring the hell out of me?"

"Hey, I was here first."

"I hope you don't mind if I hide here with you." Payne sucked his cigarette and slumped in a chair.

"Dad smoked three packs a day," Carly said, watching Payne finish the smoke with three hard drags. "The doctor said his lungs looked like coal mines."

Payne smashed the butt in an ashtray and lit another. "I'm not in the mood for a lecture right now."

"Sorry. I guess I have an aversion to self-destruction. You don't strike me as the suicidal type."

"I'll work on it. Where's K.J.?"

"Taking a walk. Seth's testimony isn't doing much for his sanity."

"Sanity's in short supply." He leaned back and puffed.

Carly measured Payne. "I'm scared, Marc."

"You're looking at a charter member of the club, honey. This thing's getting way too surreal . . . even for me. It keeps up, I'm gonna have to wear a diaper."

"Do you believe Seth?"

"He's telling the truth. What I believe doesn't matter."

Carly heaved a sigh. "Spoken like a true lawyer. I don't know if I came up here to hide from Carswall, Seth, or you."

Payne managed a chuckle. "For what it's worth, I don't

think Carswall will try any more 'accidents' in light of the publicity. It'll probably cost you and K.J. your jobs, but it beats slow torture."

Carly shrugged with resignation. "Kenny and I can start over; but what about you?"

"What about me? They can lift my license and frame it around Carswall's butt for all I care. I'm sure they'll tighten the nut on me - probably the IRS for starters, but I wish them luck. Hell, I have money stashed all over the world. When this ends, I'm going dark, I assure you."

"You lawyers have it all figured out, don't you?" Carly grumbled.

"You don't like me much, huh?"

"With you and Aaron, I make an exception; but as a rule, defense lawyers and I don't mix."

"The old 'cop hates lawyers thing,' right?"

She nodded with a smile. "I'll tell you one thing - before all this happened, you have no idea how much I especially hated lawyers like you."

"I hope you'll hang on to that exception."

"Marc, you're a brilliant man; you could be anything you put your mind to. Why did you side up on the wrong team?"

"I could have answered that two years ago, but I have no idea now."

Carly shook her head. "Pardon me, but those of us who'd like to stop the tailspin this world's in don't have much use for lawyers who keep criminals out of jail."

"The job comes with a steep price tag. . ."

She felt a sudden burst of sadness. "I'm sorry for being so hard on you. You didn't deserve the kind of retribution you got."

Payne crushed his cigarette. "Lori didn't deserve it." He tried to break the spell. Sympathy angered him, no matter how well intended. "So, why so much bitterness toward lovable me?"

She shrugged. "It's not you; it's the whole damned system."

"And I'm part of it . . ."

"Yeah, you are." She nervously wrung her hands. "Before I moved here, my brother and I were on the job with the Harrisburg Police Department. A couple years ago, a four-teen-year-old kid shot him to death."

"Oh, god . . . Carly, I didn't know that. . ."

"I watched that little bastard's trial, and listened to his attorney dish out blame. He blamed gun makers. He cried racism. He blamed drugs. He blamed the cops. Everybody got blamed but the son of a bitch who pulled the trigger. Suddenly, the punk was the victim, and his lawyer had the jury in tears. Instead of the lethal injection he deserved, he went down for manslaughter - seven-to-twenty plus time served . . ."

Payne lit a third cigarette. He had no reply.

"The only consolation is that Dad smoked himself to death before it happened. He didn't have to listen to lawyers debate sociology. He didn't have to watch that jury put a seven-year price tag on his son's life. But you know what makes me hate lawyers and judges most? That little gang banger will kill somebody again when he gets out; and when he does, someone else buries their brother, while another lawyer like you sings the same old tune."

"You're blaming the singer instead of the song, Carly," Payne sadly said. "I didn't invent the game; I just play it better than anybody else."

"And that's a crock of shit, Marc," she said. "Maybe you ought to do a five-year tour in a patrol car and try playing your game in the real world."

"You're lecturing again."

"I'm making a point!" Carly said.

"Point taken. You're right, lawyers don't see it from your perch, but what you don't understand is that you simply don't count."

"What the hell does that mean?"

"You're a cop, Carly; you're not a player. The system isn't about justice for the victim and punishment of the guilty. It's about lawyers winning or losing the big prize. The judge keeps score - one lawyer wins, one loses. The winners go to

Congress and make more rules for the game, and the losers keep on trying to win."

"What about the victims?"

"Victims, defendants, they're at the bottom of the food chain in the criminal justice system. It's a game, girl. There are lots of pawns, but there's only one king."

"Oh, please! That's your idea of justice?"

"Justice exists only in your 'real world.' If you kill a fleeing bank robber, you got justice. If you book him and leave it for us to decide - then justice yields to power. We deal, we profit, we move on."

Carly ruefully shook her head. "Don't you have some fraternal code of silence that prevents you from admitting that?"

Payne playfully smiled. "Who are you gonna tell - a judge? Hell, a judge is just a lawyer in a choir robe."

Payne's words echoed into a thick silence. Carly shook her head and stared out the window. "You know, Marc, I don't know why, but I do like you. Your attitude sucks - but I like you. I don't understand why a man with such a big heart can be so cynical."

"You check your heart at the door when you take the bar exam."

"I don't buy that. Behind that hard-ass wall, you're a good man."

"Good man? Sure - I'm the best. But as attorneys go, I'm pure, uncut poison." Payne puffed a good smoke ring.

"So, why do you care enough to risk your life for Seth and a couple of no-count cops?"

"Experience is a cruel teacher," Payne said. "And I don't count any more than you these days."

Carly stared at Payne like a perplexed judge.

Payne sighed. "Look, Carly, it's a long shot, but a smart pawn can take a king - or at least make him run."

"Maybe," Carly said.

"You just listen to me; this isn't the scumbag defense lawyer talking now. I'm a friend who loves you and that insane boyfriend of yours. I know what's going on in K.J.'s heart. The only time I've ever seen a man's eyes reflect so much love for a woman was when I looked in the mirror a few years ago. Just look out for each other and forget about changing the world. The only thing you'll change is you."

Carly looked into a face that now revealed the real man. She wiped a tear and walked to him. After some hesitation, she gently hugged him. Payne clumsily returned the embrace, his heart aching for the indescribable feeling of a woman's touch.

In a moment, Carly finally let go, and Payne flashed a perfect smile. "See? That wasn't so bad. . ."

Carly shrugged and walked out the door.

Payne watched her leave. He then went to the old paper bag full of photographs in the drawer. Lori had her arm around Payne. In another moment, she would kiss him . . .

* * *

Payne circled the jury. He looked at Seth, whose eyes were flat. "Alright, Seth, let's resume. We stopped just as you explained how you and Linville were lying on the ground, and your assailants dragged Mary and Lisa nearby. You all were paralyzed by the numbing effects of some type of electrical current. And then you watched one assailant stab Linville in the neck. It is your testimony that Linville died at that time, as you believe the apparatus in his neck drained his blood. Is that correct?"

"Yes, sir," Cameron said.

"Please tell us what happened next."

"Well, this ain't pretty, but I ain't got no good way to tell it. After they killed Linville, they pulled that shiv out of his neck. Then they both get down close to him, and one of 'em has that gun I told ya about earlier. He points it at Linville's head, and this tiny red light starts a-tracing across Linville's forehead. And I suddenlike see smoke risin' up from his head, and then I smelled somethin' awful. I tried to scream out, and about that time I hear Mary trying to scream, too, but we both just couldn't make nothing much come out. I couldn't move, I swear.

"I'm just down with my face in the dirt, and I'm trying to see what they's doing to Linville, but mostly all I can see is his head . . . and it's opening up as they's burning away with that red light. I just can't believe what I'm seeing. And then, all a-sudden one of them bastards starts to pullin' at Linville's hair, and lord a-god if the top of Linville's head don't just come right off, easy as ya please."

Seth's voice choked up, and he looked at the jury box. The eyes that met him ran from shock to utter horror, while a few seemed more perplexed than anything else. Judge Falco lightly rapped her gavel to bring the muttering gallery to order.

Payne glided by the jury box, as if he was now defending them. "Go on, Seth."

"They took the top of his head off, and then they starts in again with that light, and next thing I know, they pulled his brain right outa his skull. I know it sounds crazy, but I swear that's what they done."

The courtroom was now deathly silent. Spectators in the gallery looked at each other with incredulous eyes. In press row, most of the reporters had stopped writing.

Payne swallowed hard. "Go on, Seth."

"I was scared outa my wits now, and I know Mary was, too, 'cause I could hear her gruntin' and whimperin'. And then, they start cuttin' Linville with that light again. They burn him at his throat, and they cut right down the front of his chest and on down to his loins. Then they commenced to taking out his insides, and one of 'em, real careful-like, just plucks Linville's eyes right out of his head. They worked on him like Linville was some kinda bug." Cameron winced and rubbed his head.

Payne steadied Cameron - and the jury. "Ok, Seth, just take it slowly. I know this is difficult, but you must tell us everything you remember. Now, the two assailants removed Linville's internal organs. Was there a lot of blood?"

"No, sir. That's what I mean when I say they musta pumped the blood outa him earlier, 'cause there wasn't no blood at all. Linville looked like he was made of wax or something."

"What did they do with the brain and the organs that they cut out?"

"I don't rightly know. Like I say, I couldn't move too good. They pulled that stuff outa him, and then they'd move around outa my sight, so I just can't tell ya."

"Ok, Seth, continue. What happened next?"

"So then them two bastards wandered off towards the farm and left us all layin' there for a real long time, maybe an hour or more. I remember tryin' to move, and looking at poor old Linville. And then I hear some rustling around, and they come back and head for their ship, carryin' some kinda cases with them. They was outa sight for a time, and I prayed maybe they was gonna leave, but they come back and starts payin' real close attention to the girls. I was thinking we was next to get stripped and sliced up. About then, I hear Mary scream. I tried to move, but it made me feel like I was on fire again, and I couldn't really see what they was doing. But I know them bastards was going at her."

"Did they cut Mary open, too?"

"No, sir."

"Then what happened to Mary and Lisa?"

"Well," Cameron said, taking a deep breath, "what I could see was they commenced to strip their bedclothes off. Then they kneels down and started doin' something to them - I think they was . . . they was maybe doing something bad to their privates."

"Do you mean they were raping the women?"

"No," Cameron said. He squirmed in his chair. "Not like they was jumping on them and having their way. They was in those big, bulky suits, ya know. What I mean was, from what I could see, it looked almost like they was treating them like lab rats or something."

"Seth, the evidence presented in this case clearly indicates both women were bruised in and around their 'privates,' as you call them. Do you know how Mary and Lisa suffered this abuse?"

"You don't have to be so like a fox, Mr. Payne. I ain't too book-smart, but I ain't stupid. You're asking me if I raped them."

"Just answer the question, Seth. Do you know how Mary and Lisa suffered this sexual abuse?"

"Hell, yeah, I do. Ain't it pretty obvious?"

Judge Falco moved in before Whittaker had a chance to object. "Mr. Cameron, just answer Mr. Payne's question and don't argue."

"Yes, ma'am," Cameron said. "Them bastards was the ones that hurt Mary and Lisa. I don't rightly know what it was they done, or how they done it, but I did see enough to know they was abusin' them in their privates. Maybe I ain't much for nothin' and drinks and makes a fool of myself sometimes, but I never raped no woman! And I sure as hell would kill myself before I ever hurt Mary or Lisa or Linville, god dammit!"

"Mr. Cameron," Falco said. "Do not use that language in my courtroom."

Cameron gritted his teeth and rubbed a sharp pain from his head. "I . . . don't mean no offense to you or your court, ma'am."

"Very well," Falco said. "Continue, Mr. Payne."

Payne approached Seth and gave him a gentle smile. "Alright, Seth. Your testimony is very shocking, in light of the evidence that the prosecutor presented. As a matter of fact, everything you've told us so far doesn't match up with the physical evidence. First of all, the medical examiner seems to think Linville was shot in the head with a shotgun."

"Objection!" Whittaker said. "Counsel misstates the medical examiner's testimony."

"The medical examiner clearly testified that he never established positive identification of the body," Payne said. "Therefore, his testimony that the dead man he examined was Linville Reeves is presumptive and not based on personal knowledge."

Falco wavered as Payne stared at her. After a moment's hesitation, she ruled. "Objection overruled, Mr. Whittaker."

Payne returned to Cameron. "The medical examiner thinks Linville was shot with a shotgun, Seth. What do you have to say to that?"

Cameron shook his head. "That ain't how Linville was killed. I shot the rifle straight up in the air, like I told you earlier - way back when I had it in mind to shoot one of them bastards from the ship."

"Seth, there is solid evidence, however, that proves Mary and Lisa were killed with your knife. If you know, how did Mary and Lisa Reeves die?"

"Well, I was so mad that I wanted to kill both them bastards before they'd do the girls like they done Linville. I got real hateful, and the madder I got, the more my head burned up inside."

"Describe this feeling, Seth."

"It's that thing they shot inside my head. Every time I got myself riled enough to fight, I'd see stars and feel that burn. It's the same feeling I got later when I hurt the sheriff."

"Do you still experience this sensation?"

"I feel it coming on sometimes when I remember all this. Like now, when I talk about it, I gotta keep from getting too riled, 'cause I'm afraid them stars and the burning might come back."

"So, you felt this burn when they attacked the women; what did you do?"

"I seen my knife laying close to me, and I'm thinking I wanna kill them bastards. So - pain running through me or not - I was gonna try. My head was burning up, and I see lots of stars. Next thing I know, I jumped for my knife. The pain was killing me and I was real clumsy and stiff, but I was crazy mad. I remember grabbing my knife and going after one of them bastards, but I was just too clumsy. I swing that knife like all get-out, and I'm all a-sudden blowing up with pain. I only remember a little of it, but I know I came down on Lisa. I started stabbing and stabbing. I couldn't help myself, I swear!"

"Seth, Mary was found with your knife still lodged in her chest. . ."

"I know! I seen her! I musta stabbed her, too! And them bastards, now they're acting pretty shook up, 'cause there's the two dead girls laying there, and I'm squirimin' around and trying to get back up, and there's blood everywhere. Goddam!" Cameron scrubbed the tears from his eyes.

"Take your time, Seth. What happened next?"

"They back off, and they pick up their cases and gadgets, and they head towards the ship like they're done with it and wanna get out of there. I was still crazy mad, and that old wind was blowing hard - it was like hate blowing into my brain. I don't know how, but suddenlike, I feel like maybe I can move again. I see this big old rock next to me, so I pick it up. Them bastards ain't even looking my way, so I run just as hard as I can, and I whumped that old rock right upside one of them bastard's head. Lickety-split, his helmet cracks open in the back, and he falls down. He's down and kinda stunned, so I whumped him another good one, and I drop down on him and starts ripping at him. I was shredding him up like I was an old wildcat, and I rip this blue patch off his arm."

"What did he do?"

"On his back, he wasn't much for a fight, and I was getting the best of him. But then - wham! The other one came down atop of me and hit me on the head. I stagger and drop right next to Linville like I was dead. Last thing I remember is the bastard comes up and commences to kicking hell outa me."

Cameron stopped and stared at the floor. "I must have passed out, 'cause that's all I remember until the next morning. I come-to around sunup, and I found them bodies next to me. So, I pulled myself up and I run to town the best I could to get help . . ."

Payne stalked, carefully inspecting the shell shocked jury. "Seth, you have testified before this court and promised to tell the truth. I'll ask you now, do you stand by your testimony?"

"It's what happened, Mr. Payne. Them bastards killed the only family I ever had." Cameron's eyes suddenly turned to the jurors, who sat with their mouths agape. "Maybe you think I'm crazy. If that's what you wanna believe, more power to ya. But if any of you got family - little kids and such - you better take care, 'cause them bastards are still out there. That's all I got to say."

Payne slowly walked back to his table and sat. "I have no

more questions, Your Honor."

Judge Falco looked at the jury. Some of them appeared on the verge of nausea. She turned her eyes to Whittaker, who blankly stared back. She then looked at Seth Cameron, who rested his head in his hands.

This isn't going to work, Falco thought, nobody's home.

She cleared her throat. "We'll recess until nine tomorrow morning, at which time the prosecutor may cross-examine the witness."

The reporters bolted for the doors. Everyone else in the courtroom had trouble finding their feet . . .

23

For what it was worth, Seth found dinner pretty tasty. Jail food wasn't all that bad. Seth figured he'd be eating it the rest of his life, so there ain't no use in running it down.

Seth looked forward to prison. The county lockup was dismal, the cells dingy and small, and Seth never had a chance to get acquainted with other prisoners. He was lonely for friends and conversation. The county guards weren't mean to him, but they didn't have much time to converse. In fact, since this nightmare began, Seth's only solid contact came from Officer Jackson, Mr. Payne, and Mr. Aaron, but Seth thought he fit in their company like a fish fits in a tree.

Prison will be a good change, Seth reckoned. Probably some fearful types to look out for, but he wasn't particularly scared of fearful types anymore.

Seth pushed the table away and leaned back on his cot, propping a leg up. He held a cigarette between his thumb and first finger, watching the smoke rise and fall. Contentment tasted good - better than he could ever recall. His story was told. Months of anticipation fell off his small back in just a few tough hours. To his surprise, the telling had been far easier than the waiting.

Yeah, prison won't be so bad, he thought. If they vote to stick me with a needle and kill me, they'll just make things easier, but a life sentence will do me fine, too. It ain't such a bad deal - hot meals, a roof over my head, maybe a job in the laundry. They say pick your friends real careful in stir, though. Ya don't want to end up somebody's girlfriend. Mainly, mind your own knittin', don't sass no guards, don't snitch, keep your chute to the wall, and survive. Hell, he thought, rules in stir ain't no different from rules outside.

One more step, that's all.

Tomorrow, just answer some questions from that persecutor - that district what-you-call-him. Mr. Payne said it'll be tough - like answering questions from some egghead is tougher than watching Linville's brains roll out of his goddam head . . .

Seth shrugged off his thoughts. He crushed the cigarette in his dinner plate and shuffled a deck of playing cards for a game of Solitaire. "Go ahead, ask your questions and get it done. Then kill me, or take my ass to prison and leave me be."

"You finished, Seth?"

Seth looked up and found Luke Chambers, the best guard at the county lockup. Chambers was forty, and had a good disposition. He just did his job and always gave inmates a chance to behave.

"Yes, sir," Seth said. "Cook didn't burn the chicken tonight."

Chambers smiled and unlocked the cell door. His obese frame barely cleared the opening. He picked up the tray and pulled out two packages of cigarettes from his pocket. "Here's a little thank-God-it's-over present, 'ol buddy."

"Well - ain't over quite yet, but much obliged, Luke."

"We watched you give 'em hell on TV. You did good."

Cameron shrugged. "Yeah, like anybody's gonna believe me . . ."

Chambers lingered at the door, his puffy arms making the dinner tray look small. "Keep the faith, Seth; I got twenty bucks on you."

"Hope ya win. Ya wanna play some rummy?"

"Can't right now. I got two intakes waiting. Maybe later." Chambers winked and walked down the corridor.

Seth sighed. He wished they'd let him go to the chow hall just once. Loneliness was something nobody could get used to.

He closed his eyes. Until now, he didn't realize how tired he was. Spilling your gut taxes a man. His head felt the cool cement wall. It was quiet tonight. The jail cell drifted away.

Dreams . . .

A silver boot coming down in his stomach. Once, twice, three times. . .

Momma's naked. Pearly's been pounding her hard tonight. Momma calls it rape. Pearly says she wants it real bad, the whore. You get it for money, but you give it to me for free, whore! Pearly's pounding her face with his fists, and pounding her chute - whore! - she's bleeding and screaming; she's kicking until she kicks the right place and sends Pearly howling to the floor. He's doubled up, yowling. 'That's it, whore! That's it!'

Pearly's back on momma and beating hell outa her face . . . beating hell outa her teats . . . beating hell outa her. No more! Seth shoves the door open and leaps on Pearly. Hit him! Hit him! Hit him!

Pearly tosses little Seth across the room. He hits the wall, and everything goes red-black. 'You want somma me, little dog?' He comes up on Seth, his skin wet and smelly. Pearly whumps Seth upside the head, four, five times. He yanks on Seth's dirty shorts and wraps them around his ankles. 'I'll give you some, little dog!' Pearly rolls little Seth onto his knees. 'Bark at me, little dog! Bark! Bark!' Little Seth cries. A sudden crash of glass and metal drops on his back and cuts his skin. Pearly falls over - his head split - blood squirting out of his greasy black hair. Momma whumped him a good one with that table lamp.

'Whore!' Pearly drags himself up, holding his head and screaming, 'Whore! Whore! Whore!' Seth scampers under the bed. He coils underneath and peers out. Pearly whumps Momma to the floor. Pearly reels to the closet. His shotgun! He's got his gun!

Momma screams and her head explodes into a million pieces. Her headless body twists and turns, blood squirting like a fountain. She hits the floor.

'Next one's for you, little doggy!'

Seth ducks back in under the bed. That big gun barrel comes right in after him.

'Say bye-bye, little barkin' dog!'

Seth kicks the barrel away and rolls out the other side of the bed. Pearly's still pointing the gun underneath. Seth crawls over and grabs Pearly's head, poking his dirty fingernails into Pearly's eyes. Pearly yowls.

'You gonna die, stinking dog!'

Pearly's got too much strength. Little Seth flies across the room and lands in Momma's blood. He sees the butt of that gun coming right for his head. Seth jumps away, and the butt hits the floor.

BOOM!

Little Seth closes his eyes. He is deaf, but he can still see when he looks again. Pearly's in two pieces as his head and chest fall one way, his legs another . . .

Big Luke Chambers flashed his light in Seth's cell. He squinted through the bars and saw the little man curled on his cot. Luke's heart became a pool of hot water. Seth clutched his knees, blowing a hard, labored sleep. He mumbled now and then. The words weren't discernible. His thumb was jammed to his throat . . .

* * *

District Attorney Roland Whittaker abandoned the dais and placed himself directly in front of Seth Cameron, pushing aside visions of a poisoned video playing across the nightly news.

The courtroom was packed beyond capacity. Whittaker coldly stared at Seth as his mind gave him final instructions: Cameron has a fuse. Light it . . .

"Well, well," Whittaker said, "we finally heard the truth, did we, Mr. Cameron?" He tossed a wicked smile at the jury. "The truth, according to the defendant, that is. Space monsters, space ships, high-tech body dissection. You know, I'll bet somebody's gonna score a bestseller and a blockbuster movie deal out of this one, folks. They're making fools out of you!"

"Objection, Your Honor," Payne said.

"Sustained," Judge Falco said. "Mr. Whittaker, are you going to cross-examine the witness, or run for Mayor?"

Whittaker glanced at Falco's 'no bullshit' stare and

resumed. "Mr. Cameron, I just reviewed the autopsy reports again to see if I missed something. Lisa Reeves, twenty-one stab wounds; Mary Reeves, three stab wounds; Linville Reeves, shotgun wound to the head. I read it five times to be sure brain surgery wasn't mentioned."

"Counsel," Falco said, "ask a question."

"Sir, you blew Linville Reeves' head off, didn't you?"

Seth kept looking at his interlaced fingers. "No, sir."

"Did you not tell Sheriff White you killed them?"

"I was talkin' outa my head then. I didn't kill Linville."

"Answer the question, sir," Whittaker barked. "Did you, or did you not confess all three murders to Sheriff White?"

"I said I done it, but I was scared back then. I didn't kill Linville, and I didn't mean to hurt Mary -"

"The evidence contradicts you, sir! Linville Reeves died of a gunshot wound. Your prints are on the weapon. You shot him, didn't you?"

"No, sir!"

Whittaker shook his head and paced in front of Cameron. "You want to stick to your story that outer space monsters killed him?"

"I don't know where they came from."

"Sir, did Mr. Payne tell you to testify that Linville Reeves was killed by space monsters?"

"No, sir."

"Has anyone ever told you that your claiming a UFO landed on that farm - and this cattle mutilation nonsense - would be a way out of admitting you murdered the Reeves family?"

"Nobody told me nothing."

"The evidence is not there, Mr. Cameron! Linville Reeves died of a gunshot. Did you lie to the court about killing one person, when you admit to killing the other two?"

"I ain't lying."

"How do you explain Linville Reeves' body? No mutilation. No innards missing. His head was blown off by that shotgun over there on the table. How do you explain that?"

"I told the truth. You explain it."

"Did you rape the women before - or after they were dead?"

"Objection!" Payne said.

"I didn't rape nobody!"

"Before or after they were dead, Mr. Cameron?"

"Your Honor, argumentative!"

"That's enough, Mr. Whittaker," Judge Falco said.

Whittaker stood back to reload. He smelled blood. "Lisa made fun of you, didn't you say that, sir?"

Cameron shrugged. "Everybody makes fun of me."

"Lisa teased you with sex, didn't she?"

"Misstates the evidence," Payne said.

Judge Falco agreed. "Rephrase the question, Mr. Whittaker."

"Did Lisa ever tease you with sex?"

"Yeah, I guess she did."

"When did she do that?"

"Once when I was kinda drunk."

"Kinda drunk? With a teen-age girl?"

"I didn't do nothing to her!"

"At autopsy, Lisa's body had evidence of sexual abuse, Mr. Cameron! Did you rape her?"

"No! I told ya them bastards done that to her and Mary."

"The space monsters raped the women? Is that what you want us to believe?"

"Objection!" Payne said. "Misstates Mr. Cameron's testimony."

"Sustained," Falco said.

Cameron sputtered and shook his head. "I didn't hurt them."

"You testified that you stabbed them to death! I'd say you hurt them badly!" Whittaker said.

"Argumentative!" Payne said.

"Sustained," Falco barked.

"I reckon I hurt 'em," Cameron said.

"You reckon?" Whittaker stalked. "What about Mary? You told this court that you were treated like family. Was Mary like a mother to you?"

"Mary was a good lady."

"Just like a mother?"

"Yeah, kinda like that."

"You had a mother once. But she was more than just a mother, wasn't she? She and Pearly Scott were all kinds of things to you, weren't they?"

"Objection!" Payne said. "Why doesn't Counsel just assassinate Mr. Cameron now?"

"They wasn't nothing to me, goddamit!" Cameron hollered.

"Mr. Cameron, control yourself," Falco ordered.

"They was animals! Is that what you wanna hear? I thought we was gonna talk about them bastards killing Linville, but you wanna talk about Momma? Go ahead - and kiss my ass while you're at it!"

"Mr. Cameron! Stop right now!" Falco said.

Seth felt a familiar burn. He clenched his teeth and sat back.

Before Payne could speak, Judge Falco intervened. "Everyone, calm down!" she said. "Mr. Whittaker, this is not a shooting gallery. Your questions concerning Mr. Cameron's mother are inappropriate. You will confine your cross-examination to his testimony." Falco dragged the time for another minute while the dust settled. "I order the comments regarding Mrs. Cameron stricken from the record. The jury will disregard those questions. And you, Mr. Whittaker, will back off and proceed with a little less venom!"

Whittaker came back out of his corner like a heavyweight stalking a quick kill. "Okay, sir, by your own admission, you brutally pounded your knife into the women. The only question is the matter of Linville. Your explanation about him being sliced and diced is a lie, pure and simple, isn't it?"

"Fuck you . . ."

Several spectators in the gallery stood up and cheered.

"Order!" Falco said. The gallery rumbled, and several others hollered back. "Order!" Falco said, pounding her gavel. "Bailiff, I want those people removed - now!"

The bailiff and several police officers selected the loud-mouths and roughly escorted them from the courtroom. Several minutes passed before things eased.

"Mr. Cameron," Falco said. "This is my last warning. I will not tolerate that kind of language, is that clear?"

Cameron refused to look at her.

Falco turned her ire to Payne. "Mr. Payne, your client is just about out of here."

Payne shrugged. "I think his answer was succinct and to the point, Your Honor."

"Sir, would you care to share space in his cell?" she said.

"I guess not," Payne said. He shot a glance at Seth, who responded with a resigned nod.

"Mr. Cameron," Falco said, "please just answer the questions."

Seth's eyes bobbed to her. "I meant no offense to you, ma'am."

Whittaker moved back in. "Mr. Cameron, did Linville yell at you about your drinking?"

"Some," Cameron said.

"He frequently bailed you out of jail, didn't he?"

"Yeah, I guess he did."

"Did you ever think he was pushing you around?"

"Yeah, sometimes. But he was paying me to work for him, so he had a right."

"He treated you like a child! That angered you, didn't it?"

"I don't reckon I know how a child is supposed to be treated."

"You lived with a man who always told you what to do, a woman who scolded you like a child, and a little girl who teased you with sex! So, you got even with them in one big rampage! You raped and stabbed the women, and you hunted Linville down and blew his head off, didn't you?"

"I told ya," Cameron said, "I stabbed them because them bastards shot somethin' inta my head that made me crazy! And I didn't shoot Linville!"

"Oh, so you admit he was shot?" Whittaker said.

"They didn't shoot . . . I didn't do it! Nobody shot him!"

"The autopsy clearly points out Linville Reeves was shot!"

"Your Honor! He's using my client for target practice! Do something!" Payne hollered.

"Mr. Whittaker!" Falco said. "Stop this line of attack - now!"

"I told ya what happened, that's all!" Cameron said, his hands shaking.

Whittaker kept pounding. "You testified that you looked at the Reeves bedroom window. Have you been in Mary Reeves' bedroom?"

"Huh?"

"Did you ever see Mary naked, Mr. Cameron?"

"Objection!"

"Out of line, Mr. Whittaker," Falco said. "I order you to - "

"Why did you stab her to death?"

"I told ya, I couldn't help myself!"

"You couldn't help ramming a knife into her chest?"

"No!"

"Your Honor!" Payne stood.

"She was raped! Could you not help raping Lisa?"

"I didn't rape nobody!"

"You raped Lisa and stabbed her twenty-one times! You couldn't help that?"

"No!"

"Oh, so you did rape her!"

"Judge!" Payne stepped around the table.

"Stop this, Mr. Whittaker!" Falco said. "And Mr. Payne, back off!"

Whittaker paced in front of Cameron. "Why don't you quit this nonsense and admit you shot Linville Reeves?"

"I didn't!"

"You're lying!"

Payne moved forward. "Judge! End this!"

"I ain't lying!"

"Mr. Payne, sit down! Whittaker, approach the bench!"

"You hated those people! Linville pushed you around! Pearly pushed you around! Mary was like your mother! Lisa teased you! Momma teased you! Tell the truth!"

"I told the truth!"

"You shot Linville Reeves!"

"No!"

"What are you doing, Judge?" Payne cried. "Stop him!"

"Mr. Whittaker, approach the bench!" Falco hollered.

Whittaker slammed his hands on the railing in front of Cameron. "Did Mary look like your mother? Is that why you killed her?"

"Your Honor, put a goddam muzzle on him!"

"Looked just like her, didn't she?" Whittaker said, his hot breath spraying Cameron.

"What? Momma?"

"Mr. Whittaker, back away from the witness and approach the bench!" Falco said.

"Did you kill your momma, too?"

"Momma?"

Falco stood. "You're in contempt, Counsel!"

"Did Momma tease you with sex? Did you kill Momma?"

"Momma? I didn't kill -"

"You killed them!"

"No!" Seth's brain turned black.

Payne charged. "Judge, either you stop this, or I will!"

"Freeze, Mr. Payne! Bailiff, remove Mr. Whittaker!"

"You killed them! You killed them!"

"No! Noooo!"

Seth's eyes rolled into the back of his skull. He suddenly pounced on Whittaker with a guttural scream.

"Seth!" Payne cried.

Seth's mouth popped open, his brain frying like bacon on a griddle. He grabbed Whittaker's throat. The prosecutor's face bulged to a hot shade of crimson. Two officers followed Jackson to the stand.

Payne ran up, but Cameron caught him with one quick arm whip across the face.

Whittaker's head was about to burst.

Seth's brain slowly burned to gray ash. He reared back from the deputies, hoisting Whittaker off the floor by his neck.

"Stop it, Seth!" Payne hollered.

Seth twisted Whittaker's head until his neck shattered

with a freakish, gut-churning CRACK!

The courtroom imploded. People banged off each other as if a gigantic child had picked the building up and shook it. Seth tossed Whittaker like a baseball, the dead attorney's body crashing into Jackson. Seth, his eyes weaving, danced a lethal two-step.

"Seth," Jackson said sternly, "you just hold yourself right there! Don't move!"

Seth's head shuddered, stars and lights ripping his skull. He let out a coyote-like yowl and mowed into Jackson. The cop somersaulted into the defense table, splintering it like a wooden crate. The other two cops flew along separate routes when they tried to subdue Seth. One hit the jury box, and the other took out five terrified reporters. Seth beat a path to the window, bodies rolling in his wake, and crashed through the glass. He landed eight feet below in the snow, rolling and breaking into a dead run.

The courtroom tumbled and landed upside down. Sheriff White threw people out of the way with his bandaged arms. "Go after him!"

The dumbstruck cops bolted, some jumping out the broken window to pursue Cameron.

Jackson pulled himself out of the debris and took a knee, checking for more broken bones to add to the list. Carly pushed through and helped him stand. Payne joined them, his ribs howling. He suddenly stopped and stared in horror at Roland Whittaker.

Whittaker, video king and former lover of little boys, lay twisted on the floor near the prosecutor's table. His assistant knelt over the corpse in utter disbelief. Whittaker's head pointed backwards, looking at the flag in the corner. His eyes were frozen in confusion as if there might be a few ounces of life in them.

Screams fell on the body as Virgil White blew a curse and stripped the suit coat off the assistant D.A.'s back. White dropped the coat over Whittaker's twisted head, tossing a creative string of obscenities at three busy news photographers who jockeyed for a good photo op.

Carly put her hand to her mouth and turned away. She grabbed Jackson's arm for support.

Jackson looked back at Payne. "You okay, Marc?"

Payne was out of courtroom strategies. He managed a weak nod at Jackson as he turned away from Whittaker. His eyes stumbled over the crowd until he saw a tall, silver-haired man with black eyes near the doors.

Jonathan Carswall could have left earlier, but he wanted to make sure Payne saw him. He threw a mocking wave and walked out.

Payne watched the doors sling shut. He looked back at Jackson and Carly.

"What the hell just happened here, Marc?" Jackson said.

Payne looked at Jackson stupidly. "Seth was convicted..."

Judge Kathryn Falco sat at the bench. Indeed, she jumped up when the room caved in; she dutifully screamed and hollered with everyone; she was even within a few feet of breaking her gavel over Cameron's head if she'd had the chance. And, like everyone else, she had to choke back her breakfast when Whittaker's snapping neck echoed through the place. She really wasn't much different from the rest - but she was a judge, after all, presiding over a court that just finished business.

Finally, Falco brought her gavel down with a resounding bang . . .

24

Reed Aaron stared vacantly out the window from his hospital bed, rigged in a grid of traction pulleys like a twisted marionette. His mind was clear enough to understand everything Marcus had told him. It seemed this nightmare was endless. Aaron's eyes slowly rolled back into the room, his head encased in a cervical collar.

Payne tried to dislodge the shock from his bones. He sat next to Gracie Aaron, who was clamped into a wheelchair. He held her hand, which disappeared into a cast that ran to her elbow. Gracie was puny in her chair, eight pounds lighter than the night she was hurled into this atrocity. The only thing that looked large on Gracie was her pumpkin-sized face, still battered and blue. Her other arm and hand were enclosed in a fiberglass cast, bent awkwardly at the elbow. Her right leg poked straight out, supported by a brace. A single red rose stuck out between two blue toes.

Payne tried to buck up and give Gracie a smile, and she returned it with a hint of teenage optimism. A visit today from three of her best girlfriends and eight hunks from the A.H.S. football team put fresh light in her eyes. They playfully turned her hair into one big ponytail that stuck out of the top of her head. She had a lipstick message on her forehead, written backwards so she could read it in the mirror: "Get well fast! We love you!"

Until today, Gracie hadn't smiled. Smiling hurt her wired jaw. It hurt to smile, it hurt to cry. Not much to do but hurt these days.

Sybil Aaron occupied the bed next to Reed. Both legs were in traction. One was pinned in three places, and she was due for more surgery at the end of the week. She needed a ton of painkillers to keep her head into reality. The constant pain was a burdensome companion, but Sybil's wispy eyes burned with life.

A nurse appeared at the door with a genuinely kind smile. God knew Reed loved Sybil forever, but he was having a short affair of the mind with this angel of mercy. She walked in with a tray of ice cream containers and an orange soda for Gracie.

"How about some treats for my favorite patients?"

Aaron smiled weakly. "Doctor's orders?"

"Yup," she said. "Doctor Gracie, that is." She put the soda on the table and gave Payne the job of assistant. Sybil politely declined the ice cream, deferring to her stomach that reeled from a recent drug fix. Reed was only now getting an appetite, and he allowed the angel to shovel in a few mouthfuls.

"Okay, this'll be tricky," Payne said softly as he worked the straw through Gracie's lips.

"Yust, shick it hin," Gracie said.

Payne wanted to kid her about her new vocabulary, but he knew an unexpected laugh would be messy. If anybody could make Gracie giggle in this condition, it was Doc. She managed the soft drink pretty well, occasionally squirting a drop into the tissue Payne held under her fat chin. She let out a cry when she moved her jaw the wrong way.

Payne pulled the straw out as if he just killed her. "I'm sorry, honey." His faced paled and he dropped his head. "Sweet Thing, I'm so sorry I did this to you." He hated himself for a lot of things, but mostly for breaking down in front of everyone.

"Stof hit," Gracie murmured. She clumsily dropped her cast on his wrist.

The nurse suddenly felt like a nasty voyeur. She politely smiled at Aaron and got out as fast as she could.

"Marcus," Reed said. "Don't beat yourself. We're out of beds."

Payne jammed his hand in his cheek and rubbed a tear away.

"Goc?" Gracie said.

"Yeah, honey?"

"I uv ooh."

He tried to laugh as he dabbed the tissue in her eye. "I love you, too."

"Dwink."

Payne quickly plugged the straw back into her lips.

"You owe us big, Payne," Sybil drunkenly said. "I like the idea of a thousand-buck-an-hour lawyer waiting on us."

"Yeah? Well the docs say your old man is gonna walk again. He won't need a valet by next summer; right, Counselor?"

Aaron gave a hopeful smile and managed to make his right foot flutter under the sheet. He rolled his eyes back to the window with a sigh. "Where do you think he went?"

"He can't get far," Payne said, wiping more orange from Gracie's mouth. She signaled 'all full,' and he set the cup on the table. "It's getting dark. It's cold. Where can he hide?"

"Where," Aaron parroted.

"I thought I'd seen it all," Payne said, shaking his head.

"From the way Seth was worked up," Aaron said, "I'd say it proves what he's tried to say all along."

Dan Williams' devilish grin lit up the doorway. "Excuse me, but did anyone order a pest?"

"Come," Aaron said.

Willy plodded in, tracking ghosts of mud and snow on the floor. The room instantly reeked of whiskey. He pulled off his heavy coat and threw a longing glance at the last ice cream container on the table. "I'll give a hundred dollars for that."

"Cash?" Payne said.

Willy smiled and lustily attacked. "I haven't had a bite all day." He spoke through each slurp. "How's everyone feeling? You ready to go dancing, Counselor?"

Aaron sighed.

"What have you heard?" Payne asked.

Willy's table manners were disgusting. The ice cream didn't have a chance. "There's a statewide A.P.B. out. White's got every hound on the force sniffing. Roadblocks, door-to-doors - the works. He figures Seth is close by - maybe slumped down under some bushes in a park or back yard."

"Did he check the farm?"

"No. He doesn't think Seth can get that far in this cold, but Jackson's watching the road out of town anyway."

"I thought Jackson was suspended."

"He is, but White isn't turning away any help right now."

"I just wonder who else is looking for Seth," Aaron said.

"Somebody smarter than Virgil," Payne said.

Williams dropped the cup and wiped a smirk on his sleeve. "Well, I hate to gobble and run, but I have a deadline. Just wanted to say my 'get wells,' and tell you what I've heard. I appreciate the dinner - let's do it again sometime." He stood and put his coat on.

Payne's cell phone rang. Williams stopped and turned an ear.

Payne answered.

Jackson's voice crackled over the receiver. "Marc? There's a light in Seth's cabin. I think he's out here."

"What? Where are you?"

"I'm parked down the road from the farm. We gotta get to Seth before Carswall. I need back-up – I need you - hurry!"

Payne jumped up and quickly grabbed his coat.

"Who was that?" Aaron said.

"I'll be back." Payne hurried past Williams . . .

Willy scuffed down the hospital corridor on Payne's heels. "You found him?"

"No. Gotta take a leak."

Willy caught Payne's arm as they pounded into the elevator. "Where is he?"

Payne quickly evaluated the situation.

"Look," Williams said, "you know I'll follow you anyway. Let's split the gas."

"He's at the farm. K.J. saw a light in his cabin. If he saw it, Carswall will see it."

The elevator landed, and Williams matched Payne's steps across the hospital lobby. "I'll go with you."

"It's dangerous, Willy. You know this game."

"Hey, this could be the 'thirty' to my story; besides, who's gonna watch your back?"

Payne didn't answer. He didn't argue. In fact, he thought, the joker just asked a damn good question . . .

* * *

A harsh wind whipped the snow into misty swirls. The cold, dead winter night swallowed the countryside whole. The bleak, shadowy darkness stood in stark contrast to a sweltering summer morning when Ken Jackson first set this entire affair in motion.

The Reeves farm, dark and silent, was frozen solid. The house and barn were boarded up, awaiting new tenants in the spring.

Jackson's shopworn car sat in the same spot where he parked his patrol car last summer. His weapon - drawn and cocked - stalked the darkness. He slowed near the barn, peering at Seth's cabin across the field. Seth was his friend, but after what happened today, Jackson took no chances. Blood beat his temples - identical to the rush he felt the last time he crept by this barn. Seth's cabin was stark and gray in the frozen air. It sat like a lonely sentry in front of the barren wheat fields beyond. Jackson blinked away the memory of the Reeves family lying out there, ravaged by some unspeakable terror.

Indeed, a light flickered in the cabin window. It was not constant. It jumped intermittently against the curtained glass like an orange phantom. Jackson slowly took one step and then another, ice and sticks crackling beneath his boots. Light snow began to fall, an occasional gust from an icy norther tossing the flakes into the air. Jackson saw scores of footprints, some fresh, some cracked and old. The farm had been shown to prospective buyers all winter, and there was no way to tell what prints were new.

Jackson reached the side of the farmhouse and stopped. Again, an ominous flicker of light danced on the cabin window. It wasn't an illusion. It came from inside.

As Jackson carefully watched the cabin, he didn't notice a

slight shadowy movement behind him.

He crouched and gingerly stepped through the snow as if it were thin glass. His chest bounced against his leather jacket. Even in this darkness he felt naked - and watched. He prayed Seth was inside, perhaps passed out drunk from booze hidden away, or sleeping from exhaustion. Jackson's memory of the sickening crack of Roland Whittaker's neck rustled in the barren trees. He could see that hideous twisted head, and could only believe that Jonathan Carswall may have carved another notch in his gun.

As Jackson reached the cabin, the shadow behind him dodged and disappeared near the farmhouse.

The cabin door. Jackson stepped up and gently moved to the side of the opening. He stood still for a moment and then carefully slid his hand to the door and pushed. The hinges protested, and the cold air opened the door.

"Yo, Seth?" Jackson said. "It's Jackson. You in there?"

Nothing . . .

He saw light dance along the door's threshold. Jackson brought his weapon up, his finger lightly on the trigger, and he edged to the door. He quickly popped his head in and out, asking his eyes for a report. Dark. Table. Candle. Jackson repeated the action. Dark. Candle. No Seth.

He dropped to a new position and slowly exposed one eye. A bare cot sat on one side of the room. In the middle was a crude handmade wooden table, upon which a lighted candle threw orange streaks at the walls. Jackson carefully pulled a flashlight from his belt and flicked it on, bracing it with the gun to illuminate a target. He quickly stepped into the doorway, aiming at the table, and then drew circles in the room. The cabin leaked a residue of the madness in the courthouse today.

Seth was in here. Jackson could feel him.

He took one step inside, scanning with the flashlight. It seemed much larger in here than it looked from the outside.

"Momma?"

Jackson jumped and came no farther. Seth's tiny voice bounced off the walls, but Jackson was sure it came from a blind spot behind the open door.

"Seth? It's me, Jackson. Where are you?"

"In here, Momma."

Jackson's heart ached both with terror and pity. He took another step. "I'm not gonna hurt you, Seth. You know me."

"They tried to kill me, Momma."

"It's okay, Seth. Nobody's gonna hurt you."

Jackson cleared the door. He stepped once more and gasped. Someone huge stood just to his left! Jackson spun wildly and almost shot a familiar black man in the mirror. He nearly bit his tongue with relief.

"Momma?"

The strange acoustics in the wooden cabin made it impossible to locate sounds. "Where are you, Seth?"

"Them lights, Momma. They was so bright. I couldn't help myself. Them bastards made me kill you. I'm sorry I killed you."

Jackson's spine was brittle. Seth's monotonous voice sounded distant and unfamiliar. Most of his brain cells were cauterized, and he had very little sensory awareness outside his memory.

"Wasn't anything you could do, Seth," Jackson said, now realizing he was dealing with a talking turnip - a potentially poisonous talking turnip. He slowly revolved in a tight circle with the flashlight pointed forward.

"Terrible, Momma. Lots of blood."

"I know, Seth. But you're safe now. Nothing to be afraid of."

"I just seen that light again, Momma. Them bastards is back. One of 'em's in here now!"

"No, Seth. It's just me, Ken Jackson."

"I killed Jackson. He can't help me."

"Sure he can."

Seth heard a shotgun blast in his mind. "No!"

Seth's scream shot acid into Jackson's stomach. He froze. "Seth, you're okay, pal."

"Them bastards is in here! They're gonna cut me open!"

Jackson made the full circle but still didn't see Seth. He

came back around to the mirror. The familiar black guy with the gun looked even more scared than him.

Seth popped over his shoulder.

"Nooooo!"

Jackson gasped horribly as Seth's hands grabbed his throat. He tumbled to the floor, and the gun flew from his hand. Jackson clutched Seth's hands, summoning his own formidable strength to roll the little man over.

"No! No! No!"

Jackson's brown eyes bulged. He had no air. He valiantly pulled on Seth's hands and rolled again.

No air! Seth's red eyes faded into a bevy of stars as Jackson felt his own grip dying. God! Air! He could barely see his killer now. It was ending. It was over. Jackson's hands fell.

A sudden deafening bang rocked the cabin. Frozen air inflated Jackson's lungs as Seth cried out and slumped to the floor. Jackson pulled himself up. Seth pitifully rolled on his back in a growing pool of blood. He stared at the ceiling, a clean hole in the center of his forehead. Jackson reeled himself to his knees and bobbed his head to the door. He saw a tall, silver-haired man with coal black eyes. Carswall's gun was still aimed at Seth.

Carswall's eyes rolled to Jackson, and his outstretched arms followed. Jackson looked down the barrel of the gun.

He panted and gritted his teeth defiantly. "If you're gonna shoot, get it over with. Begging ain't my style."

"Pulling this trigger would be gratifying," Carswall coldly said. "You've made things very difficult for me."

"Yeah - too bad blowing me away would untie your package again."

Carswall's black eyes glowed. "Nothing I couldn't fix, Officer. But it's more fun watching you grovel. Kind of takes you back to the good old days, doesn't it?"

"Goodnight," Jackson said with a hazy smile.

"What?" Carswall heard a sudden ring in his ears. He looked dumbly at the wall and dropped the gun. The room turned upside down when the pain kicked in. His knees buckled and he dipped down, landing on his chin - his ass pointing mightily in the air. Finally, Carswall keeled over like a waterlogged frigate.

Carly walked in with her heavy flashlight poised for another swing. She watched Carswall roll like a drunk in a gutter. He grunted from his bowels, trying to lift his head.

She leered at him. "Son of a bitch . . ."

Payne and Williams skidded into the back bumper of Jackson's sports car. The panic started at the hospital, escalated as they drove around a black sedan in front of the farm, and erupted into terror when they heard gunfire.

"Shit!" Payne said, bolting from the car. He stumbled to the ground as a patch of ice kicked his shoes. Williams helped Payne regain his balance, and they skated toward Seth's cabin. As they rounded the farmhouse, they slowed in terror. A shadow stood in the doorway, a body at its feet.

"Hey, we don't have a gun," Williams whispered, reluctant to move.

Payne didn't hear. He took careful steps until the shadow at the door appeared less deadly. "Carly?" Payne called, ready to dive for cover in case he was wrong.

Carly turned and looked at Payne as he trotted to her. Williams got brave again and followed. As Carly's face grew familiar, Payne saw her tears. She grabbed his coat lapel, trying hard to keep from breaking. Payne gently moved her aside and peered in. He saw Carswall floundering about near the body of Seth Cameron. Seth's head rested in Jackson's lap.

"Oh, god," Payne choked. He fell to his knees and crawled. His trembling hands fell on Seth's head as he looked into a pair of glazed, dying eyes. "Oh, Seth - no . . ."

Seth's eyes fluttered. His breath was nearly gone. He looked first at Jackson and then at Payne. "Momma?" he breathed.

And then, he died.

"Aw, Seth," Jackson said. He wept hard.

Payne buried his head in Seth's tiny chest. Carly slowly approached and knelt beside them. She put her arms on Jackson and Payne, and they cried together.

Dan Williams sadly stood in the doorway, his eyes burning with rage as he glared at Carswall. Silver Hair was napping. Williams thought for one insane moment that he could kick a man to death.

Instead, he turned and let himself drop to a crouch. His sandy hair fell over his eyes, and he covered his face . . .

KNIGHTS

"The wicked are not so,
but are like chaff that the wind drives away."

Psalm 1:1-6

25

Marcus Payne leaned in the doorway of Seth Cameron's cabin, watching the winter sun inexorably crawl toward the horizon. He flicked his cigarette into the wind. This was his sixth visit here the past week. He'd come here and sit. He'd come here and wander. He'd come here and sketch. Yesterday, he climbed on the cabin roof and simply gazed at the sky. With each visit, he asked the same question and came up with no answer: What the hell happened out here?

It was a pleasant day today - not too cold - but Payne had to pull his collar up when the wind picked up. He turned his back to the breeze and lit another cigarette. He couldn't help a sad smile at what a peaceful place this was - the sturdy wood frame farmhouse, the barn, the pens, and the vast wheat fields surrounding him. He leaned against the porch railing and watched the smoke rip from his mouth and run for the sky.

The distant fields were silent. Whatever secret was told out there last summer, the flattened wheat stalks revealed no clues. Even the burned scar was gone now. Payne tried to imagine a giant, unfathomable aircraft slowly descending out there, but now that Seth Cameron was dead for more than a week, the whole idea seemed increasingly ludicrous. Payne chuckled softly to himself, torn between grieving for Seth and wondering if the poor little guy was nothing more than a sad case haunted by cinematic hallucinations. He looked back at the farm, incessantly puffing. Out here, Payne felt like the only living creature in the universe. He slipped a worn photograph from his pocket and looked at Lori Payne.

His attention perked to a patrol car rolling behind the

Aaron mini van. He put the photo back in his pocket and watched Ken Jackson climb out. Dan Williams emerged from the other side.

There's an unlikely pair, Payne thought, returning Willy's wave.

They casually walked past the farmhouse and approached the cabin. "We thought we might find you out here," Willy said. His sandy hair stood straight up in the wind.

Payne nodded and smoked. "We all have to be somewhere."

Willy turned his back to the wind and formed his hands around his pipe like a tent. He stoked his pipe, smoke leaping from the briar bowl. He took a pull from his flask.

"K.J.?" Payne said. "The uniform? The badge? Did I miss something?"

Williams kept grinning. "We're celebrating the exoneration of the intrepid officers Jackson and Farrel, who've returned to active duty."

"You're not suspended anymore?" Payne said.

Jackson shrugged at Payne. "White called Carly this afternoon. He says Judge Falco called in some favors at the Harrisburg District Attorney's Office, and they suddenly closed the whole investigation."

"No fanfare, no press conference," Williams said. "A press release simply states the matter is closed - no evidence to implicate the mortuary burglars, because there is no mortuary; end of story. Jackson and Farrel committed the perfect crime."

"Nice work, K.J.," Payne grinned.

"I'm a retired burglar," Jackson said. "Crime don't pay - unless you're with the State Department."

"The only concern is all the publicity some irresponsible reporter printed about the break-in," Willy said, taking another pull of gin. "I don't think it'll hurt Jackson's credibility, though. Nobody believes anything they read in the papers..."

"And I don't suppose your editor gave you a pink slip," Payne said.

"Are you joking?" Williams laughed. "The online advertising revenue is at a record high! I got a raise!"

Jackson rolled his eyes, and Payne laughed.

"So you and your lady are cops again," Payne said.

Jackson drew lines in the dirt with his foot. "I am, but Carly's gonna resign soon. She's pregnant."

"What?" Payne exclaimed. "That's fantastic!"

"Yeah," Jackson shyly said. "I'm pretty happy about it, too. So, uh, Marc, we're gonna get married pretty quick, and I was wondering if you might stand up with me."

Payne smiled. "I'd be honored."

Jackson smirked. "Me and Carly, and the master of deception leading the wedding party. Ain't that gonna go over big in this town? We thought it might be smart to invite the fire department, just in case . . ."

Williams laughed. "Let me drop ranks for a minute and say congratulations. I mean that."

Jackson snatched Willy's flask and raised it in toast.

"You're on duty," Williams smirked.

"Officially – not until tomorrow." Jackson took a healthy slug and winced. "Woah. No wonder I don't drink. What's in here, kerosene?"

"High octane," Williams chuckled. "Marc?" He offered the flask.

Payne was tempted. "Better not. One vice is enough." He took another drag from his cigarette. "Why isn't Carly out here celebrating?"

"She's been in the tub all day," Jackson said. "Says she's not gonna get out for a week."

"Have you heard the latest news, Counselor?" Williams said, drinking again.

"What news?"

"The Attorney General released his report on the UFO Trial investigation this morning."

"That was fast. What a surprise."

"He concluded that Seth was obviously insane, and recommended Marcus Payne be investigated for possible misconduct. Your conspiracy allegations against a loyal government agency apparently ruffled the right feathers. They're threatening disbarment."

Payne nodded. "Too bad. I had a lot of potential."

"I wouldn't joke, Counselor. It's an election year, and the President's platform includes a crackdown on crime. Hanging you would look good to the voters."

"You're apparently under the impression that I give a shit," Payne said.

"This is serious, Payne," Williams said.

"So am I."

"Are you going to tell me why?"

"If you want to print this, you can say I'm pursuing other interests. My family needs somebody to clean bedpans and buy them a new house."

"But that won't last forever," Willy said. "What will you do?"

"Who knows?" Payne said. "I picture myself painting atop a nice quiet mountain somewhere - maybe talking to myself now and then."

"Oh, by all means, that's you," Williams sarcastically said. "A hermit painter? Come now - the world's full of murderers to set free."

"The world can kiss my ass," Payne said.

"But what about me?"

"Oh, don't worry, you can kiss it, too," Payne said.

"But I'm hot right now. People are throwing money at me. I just sold a national piece condemning the deteriorating morality of the legal profession. I'm getting offers every day to bend you over good. How can I do that if you vanish into the wilderness?"

"You'll sell papers, Willy. If you like, I'll write some rebuttals, and we can yell at each other on the cable talk shows for as long as it plays out."

Williams had to laugh. "Are you serious? You'd do that for me?"

"Willy, I get a dozen requests from the networks every week. If you want to go prime time, I'll play. Just let me do the negotiations so we charge them up the ass. I'll sign my checks over to Aaron."

"I don't believe it. Why are you throwing me bones now?"

"You pulled K.J. and Carly out of the fire. I owe you. Just do me one favor and leave them out of it."

"Oh, absolutely - we're going to support Jackson's election bid next fall, so we can't very well crucify him first. We'll just claim they were puppets, their strings pulled by the master of deception. It's P-A-Y-N-E, correct?"

"Marcus Andrew."

"Willy, you're a goddam hypocrite," Jackson said.

"Hey, I'm a reporter, that's my job."

"You're a trash bag."

"Well, at least Mr. Payne is grateful I saved your bottoms."

"I'm grateful, but you're still scum."

Willy sighed. "At least things are getting back to normal around here."

Payne heaved a good laugh that infected Willy and Jackson. It felt good and took some time to wring itself out. Payne settled and lit another cigarette. Williams turned his back to the wind and fired up his pipe. Jackson disgustedly waved the blowing smoke and wondered which one of these smokestacks would die first.

"Counselor, if I may," Williams said, "and this is strictly off the record of course."

"Of course," Payne said.

"Do you believe in space buggers?"

Payne leaned against the post. "I don't believe in anything."

"Hedge! Come on, Counselor, we're not in the courtroom, so you don't have to lie."

Payne smiled and simply replied, "I owe it to Seth."

Williams pondered the comment and then nodded. "I'll deny it if you ever tell anybody, but I believed him, too. Something landed out here . . ."

Jackson folded his arms for warmth against the breeze. "Who do you think they were?"

A long silence followed.

Payne looked across the big spread, opting to forget the

last question. "How about you, Dad? You gonna win that election?"

Jackson pensively kicked at the ground. "I ain't so sure I want to anymore."

"Oh, poor Officer Jackson," Williams said. "Are you going to let some empty-headed rednecks ruin your career? And what about me? I can't wait for you to pin on that sheriff's badge."

"I've had happier thoughts."

"What else are you qualified for, anyway?" Williams said. "God knows you'd make a terrible mortician!"

They laughed again. Jackson put a finger in Willy's face. "If I am the sheriff, you may need a mortician, pal."

"Counselor, you heard that threat. Let's sue."

"I'm retired. You're on your own," Payne laughed.

Jackson kicked at the ice and snow, his laughter dying quickly. He looked around the farm, recalling the horror. "Poor Seth. We were so close."

"To the wire," Payne agreed, sharing the sadness.

"Instead," Jackson continued, "Carswall blows him away and gets a commendation for saving my life. Ain't that just perfect?"

"A perfect fit," Willy added. "It gave the feds a reason to investigate and perform Seth's autopsy. By God, they found no brain anomaly of any kind - outside of a well-placed slug."

Jackson sighed. "It was generous of them to pick up the cremation bill, too. I get a lot of comfort knowing these boys are spending my taxes so well."

"Gentlemen," Williams said, "we are little bugs in this world. As long as we stay under our rocks, we don't get crushed by the boot of democracy."

"Oh, brother," Jackson said. "You're a bug, Willy."

"He's a journalist," Payne said.

Jackson was tired of laughing now. "I keep thinking about that patch Seth said he ripped off in the fight. He said it had symbols on it. Man, can you imagine if we'd found that thing?"

"Way ahead of you," Payne said. "Reed and I crawled all

over this place looking for it last summer."

"Carswall probably combed it up the morning of the murders," Williams said.

"Damn," Jackson said. "If I'd kept my head, maybe I would have seen something."

"Woulda-coulda, K.J.," Payne said. "No use worrying about it now." Payne watched his smoke dash into the wind. He took another drag and stopped suddenly. "Wait a minute..."

Jackson and Williams watched Payne blow smoke again.

"Careful, Jackson," Williams said, curiously watching Payne. "He's getting one of those looks."

"What's wrong with this picture?" Payne said, blowing another mouthful of smoke.

Williams shook his head. "You can't blow smoke rings in the wind? That's har-dl-y . . ."

"The wind," Jackson said. "The wind was blowing. Hell, it whips the countryside every summer night."

"Seth mentioned it," Payne said. He stepped off the porch and pulled some wet sticks and weeds from the snow. They jumped away when he tossed them.

"Maybe the wind took it," Jackson said.

Willy shrugged. "If so, that patch is five hundred miles from here now."

Payne looked out to the wheat fields. "K.J., what's out there over that rise?"

"Land, and more land. The property extends at least two miles or more downwind." Jackson thought about the years he spent sweating out there. "And you know what? I helped mend a fence line out there maybe a hundred times - heavy barbed wire that shredded my hands more than once. Linville used to send me out there to pick up all the trash it snagged."

Payne smiled at Jackson. "No kidding? Snagged a lot of trash?"

Jackson's smile was almost stupid. "Damn thing caught just about anything that blew by."

"Stop the presses," Williams said. "At this juncture, I respectfully request that you two stop thinking what I just thought. Being the only one of sound mind here, I dismiss it."

"The wind's blowing," Jackson said. "Seth rips that patch off -"

"And it blows away," Payne said. "Willy, did Seth mention the wind when you interviewed him?"

Williams puffed. "Hell, I don't remember. I doubt I wrote about it if he did."

"So Carswall doesn't make the connection and come looking later," Payne said. "And when he was out here taking over the crime scene, the wind isn't even a consideration."

"No," Jackson said. "Besides, he's too busy hiding Linville's body in the barn."

"Did you hear me?" Williams asked. "You're talking seven months ago. Why is the drunk reporter here the only one who's thinking rationally?"

Payne checked his watch. "We still have some daylight."

"And if we run out, we can come back tomorrow, and the day after that," Jackson said.

They started walking.

"Fellas. Is anyone listening to me?" Williams asked.

"Sorry, Willy," Jackson said, "did you say something?"

Williams sucked his pipe and incredulously watched. "You can't be serious!"

Payne and Jackson continued without looking back.

Williams kept drinking and mumbled to himself. "I'm not going out in that mud. I have new shoes on. They won't find anything." He watched Payne and Jackson plod into the fields. He plugged the flask in his coat pocket. "Aw, dammit!" He ran to catch up . . .

* * *

On the road beyond the Reeves drive, Jonathan Carswall approached a huge man who leaned against his car. The agent looked at Carswall and then peered back into his binoculars. He wore a headset attached to a listening device that pointed out towards the wheat fields.

"What's going on?" Carswall said.

He pulled the headset off. "Something's up. The lawyer's been here all afternoon - hanging around, snooping like he has the last two days. But the reporter and the cop showed up today. That's why I called you."

Carswall borrowed the glasses and peered into the fields. "Where are they going?"

"Just before you got here, they had an interesting conversation about that patch."

Carswall stopped and looked at the agent. "Patch? . . ."

It was a numbing walk in the country. Thankfully, the wind was at their backs, but that left bleak prospects for the walk back. Williams slipped twice. The first time, he scraped and bloodied his hand; the second fall soaked his left trouser leg. He wasn't having much fun, and he didn't hesitate to mention it. Beyond the murder site, the wheat field gently rose uphill about a half mile. At the crest of the hill, the fence came into view another mile away. The matted ground was patched by ice, snow, and mud, and everyone's feet complained long before the fence came within reach. The wiry snake ran to each horizon, and it indeed possessed a collection of interesting travelers of the wind, caught primarily in the heavy wire strands close to the ground.

Payne couldn't see the farmhouse from here, but he estimated they'd walked a fairly straight line. "If it did get this far, I'd guess it might be in this range." He swept his arm to cover a fifty-yard-wide swatch. "Like you said, we can come back, so let's just work around here until one of us collapses from the cold."

"I'm about to die now," Williams said. "This is a waste of time."

"Then why did you come with us?" Jackson said, panning out to the left.

"I live for intrigue."

Payne ranged out to the right, and Williams went forward. Jackson reached the fence first. The trash wasn't heavy in any single area. In some places, there was none at all. The first clump he found was a wad of wet yellow paper. He untangled the mess and clenched his teeth at the goo. It was just and old paper sack with a few unidentifiable partners stuck to it. Jackson tossed it aside, suddenly thinking Williams was probably right - this could be an exercise in futility. But Jackson remembered what Reed Aaron once said about 'Payne's Magic.'

Williams searched with less enthusiasm. His hands didn't come out of his pockets unless it was an emergency. He fumbled and kicked at the trash. A paper cup; a farm implement catalogue with a quart of slime all over it; a single broadsheet piece of newsprint. Williams perked. The *Attica Sentinel,* and by god, a Dan Williams story about a burglary at the Dairy Dip. One of my hard-hitting investigative pieces, he thought.

"Woah, what have we here?" Willy picked up a tattered magazine - a genuine nudist periodical. He hadn't seen one of these since he was a kid. A grin dripped over his chin as he flipped through the muddy pages. Nude people by a swimming pool, playing croquet, laughing and mingling at a buffet line. Big nudes, fat nudes, skinny nudes, look-at-the-size-of-that-wanger nudes, children nudes - even a dog in the buff. Williams folded the magazine and stuffed it in his coat pocket for later . . .

Payne didn't mind hitting a knee as he rummaged. His hands were a little achy, but not unbearably so. He found a three-year-old Attica High School football program, littered with local advertisements for trophies, sports equipment, the soda shop. He moved to another clump and came up with a brown paper bag just the right size for a liquor bottle. An old cigarette package. A Big Slop soft drink cup. A roll of muddy butcher paper. What a mess . . .

Williams found a paper plate with something disgusting crusted all over it. He kicked and scrounged. A heavy fence barb suddenly jammed through the toe of his new shoe and poked him good. "Dammit to hell!" Williams limped while selecting more obscenities. I'm a fool, that's what I am, he thought. Out here in the cold with these pathetic idealists -

looking for space litter. Come on, sun, go down fast so I can go home . . .

Time ran quickly. The afternoon light grew pale. Jackson straightened and arched his back, believing what everybody says about your mid thirties is true. Muscles and joints just don't behave like they used to, and the wearisome injuries of the last few weeks didn't help either. He rubbed his hands and blew into them. He guessed they'd been at it for a good hour or more. It might make sense to blow this off and get a good start tomorrow. Downrange, Willy was reading something. Big help, Willy, Jackson thought. Farther down, he saw Payne with his nose buried in a tangle of tumbleweeds.

Jackson resumed his search. The trash seemed to clump together - probably wind currents and swirls and such, he thought. He sifted through some old newspapers and stopped when his eyes fell on a headline that gave his heart a tug: ATTICA FAMILY IN MACABRE SLAYINGS. Most of the story was obliterated by mud and time. It dispatched a tingle down Jackson's spine, that horrible morning coming back to him as if it happened yesterday. The heat, the birds, the stench, the animals. Linville Reeves.

He looked up and saw a willowy contrail in the sky. The condensed vapors thinned down to a tiny airplane streaking north. Its tail had an orange hue given by the setting sun.

Jackson was suddenly startled by a shrill whistle. Payne was seventy-five yards past Williams. He whistled again, frantically waving. Jackson felt very small. My god, he thought.

He broke into a run and caught Williams about thirty feet from Payne, who was on his knees in the mud. Payne watched them approach. He tossed a coiled smile and pointed at the fence.

Caught on a barb on the lowest wire strand was a piece of heavy, coarse cloth. Payne plucked it and stood, Williams and Jackson huddling close. The dark blue patch was grainy and thick, eight inches long and four wide, tapered at the long ends. It was tattered by the punishing wind, but had survived in remarkably good condition. Payne almost laughed as he passed it to Jackson.

"Good god grief," Williams whispered, peering through his sandy hair.

Jackson looked at the strange, unrecognizable symbols on the cloth. "This is it," Jackson said. "It's gotta be."

"Let me," Williams said, taking the patch.

"Okay, Willy," Jackson said, "you're a writer. What does it say?"

Williams cocked his head, turning the patch over and over. "It says, 'Property of Jonathan Carswall. If found please return to . . .'" He looked for a laugh, but got only two dour smiles. "I have no idea. They aren't numbers, and they sure as hell aren't letters - even hieroglyphics possess some type of recognizable symbolism. I've never seen anything like it."

"It's fantastic," Payne said, his voice childlike.

"I can take this to the university," Williams said. "Language experts - anthropologists. Oh, this could be delightful!"

They stopped and looked at each other. Suddenly, they broke into uproarious laughter, high-fiving and backslapping like champions.

"You are indeed a sorcerer, Counselor!" Williams said.

"Gimme that," Payne said. He plugged the patch in his pocket . . .

They began the long trek back to the farmhouse, laughing and discussing possibilities. One adventure was over, but a second just beginning. The sun was almost below the horizon now, and the wind picked up, but the three unlikely friends burned with ideas.

They came over the rise, finding the Cameron cabin and Reeves farmhouse directly ahead. Williams and Payne still verbally jousted, but Jackson grew silent. He stopped. Payne chuckled, and then curiously looked back at Jackson.

"K.J.?" Payne said. "Good evening? K.J.?"

"God . . . damn," Jackson whispered. His eyes glared at the farm.

Payne and Willy looked with him. Jonathan Carswall and something that looked like a mountain with legs stood by the barn . . .

Carswall and the mountain met them as they reached the cabin. "Gentlemen," Carswall said with a nod. "A chilly afternoon for a walk, isn't it?"

Nobody spoke. They continued walking, but their gait slowed when they saw four more agents on the road, standing by their cars.

Carswall and his friend stepped in front of them. He looked first at Jackson. "You don't look any worse for wear, Officer. I trust you've recovered from your brush with the madman last week?"

"I've gotten used to people trying to kill me," Jackson said. He looked through those soulless black eyes.

"Maybe I'm missing something," Carswall said. "I would expect some gesture of gratitude. After all, Cameron would have killed you if not for me."

"You're right. You are missing something," Jackson said.

"Your girlfriend certainly packs a wallop. I'm lucky she didn't fracture my skull. She also assaulted a federal agent. Under the circumstances, I chose to overlook that. I guess gratitude is something you people don't understand."

"Understand this," Jackson said. He flipped a perfectly formed, and very nasty bird.

Carswall turned to the agent and theatrically sighed. "The manners of these small town people." The thug didn't do anything but spray his intimidating scowl. "What were you doing out there, gentlemen?"

Williams lit his pipe. "We were thinking about choosing up sides for softball. Did you guys bring your gloves?"

"What was the big discovery out by the fence?"

Payne looked at Jackson and Williams. He took the lead. "We tried to find you a personality, Jonny. No luck."

Carswall sighed. "Are you going to make this difficult, too? Very well, have it your way." He approached Williams first and reached for the reporter's coat pockets.

Williams shoved Carswall's hands away. He stopped short at an ominous CLICK! Carswall's man pointed a 9mm semiautomatic at Williams' head. Payne stepped back and held his hands out, but Jackson started to advance.

"Don't do it, Officer," Carswall said. He walked to Jackson and got in his face. "Don't *fuck* with me!" His black eyes boiled.

Jackson froze.

Carswall smiled and spoke over his shoulder. "You just have to know how to communicate with these hicks. If he breathes, splatter his black brains all over the snow."

"With pleasure," the agent said, turning his gun at Jackson.

"Now, Mr. Williams, if you please?" Williams was more cooperative now. He held his arms out and Carswall searched his pockets.

"Constitutional rights," Williams said. "Ever hear of them?"

"Call a cop," Carswall muttered. He pulled out Williams' nudist magazine.

"I'd like that back when you're done with it."

Carswall gave Williams a hollow stare and tossed the magazine on the ground. He turned to Payne. "Counsel, arms up, please." Payne tried to step back, but the thug moved his gun closer to Jackson's head. "Mr. Payne, haven't you gotten enough people killed already?"

Payne stared at the gun and raised his arms.

"What have we here?" Carswall pulled the blue patch from Payne's pocket. He turned it over in his hand. "So, that little degenerate was right. Pretty stupid of us to not know about this until his testimony. Ah, well, you can't know everything." He pocketed the patch and then pulled out a piece of paper, holding it for Payne to see. On it were symbols, crudely resembling those on the patch.

"What the hell is that?" Payne said.

"A proposal." He put the paper back in his pocket and looked at all three in wicked triumph. "Questions?"

"What do the symbols mean?" Payne finally said.

"You got me," Carswall said. "I can tell you this, they don't coincide with any known language. Nobody has a clue." He shrugged matter-of-factly.

"Where did you get the symbols?" Williams asked.

"From their spacecraft, Mr. Williams, where else?" Carswall looked at him dumbly. "Gentlemen, haven't you figured this out yet? Are you just waiting for me to confirm it before you believe?"

"Who are they?" Payne said.

"No clue," Carswall said. "I'm in Intelligence and Enforcement - I'm not a scientist. However, I don't think those bookworms know any more than me." Carswall loved this game. "Okay, you all nearly froze to death out there; I'm willing to show a little gratitude by telling you. Evidence of the craft started piling up a month before this sloppy incident out here. Mutilated cattle, bodies strewn about - whomever these beings were, they weren't very tidy."

"Were?" Williams said.

"The Air Force started tracking sectors where they kept returning. The spacecraft was too fast to chase, so they looked for patterns. With a little high-tech sleuthing, and some dumb luck, a fighter patrol caught their trail and shot them down over the ocean. The Navy is still conducting a salvage and recovery mission as we speak. So far, they've come up with some remarkable undersea photos that show markings like the one on my little patch here."

Payne's astounded eyes popped from Jackson to Williams.

"Oh, I know I have a habit of stretching the truth," Carswall said, "but this one makes more sense than tales of nuclear waste and rogue black helicopters. I mean, it's too ridiculous to not be true, don't you think?"

"So, what's with the masquerade?" Jackson asked.

"Masquerade?" Carswall said. "Are you really that stupid? Aliens were buzzing our skies, landing in remote regions and harvesting live creatures. If that isn't enough to trigger mass hysteria, what about the thought that somewhere out there is a civilization that may come looking for its two missing pioneers? If they managed a distress call and communicated that they were under attack, we may be in for a retaliation some day."

"So this is all about a cover-up," Jackson said. "And you kill whoever gets in the way . . ."

"Grow up, Jackson. Anyone who threatens national security is an enemy of the state, so save your tears. You're all lucky you've survived this far. I've never seen such impossible good fortune."

"So, how long should we expect to be around now that you've told us?" Jackson said.

"Depends, Officer," Carswall said. "I'm willing to deal. In fact, you have a good chance of telling your grandchildren about the day little green men roamed your town - that is, if any of us survive the next ten years or so."

"I don't get it," Jackson said.

"No, I wouldn't expect you to."

"Look, you sanctimonious motherfuc- "

"K.J.!" Payne said, grabbing Jackson's arm.

Jackson backed off. At first, he didn't give a damn about the gun pointed at him, but the thought of coming out of this a grandfather was more appealing than dying here in the mud.

Carswall continued. "Let me explain, so there's no misunderstanding. You now know the truth. In a way, you are in the confidence of your government and will be treated like any intelligence-level agent. The information you have is yours to do with as you see fit. Of course, we prefer you keep our secret, because eliminating you costs us time and money."

"You're all heart," Payne said.

"Mr. Payne, you were very clever the way you covered yourself and your friends thus far. I commend you for that, but all bets are off now that you discovered this patch. I promise you, had I not shared the truth with you, you'd be dead now, and we'd take our chances with the cleanup. Luckily for you, the patch no longer exists, and you have a very safe and simple alternative. To walk away from this, you only need to agree to remain silent."

"Or?" Payne said.

Carswall shook his head. "Alright, Counselor, there are a few incentives. I know you'll probably tell Mr. Aaron. I suppose he deserves to know. Maybe Jackson will tell Officer Farrel. That's acceptable - it doesn't concern me. But I insist you not make a public revelation."

"The world has a right to know about this," Jackson said.

"Does it? I have news for you, Officer Jackson, the world's rights end at your nation's shores. We're talking about worldwide panic. Global collapse of financial markets. Third World dictators, terrorists, domestic radical elements on both the left and right - they lie in wait for an opportunity to destroy this country. How might they respond to a world torn by fear of extraterrestrial pirates?"

Williams had been puffing and relighting through the conversation. "Hate to say it, but he's got a point, Jackson. If word got out that the military may have provoked a future holocaust, there could be chaos."

"It could trigger anarchy in the only country left on this planet with a chance to defend itself," Carswall said. "We're salvaging the craft, don't forget. It will reveal their physiology, their power source and weaponry; it will strengthen our ability to wage war on any opponent. These are high stakes, gentlemen. Maybe they'll never return, but we don't bank on maybes, and neither can you."

"We tell, we die. That's it?" Jackson said.

"Not exactly. We're aware that you're the type who would die for nothing, if it fit your illusion of justice. Therefore, I offer an incentive. Mr. Payne, the famed sentry of organized crime, understands the principle of persuasive motivation. It's a procedure that, forgive me for bragging, the Mafia learned from us.

"I'll give you a hypothetical. Let's say Mr. Williams proposes a revealing story about this meeting to his editor. Now there's a way of telling the world, isn't it? But Mr. Williams won't do that because he knows such foolishness will exact a severe consequence for someone like, say Carly Farrel. And you want to know the kicker? Even if Williams was so foolish, we can persuasively motivate his newspaper to reject any more stories about government conspiracies and UFO non-sense. In fact, I'd wager he can't sell his story to any news organization in the country right now. If he tried, all he'd accomplish is arranging Carly's funeral. The death of her and your unborn child would lie squarely on his shoulders."

"You son of a bitch," Jackson said.

"I admit my mother was no prize, but that aside, I think you understand the consequences of violating our contract. I'd say you all have good reason to encourage each other to behave. And, Jackson, you surely understand the break I'm giving you. I went to the mat to persuade my superiors to forgive you and Carly for murdering two expensive government employees at Crane Lodge."

Jackson breathed a heavy sigh. Payne and Williams were less indignant. They simply stared at the ground.

"Gentlemen," Carswall said, "this is a fair compromise. You remain silent, and in return I guarantee the safety of your loved ones. If money is an issue, your government is willing to listen to a reasonable request. I'm sure a tax-free stipend can be worked out for all of you."

"Oh, fuck you," Jackson grumbled. He shook his head and threw his hands in the air.

"Hold on a second," Williams said. "Did you say, tax-free?"

Williams looked at Jackson and Payne. "Oh, uh, never mind . . ."

Carswall chuckled. "Don't say I didn't offer. Mr. Payne, as attorney of record, you can speak for your clients. Do you accept our terms?"

Payne didn't look at Jackson. "You win," he sighed.

"We both win," Carswall said. "That's the beauty of a free society. Reasonable men can barter for an equitable conclusion without resorting to violence." Carswall clapped his hands. "I for one, am getting cold, and I know you all have family and friends to go home to. Gentlemen, your government thanks you for your cooperation - you are true patriots. Barring any future misunderstandings, I don't believe we'll be seeing each other again. It's been fun."

He turned and brushed by the thug, who, because it looked good, backed away with his gun still pointed at them. The agents crunched through the snow and slowly pounded a path to County 84. In a moment, the sound of car engines tore the icy air, and their headlights streaked the night . . .

Payne lit a cigarette, Williams lit his pipe, and Jackson waved the smoke away. The sedans rolled toward Attica and blinked out over the hill, leaving County 84 dark and deserted.

"You know," Williams said, "I don't feel all that patriotic."

"I don't believe you," Jackson said. "You were gonna take a bribe from that prick?"

"Jackson, I need a new car," Williams said.

Payne looked at Jackson, who stared into the night. He put a hand on his friend's shoulder. "You okay?"

"Yeah, I'm okay."

"You didn't really want to be a hero, did you?"

"Dead hero," Williams added.

"Dead heroes aren't heroes," Jackson said. "They're just dead."

Williams puffed and found his old grin. It wasn't as happy as usual, but it was a grin. "I prefer to remain a live coward."

"Kind of ruins your plans, does it?" Payne asked.

The grin got better. Williams sighed with resignation. "I guess I didn't really want to be a TV star. I don't photograph well . . ."

"Is this the right thing, Marc?" Jackson asked. "Is cutting bait our only alternative?"

Payne glared knowingly. "You remember a long time ago when I told you to run if I said so?"

Jackson nodded and kicked more dirt.

They stood silently for a few more minutes. Williams just about killed his pipe. It was hot to the touch, and the smoke gave him a bad buzz. He banged it off his hand, and the black soot fell to the ground. "You know," he said, "for a long time I've thought about giving up journalism and taking a shot at fiction. Novels are safer. Publishers can humiliate you like this, but at least they don't threaten to kill your mother."

Payne chuckled, but he really wasn't thinking about Willy.

Jackson was thinking about Carly and babies. He was thinking about a woman who saved his life twice and made a mean pizza. He suddenly needed to hold her. He needed to argue about his leaving wet towels on the floor, and her hanging pantyhose over the shower curtain. He needed to face an alarm clock, and roll call, and the agenda for his upcoming political campaign. It might be nice to go back to pulling over drunks in front of Rusty's, and going home to a bed full of the love he'd searched for all his life.

Grandpa. It did sound good . . .

Marcus Payne thought about Lori Payne.

Nobody thought about Seth Cameron.

Payne told Jackson and Williams to go on. He needed another moment alone.

Willy trudged to the patrol car, but Jackson hesitated. He looked at Payne sadly. "Catch you soon?"

"You know where to find me," Payne said.

"Thanks, Marc."

Payne couldn't help a frustrated chuckle. "For what?"

"For helping me. I don't think I'd be here right now if not for you. And thanks, too, for being my friend." He offered his hand.

Payne took it after a moment. "I'm not so sure you'll consider that a favor in the long run."

Jackson smiled. He grabbed Payne with his other hand. "I hope you hang around for awhile."

"I'll get my tuxedo pressed," Payne said with that endearing smile . . .

Payne watched Jackson slowly walk to the car. In moments, he and Williams disappeared over County 84.

The wind picked up. It was getting damned cold. Payne strolled back to Seth's cabin. He hesitated and then hopped on the porch fence railing. His aching ribs were numb from the cold, so he had a little problem hoisting himself on the roof.

He sat and looked at the clear, black sky. Several hundred stars twinkled brightly. Payne stiffened himself to the biting wind, and he thought about that damned patch. The undecipherable symbols were recorded in his mind:

ited States of Ameri

Payne looked into the sky and stared at the moons. They stared back without an answer.

He shrugged and fetched the old photograph from his pocket. He held it in the darkness, closing his eyes. Someday, Lori would kiss him . . .